D0410944

BULLION

By the same author

MRS MOUNT ASCENDANT

THE ICING OF BALTHAZAR

VOYAGE IN THE BEAGLE

EXODUS GENESIS

BULLION

a novel by

JOHN GOLDSMITH

'Novels serve a useful purpose: they
inoculate the public to the truth'
Anonymous Swiss Banker
1981

BOOK CLUB ASSOCIATES LONDON

This edition published 1983 by
Book Club Associates
by arrangement with Sidgwick and Jackson Ltd

Copyright © 1982 John Goldsmith

Printed in Great Britain by
Richard Clay (The Chaucer Press) Ltd
Bungay, Suffolk

To W.A., M.W. and V.S.

PROLOGUE

The gold rush began in early December 1979, but at first it wasn't news.

On 4 December the business section of *The Times* of London reported a sudden jump in the gold price from $415.75 an ounce to $432.25, but attached no great significance to the fact. During the next three weeks the price of gold bullion continued to rise but press reports were still confined to the financial pages. It was only when the price broke through the $500 barrier, on 27 December, that gold hit the front pages. By the first week of the New Year, 1980, bullion was headline news.

'PANIC BUYING AS GOLD SOARS TO RECORD $630' *The Times* reported breathlessly. For some it was an exceptionally merry Christmas and a New Year full of golden promise: a leading article declared that investors who had bought gold bullion between 1971 and 1980 could be looking at anything up to a 1,700 per cent profit.

There was a brief lull, then the gold bonanza went on. By Thursday 17 January 1980 the price of gold on the London Gold Market stood at $755 an ounce. On that same day, in Washington, finance ministers from five countries – the United States, Great Britain, France, West Germany and Japan – met in secret to discuss the situation: the prices of other commodities were soaring alarmingly in the wake of gold; millions of small investors were leaping onto the gold bandwagon; the stability of the international financial system seemed threatened.

On 18 January the gold price topped $800. Dealers were predicting that it would go beyond $1,000. The price of bullion had doubled in six weeks, risen by a staggering $308.5 since the beginning of the New Year. The world was gold crazy.

Perhaps nowhere was this craziness more apparent than in phlegmatic England. In London's Hatton Garden, the oddly drab street where the leading dealers in bullion and precious stones

7

operate, there were bizarre scenes. Long lines formed outside the dealers' offices as people of all classes and types were suddenly drawn together by a common fever: to sell their gold. There were old women in plastic mackintoshes clutching paper bags that jingled with cherished trinkets – Grandmother's old locket and rings, Uncle Arthur's golfing trophies. There were city gents in immaculately cut overcoats, their briefcases bulging with family heirlooms. Antiques of exquisite craftsmanship, whose historical and aesthetic value far outweighed their bullion content, were assayed, smashed, and melted into bars.

The dealers themselves entered into the spirit of the thing. They turned Hatton Garden into a casbah. Hand-written notices, announcing 'Best Prices Paid Here', appeared in the windows of discreet establishments whose proprietors normally dealt only with Cabots, Saltonstalls, and God. Magnificent commission-aires, whose usual job was to usher millionaires in and out of bullet-proof limousines, found themselves controlling crowds and touting for business like hucksters outside strip joints.

But if there was a fever to sell gold, there was a frenzy to buy. At street level, sales of Krugerrands, sovereigns, jewellery, ingots, and small bars broke records all over the world. At higher levels, the gold-futures market went stark mad as speculators fought and clawed to climb onto the gold train and pension- and investment-fund managers, responsible for billions of dollars belonging to ordinary people, scrambled to invest in bullion.

In the meantime, financial journalists and government spokesmen tried to explain the phenomenon. The *Wall Street Journal* attributed the sudden rise to rumours that Soviet troops were massing on the borders of Iran, stressing that the Pentagon had denied the rumours. United States Treasury Secretary G. William Miller was quoted as saying that the gold rush was 'a sign of troubled times'. The *Washington Post* reported that it was rumours of *Chinese* troops massing on the border of *Afghanistan* that had triggered the panic. In London the *Financial Times* also cited Afghanistan. The Soviet invasion, combined with the continuing deadlock over the US hostages in Tehran, they said, had caused the sudden flight into gold.

Among other explanations offered were: a worldwide psychological fear of inflation; a general atmosphere of political tension; and a stampede out of paper money led by the OPEC countries – in other words, those handy universal bogeymen, the Arabs, were to blame.

8

A few commentators, however, hinted at a less cosmic cause. On 6 January the London *Sunday Times* published an article by its 'Insight' team. Entitled 'Why The Price Of Gold Went Mad', the article quoted a $2,000-an-hour New York financial consultant, Harry Schultz. Mr Schultz declared that the rise in the gold price was 'wholly artificial' and advised readers against investing in bullion. The article went on to point out that the immediate cause of the gold rush had been a flood of orders to buy that had overwhelmed the world's gold markets. The orders had been placed by banks on behalf of anonymous clients. A fog of secrecy protected the identities of these clients, a fog that even a top-level CIA probe had failed to penetrate.

And then, on 26 January, the gold price suddenly plummeted to $670. Within a few weeks it had dropped back to below $500.

Hundreds of thousands of investors, great and small, lost incalculable billions of dollars. Reviewing the disaster, the press repeated that it had been caused by forces beyond the control of individuals or even governments. There was much talk of the folly of speculating in gold but very little about the fact that if some people had lost millions, other people must have gained millions – one man's loss being, after all, another man's profit. It was as if the money had simply evaporated. Yet money does not evaporate: *it changes hands.* Exactly into whose hands the colossal profits of the gold rush had fallen was a question curiously few people were asking in March 1980.

There were, however, at least two men who knew the answer – and one of them, Dan Daniels, was trying to find somewhere in the world to hide. His partner, Eddy Polonski, had all the strands of the story in his hands but he still had to weave them into a rope strong enough to hang a very powerful and utterly unprincipled man. Nine months before Eddy had never heard of Anthony Melldrum; but then nine months before Eddy had been on the brink of making his first million. And it had all started for him on the night when he lost everything, when the achievements of thirty-eight years were obliterated in an hour.

9

1

Eddy was squatting by the single candle that filled the cold cellar with shadows, his father was trying to prime the *samovar*, they were waiting for the Russian tanks to grind through the heaped rubble which was all that remained of Warsaw, each could sense the other's fear, and – crazily – there was a phone ringing. It was a modern American sound, a purring *draung-draung*, the signature tune of the Bell Telephone Company, and it was dragging Eddy out of his dream, out of sleep.

He lay still for a moment, letting his mind make the adjustment from dream to reality, from Poland 1945 to Houston 1979, cursing the overseas caller who'd got his time zones screwed up, yet knowing intuitively that it would not be London or Hong Kong on the line, but something worse. He rolled over, switched on the light, and picked up the phone.

'Polonski.'

'Mr Polonski? This is the South West Houston Fire Department.'

It was a girl's voice, a bland, switchboard voice, and it tightened a knot in Eddy's throat.

'We have a report of a fire at your facility at' – a pause – 'Fork Road, Westpark Drive. Chief Gruder has requested that you get over there as soon as possible.'

The knot in Eddy's throat tightened again. He made himself breathe deeply, in and out, three or four times.

'Mr Polonski?' The girl's voice was hesitant, puzzled.

He was able to reply in his normal, soft voice.

'D'you know how bad it is? When it started?'

'I'm sorry. I do not have that information.'

There was no more time to be wasted. He said: 'Okay. I'll get over there. Thanks.'

He put down the phone, swung out of bed, and ripped the curtains open. There it was: an orange-white glow ten blocks

11

away. He pulled on jeans and a tee shirt, shuffled into a pair of kickers, scooped up his keys, and ran out of the apartment.

He swung his Chevrolet El Camino SS out into Landren and stamped on the throttle. It was three in the morning, the wide streets were deserted – not even a truck in sight – and he took the car up to eighty and held her there before breaking hard for the right turn into Red Creek. He passed Denny's 24-Hour Restaurant at ninety, slowed, skidded into Westpark, and was accelerating towards the chaos of blue and red flashing lights and the sky-lighting torch of fire in Fork Road less than five minutes after receiving the call.

As he flung himself out of his car the roof of the laboratory building behind the offices collapsed inwards and a tongue of flame licked thirty feet into the air. But the office was not burning yet. Instinct told him: go in there now, before it's too late. Common sense said: the Fire Chief'll stop you, you have to talk to him.

Two fire-trucks and four or five cars were parked haphazardly on the driveway and the St Augustine's grass lawn. Thick hoses snaked everywhere, there were men in yellow slickers running and bawling, there were five arcs of water splashing impotently into the fire. Eddy thrust through the bedlam, feeling the heat brush his cheeks, shouting: 'Where's Gruder?' Somebody thrust out an arm, pointing to a man in a blue denim uniform leaning on the open door of a car, and drawling into a radio-telephone. He was a big bear of a man, with the look of a typical Texan good-ol'-boy, except for an intelligent, humorous glint in his eyes.

'Chief Gruder? I'm Polonski.'

'Well, praise the Lord for that. Okay Mr Polonski. Number one, any people inside?'

'No.'

'Halleluiah. Two, any way I can get my trucks round the back?'

'I don't think so. The bayou runs past the back.'

'Shee-it. Three, I want to know what you've got in there – like chemicals, combustibles, explosives.'

'There's a list of everything filed with the Fire Department.'

Gruder scratched his grizzled hair. 'Boy, if I could get that information out of our wonderful computer, I'd do it. But I can't. So I'm asking.'

As he spoke there was an explosion from within the laboratories. Eddy thought: the butane bottles.

'I'm asking,' Gruder repeated.

12

Eddy looked towards the offices. There was smoke curling thickly from under the flat roof, but no sign of flame. There was still time. There had to be time. But he must get Gruder on his side. How? He looked directly at the big man.

'We have tanks of nitric acid, butane gas, we've got a list of combustibles as long as a Turk's prick. Think of a disaster, double it, add the first holocaust you thought of——' Eddy shrugged his shoulders and a slow grin spread over Gruder's face. Then Gruder chuckled.

'Okay, Mr Polonski. I apologize.'

'Chief, you can help me. How long before the offices go?'

Gruder's eyes narrowed. 'You got fire-doors – between the offices and whatever?'

'Yes.'

He looked, assessed, shrugged. 'Five, maybe ten, minutes.'

'If I went in, what would my chances be?'

Gruder squinted at Eddy. 'Zero, boy, because I'm not letting anyone, and I mean *anyone*, within thirty feet of that fucking time-bomb. In fact I'm pulling my men back.'

'I've got to go in, if there's a chance I can get out. Is there?'

He'd spoken calmly, levelly, but the appeal had been all the more powerful for that.

'I can't let you, Mr Polonski. You know I can't. It'd be my ass.'

'You don't know. You haven't seen me. This conversation never took place.'

'What the hell've you got in there that's so all-fired important?'

'The rest of my life,' Eddy said quietly.

Gruder looked away. 'You'd have to have a moon suit.'

'No time. What I have to do'll take a minute – less.'

Gruder was looking at the ground. 'Don't hold your breath. Breathe normal – but shallow.'

'Thanks Gruder.'

Eddy sprinted across the grass. Close to, the fire was scorching; the heat was so intense that he felt as if his beard and hair would start smouldering. He fitted his key into the lock, opened the outer door, stepped inside the lobby, and quickly pulled the door shut behind him.

Instantly it was cooler – and uncannily quiet. The booming of the fire seemed a mile away. The light was pale red, as in a dark-room. Horizontal layers of smoke were shifting sluggishly across the room and his eyes began to smart and water. He choked. He

13

told himself: absolute calm, absolute control, and you'll survive this. He strode rather than ran past Linda-Lee's desk, with its shrouded typewriter, to the door of his own office. He paused for a second. Would there be a furnace or a gas-chamber behind the door?

He gripped the handle, turned, and pushed. A wave of heat blasted him, blinding him momentarily. He wiped his eyes, blinking. An acrid haze hung in the familiar office. The wall opposite, which abutted directly onto the labs and contained the safe, was bubbling and blistering. The temptation to hold his breath was overwhelming, but he resisted it, even though there was acid in his throat and lungs. He forced himself to walk over to the safe as unhurriedly as if this was the beginning of a normal, working day and he was getting the research files for Andrews and Miller.

The metal of the dial was hot to the touch, it burned the tips of his fingers as he twisted out the combination. He ignored the pain. His only fear was that the heat might have damaged the lock mechanism, that the safe wouldn't open. It did.

He put a hand inside and cried out at the pain, thinking: *now I must run.*

In the lobby, the fire-door shattered. Eddy had been halfway to the office door when the vortex of airless heat sliced his feet from under him and slammed him against the wall. He was winded. His lungs automatically heaved and drew in pure poison and he knew he'd lost.

Distantly he heard himself retching; dimly he saw a figure like an astronaut lumbering towards him.

Gruder knelt by him and tried to grab his right arm so he could hoist him onto his shoulders. But the crazy Polak's arms were locked round his belly. He was clutching something so tightly that it was impossible to prise a hand away. Emitting a stream of profanities, Gruder pulled Eddy forwards, lifted him in a bear hug, and carried him out of the office and through the flaming lobby. There was a terrible moment when he had to support Eddy with one arm, while he fumbled for the door-handle with the other, then they were both out, men were helping them across the grass to the shelter of the trucks, and they were clamping an oxygen mask over the Polak's face.

Gruder took off his helmet and said to the world in general: 'Crazy son-of-a-bitch.' Then he knelt by Eddy and examined him. He was blacked out but breathing normally. He was lying on his

14

back and suddenly his arms fell away to his sides and there, lying across his stomach, was a bar of metal ten inches long, three inches wide and perhaps an inch and a half thick. In the confused light of the fire, flashlights, and car headlamps, it glowed with a dull, steady luminescence that seemed to be generated from within.

'Well I'll be——' Gruder said.

'What the hell is it, Chief?' someone said.

'Whaddaya think it is, lame-brain? It's gold.'

He'd pulled off his protective gloves and now he put out a hand to touch the bar. As his fingers made contact with the metal he whipped them away.

'Jesus. It's red hot.'

He quickly drew on a glove, got his fingers under the bar, and heaved it off Eddy's body.

'Sheeit. Look at that,' a voice said.

The bar had scorched away the thin cotton of Eddy's tee-shirt, and branded the skin of his stomach.

Eddy came round as the *whoop-whoop-whoop* of a siren announced the arrival of an ambulance. His hands went automatically to his belly and found nothing. He tried to rise but fainted away. He was only out for a moment and when consciousness came surging back he found Gruder looming over him.

'Relax Goldfinger,' he said. 'It's safe. Here.'

He hefted a paper carrier bag with 'Joske's' printed on it.

One of the ambulancemen said: 'Okay pal, we're gonna lift you onto a stretcher. Just take it easy.'

'Like hell you are,' Eddy said. He struggled into a sitting position. 'Help me up, Gruder.'

He refused to be taken to the Herman Hospital, but let them treat and bandage his burns. Then he stood next to Gruder and watched the fire burn itself out. There were no other buildings within a hundred yards, therefore no danger of the fire's spreading, and Gruder let it, in his own phrase, 'eat its own meat'.

The sun came up, flushing the sky coral, and the dawn seemed to erase the last smudges of black smoke. The fire-trucks and cars drove away leaving only Eddy and Gruder contemplating a heap of blackened rubble.

'Until this morning those buildings housed the most advanced system of precious-metal extraction in America,' Eddy said.

Gruder sniffed. 'You must ha' been making money.'

'I was.'

'Maybe too much.' Gruder spat and shrugged. 'Pro job, Polonski. You can forget about evidence.' He went on: 'Maybe nothing, but there was a guy loafing around while you were out. Said he was press. Hogwash. He wasn't one of the regular boys. Seemed very interested in your gold. I told him to shift his ass.'

'Thanks, Gruder. And thank's for what you did.'

Gruder looked at him. 'Stay small, Polonski. It's better. You can sleep nights – and you can bet on waking up in the morning.'

Eddy drove slowly back to the apartment. He opened the car windows and let the sweet, humid air flow in; the hedgerows along Red Creek were a mass of dark pink crepe – myrtle. Traffic was beginning to crowd the highway, the giant city was stirring, coming alive. But in spite of the traffic, and in spite of his burns and exhaustion, he was aware that he had company – a red compact with two men inside. When he turned into his own street, a cul-de-sac, and parked, he saw the red car drive on down Landren then pull into the kerb.

He brewed himself a big pot of tea and – for once – drank it with sugar, to allay shock. He washed carefully, avoiding the fresh bandages, put on clean jeans and a shirt and sat down to call each one of his eight employees.

There was no answer from Miller's phone – and that didn't surprise him at all.

He broke the news to the others as gently and succinctly as he could and told everybody to come to his apartment at ten o'clock. The little gathering had the air of a funeral party: solemn, but ready to tip into nervous laughter. Linda-Lee, Eddy's secretary, had been crying and was still sniffing into a pink handkerchief. Like all of them, except the senior researcher Ben Andrews, she had come by the labs and seen the remains for herself. She kept saying: 'I just can't believe it. I just can't believe it happened.'

Lamarque, the office manager, said: 'It's an insurance job, right, Eddy? We're opening up again in Malibu?'

Billy, one of the three, black, technical assistants said: 'I left my old lady's birthday present in there, goddammit, a five-hundred-dollar bracelet. Jeezus. No coffee, Mr Polonski, I'll take bourbon.'

Ben Andrews said nothing and Eddy watched him carefully.

16

Andrews had worked for Westmacott. He had known the gold cartel from the inside – he would understand.

'Okay,' Eddy said, 'this is it. I've never had secrets from you and I'm not going to start now. Yesterday I was making a clear sixteen thousand dollars a day. This morning I'm wiped out.'

'Just a moment,' Andrews said. 'Where's Miller?'

'I don't think Mr Miller will be joining us this morning.'

Andrews nodded. 'Okay. Sorry, Eddy, go on.'

Eddy began to talk to them, in his soft voice, in which only a trace of a Polish accent remained. They listened in silence – he'd always been able to compel them. He owed money to the bank, to the miners in Nevada and New Mexico, to the trucking company, the South Pacific Railroad, and three leasing companies. The insurance payment would cover perhaps three-quarters of these debts, if he was lucky, but he explained that insurance companies fought such cases. Their lawyers could hold up payment for months, even years.

'Now each of you has a contract with me that entitles you to compensation for dismissal without notice,' he said. 'I have enough cash put by to cover that, so I don't want any of you to worry about your immediate financial situation. I'm going to make some calls and I don't think you'll be out of jobs for long.'

Billy said: 'Screw our contracts. You can start again, Mr Polonski. We'll wait.' He looked round, gathering agreement.

'That's right,' someone said.

Eddy smiled. 'Thanks, Billy. Thank you – all of you. But it's not possible.'

'I don't understand,' Lamarque said. 'You did it before, Eddy. You can do it again. We'll all back you till hell freezes.'

'Well, hell has already frozen for me, Tom. But I appreciate your offer. I really do. Maybe one day.'

'I don't get it.'

'Wait a minute, Eddy,' Andrews said. 'Surely we could handle a smaller operation? It's no secret that you bought the house for me when I joined you. Mortgage it. Raise cash. Hell, we can keep going.'

Eddy looked directly at Andrews. 'I don't think so, Ben.'

Suddenly there was a hubbub of talk, most of it wild and irrational – partnerships, co-operatives: they all wanted to put themselves in hock to help him out. It moved him. But in the end he convinced them that Fork·Road Metals was a dead thing. Gradually he ushered them out of the apartment, promising to be

17

in touch soon. Only Ben Andrews lingered. Eddy poured him a Scotch and made himself a fresh pot of tea.

'It was good of you, Ben, to offer the house. But keep it. You've earned it.'

Ben took a sip of his drink and looked sidelong at Eddy. 'They timed it beautifully, didn't they?' he said.

Eddy nodded. 'In three months I'd have been clear of debt. In six months I'd have had enough to buy foolproof security. In a year I'd have been unassailable.' He shrugged. 'They just hit me when I was most vulnerable.'

'Miller. Miller was the mole.'

'It looks that way.'

'Bastard.'

'Maybe not, Ben. We don't know.'

'Jesus.' He shifted restlessly in his chair. 'How can you be so goddam cool about it, Eddy?'

Eddy shrugged. 'I knew it could happen. You must have known it could happen. We've both seen it before. Remember Markstein?'

Ben nodded. Markstein had run a small refinery in Dallas, very similar to Eddy's. Like Eddy he'd been buying tailings – used ore – from the miners and by applying advanced auto-leaching techniques had been getting the same amount of gold and a lot more platinum out of the dross as the miners got out of the prime ore. Like Eddy, Markstein had grown big, fast. One afternoon a man had walked into his office and told him: 'You have three minutes, Mr Markstein.' Precisely three minutes later a controlled implosion had demolished Markstein's building. An enquiry later established – 'officially' – that the disaster had been caused by a gas leak.

'Markstein took barbiturate pills and forgot to count,' Ben said.

'Don't worry, Ben. I won't do that.'

Eddy went over to his desk, unlocked a drawer, and took out the gold bar. 'I didn't tell them the whole story,' he said. 'I'm not bankrupt. Not quite. That's what our friends were playing for, of course, but they've failed. I can pay everybody who has to be paid, and I'll have some left over.'

'I'll work with you. I'm not afraid of the bastards.'

Eddy sat down. 'Then you should be, Ben. You've got a wife and three kids. Anyway I won't be doing that sort of work. Not for a while.'

'Come on, Eddy. All you know is gold.'

'I know how to make a living on this planet, Ben. There are hundreds of ways.' He wanted to change the subject. 'I'm going to call Conolly at Lone Star Chemicals. He owes me a favour and he needs a new Head of Research in Metallurgy. I'm going to recommend you for the job.'

'I don't want the job. I wanted out – out of that whole damned rip-off. That's why I joined you.'

'I know. But take the job anyway. I told the others I'd live to fight another day and I meant it. We'll work together again. Trust me.'

Andrews looked at him – the long, lean body, the eagle's face with its pointed beard. A masterful man and one to trust, but God – lonely.

'Listen, Eddy, why don't you come on over to the house tonight and have dinner. You've never even met Susan.'

Eddy smiled. 'Thanks Ben, but I have other plans.'

'Well I hope they include getting good and drunk.'

'I don't drink.'

'Well at least get laid.'

Eddy grinned. 'That,' he said, 'I might just do.'

When Andrews had gone Eddy sat down at his desk and did some calculations. The gold was worth between $110,000 and $120,000. That would cover his outstanding debts and leave him a small balance of cash. The insurance cheque would cover the bank overdraft eventually. There'd be a battle over the claim but the bank's lawyers could fight it for him. Dog could eat dog.

What he needed now was rest and time, time to re-orientate himself. To achieve that he needed to vanish. He put the gold bar into his attaché case – he was going to keep it right by his side until he sold it – and left the apartment.

Walking from the front door to his car was like walking through steam. The July sun was merciless and the humidity was crawling up into the nineties. As he turned into Landren he kept his eyes on the rear-view mirror until the red compact appeared. He drove slowly and was relieved to see that his tail was content to leave three or four cars between them. He grinned. It was never difficult to lose a tail if he assumed you weren't aware of him. All you needed was the right set of circumstances.

He got him at the intersection of Landren and Teesdale. As he approached the traffic light he slowed right down and willed it to go red. It obeyed. When he stopped he was therefore first in line in the right-hand lane. He waited. Two cars drew up behind him, then the tail. Three or four other cars halted behind the tail. The left-hand lane was filling up too, with cars and a couple of big trucks. He glanced to his right. There was a wire-mesh pedestrian safety-barrier. It was all set. The tail was boxed in on all sides, couldn't even mount the side-walk. The light was still red, traffic was streaming in both directions across the intersection. Eddy waited for a gap, then stamped on the gas and simultaneously spun the wheel. The Camino slalomed out into Teesdale under the bows of a bus and burned away amid panicky horn-blasts. When the needle touched eighty he braked. There was a left turn up ahead, a street that led into a residential labyrinth. He slowed, darted in front of a sluggish station-wagon, and disappeared. The whole exercise had taken under thirty seconds. He reckoned the tail would still be stuck at the lights. Even so he dodged and doubled for a few miles and then turned north until he hit Westheimer. On Westheimer he turned east. Downtown.

In the heat haze the perpendicular heart of the horizontal city was strange and beautiful. The slender glass towers, some black, some gold, some kaleidoscopically reflecting the sky and the neighbouring high-rises, looked like minarets in an Arabian-Nights fantasy of the future. He skirted the centre to the south, turned into Telephone Road, and cruised past the gimcrack motels, and the clubs, bars, and discos the Houstonians called 'pressure-cookers' because, between the hours of 10 am and 2 pm they were haunted by a small army of frustrated housewives, in desperate pursuit of adultery, who relied on pressure-cookers to provide instant dinners and alibis for their husbands. Eddy had never messed with marriages, however empty, but he occasionally visited a club, wryly called 'The Tick Over', to which divorced women resorted.

At three o'clock the place was almost deserted, but Connie was sitting in her usual place between the bar and the bandstand drinking a screwdriver. Her greeting was characteristic.

'Eddy! My perfect stranger. Where the hell've you been, Paderewski?'

She was a plump brunette masquerading as a slim blonde. She described her age as 'over twenty-one', she was divorced from a prosperous auto-dealer called Zak, and she was fun. Eddy knew almost more about Zak than he did about Connie. She was still obsessed with Zak, his myriad infidelities, and the catastrophic course of his new marriage which Connie charted through an undercover network of neighbours. She was the only woman Eddy had ever met who could theorize about her ex-husband's psychological problems while unzipping a man's fly, who could earnestly misquote Jung while going down on him, and who stopped talking only when her mouth was full.

On this occasion Connie paused only to down her screwdriver before launching into the inevitable topic.

'I've sussed Zak's problem,' she said. 'I've finally got him figured. Fundamentally he's gay. All the two-bit typists and one night stands – it's a classic case of Don Juanism. He's trying to prove to the world – and to himself, see – that he's a normal man. The poor bastard's locked in the closet and that bitch he married's too stupid to see it.'

He let her develop her thesis, bought her two more screwdrivers, drank tea, and subtly began the business of exciting her. When he judged the moment to be appropriate he stopped her discourse with a kiss.

'Why don't we check in next door?'

'I was beginning to think you'd never get round to asking, Paderewski,' she said.

Eddy took a room in the name of Mr Edwards in the neighbouring motel for two nights and paid in advance. Connie recoiled from the bandages on his stomach and forearms.

'Jesus, whatever happened to you?'

'Oh – there was a fire at the labs. I'm fine – but we'll have to be inventive. I'm not into S and M.'

She laughed. 'Was anyone else hurt?' He shook his head. 'Well you just lie back and leave it to me, lover.'

A long time later – neither of them believed in rushing such matters – Eddy swung off the bed and padded into the bathroom to get her a glass of water. When he came back into the bedroom she was crying quietly into the pillow. He sat down beside her and stroked her cheek.

'Connie, what's the matter? Here.' He held out the glass. She gulped down some water and tried to laugh. 'What is it?'

'Every time I see you, Paderewski,' she said, 'I fall in love with you.'

'Come on, Connie. You're in love with Zak.'

'I guess I am, too. Fetch me a cigarette, Eddy.' She was silent as she drew on her cigarette. Eddy stretched out beside her. She turned to him and laid a hand on his chest. 'Are you a very lonely man?'

He thought for a moment, then: 'No. I'm solitary.'

'I guess somebody hurt you, way back.'

He smiled. 'Careful, Anna Freud. You'll have me in the closet with Zak in a minute.'

'I'm lonely,' she said.

'I know.'

There was a silence. She was combing her fingers through the hair on his chest.

'I suppose I use you,' he said.

She laughed then, and gave his beard a little tug.

'Not so, Paderewski. You're medication. I love you in small doses now and then. You're not a cure.'

'I want to sleep now, Connie.'

'Sure.'

She kissed him, then began to get dressed. When she left he was already drowning in sleep. He heard her say: 'See you around, Eddy,' felt the brush of her lips, then his mind and his body surrendered gratefully to oblivion.

2

He spent that night, the whole of the following day, and the next night, in the motel, watching old movies on the television, eating in the Howard Johnson's opposite, letting his mind and body lie fallow.

He got back to his apartment at ten o'clock on another super-heated morning and found his neighbour, Tom Hayes, tinkering with his ancient but cherished Oldsmobile out in the street. Tom Hayes was an accountant who made good money working for Exxon and lost most of it in wild stock-market speculations. He and his wife, and two teenage boys, were about the only friends Eddy had. He always spent Thanksgiving and Christmas with them.

'Eddy – we read about it in the *Star*. Gee, I'm sorry.'

'Thanks Tom.'

'Where the hell've you been? Your phone's been ringing day and night.'

'I took a little vacation.'

'Listen, Barbara's baking a meatloaf. Why don't you come on over tonight and bring a hatchet with you?'

Eddy grinned. 'Thanks, Tom, that'd be great.'

The phone began to ring as he let himself into the apartment and when he picked it up he recognized the soft drawl of Henry Querby, senior Vice-President of the Westmacott Copper Corporation.

'Eddy – I've been chasing you-all all over town.'

'What do you want, Henry?'

'Why, I want to buy you a lunch. I heard about – your singular misfortune.'

'Don't tell me. You read about it in the *Star*. Well, you did a great job, Henry. Did you set the fuses personally?'

He heard Querby's lazy, artificial laugh. Then: 'What say to the Côte D'Azur round noon?'

'I say no.'

Again that laugh – canned. Querby said: 'You know sooner or later y'all and I are going to have to have a little talk, Eddy. What's wrong with sooner?'

It was true, of course. He'd have to have it out with Querby, if only to find out what the bastard was up to.

'Okay Henry,' he said. 'But let's make it James Coney Island at one.'

'James Coney Island! Are you kidding me? What's wrong with the Côte D'Azur?'

'Nothing much except that the prices are even higher than the steaks – and I'm buying.'

There was a pause.

'Anything you say, Eddy.'

Eddy hung up.

James Coney Island was an old-fangled fly preserved in the space-age amber of downtown Houston. Mr James opened his hot-dog parlour on Rusk Street in the late twenties and he called it Coney Island hoping that the association with the beach resort would give it glamour and attract customers. The customers were attracted, but not by the name. They came for the unique chilli sauce and cheese and onion garnish whereby Mr James transformed the humble hot dog into a gourmet speciality. Later Mr James expanded, dotting Coney Islands all over the greater Houston area, but the original parlour remained, untouched, untouchable, a much-loved Houston landmark and a famous meeting-place, patronized by truck-drivers and oil tycoons, janitors and corporation presidents, where billion-dollar oil deals were sealed with a handshake over a salt beef on rye and a mint julep.

Whenever Eddy went there he felt as if he was walking into a time capsule. There was a high bar-counter from which old men in grubby, white smocks served food with terrifying speed. Opposite were rows of wooden armchairs fixed to the floor. The right arm of each chair formed a little table, big enough to take a plate and a glass. The customers sat in rows, twisting round to talk to their neighbours. Absolutely nothing had changed in over half a century, except that incalculable clouds of greasy steam had gradually taken the shine off Mr James's pride and joy, leaving it tatty and down-at-heel. In the back there were some rickety chairs and tables, one of which Eddy secured. He had deliberately arrived ten minutes early. The place was crowded. At the next table two blacks in mechanics' overalls were hotly debating the merits of a new quarter-back hired by the Houston Oilers and slapping back beers.

At a minute past one o'clock a man Eddy recognized instantly walked in off the street. But it was not Henry Querby. Eddy had last seen this man in Johannesburg. This was the man who had once told him, in a tin shack on the edge of the Kalahari desert: 'The price of your freedom is ten years of your life, Polonski.'

Jan Pienaar raised a hand in greeting, then joined the line at the counter. Eddy had to admire the cool with which he handled the quickfire questions of the waiters and collected a hot-dog and a root beer as if he'd eaten his lunch in James Coney Island all his life. As Pienaar carried his tray towards the table, Eddy stood up. He was a head taller than the South African.

'*Goeie middaj, meneer*,' Eddy said.

Pienaar smiled and set down his tray.

'*Goeie middaj*, Eddy.'

Pienaar was still the same lithe, stooping man whose high-bridged nose, deeply chiselled chin, and startling violet eyes proclaimed his Boer ancestry. He wore an expensive, stylized bush-jacket, that Eddy guessed had been made for him by Edelstein in Eloff Street. He was greyer, there was a tracery of fine lines under his eyes, but there was none of the softening of advancing years in either his body or his will. You could tell that at a glance. He was the eternal hardliner, the *Broederbonder*, a man who would sanction any action, however brutal, in defence of the twin causes of South Africa and monopoly control of world gold production, which, in his mind, were indivisible. Eddy had long ago decided that when you got right down to it Pienaar was a Nazi.

Neither man offered to shake hands. They both sat down and Pienaar sipped his drink.

'I'm honoured, Jan,' Eddy said. 'I didn't realize I was so important. I feel like a dissident being shot by Uncle Joe Stalin in person. Except that I'm still alive.'

Pienaar smiled. 'Are you indeed, Eddy?'

'Very much.'

Pienaar took a bite of his hot-dog – neatly, like a weasel.

'Answer one question, Jan,' Eddy said. 'Did you pay Miller or was he under pressure?'

'Does it really matter?'

'Yes it does.'

Pienaar shrugged faintly. 'I believe that Mr Miller was under a certain obligation to us.'

'I'll just bet he was. Well, you can tell Miller when you next see him that he's in no danger from me. In fact, he has my sympathy. But you might warn him that his former colleagues are in a more militant mood. He might find it prudent to get his ass out of Houston.'

'Mr Miller is already on his way to Jo'burg.'

There was a silence as Eddy sipped his tea and Pienaar took another delicate mouthful of his hot-dog, fastidiously wiping a splash of chilli sauce from his lip with a handkerchief.

'I'm puzzled, Jan,' Eddy said after a moment. 'Am I that big a threat? Why does it suddenly take a five-star general to settle a little local difficulty?'

'My dear Eddy, you were neither little nor local. Particularly not local. When it comes to my notice that you are selling 999.9 fine to the West German electronics industry, to our mutual friends in Hong Kong, and even to our own people in London, you really cannot expect me to take it lying down.'

Pienaar's nasal Afrikaans accent added a sneer to everything he said. 'That transaction in London, Eddy,' he went on. 'It was insolent. And very foolish.'

'I thought I'd covered my tracks.'

'My dear Eddy! Covered your tracks? You left a scent like a trail of blood through the bush.'

Eddy took a sip of tea to mask his excitement. Pienaar was lying. The London deal had been a hundred per cent discreet. For Pienaar to have found out about it meant that the Fork Road operation had been under very heavy surveillance, and nobody went to that kind of trouble to prevent a little fish turning into a big fish. There was something else.

'Did you come here to sample the chilli sauce or to tell me something, Jan?' he said.

'To offer you something, Eddy. Your debts paid, a hundred thousand a year, and an unlimited-research budget.'

Eddy laughed – so sharply that the two blacks at the next table glanced round.

'Working for you?'

'Working for me.'

'Here or in South Africa?'

'In Jo'burg.'

Eddy smiled. 'Jan,' he said, 'I'd rather spend the rest of my life drawing social security in Nicaragua.'

'That's exactly what you may have to do, Eddy. You're bankrupt. Face the fact.'

Eddy felt the hard edge of his attaché case under the table. He shrugged.

'Nobody starves in America.'

'There are other pressures I could apply. Entirely thanks to me the Soviets think you are dead. It would be very inconvenient for you if I chose to organize a resurrection.'

'It would be even more inconvenient for _you_ if on hearing the good news they offered me a hundred thousand roubles a year and I accepted. If blackmail's the name of the game, Jan, I already hold the aces. A word from me to the Department of Internal Revenue and Henry Querby would spend the next five years in a Federal penitentiary.'

It was not an idle threat. Eddy had spent six years working for Westmacott Copper – the front for Pienaar's company, Mining Consolidated International. Part of his job had been to make it technically possible for Henry Querby to run one of the neatest scams in America. Westmacott mined copper ore. They refined out the copper, then concentrated the platinum-rich tailings into black granules which, officially classified as copper concentrate, were shipped to London free of Federal taxes. In London, thanks to a colorimetric process invented by Eddy, the platinum was unscrambled, melted into bars, and sent to South Africa.

Pienaar shrugged. 'You cannot fight us, Eddy. Face up to it. When you defected twelve years ago you put your future in my hands.'

For a moment Eddy remembered the pulverizing heat of the desert, the brackish taste of his own urine, the vultures lifting their heads, and remembered Pienaar's silken sneer: 'We wanted to make your death as authentic as possible.'

Pienaar was lifting his hot-dog to his mouth. Eddy leaned forward and seized his wrist. Slowly he forced down Pienaar's hand so that a mess of hot-dog, brown sauce, onion shreds, and cheese were smeared over his elegant jacket. Then he released him, picked up his case, and rose.

The two blacks were goggling. Eddy smiled at them and said: 'The South African gentleman seems to have got dirt on his shirt.'

The blacks gaped, then grinned. Eddy turned and walked out.

27

He picked his car up from Foley's Parking Garage and drove the fifteen blocks down to Kreisky's office. Kreisky was not the biggest precious-metals dealer in Houston but he was certainly the least grasping. The secretary told him that Kreisky was out of town. Eddy had noticed a Mercedes parked in Kreisky's space in the parking lot but he didn't press the point. He took Main Boulevard south, then turned east on The Loop, past the monumental mushroom of the Astrodome, wondering what sort of pressure Pienaar had put on Kreisky. He reached the Culver-Kahn Electronics complex providentially as Nat Culver, its founder and president, was climbing out of his Lincoln, having returned from lunch. Culver-Kahn was one of the high-technology, high-profit children of the Apollo space programme. Political horse-trading on an epic scale had decreed that the NASA Space Center should be located at Houston and the result had been the first moon-boom in history, with four thousand people moving into the area, and one thousand new cars being registered, every week. Nat Culver was part of the boom – it had transformed him from a New England research scientist into a Texan millionaire. Eddy was part of it too, but in a different way. Culver sold technology, Eddy bought it. Or had. The ceramic filters that had been the key to his system for extracting complex gold were a direct spin-off from heat-shield experiments.

Culver took Eddy up to his office and listened to him in silence. When Eddy had finished he ran a hand through his thick, grey hair and said: 'Eddy, I'm sorry. I can't buy the gold. Not even at bargain basement prices.'

Eddy nodded and said very quietly: 'Whatever happened to rugged independence, Nat?'

'You did, Eddy. Now that you're out of business I'll have to rely one hundred per cent on the cartel for my precious and strategic metals and the word has already gone out. You know how subtle and tactful Henry Querby can be.'

Eddy laughed. 'A last fling, Nat,' he said. 'For old times' sake. As you pointed out, you won't be buying any more from me.'

Culver was genuinely distressed.

'It can't be done, Eddy. Querby knows what I order every month. An amount like four hundred ounces would stand out. People would talk and Querby would find out. If it was just me I'd say to hell with the cartel. But I have two hundred people working for me here. I just can't take the risk.'

The classic response of the protection racket victim. Eddy said:

'I understand that, Nat. You've been a damned good friend to me.'

'Come and work for me, Eddy. Vice-President in charge of research. Name your own salary.'

Eddy shook his head. 'Jan Pienaar wouldn't like it, Nat. He wants me for himself.'

'Bastards. Think they run the whole goddam world.'

'They do, Nat. At least they run their own particular world. Anyway, I wouldn't want to work for you. I'd prefer to remain a friend.'

Culver looked up. He put a hand on the gold bar.

'We should stay friends,' he said.

Minutes later they shook hands and Eddy left.

Eddy drove back to the apartment asking himself not *how*, but *why*. The how was obvious: MCI was one of the biggest multi-national mining corporations in the world and Pienaar was its chief point-man: he had the power to close all doors, make Eddy's gold unsaleable. But the why? That was more puzzling. Why was it suddenly so important to force Eddy Polonski back into the fold?

He found out in an unexpected way, at dinner that evening with the Hayes family.

The Hayes home was a three-bedroomed clone of his own one-bedroomed 'garden' apartment, part of a medium-priced development constructed in a style invented by real-estate speculators and known as 'Rustic Regency'. With two teenage sons Tom and Barbara Hayes were bursting out of their apartment, and but for Tom's disastrous stock-market speculations they would have moved long before. Eddy was glad they hadn't been able to; they were warm, intelligent, uninquisitive people and, in spite of permanent minor feuds, a loving, united family.

Tom handed Eddy a glass of tea and mixed a powerful dry martini for himself.

'Eddy, I meant to tell you. There was something else in the *Star*. Maybe you've seen it?'

'I haven't looked at a paper today.'

Tom searched among an untidy pile of magazines and comics.

'It's about that Russian professor. The guy who was your teacher. He died. Look, here it is. Igor Shulov – that's the guy isn't it?'

Eddy stared at the six or seven lines at the bottom right-hand corner of the page. It was a bald Agency release stating that Professor Anton Shulov, the Nobel Prize physicist, had died in Moscow at the age of seventy-one.

It was always difficult to read anything in Eddy's face but Tom knew that the news had hit his neighbour hard.

'Eddy, I'm sorry. I didn't realize – I guess you must have been pretty close to him. I'm sorry.'

'That's okay, Tom. Yes, I was close to him – a long time ago.'

'I shouldn't have sprung it on you like that. God damn my loud mouth. Here. I'm going to mix you a real drink.'

Eddy folded the paper away, smiled, and shook his head.

'It was Shulov who taught me not to drink. He used to say, that in a nation addicted to vodka, the *nwunya* – the pussyfoot – was the strong man.'

'Well you're in the land of the free now.'

'In the land of illusion, Tom – where a clear head's just as important.'

Barbara came in and announced that dinner was on the table. The boys were enticed away from the television and they all went into the kitchen.

It was towards the end of dinner, when there was a momentary silence, that Eddy heard a sound coming from his own apartment next door. It was the sound of a heavy object falling. The silence had been caused by Tom ordering his elder son to shut his mouth. Peter, a sixteen-year-old Marxist, had been telling Eddy what to think about Poland.

Eddy said: 'I've got a couple of books in the apartment you should read, Pete. I'll go get them.'

Before anyone could protest Eddy was outside. It was very dark – the sky was overcast. He paused to let his eyes adjust and to scan the line of parked cars opposite. He thought he detected the figure of a man in a white Mustang fifty yards up the street. He vaulted the low fence that separated the Hayes's strip of front lawn from his own. The second he appeared in the dim light of the carriage lamp by his front door there was a triple shriek of high-pitched horns from the Mustang and the car took off.

Eddy kicked open the door and ran across the lobby into the living room. He stumbled over something, half falling. From the bedroom he heard glass shatter and, as he recovered, and flung himself into the bedroom, he saw, through the smashed window, a dark figure throwing an attaché case over the white palings at the end of the tiny back garden, then jumping after it.

He switched on the light. The room looked as if Hurricane Betsy had hit it. Every drawer had been pulled out and up-ended. The bed had been ripped apart, pictures torn down, closets ransacked. In the living room it was the same. The floor was heaped with hundreds of books. Tom Hayes appeared in the doorway.

'Jesus H——. What the hell's going on?'

'Sorry I broke up the party, Tom.'

'Shouldn't you call the cops?'

Eddy laughed shortly and shook his head. Tom sat down on the edge of the couch. 'What's going on, Eddy? First your place burns to the ground, now you get burgled. I know it's none of my business, but maybe I can help. Are you in some kinda trouble?'

Eddy began picking up books. 'You could say that.'

'You haven't got yourself mixed up with——' Tom hesitated nervously.

'It's okay, Tom. Really. The police wouldn't be interested.'

'You're a strange man, Eddy. Sometimes I think I don't know you at all.'

'Apologize to Barbara for me. I must get this mess cleaned up.'

'I'll get the boys. We'll help.'

'No. You go home, Tom. I can handle it.'

Tom hesitated, then: 'We'd stand by you, you know.'

'I know that, Tom. Thanks. And goodnight. Forget about it, huh?'

'What'll I tell the others?'

'Tell them I got burgled and that nothing was taken.'

'And what's the truth?'

'I don't know yet, Tom.'

But he did. Shulov's death was the key. When Tom had gone he searched among the scattered books until he found what he wanted: Shulov's paper on the organic origins of gold, the paper that had made him the laughing stock of the academic establishment and the privileged prisoner-for-life of the men whose task it was to explore and exploit the gold resources of the Soviet empire. Shulov's photograph was on the front page. It had been taken in 1958, the year when Eddy, the seventeen-year-old prodigy of the Physics Department of Warsaw University, had been taken to Moscow to work in Shulov's laboratories. As he gazed at the photograph – the dark hair cut *en brosse*, the far-away eyes behind those absurd steel-rimmed glasses – Eddy could

31

hardly believe that his old tutor and mentor was dead. He felt bereaved in a way he could not remember feeling when his own father had vanished in Stalin's first Polish purge. Shulov had given him more than knowledge, he had given him wisdom, had shown him how to survive in a society steeped in fear and betrayal. The phone broke into Eddy's reverie. Predictably, it was Pienaar on the line.

'I just wanted to remind you, my dear Eddy, that my offer is still open, and will remain open until you accept it. And to thank you for a delightful luncheon, of course.'

Eddy thought for a moment, then said: 'To save you the trouble of breaking it open, the combination of my attaché case is 30545.'

There was a silence. 'Very well, Eddy. I'll buy the bar from you. When you've signed a ten-year contract with Mining Consolidated.'

'It's already sold, Jan. Don't bother to send your morons back to look for it.'

'Bluff, Eddy? It's unworthy of you.'

'Truth, Jan. There's one factor you've left out of your calculations.'

'Really, my dear Eddy? And what is that?'

'Friendship.'

He hung up. Then he took the phone off the hook. He smiled as he remembered the delighted grin that had spread over Nat Culver's face. 'I can't buy the gold for the company,' Culver had said, 'but, by Christ, I don't need anybody's permission to make a *personal* investment. What'll you take for it, Eddy? As a friend.'

Eddy went into the bedroom and mechanically began to clear up the mess, re-make the bed. The news of Shulov's death had put everything into perspective: the fire, Pienaar's visit to Houston, the harassment. With Shulov gone there was only one man left capable of carrying on the Russian scientist's quest. That man was his pupil and surrogate son, Eddy Polonski.

As he hunted for a packet of tea in the chaotic kitchen Eddy assessed his situation. His problem had always been to find the money necessary to pursue Shulov's line of research and to buy protection while doing so. He'd been on the brink of making enough money, with the laboratory. Pienaar had known that and had struck in time. Now, with a starting capital of less than twenty thousand dollars, and the full forces of an all-powerful monopoly massed against him, how the hell was he going to survive, let alone start building another fortune?

The answer came two days later. It came in the unlikely form of a down-at-heel lawyer called Walter Shipley.

Mr Shipley was in his fifties. He wore a cheap, blue suit bought off the rack at Sakowitz, a string tie, and a drooping tweed hat. He looked like a typical ambulance-chaser, a tenth-rate attorney who hung around hospitals, mortuaries, crematoria, and police stations, grubbing a miserable living out of the fear and desperation of the very poor. In fact, Eddy recalled as he ushered the lawyer into his living room, Shipley worked for one of Houston's most prestigious law firms: Landau & Landau.

Mr Shipley accepted a Scotch on the rocks, sat down on the couch, with his briefcase beside him, and lit an acrid little cigar.

'I'm sorry to come knocking on your door like this, Mr Polonski,' he said. 'But I've beeen trying to call you for two days and your number's been busy.'

'I took the phone off the hook.'

'I decided that must be the case. Chin-chin.'

'What can I do for you, Mr Shipley?'

'Well, sir. You recall that a year or two back I approached you on behalf of some clients?'

Eddy remembered perfectly. He'd made a hundred thousand out of the deal, enough for a down-payment on a Jarrel-Ash spectroscope. He'd designed and installed a simple auto-leaching system for a Nevada mining company. It hadn't taken him very long to realize that the company was owned by a certain 'family' more celebrated for its interests in drugs, prostitution, pornography, and gambling than in mining. He remembered being mildly surprised that Landau & Landau should have such connections.

'I hope there are no problems with the system I sold them,' he said.

'On the contrary, Mr Polonski. I believe it turned out to be highly satisfactory. The fact is that – my clients would once again like the benefit of your advice.'

Eddy smiled. Who can ever resist being asked for his advice?

'I should warn you', Eddy said, 'that just at the moment I'm in no position to do business.'

'I'm aware of your problems, Mr Polonski.'

'Are you?'

'Oh yes. My clients have a proposition to put to you. They would very much like to make a meeting. In Las Vegas.'

Eddy stood up and wandered over to his desk.

33

'Mr Shipley, I don't want to sound offensive. But I am perfectly well aware who and what your clients are, and, frankly, they're not the sort of people I would care to advise.'

Shipley smiled. 'I appreciate that. But I can assure you that this is a perfectly legitimate proposition. A business transaction of some magnitude.'

Eddy shrugged. 'I really don't think I'm interested.'

'It concerns gold, Mr Polonski.'

Eddy's immediate thought was that this was a ploy of Pienaar's. But no. Shipley had nothing to do with the cartel. Then what?

'You'll have to give me more detail,' he said.

'That's all I know, Mr Polonski. That's all you'd expect me to know.'

Eddy continued to hesitate.

'I have a private jet ready to fly you down to Vegas. There's a suite reserved for you at the Eldorado. Surely a week's free vacation – with no strings – is attractive?'

'No strings? Come on, Shipley.'

'Really. No strings.'

Eddy thought for a moment. Then he said: 'Okay. But you can cancel the plane and the suite. I'll make my own way. I'll be in Vegas on Thursday. Your people can contact me at the Fremont.'

'But everything's arranged——.'

'Mr Shipley, I don't like being under an obligation to *anybody*. If the business is legitimate what difference does it make?'

Shipley rose. 'Okay, Mr Polonski. I'll inform my clients.'

3

Vegas greets the visitor with a metal handshake. Eddy strode past a row of one-armed bandits in the arrival lounge of McCarran International. There's even a bandit in the damned lavatory, he thought – a gleaming machine with flashing eyes and one saluting arm, waiting to relieve the sucker of the first few dollars before permitting him to relieve himself.

He'd flown in just as the sun was sinking over the desert, blurring the outline of the treeless mountains, flushing the mineral-rich Nevada soil with earthenware hues of ochres and umbers. The day temperature had been in the low hundreds and was still well over ninety, but it was a dry heat, bearable. Eddy slung his small overnight case into the back of a cab and asked the driver to take him to the Fremont. He was dressed in the clothes he invariably wore on business: an anonymous, dark grey, lightweight wool suit, white shirt, and plain blue tie.

The cab driver was a loquacious New Yorker who began his life story before they'd left the airport maze and turned west for The Strip. It was a standard tale of living like a multi-millionaire when lady luck smiled and driving a cab when she scowled. After thirty years in Las Vegas the driver was still able to ignore the fact that everybody in the town was a loser except the people who owned it. They turned north-west on The Strip and Eddy looked back to check that the yellow station-wagon was still behind them. It was. A traffic snarl-up halted them by the Flamingo Hilton, where huge, mechanical flamingoes, pink and orange in the neon lights, ducked and waded amongst plastic reeds.

The driver turned to Eddy and said: 'They shoulda made 'em pink elephants.'

They moved on, past the Sands, the Riviera, and the golden portals of the Eldorado, and the yellow station-wagon kept right behind. As they came to the intersection of Las Vegas Boulevard and Charleston, Eddy asked the driver to make a left, double through the back streets onto South Main, and rejoin The Strip opposite the Sahara.

'Are you kidding me?' he said, then shrugged and pulled over.

When they'd completed the circle, the station-wagon was still with them.

'Okay,' Eddy said, 'now the Fremont.'

The driver grinned. 'You're pickin' up the tab.'

They drove into the flashing, swirling, multi-coloured light explosion of downtown Vegas where, in Eddy's book, the heart of the city beat more brashly, openly, and honestly than in the gilded cages of The Strip. Here you could gamble in barbers' shops, hamburger joints, bars, even on the street. He paid off his cab and went into the Fremont via the Casino Center Boulevard entrance, to avoid having to thread his way through a barrier of slots on the way to the reception desk. He checked in, waived the services of a bell-hop, and waited by the phones and elevator doors near the entrance. He saw the station-wagon pull up and two men get out. A parking attendant took the car away and the two men came through the glass doors. Both were in their mid-thirties, conservatively dressed, with the look of business executives. Eddy put them down as middle- to lower-grade pros from a private detection agency hired by the day by Pienaar. He heard them check in and ask for Mr Polonski's room number. He strolled over and touched one of them on the elbow.

'I'm Polonski.'

The man smiled. 'I know,' he said.

So that was that. Open surveillance, KGB style. A war of nerves.

'Well, I hope you enjoy my stay,' Eddy said and walked away towards the elevators.

His room was a standard assemblage of professionally matched mustard curtains, bedspread, and carpet; there were padded black armchairs, a colour TV, and a mirror-backed desk. It was modest, comfortable, and at thirty-eight dollars a night, dirt cheap. But then in Vegas the hoteliers didn't reckon to make their money out of letting rooms or selling meals. What they lost in the kitchens they gained, a thousand times over, on the tables. Eddy showered, drank a glass of water, switched on the TV, and lay down on the bed to wait.

The call came halfway through the commercial spiel of a local loan shark. A quiet, educated voice said: 'Mr Polonski? Welcome to Vegas, Mr Polonski. My name is Collins. Jim Collins. I am a friend of Shipley. I'd be glad if you'd join me and my associate for dinner tonight.'

'Certainly.'

'Are you familiar with the Eldorado?'

'Sure.'

'Shall we say the Sun God Restaurant at ten? The Maitre D will show you my table.'

'Fine.'

'Ten o'clock then. Goodbye now.'

Pienaar's men stayed with Eddy all the way to the Eldorado. As his cab pulled up under the massive portico, supposedly a reconstruction of the gateway of the Inca fortress at Cuzco, theirs was only seconds behind.

As in virtually all The Strip hotels, even the upper crust Riviera, you entered directly into an inferno of slots, crap tables, keno, and roulette wheels. The Eldorado was packed that night – as always there were several big conventions in town – and the racket from the bandits was shattering. There must have been over two thousand people of every age, type, class, and colour yanking the handles with robotic regularity, feeding silver tokens into the gluttonous machines, waiting for the hollow belch and the glittering vomit that would signal a win.

Eddy threaded his way through the mêlée, more interested by the ceaselessly patrolling security guards, both uniformed and plain-clothed, the hundreds of closed-circuit TV cameras, and the black holes in the ceiling through which teams of watchers kept up a twenty-four hour surveillance from hidden catwalks. The reception area was dominated by a thirty-foot statue of an Inca sun god. He remembered having read somewhere that the statue was covered with over a million dollars' worth of gold leaf. He paused to examine a bulbous toe. It was not gold leaf but *schlag* metal, a cheap substitute. Glancing at his watch – a clock was never to be seen in a Las Vegas casino – he took the elevator four floors up to the restaurant.

It was a dim, candle-lit cavern cantilevered out over the floodlit pool. He followed the Maître d'Hôtel to an alcove overlooking the water and two men rose. The elder of them, a short, chunky, greying man in his mid-fifties, was soberly dressed in a dark business suit. His sole concession to sartorial frivolity was a red and white spotted bow tie. It gave him the look of an academic. He introduced himself as Jim Collins and handed Eddy his card. This told Eddy that Mr Collins was the Investment Manager of a Nevada trade union.

The other was tall, tanned, and good-looking in a conventional, Latin-lover way. He wore a white jacket with a silk handkerchief in the breast pocket, a black shirt open to his navel, and dark glasses. A gold medallion nestled in his chest-hair, and the thick, platinum identity bracelet on his wrist vied in ostentation with three or four globular rings.

'Paul Delgado,' he said. 'Great to meet you.'

Delgado's card proclaimed him to be Executive President of the Canyon Bank. They sat down, ordered their food and quietly assessed each other. Eddy found Delgado easy to read: overdressed, vain about his body, a conspicuous spender – he would be easily bought, intimidated, and manipulated.

Collins was a different matter. On the surface he seemed to be a typical Middle American. One could imagine a spacious ranch house out near Lake Mead, a wife dedicated to bridge and European fashions, a pool, a barbecue pit, a den full of militaria, and a dog. Maybe Collins had all those things, maybe he was a family man in both senses of the expression, but if so the *bon-bourgeois* image was as much a front as his position in his trade union.

Eddy saw Pienaar's two pros sitting down at a table on the far side of the room and thought about asking Collins to have them thrown out. But that would be wrong. Initially he must keep his distance from Mr Collins.

After a certain amount of small talk and the fluster when Eddy asked for tea rather than wine, Delgado broached the subject of gold.

'We believe you have a certain expertise, Mr Polonski,' he said. 'Not just at the refining end but in selling. Is that correct?'

'I have sold, yes.'

'Direct? Not through the bullion markets?'

Eddy nodded.

'What sort of quantities?'

'Small quantities. Tranches of a hundred, maybe two hundred ounces.'

'If you were asked to shift a large quantity, I mean, a really substantial amount, would you go to the market or try for a private deal?'

'That would depend on the amount.'

Delgado produced a document. 'Take a look at that, Mr Polonski.'

It was a letter on the headed writing-paper of a Swiss bank – Limmatbank CS of Zurich – addressed to Delgado at Canyon Bank. It was confirmation that Limmatbank held a certain quantity of gold bullion to the metal account of 'a client'. The amount was coded as *Rampa/mercantus/WTM2000*. Delgado clearly regarded this as the first test: if Eddy could show that he understood the code it would prove that he was familiar with the terminology of bank-to-bank letters. Such letters were the basis of all major bullion transactions outside the market.

'*Two thousand tons* of gold?' Eddy said. He laid the letter down and looked first at Delgado, then at Collins. 'I have no means of checking whether the signatures are genuine, but even if they are I suggest that somebody at Limmatbank is giving you the rush.'

'Why do you say that, Mr Polonski?'

It was Collins who had spoken. His enunciation was cultivated; Eddy placed him as a native of the east coast, Connecticut probably.

'Because,' he said, 'the wording of the letter suggests that the gold belongs to an individual and no individual could have that much bullion.'

'Why not, Mr Polonski?'

'Because two thousand tons is a little in excess of two per cent of the world's entire official stock of gold.'

Delgado laughed shortly, contemptuously. 'Come on, Mr Polonski.'

Eddy was interested. Delgado's reaction had been genuine and that meant that he knew less about gold than he pretended.

'You can find the statistics in any library,' he said. 'In seven or eight thousand years of gold mining the human race has accumulated approximately eighty-eight thousand tons, according to official figures.'

'I didn't know that,' Collins said.

'If you took all the gold in the world', Eddy went on, 'and refined it to maximum purity it would make a cube fifty feet by fifty feet by fifty. You could probably fit the whole amount inside this restaurant.'

'That's fascinating,' Collins said, 'but I still don't see why it would be impossible for an individual to own two thousand tons.'

Eddy spread his hands. 'The entire official gold reserves of the Soviet Union, for example, amount to no more than two thousand five hundred tons.'

Collins thought for a moment, then: 'Assume it's true. Assume there is a man with that much gold, and say he wanted to sell it. Would you advise him to go to the market?'

'If he did, he'd be wasting his time. That much is obvious.'

The dart was directed at Delgado and he was duly stung.

'How's that?' he said.

Eddy smiled. 'I don't have to tell a banker that a market price is basically determined by supply and demand.'

'So?'

'So the average daily turnover on the London Gold Market is roughly a hundred thousand ounces. Suddenly dump two thousand tons and the price of gold goes through the floor. Do that and you have an instant international financial crisis. The price of gold affects the price of every other commodity from copper to soya beans. It affects the relative values of foreign currencies, interest rates, and ultimately the rate of inflation.'

'That's a very simplistic view of economics,' Delgado said.

Eddy shrugged. 'It's a complex view stated in simple terms. When the price of gold was thirty-two dollars an ounce, the price of a man's suit was approximately thirty-two dollars. The price of gold is now around three hundred dollars – and so is the price of a suit. Economic theories come and go, like fashions, but the reality is that the value of gold determines the value of everything else. Besides which, the gold cartel could be wiped out by a slump. And powerful monopolies don't get wiped. My guess is that when you approached London they told you to forget it.'

Collins smiled for the first time.

'Words to that effect, Mr Polonski,' he said. 'Now listen. The gold exists. It has to be sold and sold quickly. The only way is a private deal and that's where I think you can help us – and yourself.'

Eddy looked away. All around him was the murmur of conversation, snatches of laughter, the clink and chink of knives on plates. He felt dislocated: on the outside, looking in. What Collins proposed was phenomenal, if it was true. He picked up the letter. 'I'm still sceptical,' he said. 'I know the gold world and I've never heard of a hoard this size.'

Delgado was about to say something but Collins stopped him with a look.

'Have you ever heard of a man called Gheorgis Maniatos?' he said to Eddy.

The name was a trigger to Eddy's memory. South Africa, 1966. The secret place on the edge of the Kalahari where scientists from Moscow worked side by side with Pienaar's experts to unlock the mysteries of gold. Six men sitting round a fire, talking easily together about their common obsession. A casual question; who has the biggest hoard of gold in the world? A spate of obvious suggestions: Rockefeller, Engelhard, Oppenheimer, Gulbenkian. Then one of the South Africans saying quietly: 'What about the Greek gold? Maniatos?'

'I've heard rumours about Maniatos,' Eddy said. 'That he had a lot of gold. But two thousand tons?'

'He got it in '65.' Collins said. 'He sold a fleet of tankers and some big oil refineries to the South African government. It was a secret deal and they paid him in bullion. Two thousand tons. Then worth around a billion and a half.'

It made sense. Nineteen sixty-five was the year Ian Smith declared UDI in Rhodesia and the British applied sanctions, confident that once oil supplies stopped the illegal regime would collapse in three weeks. Instead, it had survived for thirteen years, thanks to highly organized sanction-busting. A billion and a half would have been a small price for Hendrik Verwoerd to have paid to keep white Rhodesia alive.

'That explains how Maniatos got the gold,' Eddy said, 'but it doesn't explain your interest.'

Collins didn't reply for a moment. Then he said: 'I'm going to level with you, Polonski, because I believe you are an intelligent man – and a discreet man. Five years ago Maniatos ran into trouble, like a lot of the shipping people. He needed a loan, a very substantial loan, and because we'd helped him in the past, he came to us. He offered excellent security – the gold – and we felt able to accommodate him.'

Eddy could just imagine the punitive *vigarish* on that loan. 'And now you want your money back?'

'That is the position.'

Delgado said: 'Does the proposition interest you, Mr Polonski?'

After a moment Eddy said: 'You want me to sell the gold, on commission I assume. Why me?'

'We believe you have the right connections,' Collins said, 'and that you may be at a loose end right now.'

41

'What scale of commission do you have in mind?'

'That would be a matter for negotiation.'

'I'll have to think about it.'

Delgado laughed. 'What the hell is there to think about?'

'That's understandable,' said Collins quietly. 'Why don't we meet again here, in twenty-four hours?'

Eddy was thinking hard. He needed more information, he knew where he could get it, but he didn't want Pienaar's men breathing down his neck. He turned to Collins.

'I appreciate that. In the meantime – there's something you could maybe do for me. I have a couple of people on my tail. I think it would serve both our interests if they – lost track of me temporarily.'

Collins smiled, and glanced casually across the room. 'Oh them,' he said. 'Consider it done, Mr Polonski.'

That smile and Collins's tone of voice woke Eddy up. He saw what should have been obvious: that he'd been under surveillance by Collins's own men as well from the moment he'd arrived in Vegas. The garrulous cab-driver had probably been a plant. It was a salutory and timely reminder of the sort of people he was dealing with. In this town they wielded absolute power.

'Thank you. Well, gentlemen, I've had a long day.' Eddy rose and offered his hand. 'Goodnight, Mr Collins.'

'Jim. Call me Jim. We look forward to meeting with you tomorrow night.'

Eddy walked slowly out of the restaurant, took the elevator down, and waited by the false-gold statue. After five minutes there was still no sign of Pienaar's men. As he pushed through the casino he reflected that in Call-me-Jim he had found a dangerous new friend.

During the short cab ride back to the Fremont he tried to adjust his mind to the scale of the deal he'd been offered. He went straight to his room and sat down at the desk with a calculator, a pad, and a pencil. He started by converting two thousand metric tons into troy ounces and blinked at the answer: sixty-four million. At a dollar per ounce commission – the barest minimum – that meant that he could make sixty-four million dollars. He did another calculation – the total value of the Greek gold based on the current price of $300 an ounce. He stared at the figure. Over nineteen billion dollars. It was almost beyond belief. He felt crushed by it. Where in hell was he going to find people with enough cash to buy even a fraction of it?

He'd eaten very little at dinner and he was suddenly hungry and thirsty. He took the elevator down to the ground floor and ordered tea and a Chinese meal in the coffee shop. At two in the morning the Casino was crammed. He heard a siren and hysterical shrieks, meaning that someone had won a $20,000 jackpot on one of the slots. His negative mood evaporated. The jackpot. He had been offered the deal of the century, the chance for which he'd been waiting for eighteen long years of servitude, ever since Shulov had told him: 'Go to the West, Eddy. In the West you can buy freedom, if you are rich enough. Here it is not for sale.'

He strode out to the reception desk and asked them to call him at six o'clock, his usual hour for rising. Back in his room he dialled Brooks Rent-a-Car and arranged to pick up a car at their Mel Avenue office at seven. He was going to find out just how desperate Call-me-Jim was to sell the gold. And then he was going to nail a deal that would stagger even the billionaire barons of Las Vegas.

4

Six hours later Eddy was speeding north-east on Interstate 91, the road to Pioche, where the Nevada gold rush had started back in 1870. Fifty miles short of the old boom-town, and fifty miles out of Vegas, he turned north, in Moapa, and began to wind up through the naked, lunar mountains on the road to Alamo. The heat of the new day was already ferocious, the sun blinding. By mid-morning his hired car was bouncing and rattling down a dirt track through a landscape that seemed to have been devastated by fall-out from the nuclear test-site on the other side of the eastern peaks, an arid canyon of dead sagebrush and red-brown rock where it seemed nothing could live except rattlesnakes. He rounded a hairpin and there below was an ugly cluster of towers, wheels, sheds, and shacks – twentieth-century scar tissue on the primevally harsh terrain. He pulled up in the yard to the pounding sound of the ore-crushers and, as he got out of the car, breathed in the fine dust that hung in a permanent haze over the mine.

Mulligan was in his office, leaning back in an antiquated swivel chair, his belly bulging out of a check shirt, the stub of a cigar singeing his beard, a greasy baseball cap on his head.

'Well, if it ain't my favourite defaulting Polak.'

Mulligan lurched upright in his seat and pumped Eddy's hand.

'Hi, Mulligan. I've come to settle my debt.'

He handed the miner a cheque. Mulligan squinted at it and then stuffed into his shirt pocket.

'*Gracias* Eddy,' he said. 'But why the personal visit? What happened to the US Mail?'

'I was in Vegas – thought I'd run out to see you.'

'I'm charmed, Eddy, charmed.' Mulligan grinned. 'So whaddaya want?'

'Some information, Mulligan. I've been offered a deal – a very big deal – by the people behind the Eldorado in Vegas. They seem anxious to raise a lot of money, fast. You know all the Vegas

44

scam – I just wondered if you'd heard anything?'

Mulligan removed the cigar from his mouth and regarded it thoughtfully for a moment.

'It sounds like you've been havin' dealings with my old friend Just-Call-Me-Jim Collins. If so, you're keeping bad company, my son.'

'Who is Collins?'

'Accountant from out east. Runs some kinda union – but that's all boloney. He operates the biggest laundromat for mob money in Nevada.'

'But what's his panic, Mulligan?'

Mulligan sighed like a wise man wearied by long contemplation of a sinful world.

'In two words – Federal investigation.'

'How heavy?'

'Heavy. There's a hundred-million-dollar investment in Atlantic City at stake just for openers.' He killed his cigar in an ashtray overflowing with butts. 'The drums have been beating about you too, Eddy. You're in all kinds of trouble.'

Eddy nodded. 'So would you like to do me a favour?'

Mulligan was stripping the wrapper from a fresh cigar. 'Maybe.'

'I need some dust. Good stuff – ninety-two per cent. About five kilos. Will you sell it to me?'

'I'm not supposed to sell you anything.'

'I know. But will you? You'll have to give me credit.'

'Credit! I'm a poor man.'

Mulligan was worth at least two million dollars in cash and was sitting on another ten million in the ground. He lit the cigar, half closing his eyes against the smoke. 'But I kinda hate being told what I can't do.'

Five minutes later Mulligan walked with Eddy to his car – the gold dust in an ore-bag which Eddy put on the back seat. Eddy glanced towards the vibrating Carter tables where the men were sluicing crushed ore.

'You know you're throwing away a fortune in flour gold? I could give you a simple re-cycling and filtration system that recovers eighty per cent.'

Mulligan laughed. 'A great thought, Eddy. So I start to over-produce and I get into trouble. Like you. I don't need that kinda action.' He threw a hairy arm round Eddy's shoulders. 'I don't know what drives you, Eddy – never have figured it out. But watch your back with those bastards in Vegas, huh?'

'I'll do that, Mulligan.'

Mulligan laughed again and slapped Eddy's back.

'Go for it, Eddy', he said.

By mid-afternoon Eddy was back in Vegas. He returned the car, deposited the gold in the Fremont's safe, showered some of the dust of Mulligan's mine out of his hair, then sat down to think through exactly what he would say to Collins and Delgado later in the evening.

He arrived at the Eldorado punctually at ten and found Collins and Delgado at the same table. Collins was dressed exactly as he had been the night before; Delgado was sporting a black velvet tuxedo and a shirt with brown and yellow frills. Collins was effusive.

'Eddy. Great to see you!'

Delgado nodded coolly. After some talk around the subject, Eddy stated the first of the conditions under which he would undertake to move the gold: the vendors would sell the gold to him at ten dollars per ounce under the London Gold Market price on the day of the sale, and he would then pass it on to the buyer at whatever price he was able to negotiate. The difference would be his commission. Delgado almost spat.

'Ten under? That's outrageous.'

'I don't think so. What are you getting it for?'

Eddy spoke very quietly and gently, in a manner that was almost off-hand. Delgado avoided a direct answer.

'Well, it's a figure that has to be negotiable,' he said shortly.

'If I take this deal on,' Eddy said, 'I'll be the one who has to back-to-back it. You have no exposure. Level with me. Do I have to protect you?'

Delgado looked at Collins, as if seeking guidance. Collins's face remained expressionless.

'You do,' Delgado said after a moment.

'Okay,' Eddy said. 'How many points?'

'We have our own people to take care of,' Delgado said. 'Fifty cents an ounce.'

Eddy smiled. 'Thirty-two million dollars,' he said. 'That's a heap of money. I have all the exposure, I have all the risk. I don't control the gold price. It could go up like a zipper and then my buyers could back off, leaving me naked. All you have to do is sit.'

Delgado looked confused.

'Let's leave figures aside for a moment,' Collins said smoothly. 'Eddy, you mentioned that you would require documentation. What exactly would that be?'

'A copy of the letter from Limmatbank establishing that the gold exists. A further letter from the bank stating that I have the right to negotiate the sale of the gold.'

It was a tense moment: such letters could provide an unscrupulous gold-broker with free entertainment in the best hotels for the rest of his life – and Collins and Delgado might know that.

'Nothing more?' Collins said.

Eddy concealed his delight.

'You mean a contract between ourselves?' he said. 'In the event that I'm successful in finding buyers I believe market forces will provide all the protection either of us requires. You want to sell your gold. I want to make money.'

He'd got the point over neatly, not necessarily alerting Collins to the fact that he knew how anxious he was to sell, but reminding him of it just the same.

He added: 'I'm prepared to protect you on fifty cents with a bank division order at the time of the transaction.'

He judged it a timely moment to make his next demand. 'In return I require an advance. To enable me to start chasing buyers. It's a costly process – involves a lot of travel, entertaining – and you gentlemen are aware of my circumstances.'

'How much?' Delgado asked.

'A hundred thousand.'

'You're really beautiful, Polonski. First you demand ten under, now a hundred grand advance.'

'Thanks, Paul.' Collins's soft voice silenced Delgado. He turned to Eddy.

'How long would it take you to find buyers?'

'It's difficult to assess accurately. Maybe three months, four. Not more than six.'

Collins nodded, leaned back against the padded wall of the alcove, and pensively steepled his fingers.

'To return to your original request for ten under. As you have yourself suggested, we are aware of your current circumstances. In those circumstances don't you think that figure is – shall we say, optimistic?'

Eddy smiled. It was time for the straightline punch.

'Any optimism around here is entirely on your side. I'm not

47

prepared to touch this transaction until I have guarantees from you and Mr Delgado that the highly complex banking arrangements essential to the operation will be available – and will come good.'

In Wing Tsun boxing there is a move of simultaneous defence and attack. By producing its verbal equivalent Eddy saw that he had winded Collins and put Delgado right on the spot. He allowed them a brief respite before following up his advantage.

'We're not talking about exchanging a valise full of bars for a suitcase of money in an airport safety deposit. We're talking about selling billions of dollars' worth of bullion to people who will demand total security and total secrecy. In an ideal world we'd load one truck with the gold, the buyer would load another truck with the money, and then we'd exchange drivers in the middle of the desert. But you don't do that with gold. To buy and sell gold in quantities like this you have to use the banking system. I assume that Mr Delgado is fully versed in what will be required?'

Delgado shifted in his seat as if he had gastric trouble. Eddy took pity.

'I'm sure Mr Delgado wouldn't object if I explained in layman's terms for your benefit, Jim. To put it simply – at the end of the day two letters from two prime banks will be required. The first will be from a bank representing the seller. This will confirm, with the bank's full responsibility and irrevocably, that the bank's client has the gold and will sell at a stated price. The second will be from a prime bank representing the buyer. This will confirm, with full responsibility and irrevocably, that the bank's client has the money to buy the gold and will buy it at the price stated. When you have those two letters you have a transaction. But to get letters like that out of prime banks is like asking the President of the United States to get Congress to lend you the keys to Fort Knox for the weekend. Both letters being with full responsibility and irrevocable, one *is*, so to speak, the gold and the other *is* the money. Each bank is totally committed to producing either the gold or the cash. And when you're talking about two thousand tons of bullion and over nineteen billion dollars each bank will know that if there is any default it would be wiped out.'

He paused and sipped his tea, then added, in a quieter voice: 'I undertake to get the required letters from the buyers' banks. Do I have your assurance that matching letters from your bank will be forthcoming?'

After a moment Delgado said hoarsely: 'You do.'

'Good. Then I believe we have a deal, gentlemen.'

On Saturday, the three men met again at Collins's office near the Union Pacific station. Because it was the weekend, the suite was deserted. Collins handed over twenty thousand dollars in cash to Eddy and Delgado produced copies of two telexes. The first was an instruction to Canyon Bank's Swiss subsidiary instructing them to transfer the balance of Eddy's advance, eighty thousand dollars, to a numbered account in Geneva. The second was an instruction to Limmatbank requesting them to issue to Eddy, in person, a letter authorizing him to sell the gold, the letter to be handed over only on receipt by Limmatbank of a code-word. The atmosphere was neutral and businesslike. Only when Collins handed over the money was there a hint of menace.

'Don't blow it on blackjack, Eddy, and don't forget you're working for me now.'

Eddy shrugged. 'You don't have to trust me, Jim. I don't have to trust you. We can both put our trust in market forces, remember?'

'There are other forces, Eddy.'

When Eddy had gone Delgado gave vent to his feelings. He mixed himself a Scotch and Seven-up at the drinks cabinet.

'D'you realize that if that arrogant Polak bastard pulls this off he could make – Jesus if he sold the gold at full price – he could make six hundred million dollars!'

'Don't be naïve, Paul,' Collins said. 'Do you really think we're going to hand over that kind of bread? Godfathers are supposed to be generous – but not that generous. The maximum Mr Polonski is going to make out of this is his hundred grand.'

Delgado was holding his glass halfway to his mouth, staring at Collins.

'You drink too much, Paul. We meet the Greek and Landau in Houston, Monday. I want you sober and talking as if you knew the first damned thing about banking.'

Eddy booked a tourist-class seat on the eight o'clock flight on Sunday morning to Houston via New Orleans. He bought a strong, lightweight aluminium valise at El Portal's to hold the gold dust, took a cab over to the Cambridge Raquetball Club, got a game with one of the professionals, drew the match, had a swim, and ate a three-dollar dinner in the Fremont's Fiesta Buffet.

At seven-thirty the following morning he was sitting in one of the outlying departure lounges at the airport waiting for his flight to be called, and observing his fellow travellers. They all had the dazed, dehumanized look of prisoners recently released from a KGB brainwashing clinic. They sat slumped in chairs, whey-faced and speechless, in crumpled clothes and souvenir ten-gallon hats, suffering from multiple hangovers and sexual exhaustion. Vegas had robbed them of everything but their illusions: they'd had the hell of a good time and they'd be coming back next year.

The only exception seemed to be a black minister in a dark suit and a clerical collar who was sitting opposite, looking spruce, clear-eyed, and full of zeal. There were one or two diehards playing the slots and suddenly the familiar rumble of a big payout echoed through the glass and concrete lounge. The effect on Eddy's neighbours was instant. They reacted like laboratory animals in a programmed-response experiment; in twos and threes they began to drift over to the slots for a final encounter with Fortune. Eddy caught the black preacher's eye and they exchanged a smile.

'The cry of Sodom and Gomorrah is great,' the preacher said, 'because their sin is very grievous. Arise lest thou be consumed in the iniquity of the city.'

'Is that your text for today, Reverend?' Eddy said.

The preacher spread his hands. 'It's all in the Bible, sir.'

'But, Reverend, Vegas has the highest number of churches per head of population of any city in the country.'

'And the devil goes often disguised. This is the holy of holies of the temple of Mammon, sir. A disgrace to a Christian country.'

'Well, Reverend, America was founded on gambling. The money for the *Mayflower* charter was raised through a lottery.'

Before the preacher could answer, their flight was called.

'Time to arise,' Eddy said.

Three hours later, in the terminal building at Houston International Airport, he noticed the preacher standing by a carousel. He gave him a wave and received a gesture of benediction in return.

It was just before he drifted off to sleep that night that the thought occurred to him. He was lying in bed, in the dark, having reserved his flights to Los Angeles and London and arranged for Tom Hayes to take over the apartment for six months rent-free.

50

He was thinking about the astonishing opportunity life had thrown his way, when he had remembered the preacher and his strictures on the temple of Mammon. And it suddenly struck him that ministers of Deep South fundamentalist sects do not travel on Sundays. What he could not decide was whether Jan Pienaar or Call-me-Jim had planted that genial Bible-thumper on him.

5

Dan Daniels woke at five o'clock on the morning of the Monday that changed his life. He awoke to one of the most delicious smells in the world: fresh-ground coffee and frying bacon mixed with the dawn tang of forest, lake, and mountain.

Gina wasn't in the bunk beside him and he raised himself, blinking his eyes clear, and looked through the open door of the shack. She was squatting by the fire, tipping the frying-pan over the fresh flames. Her blonde hair was tied into a pony-tail and she was dressed in cut-down jeans and one of his own shirts. Earth, Dan thought, could not possibly have anything to show more fair.

Gina turned and shouted: 'Come and get it.'

He climbed out of the bunk and into the morning. The heavy dew was wet and cold on his bare feet. He put his arms round Gina and kissed her.

'Beautiful——'

'Sure. How d'you want your eggs. Sunny side up or easy over?'

He kissed her again.

'You sound like a waitress.'

'I *am* a waitress.'

'Give me five minutes?' He glanced at the lake.

'You're out of your mind. At this time in the morning even the fish are wearing wet-suits.'

'Okay, four minutes.'

He ran down through the rough grass and greasewood bushes to the lake, waded in up to his waist, gasped, and heard Gina laugh as he took the plunge. He did ten strokes of fast crawl then slowed to breast-stroke. He dived, turned, and back-stroked slowly towards the shore. Gina was waiting for him with a towel. She wrapped it round him.

'You should try it, Gina. It's the greatest feeling in the world.'

'Not on your life, Tarzan. Now will you come and eat?'

They sat opposite each other on towels in the damp grass and ate bacon and eggs and toast.

'You and this place just go together,' said Dan.

'Why not? It's wonderful. For three nights I've slept like the dead. Is it the air or what?'

'The what,' said Dan.

He got to his knees, shuffled over to her, and put his arms round her.

'Dan, you're still wet.'

They kissed before she pulled away.

'We've just had breakfast and we have to go.'

He put his hand inside her skirt, tipping her gently back onto the grass. 'I was wrong. *This* is the greatest feeling in the world.'

Gina's frown turned to a smile.

Later, they doused the fire, rinsed the dishes in the lake, threw out the left-over food for the birds, bolted shutters, and padlocked the door of the shack. They threw their bags into the canoe and Dan paddled them out across Hoke's Lake. When they were in the middle, he stopped dipping and they drifted for a moment. They were in a silent world. There was no breeze, and hardly a bird-cry to be heard; only the faintest lisp as the canoe's prow nosed the water. At that distance the crazy old wooden shack with its tin roof looked like a toy. It was dwarfed by the Texas oaks and black cherries. Gina broke the silence, but her voice was soft.

'It must be wonderful here in winter.'

Dan nodded and plied his paddle.

'Sometimes the lake freezes right over and you can walk across it. Once there was snow right up to the roof of the shack. It was like living in an igloo.'

'I'd love to come here in winter.'

'You will.'

She laughed. 'I know you. By the time winter comes I'll be a name with a line through it in your little black book.'

'Never. It's a little red book.'

'Hey – you never told me the story of old Hoke.'

'I've had other things on my mind.'

'That's your problem. You've got a one-track mind.'

'Well that was old Hoke's problem too.'

'You mean he was a sex maniac?'

'He was a gold maniac. He spent his entire life prospecting for gold and he ended up just as poor as when he started. He was a born loser.'

'Poor old Hoke.'

'Yeah. Whenever anyone struck gold, in California, Nevada, the Klondike, Alaska, Old Hoke was there – bringin' up the rear. Then one day he came here, to the Davis Mountains, looked up, said to himself: "There's gold in them-thar hills", bought himself a few acres of land, staked a claim, built himself a shack, and started digging.'

'And he didn't strike it lucky?'

Dan shook his head. 'There isn't any gold in them-thar hills. Old Hoke just went on diggin' and diggin' until he dug himself into his grave.'

The canoe scrunched onto the gravel beach on the far side of the lake and Dan jumped out. They turned the canoe over and Dan made the painter fast to a tree. They lingered for a moment, to look back over the flat, green water to the tiny shack lost in the vastness of the forest and Dan put his arm round Gina. A handsome couple. Dan was thirty-eight, trim and muscular: tennis and jogging had kept the effects of good living at bay. His curly, unruly brown hair made him look younger than he was, as did his clothes – old jeans, battered Mexican boots, and the frayed checked shirt that Gina had worn. Gina herself, in her cut-downs and a white tee shirt, looked fresh and natural, utterly in her element. For a moment they said nothing. The sun was climbing up the sky, tingeing peaks with pink and gold, sending diagonal shafts of light glacing down through aisles of pines. In the chaos and danger of the days that followed Dan would often remember this moment, remember the scent of pine, the cry of a whitetail, the round ripple of a trout rising in the lake.

'God,' he said, 'in the form of Beauregard Johnson Landau, is about to cast us out of Eden.'

He picked up the bags and they set off down the forest track for the mile-and-a-half hike to the grass strip where Dan's plane was parked.

'How did a city boy get to buy himself a piece of paradise?' Gina asked.

'Lawyer's privilege. When old Hoke died, back in the thirties, the property passed to his sister's family. They sold it off in 1970 and Landau & Landau handled the legal business. I'd just joined the firm, fresh out of law school, didn't have a nickel. But I knew old Hoke's place. I used to spend summers out here when I was a

54

kid, working on the big ranches. I just knew I had to buy myself a piece of these mountains. It's a cartel out here, you know. A handful of billionaire ranchers has got the whole area sown up and they don't like interlopers. Hoke's place was a chance in a million. So I went right to the bank and put myself in hock.' He didn't add that he'd been in hock to banks, loan sharks, and Beauregard Johnson Landau, ever since.

The Beachcraft Baron was standing where they'd left it in the clearing. Dan climbed up onto the starboard wing, unlocked the door, and slid across the passenger seat into the pilot's seat. Gina followed. They strapped themselves in and Dan flipped the master switch, opened the throttle, primed the booster, and fired the starboard engine. When both engines were idling, Gina slid the door shut.

'What it is to be a millionaire,' she said.

Dan shrugged. He began to taxi to his take-off position and set the flaps. He reflected that Gina, a three-hundred-dollar-a-week waitress, with no debts, was probably several grand ahead of him. Gina gripped the arm-rests of her seat as they took off and as they climbed and circled she shouted above the engine roar.

'Hey, Lindbergh, we're going in the wrong direction.'

'There's something I want to show you.'

He headed the plane east, skirted Blackwind Peak, and flew high over the Blackwind ranch. 'That's Blackwind. Harvey Ravenscroft's place. Made his money in gold. Buying and selling it, not digging it. But wait till you see what's over the next mountain.'

It was a perfect, white Greek Revival mansion set like a jewel in green, velvet pasture.

'That's Barraclough,' Dan shouted. 'Fifty thousand acres of mountain, forest, pasture, vineyards, rivers, and lakes. It's totally unspoiled. Old Miss Barraclough doesn't approve of the twentieth century. Owning that place'd be like having your own little country. You'd be a prince. Monarch of all you surveyed.'

'Don't tell me. You're buying it.'

'One day. One day I'll buy it.'

'I get it. From log cabin to white house.'

'Something like that.'

'Is that your dream, Dan?'

'That's my dream,' he said, and turned the plane's nose westwards.

They touched down to refuel in San Antonio and Dan winced as a hundred gallons of high-octane aviation fuel, at a dollar a gallon, was pumped into the tank. They flew on, over the endless prairies, saw the muddy ribbon of the Guadelupe River nine thousand feet below, then the Colorado, and by nine-thirty they were approaching the five-hundred-square-mile sprawl of Houston.

Gina broke a long silence.

'By the end of the century they say it's going to be the biggest city in the world. I can believe it. It's ugly.'

'Not to a Houstonian. To him it's the biggest and the best. You know what was the first word ever spoken from the moon?'

She shook her head.

'"Houston." When Apollo Eleven touched down Neil Armstrong said: "Houston. Tranquillity Base here. The Eagle has landed." Sums it up. Sums something up, anyway.'

'Give me a shack in the mountains.'

'Give me Barraclough.'

Dan began the descent towards Hobby Airport. There was heavy traffic behind him and he had to concentrate. There was that little moment of exhilarating disquiet as the wheels hit the tarmac, then the release of tension as he spoke into the radio.

'Ground, this is Baron 3306 Romeo Juliet. Parking at Mitsubishi.'

'Roger, Baron. Turn off at the first intersection and taxi to the ramp.'

When the mechanic had tapped off the tanks, they climbed out and drank the traditional toast to a safe landing with cans of Coors beer.

'From heaven to hell in three hours. Cheers,' said Gina.

Dan picked up his Mercedes, dropped Gina off, and was at his office on the thirtieth floor of One Shell Plaza by ten-thirty. He had just changed into a suit, shirt, and tie – adding a good five years to his age – when Landau's secretary called.

'Oh, Mr Daniels? Mr Landau would be glad if you'd see him in his office as soon as possible.'

His own secretary informed him: 'Dan, Mr Landau called. He said I should cancel all your afternoon appointments. Is that okay?'

As he strolled down the corridor to Landau's sanctum, Dan wondered. Now what?

Landau was sitting behind his desk. The desk was a huge thing of satinwood and glinting ormolu and Landau was a huge thing of yellowish skin, with an almost bald head, and glinting gold jewellery: tie-pin, watch, cufflinks, rings. Behind Landau the big picture window gave a superb view of the twin, black, trapezoidal towers of the Penzoil building and what Landau called 'My Houston'. Opposite Landau, slumped in a chair, and puffing at one of his poisonous little cigars, was Walter Shipley.

'Morning Dan,' Landau said. 'Good trip?'

'Terrific.'

'Don't know how you can afford that plane.'

'I can't.'

Dan turned to Shipley. 'Hi, Ship. How're things?'

'Can't complain,' Shipley said.

Dan sat down and looked at Landau. 'You cancelled my afternoon meetings, Beau. What's the panic?'

'Not a panic, Danny boy – a deal. A big one. Ever heard of a Greek shipping guy called Maniatos?'

'Gheorgis Maniatos? Sure.'

'What d'you know about him?'

Dan marshalled his facts.

'At one time he was as big as Onassis. But he didn't go for divorces, opera singers, and yachts, so the public hardly ever heard of him. Round about five years ago he went under. Or nearly went under. Something happened in his personal life – a problem with his wife, I believe – and he went to pieces. Spends his time city-hopping – Paris, London, New York, all over the world never stays more than a few days anywhere. Carries his money in an old airline bag. Pays cash for everything. He's a crazy old man.'

'You seem mighty well-informed.'

'That's what you pay me for, Beau,' Dan said. 'Another thing about Maniatos. He's into whores. I don't mean two-thousand-dollar call-girls, I mean the streets. The cheaper the better.'

Landau looked uncomfortable. He was a prude. Dan smiled cheerfully at him.

'Rumour has it that he gets them to piss in his face.'

Shipley chuckled. Landau coughed, then found his voice.

'Have you ever met Maniatos?'

'I've stayed in the same hotels, but I've never met him. He isn't a very sociable type.'

'Well, you're going to meet him at lunch today.'

'Am I? Why?'

Landau leaned forward and clasped his hands together on the desk.

'Maniatos and his associates have a problem. They have some gold they want to sell and they want to sell it privately – to Arabs. I've told them that we're the Arab experts in this city and we can help them.'

'*We*, Beau?'

Landau attempted to turn a scowl into a smile, and failed. The only time Beauregard Johnson Landau had met an Arab he'd kept his sunglasses on throughout the meeting. Dan had explained: 'They have to see your *eyes*, Beau, it's the elementary rule.' Landau had blown the deal. Dan glanced at Shipley.

'Hold on just a moment, Beau. These "associates". Would they have anything to do with Ship here?'

Landau didn't answer and Shipley, with some reluctance, took up his cue.

'They are clients of mine,' he said.

'Are they really? You can include me out, Beau.'

'Now, come on, Dan,' Landau said. 'This could be an enormous deal. Enormous.'

'I don't care if it's the Alaska Purchase, Beau, I'm not getting myself mixed up with those turkeys. I told you that six years ago and I'm telling you again now.'

'It's a totally bona fide business transaction,' Shipley volunteered.

'Walter, if you want to get yourself de-barred, or wind up with a pair of cement sneakers on your feet, or both, that's your business. I'm legit. I want to stay that way.'

Landau interposed. 'Walter – would you mind? This is something I think Dan and I should talk over in private.'

As the door closed on Shipley, Dan pre-empted Landau.

'Forget it, Beau. I'm not playing.'

Landau stood up and walked to the window.

'Danny boy,' he said, 'do you know how much money you owe me – personally owe me – at this moment?'

Dan hated him. Beauregard Johnson Landau, doyen of the Houston legal profession, who mixed with mobsters; Beauregard Johnson Landau, philanthropist, who made millions out of laundering underworld money; Beauregard Johnson Landau, Southern Gentleman, who, for nine years, had denied him a partnership or any participation in the huge profits he generated for the firm because he'd been born on the wrong side of town in a frame-house with a leaking roof, and not in a mansion with a butler at the door.

'Two hundred thousand, Dan,' Landau said. 'That's a lot of money.'

'Not to you, Beau. To you it's nickels and dimes. But I take your point. Okay. Go ahead. Break me.'

Landau moved away from the window and laid a fatherly hand on Dan's shoulder.

'I don't want to break you, Danny. I want to make you. I'm offering you a piece of this. You can pay me back, settle all your other debts. Get yourself clear.'

Danny boy stood up. 'Does this include a partnership?'

Landau looked away, once again he cleared his throat before he could speak.

'Okay, okay – you can have a goddam partnership.'

'I'll need that in writing, Beau. And *I'll* draft the document.'

Landau shrugged awkwardly.

'This must be one hell of a deal,' Dan said. 'One hell of a deal.'

6

At noon Dan and Landau walked through the glass doors of the Warwick Hotel, through the lavish foyer, floored with white marble and walled with panelling from the Murat Palace in Paris, to the elevators. There was a man lurking outside the door of Maniatos's suite, a man in a sharp, blue suit, with cropped, black hair. Dan noticed a discreet, silver ring in his left ear. An obvious pro. Dan raised an eyebrow and shrugged, making sure Landau noticed the gestures. As the door of the suite opened he said in an undertone:

'Hope you're packin' a gat, Beau.'

They entered an ornately furnished living room in which there were three men. Two of them rose. The third remained seated – in a high-backed armchair, like a throne. Dan hardly glanced at Jim Collins and Paul Delgado; his entire attention focused on the third figure, a grey wisp of a man dressed in a white, silk suit and a black, polo-neck sweater.

Gheorgis Maniatos dominated the room. He dominated with his eyes. They were visionary eyes, Napoleonic eyes, and they were staring out of the most ravaged face Dan had ever seen.

It may be that a man's future can be read in the lines of his hand; a man's past can certainly be read in the lines of his face. The Greek's face was not so much lined as crizzled, split into sections by a network of deep cracks and skinfolds – each strange fissure a seismic record of the tremors and eruptions that had made and destroyed him. Dan knew that the Greek was only fifty-five; his face was that of a man centuries old.

He realized he was staring, and turned to shake hands with Collins and Delgado. Collins, he thought, looked like a professor of English at a minor East Coast university and so, given his actual occupation, seemed sinister. Delgado looked like a *shmuck*. There was some introductory chat, in which the Greek played no part, then Landau said:

'Well, gentlemen, perhaps we should familiarize my associate with the nature of your problem.'

Dan found himself taking a letter from Delgado. It was an inter-bank letter from Limmatbank CS of Zurich, to Canyon Bank, Las Vegas. *Two thousand tons of gold.* It was impossible.

He looked up to find the Greek gazing at him intently. The Greek spoke for the first time.

'Is true,' he said.

Dan turned to the others. 'I – er – I appreciate your difficulty, gentlemen, if you want to sell this. It's – well, it's incredible.'

Delgado said: 'It's our view that the only individuals with the resources to buy such a large quantity of bullion, and who'd want to, would be Arabs. Do you agree with that assessment, Mr Daniels?'

'Maybe. Even for Arabs this is a tall order.'

'Our understanding is that many of the Gulf rulers are eager to get out of paper into bullion,' Delgado said.

'So Mr Landau has informed us,' added Collins quietly.

Mr Landau thinks a camel's a cigarette, Dan thought.

'It's a blanket statement,' he said. 'But in essence he's correct.'

Dan could see that this had not been lost on Collins. So could Landau.

'Dan is our senior international attorney,' Landau said. 'He handles the nuts and bolts. I think I can say with confidence that the name of Landau & Landau carries some considerable weight in Saudi Arabia and the Emirates.'

The Greek spoke again. He addressed Landau.

'Mist' Landau. Who you deal with in Saudi?'

Landau blandly named a senior Saudi prince.

'Know him?' the Greek asked, shifting the crag of an eyebrow upwards.

'Naturally.'

Beau having flunked, Dan decided to graduate.

'In this transaction, of course,' he said, 'we would not be dealing with that particular gentleman. Mr Landau knows that it's the custom in Arab families to share out responsibility for major deals among all the sons, in rotation. I guess that this year we'd have to approach——' He named another prince.

There was the ghost of a smile on Collins's face, and a slight tremor among the geological features of the Greek's. Dan pressed home his advantage.

'I think I can claim some credibility in Saudi,' he said. 'A year or two back I handled the contracts on the construction of an ammonia-urea plant. A five-hundred-million-dollar deal.'

'What about gold, Mr Daniels? Have you ever handled a gold transaction involving Arabs?' Delgado again.

Dan nodded. 'Sure. I've been responsible for setting up Swiss accounts and holding companies in Luxembourg for several of the Gulf princes. Acting as personal attorney, I've arranged both performance bonds and bullion purchases – for people in Dubai, Oman, Khatam.'

'Do you think it's possible that – with your contacts – you could sell the gold?' Collins said.

Before Dan could reply, the Greek said: '*All*. All gold.'

There was passion in the staccato utterance and both Landau and Delgado looked startled.

Dan said: 'I think it's possible. Yes.'

'I assume,' Delgado said, 'that you are familiar with the very complex banking arrangements the transaction would require?' He turned to Landau. 'Or would you be handling that side?' Landau looked baffled and Delgado went on: 'I mean, in an ideal world we'd load one truck up with the gold, the buyer'd load another up with the money and we'd exchange drivers in the middle of the desert.' He looked at Dan. 'But I assume that your clients will demand absolute secrecy and total security?'

'Of course. Obviously the transactions will have to be completed through prime banks. I am familiar with the procedure – but the scale of the thing. That might cause us problems.'

'What about time?' Collins said. 'How long will it take you to set it up?'

'Well, it's difficult to say. Three months maybe, if I concentrated exclusively on it.'

'And you have my guarantee, gentlemen,' Landau said, not missing the opportunity of putting Dan in his place, 'that Dan here will do just that. His time is my time and my time is yours.'

At that point there was a knock on the door and waiters arrived, wheeling in a buffet lunch. At a moment when Landau, Collins, and Delgado were in a huddle, discussing commissions, fees, and terms, Dan wandered over towards the window, where the Greek was standing, looking out. The Greek gazed up at him with his compelling eyes.

'Arabs.' He almost spat the word. 'Bad. Twist, turn. Snakes.'

'I've always found that they honour their word,' Dan said.

The Greek shook his head. 'Some, yes. Some, no. Be careful.'

'I'm always careful, sir.'

The Greek nodded and turned away. 'Not too careful,' he said. 'Bold, brave, too.' He turned back, focusing the full intensity of his gaze on Dan. He said, less jerkily, and very softly: 'You want be rich, you must be bold. You see chance, you take it by the throat.'

And it dawned on Dan that he was not being given the benefit of a billionaire's philosophy; he was being given a message.

Dan and Landau left after lunch, having arranged a further meeting, for the following morning, to discuss detail. When they'd gone, Collins turned to the Greek.

'Well – do you think Mr Daniels is hooked?'

The Greek nodded slowly. 'Clever man. Very hungry man. Very hungry.'

'He's as arrogant as the Pole,' said Delgado.

'And as smart,' Collins smiled. 'I wonder which one of them'll win the race?'

'Neither of them, presumably,' Delgado said and laughed.

They both looked at the Greek – but he seemed miles away. After a moment he shrugged and the crust of his face heaved into what would otherwise be called a grin; even Collins could not feel quite at ease.

'We see,' he said. 'Daniels – very clever man.'

As Dan and Landau stepped out of the white cool of the Warwick into the heat haze, Landau remarked: 'Amazing face the Greek has. Really weird.'

'I noticed you staring at him,' Dan said. 'I wondered if you were lookin' for traces of urine.'

Landau stopped. All the fury he had been forced to bottle up during the meeting burst out.

'Sometimes, Danny boy, I think you are the most disgusting human being in the entire Greater Houston area.'

Dan grinned. 'Beau, Beau – a true compliment coming from the master of them all.' As Landau continued to glare at him, he added: 'I think I'll take a cab back to the office. See you tomorrow, Beau.' Then he walked away.

Landau gaped after him, thinking up something cutting to shout. Inspiration failed to come. As he got into his car he comforted himself with the thought that, prick though Daniels was, he had him nailed to the floor – with two hundred thousand dollars' worth of nails.

Dan didn't take a cab. He walked, aimlessly, totally preoccupied by what the Greek had hinted. Viewing it from every angle, he finally concluded that it had been a clear invitation to stab Beau Landau in the back and handle the sale of the Greek gold himself.

He looked up, to orientate himself, and found that he was in an area he had hardly visited in twenty years – the shanty streets of the East Side, the land of the Urban Cowboy. The old house on Rosedale was still there, shabbier and more desolate than ever. The broken windows were patched with cardboard and the place had been taken over, as had most of the district, by poor blacks. As he walked on down to MacGregor Park, where as a hungry street arab he'd hunted for moccasin snakes in the bayou, he remembered how his father would come home stinking drunk at eleven in the morning and his mother would scream: 'You got yourself fired again, right?' And his father would muster what dignity he had left. 'I resigned on a matter of principle,' he'd say and subside onto the old horsehair couch while Mother cried quietly in the kitchen. He turned north and passed the pillared, Art-Deco buildings of the San Jacinto High School, the place where he'd first realized that there was a way out of the East Side, where he'd first glimpsed the American Dream.

He suddenly realized that his legs were aching. He'd walked for miles. It was six o'clock. He hailed a cab and told the driver: 'The Warwick.'

Collins didn't seem unduly surprised to see him again and the Greek said: 'By the throat,' and laughed. Delgado was out.

The discussion that followed was brief and business-like. The Greek and Collins were prepared to sell their gold at ten dollars under with a fifty-cent kickback; it was up to Dan to make the best deal he could with the buyers. They agreed to furnish Dan with a copy of the Limmatbank letter, and with another letter authorizing him to negotiate the sale of the gold. The Greek leaned forward and gripped Dan's arm.

'Have to sell all the gold. All of it.'

As if to change the subject, Collins said 'I take it we can leave it to you to inform Mr Landau of our – new arrangement.'

'It's something I've been looking forward to for a long time.'

'It doesn't mean you're on your own, Mr Daniels,' said Collins, smiling. 'You have us behind you.'

Dan wasn't sure whether that was reassurance or threat.

Dan left the hotel after an hour and took a cab back to the office to pick up his car. He remembered nothing about the cab ride; he drove to his bachelor apartment off Memorial Drive on automatic pilot. Dazed, he sat down at his desk to write a letter of resignation to Beau Landau.

The first version of the letter was angry, accusing, and self-justifying. It was also long-winded. Dan tore it up. The second version was succinct but bitter. He tore that up. The third read: 'Dear Beau, I quit. Yours, Dan.'

He called Braniff and reserved a flight to London and Zurich. Then he called his ex-wife.

'Hi, Elizabeth. Are the kids going to be home tonight? I have to go away on a long trip, I'd like to see them before I go. Okay fine. Around nine.'

At about the time that Dan was driving over to the mock-Georgian house in Hedwig Village where his married life had begun, and ended, in extravagance and debt, Paul Delgado was being ushered into a suite on the tenth floor of the Hyatt Regency Hotel. He had no idea whom he was going to meet. He had agreed to the appointment solely because the anonymous voice that had spoken to him over the phone in Vegas on Sunday night had mentioned the magic word *gold*. He had not told Collins where he was going and had made sure that none of Collins's people had tailed him. He had scented an opportunity of selling the Greek gold himself – of making an overnight fortune.

The man who rose to greet him was of middle height, lean, elderly, tanned. He had strange, violet eyes.

'Mr Delgado,' he said, 'how very kind of you to come. My name is Jan Pienaar.'

Delgado studied the card Pienaar had given him, his excitement mounting. Mining Consolidated International. Big gold people. He accepted a stinger and lit a cigarette.

'I will come straight to the point, Mr Delgado,' Pienaar said. 'You have recently been seeing something of a man called Polonski. I would be most interested to know more about the nature of your discussions, and I would be prepared to pay very handsomely for the information.'

Delgado drew on his cigarette and exhaled with a hiss. His excitement had died.

'Mr Pienaar,' he said, 'I came here tonight because I was given to understand that you were interested in buying some gold. I'm not an information service.'

Pienaar smiled. 'Buying gold, Mr Delgado? No, no – I do not buy gold. But I do give it away – in exchange for information.' With that he opened a briefcase that was lying beside him on the sofa, and took out a gold bar. He laid the bar on the low coffee table.

Delgado gaped. It was quite simply the most beautiful thing he had ever seen. He reached out to touch it, running his fingers over the surface. It was smooth and warm and there were fine creases, like the lines on the palm of a hand, from where it had lain in its mould. There was an extraordinary freshness about the metal; you could believe that only seconds before it had been liquid. It was *delicious* to look at it. He wanted to devour it.

There was a half-smile on Pienaar's face as he observed Delgado's reaction. He had seen it so many times: the wonder, the awe, the desire that made men instant slaves to gold, that enabled you to buy anybody in the world with it.

'It's four hundred ounces. Its worth is approximately one hundred and twenty thousand dollars. Do you consider that sufficient recompense for a little information, Mr Delgado?'

Shakily Delgado downed his stinger. He had forgotten the world of threats and fear in which he lived. Collins might have him maimed or killed; the risk was trivial.

'What do you want to know?' he said.

It was as he drove away from the house in Hedwig Village that Dan perceived the flaw in the scheme. He'd listened with pleasure to his daughter Annie's ambitions to follow her father into the law; with amusement to his son Joe's dreams of getting into the movies; and with weary patience to Elizabeth's long moan about her poverty. But Elizabeth's tirade against her bank manager (delivered as she casually fed ten dollars' worth of prime beef to her Alsatian) had reminded him of his own position. He was flat broke.

As he drove past the manicured lawns and floodlit mansions of the lawyers, doctors, and businessmen who had once been his neighbours, he reflected that the house he had signed over to Elizabeth as part of the divorce settlement was now worth around three hundred and fifty thousand dollars – exactly what he owed. His eighty-thousand-a-year salary – fifty-seven after tax – just about kept the raft of debt afloat, but after tomorrow he wouldn't have a salary, and he was committed to flying halfway round the world, wining and dining bankers, and entertaining Arabs. How in God's name was he going to pay for it all?

He let himself into his apartment and was surprised to see light filtering through from the bedroom.

Gina was sitting up in his bed, wearing nothing but scent.

'Daniels, you bastard. You never called me.'

He couldn't produce a flip reply. He sat heavily on the bed.

'I'm sorry, Gina. Really.'

'What's the matter, Dan? You look as if you've just been mugged.'

'Yeah. I just mugged myself. Would you like to loan me fifty thousand dollars, Gene?'

'Money troubles?'

'Like you wouldn't believe.'

'Come on, Dan. You're one of the haves.'

'I'm one of the suckers.' He lay down and clasped his hands behind his head. 'The world is divided into the rich, the poor, and the suckers. It all works on a formula, Gene, a formula. The rich manufacture dreams, and sell them to the suckers, who can't afford to pay for them. So the rich loan money to the suckers, and get richer.'

'And where does that leave the poor?'

'Free, I guess.' He shrugged. 'I'm a dreamer and a loser – like old Hoke. Goddammit Gina I've just been offered the kind of deal that happens once a century. And I haven't got enough cash for a plane ticket to London.'

'That bad?'

'That bad.'

Gina was pensive for a moment, then she said: 'I had a dream once. I was working in a bar in New York, just bust up with my boyfriend, broke, ready to kill myself. I thought why don't I just take my Diner's card, buy a ticket to somewhere ritzy and romantic, stay at the best hotel, and just go on spending until they cancel my card. I reckoned I could keep going for maybe three months. Then I'd just swim out to sea and go on till I sank. I'd go down, I thought, but I'd take a piece of the goddam system with me.' Dan was staring at her. She said: 'Your credit rating must be a hell of a lot higher than mine.'

He laughed and hugged her. 'Gina, you're beautiful and you're wise. I'll take the road to Eldorado, courtesy of American Express.'

'Eldorado? That was a legend, wasn't it?'

'Okay, Gene. But this is for real.'

She smoothed his hair. 'Are you going to spend the whole night talking, Dan Daniels?'

'Hell no.'

7

'The one thing Continentals don't understand at all is breakfast,' Lord Ilminster said.

He was sitting at a white, wrought-iron table spread with a full English breakfast of fried eggs, crisp bacon, sausages, fried tomatoes, toast, Frank Cooper's marmalade, and tea. The table was set on the balcony of a suite in the Baur au Lac Hotel, Zurich, which commanded a magnificent view of the lake, shimmering in the morning sunshine.

'I have lived in France for fifteen years,' Ilminster went on, 'but I have yet to come to terms with the *baguette*, the *croissant*, and that dreadful coffee that tastes like slurry. Are you sure you won't join me, Anthony?'

Anthony Melldrum shook his head. 'No thanks,' he said. 'I breakfasted on the plane.'

Ilminster grimaced. 'Don't tell me,' he said. 'Soggy buns wrapped in cellophane, and jam made out of coal. The thought of it quite spoils my appetite.'

It didn't appear to. The old man attacked his food with the vigour of a schoolboy. He was casually dressed in a white tennis shirt and blue slacks; you wouldn't have taken him for an English earl or even an Englishman. With his long, white hair, his narrow, crooked face, dominated by a high-bridged hook of a nose, and his short, sinewy build, he had the air of an Italian – a sculptor or a painter perhaps – aged but alert. Melldrum, his son-in-law, was quintessentially English. He was tall – well over six feet – lean, and square-shouldered. His straight, brown hair was carefully parted on the left, his hazel eyes were set wide apart above a thin, pendulous nose, and his cheeks were concave, giving a hawk-like cast to his face. He wore a Savile Row suit, a cinnamon shirt, with white collar and cuffs, and an Old Wykehamist City tie – thin, diagonal stripes of red, blue, and brown on a black background.

What Ilminster and Melldrum had in common was the voice –

69

the clipped, drawled, slightly honking voice which the English ruling class inherits along with its acres and privileges, and which cannot be acquired by lesser breeds, even through a public-school education. It was the sort of voice in which Lord Cardigan might have ordered the Light Brigade to charge.

'Well, Anthony,' Ilminster said, wiping his mouth with a napkin, 'what did you want to see me about? Something important, I trust.'

'Potentially. The Greek and his confrères have come up with a feasible method of selling their gold.'

Lord Ilminster frowned and wrinkled his nose. 'Have they indeed? I'm sorry to hear that. We have been guardians of the Greek gold for so long now, I had almost come to consider it our own property. And what is this method of disposal that you consider feasible?'

'A private sale. They have approached two men – Americans – a precious metals refiner called Polonski and an international lawyer called Daniels. I've done a preliminary check on both of them. Daniels has impressive contacts in the Middle East, and a wide experience of this sort of transaction. Polonski is a more mysterious animal but since he has been producing and selling his own gold we can presume that he knows the right people.'

'Are these two men working together?'

'On the contrary. Neither of them knows that the other exists.'

'I see.' Ilminster smiled. 'How very cynical of the Greek and his friends.'

Melldrum didn't respond immediately – he was preparing the kernel of his argument.

'I suggest that we should do everything in our power to facilitate the sale,' he said.

Ilminster's eyes narrowed. 'Go on,' he said.

Melldrum leaned forward and spoke quietly for ten minutes. His father-in-law didn't interrupt him. He stared out at the mountains that rose beyond the lake. Half his mind was absorbing the brilliant and audacious plan that Anthony was outlining, the other half was attempting to assess his son-in-law's motives for proposing it.

Ilminster had engineered Anthony's appointment as International Treasurer of the Central and Shires Bank at the early age of thirty-seven for three reasons: his only daughter, Frances, had insisted on marrying the man, even though his background was one of genteel poverty; he was an outstanding technocrat, highly qualified in the computer sciences essential to modern banking; and he was utterly unscrupulous. For three years he had performed brilliantly, maintaining the vital separation between the bank's day-to-day High-Street business and its infinitely more lucrative multi-national activities, without arousing either the hostility or the suspicions of those members of the board who were not family placemen. The question was: how wide were Anthony's personal ambitions? Did he see this bullion business as a means of establishing himself as an independent member of the élite? Was he a fit and proper person to be elected to the club? If he succeeded, would the club have the power to deny him entry?

When Melldrum had finished Ilminster was silent for a moment. Finally he said: 'What you propose is – epic. I think that's the correct word.'

Melldrum rose and leaned over the balcony, staring down at the stream of office workers disembarking from the ferry, at the orderly traffic jam in Général Guisnan Quai.

'The concept is conventional enough – only the scale is epic.' He turned and looked directly at Ilminster. 'Just how epic would depend on you. I can mobilize the South Africans but you, I think, have access to – to other spheres of influence whose co-operation would be essential and whose profits would be, well, enormous.'

Ilminster did not answer for a moment, and when he did it was, characteristically, at a tangent.

'My immediate reaction,' he said, 'is that a great deal depends on these two Americans, Daniels and ——'

'Polonski.'

'Extraordinary names Americans have.'

'Everything depends on them.'

'Quite so. And if they really are capable of finding buyers for the Greek gold, they are certainly capable of putting two and two together if things go wrong for them. Then what?'

'I think it's unlikely,' Melldrum said. 'But remember the cynicism of our Greek and his friends. It's quite clear that they have no intention of letting either Daniels or Polonski collect his commission. At the end of the day our Americans will be neutralized by their own clients.'

Ilminster nodded. 'Very neat, Anthony. However, there is a factor that seems to have been left out of these calculations. It's many years since I was directly involved in the gold world, of course, but in my day it was a very small world. I doubt if it has grown very significantly since I was put out to grass. There is a strong possibility that Daniels and Polonski will run across each other. They're chasing the same fox, after all.'

'I had thought of that possibility,' Melldrum said. 'If you think about it, it could only work to our advantage.'

Ilminster pondered for a moment. 'I see what you mean,' he said. 'Yes. Might it be a sound move to bring about just such a meeting?'

'No. I think it would be unnecessarily indiscreet.'

Ilminster replenished the tea-pot with hot water and poured himself a fresh cup.

'Do I take it that I have your backing?' Melldrum said.

Ilminster smiled. 'You have not mentioned your terms, Anthony.'

Melldrum shrugged faintly. 'Terms?' he said, as if he'd never heard the word before.

Ilminster took a sip of tea. 'I think you understand what I mean, Anthony. There are rewards other than financial rewards.'

'Isn't it rather premature to talk about that? We have no idea how Polonski and Daniels will perform. All I need at this early stage is your support in principle. Ultimately my own position would depend, as ever, on you.'

'I'm rather fond of tepid tea,' Ilminster said. 'Very well, you have my support. But you must take it step by step, Anthony. Consult me at every stage. Which of the South Africans, for instance, do you propose to approach?'

Melldrum was about to say Jan Pienaar. But he changed his mind. 'I thought Van Lennaert.'

Ilminster shook his head. 'No, no, no. Quite wrong, my dear boy. Van Lennaert's tainted with honesty. Pienaar's your man – Jan Pienaar. You know him, of course?'

'Yes, I do. An excellent suggestion.'

Melldrum was amused. The old recluse of Montillac, considered an eccentric English milord by his bucolic neighbours, still ruled: and it was no disadvantage to Melldrum to allow him an opportunity to parade his power. There had been times when Melldrum had thought that the old man would rule from beyond the grave: but not now. He glanced at his watch.

'I'd better be on my way. Our friends are both due to see Pierre today.'

'How amusing. You're flying back this afternoon?' Melldrum

nodded. 'Well give my love to Frances and the children. And keep me informed, Anthony.'

Eddy walked out of Zurich station and turned down Bahnhof Strasse. He sat down in one of the pavement cafés to drink a cup of tea, watch the world go by, and let his instincts double-check that he was alone. There was an unusually vivacious air about the stolid, antiseptic Swiss city that morning. The sun put a spring in every step and a greeting on every lip. The blue-and-white trolley buses that plied up and down the boulevard reminded him of railcars in a leisure park; they seemed so frivolously bright and clean. As he listened to the babble of French and German round him, he felt suddenly and strangely at home. He'd had the same feeling as the Paris train had hummed through the plains of northern France, those vast plains that stretched out two thousand miles east to the Urals of central Russia – those same plains that formed the heartland of his own Poland.

He finished his tea, paid for it, and strolled on in the direction of Tal Strasse. He'd phoned Limmatbank from Paris and arranged to see Pierre Schurch, the bank's president, at noon. The Limmatbank building was a forbidding concrete cube, graceless and faceless. He showed his passport to the security guard at the foot of a white marble staircase and after a few minutes an impossibly elegant secretary appeared – Valentino dress, scarf knotted at the throat   to escort him to the reception area on the first floor. He noticed that there were closed-circuit TV cameras at strategic points, exactly as in a Las Vegas casino

Pierre Schurch was a well-covered, baby-faced Swiss in his mid-fifties. He wore a grey, double-breasted suit, gold-rimmed glasses, and an obvious, white-blond wig. Eddy saw that he had no eyebrows or lashes and assumed that his body was completely hairless – probably owing to some thyroid disease. Behind the tinted lenses of his glasses Schurch's eyes blinked constantly. His manner was courteous but very reserved, typical, in fact, of a Swiss banker whose most sacred article of faith is confidentiality.

'My apologies,' Schurch said in nearly flawless English, 'but if I might examine your passport, Mr Polonski?'

While Schurch turned over the pages of the passport, Eddy glanced round the room. It was hung with abstract paintings, geometric patterns of grey and white, bland and expensive. There was also a TV camera discreetly placed in a corner, just below the ceiling.

Schurch was looking at him expectantly. Eddy nodded and pulled a jotting pad across the desk towards him. He wrote down the code-word with which Delgado had supplied him and Schurch smiled for the first time, revealing several gold teeth.

'May I say welcome to Zurich? I am under instructions to offer you every facility.'

If Eddy had chanced to glance up at the TV eye in the corner at that moment he would have seen the camera tip forward very slightly. But he had no reason to look in that direction. Even he did not suspect that the eye might be wide open – and trained directly on him. Melldrum studied Eddy's face in close-up on the monitor screen. Next to him sat another man, stocky and Germanic, his face pitted with the scars of adolescent acne. Melldrum leaned forward and adjusted the volume control. There was a frown of concentration on his brows as he listened to Schurch and Eddy exchanging technicalities. The other man looked profoundly bored. When Eddy finally rose and shook hands with Schurch, Melldrum turned to his companion.

'Well, Herr Zwingler, that's one of them. I want a complete dossier on him. Background, financial position, vices, the usual thing.' Zwingler nodded. Melldrum pressed an intercom. 'All right, Pierre,' he said, 'wheel the other one in.'

Dan saw Eddy being escorted out of Schurch's office. Instead of remaining seated in the reception area, where there was nothing more attractive than a pile of back numbers of the *International Financial Digest*, he had wandered out into the corridor to try his French on the pretty telephonist. Something about the tall, bearded man who came out of Schurch's office struck an immediate chord in his memory. He had a cinematic recall for faces. The moment passed. The man, whoever he was, was hustled away towards the stairs, and Schurch's elegant secretary returned to tell him that the banker was ready to see him.

But one of the first questions he asked Schurch, after they had introduced themselves, was: 'Who was that guy who was just in your office? I'm sure I know him from somewhere.'

Schurch blinked even more rapidly. 'A Russian. From the Narodny Bank.'

'Doesn't make any connections,' Dan said.

In the adjoining office Melldrum chuckled. He was interested that Daniels's discussion with Schurch had followed almost exactly the same pattern as Polonski's. When Dan left he went through, followed by Zwingler, and eased a thigh onto Schurch's desk.

'Well?'

'I am impressed with them,' Schurch said.

'So am I.' He turned to Zwingler. 'There you are, Herr Zwingler. You know what to do.'

Zwingler nodded. When he'd left, Schurch said: 'I don't like that man. I don't like him at all.'

'Well, he's remarkably unlikeable.'

Schurch stood up. It made him uneasy when the tall Englishman loomed over him. It was a reminder of their relative positions. He was president of an important Swiss bank, but the bank was a wholly-owned subsidiary of Central and Shires. Melldrum was fifteen years his junior, but he was the one who, ultimately, issued the orders.

'With people like Zwingler around I get nervous,' he said.

Melldrum smiled and looked at Schurch quizzically. He was a typical arms-length man, didn't like to get his hands dirty, an administrator rather than a buccaneer, effective but unimaginative. However he was discreet – fanatically discreet.

'Don't worry, Pierre. Comfort yourself with the thought that you are shortly going to make an awful lot of money. Shall we have some lunch?'

8

A summer rainstorm had deluged Hong Kong during the night, perpendicular cataracts of water turning the new glass and concrete canyons of the Wanchai district into wild gorges. But by six o'clock in the morning, when Eddy left the Harbour Hotel and began to walk along Gloucester Road in the direction of Victoria Park, the monsoon had blown itself out, and the sun was climbing out of the China Sea. The only remaining traces of the storm were three thick fingers of silver-grey cloud curled round the exclusive heights of The Peak. There were stray taxis about, splashing through the lakes left by the storm; some boys in bathing shorts were loading a lorry with lengths of bamboo scaffolding; Mr Wang, who owned the tiny photocopying booth on the corner of Stewart Street, was up and about and gave Eddy a wave and a greeting; otherwise the streets were deserted. Victoria Park by contrast was the centre of a great and strange activity. The municipal – one-time colonial – lawns and groves had been taken over by a motley army of Chinese, split up into military-style platoons, and performing a weird, slow-motion ballet, the ritual dance of *tai-chi*.

Some of the groups were uniformly dressed in white smocks and trousers, and were being directed by a master, but the majority were composed of ordinary people – old women, smartly dressed secretaries, youths in jeans and tee-shirts, businessmen in shiny suits. All these diverse types were united in the fluid shadow-boxing – arms, legs, hands, feet, rising, falling, twisting, turning in perfect unison. One old lady in particular caught Eddy's eye. She wore a hideous, pink trouser-suit, she was fat and squat, but she moved with the undulating grace of a nautch dancer. Eddy stepped over the low post-and-chain barrier onto the lawn and fell in behind the pink lady. He found his body slipping naturally into the movements even though he had practised them only intermittently in recent years. When the dance was over there was a moment of silence and repose then the groups began to disperse.

'You move like an old water-buffalo, brother Eddy.'

It was a quavery, parsonical voice and Eddy recognized it instantly. He turned. Lim San Feng was standing a few feet away, a faint smile on his wizened face. He was dressed in the dark suit and fawn raincoat of the free world. The last time Eddy had seen him he had worn the tunic and trousers of Mao's China, and had been teaching special army cadres in Peking. Eddy strode over and grasped his hand.

'Master Lim – this is wonderful.'

Several of the boys pricked up their ears at the legendary name Lim and edged nearer to stare.

'I recognized you – even with your beard and even with my old eyes,' Lim said.

He was completely bald now, Eddy saw, but still carried himself erect despite his great age. They began to walk. Lim, it transpired, had left China five years ago and now had a school at Sham Tseng in the New Territories. There was a car waiting in Causeway Road, with one of Lim's pupils at the wheel.

'I visit Hong Kong only rarely now,' Lim said. 'But when I do I like to observe the new generation. Our meeting was providential. Will you come and see me at my school?'

Eddy made a rapid mental review of his schedule.

'Could I come tonight, Master?'

Lim nodded. 'It will be a pleasure to entertain you.'

Eddy walked back to the hotel. It was comfortable, moderately priced, and seemed to be patronized by Asian businessmen and delegates to some religious conference. His room had a magnificent view of Victoria Harbour and the skyscrapers of Kowloon.

'Hiya, Mr Eddy,' Johnny, the twelfth-floor house-boy, said cheerfully as he went to his room. Suitably tipped, Johnny valeted him and ran errands, in the manner of an old-fashioned colonial servant. Eddy changed into a suit and collected his valise, containing Mulligan's gold dust, from the hotel safe. He had air-freighted the dust direct to Hong Kong and had collected it from the airport the previous day. He left the hotel through the side-entrance and strolled through the Wanchai streets where at night the spirit of Suzie Wong still lingered in the topless bars, blue cinemas, and brothels, and the locals still relied on the glands of American sailors for a living. At the top of Queensway he waited in line for a street-car, gearing himself up for a crowded ten minutes. The car came rattling up – bursting with its usual quota of humanity – and he fought his way on board. He had thirty cents ready to drop into the ticket dispenser. The car started off again, with a lurch. By the time they reached the next stop he was wedged between the barrier behind the driver and an old man with a live chicken in a rattan basket. He waited until the last moment then forced his way to the door and jumped out. As the street-car lumbered away he made a leap and re-boarded it. Once again he worked his way through to the front, but this time, when he jumped off, it was to hail a passing cab. He told the driver to take him to the Central Market and at a convenient traffic snarl-up shoved a twenty-dollar bill at him and vanished. Two further cabs and a number four bus later he was plodding along Chater Road, sweating heavily, grateful for the air-conditioned winds that blasted prodigally out of the open doors of shops and office buildings.

Mulligan's gold dust formed an untidy pyramid on Cabererras's desk, a pyramid worth approximately sixty thousand dollars. In the strong sunlight shafting through the window the flecks of pure gold outshone the dealer's ring – a platinum V set with sapphires, rubies, and white diamonds to reproduce the colours of the American flag. Cabererras, the Filipino, was pro-American to the point of idolatry. He had put his three sons through Harvard and the office was decorated with enlarged photographs of his off-spring collecting their degrees and posing with their fraternities.

'But I don't buy dust,' Cabererras said. He was intrigued.

'I'm not selling it to you. I'm giving it to you. Before you ask any questions, take a look at these.'

Eddy handed him the Limmatbank letter and Schurch's letter of authority. Cabererras read them. He had been a banker in his time – as well as a gun-runner, a gold-smuggler, and a war hero.

'Such a quantity,' he said after a moment, trying to keep the awe out of his voice and so losing his carefully cultivated Yankee accent. 'Impossible for me.'

'Obviously,' Eddy said. 'You might want to take a few hundred thousand ounces at say nine under, but I'm not here to sell you anything, I'm here to buy.'

Cabererras was twisting his ring round and round his finger.

'You want to buy a name, I presume,' he said.

'A name, an address, and a personal introduction from you. I

78

want to get into the holy of holies. I want to meet the King.'

Cabererras scooped up a handful of gold dust and let it trickle through his fingers.

'All that in exchange for a little dust?'

'I do have a sense of values. All that for five million dollars. Paid on the day a certain transaction is completed.'

Cabererras pursed his thin lips. His face was round, smooth and feminine. He looked for a moment like a petulant old lady.

'How long have we known each other, Eddy?' he said.

'Two years.'

'Two years. Yes. A very short time. The blink of an eye as we – they – say here. Yet you are my friend. I trust you. That's my way – I work from my gut – I learned that in America. But it's not the Chinese way. The Chinese test you and test you, over and over again. I have known the King for twenty years and it has taken me all that time to gain his trust.'

'I appreciate that.'

'Perhaps you do. You're smart. You know a little of the East. But do you appreciate what the King's trust means to me? What it does for me in this city?'

'Yes I do. That's why I've come to you.'

Cabererras clasped his hands together on his chest in a gesture that might have been one of piety. He looked away.

'You, my friend,' he said, 'yes. But what about the army of Triads who've been chasing you all over town for the last three days?'

Eddy sat very still.

'Triads?'

'Why didn't you level with me, Eddy? Did you really think I wouldn't have heard? This is a Chinese city. It runs on whispers.'

'Heard what?'

Cabererras smoothed his sparse hair. 'You're under surveillance, friend Eddy.'

'I know that. But what have the Triads got to do with it?'

'It's nothing personal. Triads are for hire. Somebody hired them.'

'Can you un-hire them for me?'

Cabererras laughed. 'I am a man of influence, but not Superman.' He fingered the two bank letters. 'Tell me about this gold, Eddy. I don't know if I believe it.'

Eddy gave a bowdlerized version, not mentioning the Greek or Collins by name. Cabererras listened with his brown eyes

79

glistening, responding to the story with the excitement of a man who had lived and breathed gold for twenty years. When Eddy finished he said:

'I'll speak to the King. I don't make any promises. You'd better call me tomorrow afternoon. Not from your hotel.' He escorted Eddy out of the office, pausing at the door. 'Eddy, do you want some people – to watch your back?'

'Thank you, but it's okay. I'm spending the night in the safest place in South China.'

Eddy enjoyed the half-hour ferry ride to Tsuen Wan on the mainland. There was just a touch of a sea breeze freshening the air and plenty of shipping – rusty little coasters, squat hovercraft, a sleek American cruiser, and an old sailing junk that a few weeks before must have been smelling the brackish waters of the Yangtze. It was a vessel that seemed to drift out of another time. Its sails, like half-opened fans, were a patchwork of greys and magnolias; the timbers of its steep stern and high prow were paper-thin, worn by ocean and wind.

They docked at Tsuen Wan a few minutes later, amidst rotting blocks of high-rise housing, traffic jams, and urban ugliness. Eddy picked up a cab and drove west along the coast road. They passed through Sham Tseng, with its brewery and famous roadside chicken restaurants where plump, plucked birds were strung in lines along the kerb. A few miles further on they passed a massive gateway, crowned with gilded dragons, then turned right, up a stony track, into the hills. The track soon petered out and Eddy paid off the driver. He toiled up a steep path through banana plantations. On a promontory above was a low, rambling 1930s house, all flat roofs and oblong, metal windows like the upper deck of an old transatlantic liner. Hanging by the front door was a square wooden plaque, intricately carved with Chinese characters, the shield of Lim San Feng's office as a Wing Tsun Master. Eddy arrived at the door and ran his fingers over the worn ebony, remembering the first time he had seen the plaque, in the corner of a vast parade ground in the suburbs of Peking. He rang the bell. A student opened the door and bowed. Inside the house there was the institutional smell of sweat, mingled with the scent of joss-sticks. The student led him down a bare passage and opened a door into a large, square room, lit by high windows. In one corner stood the *muk yan chong*, the practice dummy, a polished tree-trunk, five feet high, with wooden projections representing arms and legs. On the walls were framed photographs of Grandmaster Yip Man and Master Lim. In between was a clean patch of wall from which a third photograph had evidently been removed.

Ten or twelve students were standing in a circle. They were all dressed alike in black tunics, trimmed with purple ribbons, with the Chinese symbols of Wing Tsun embroidered on the left breast, and loose, black trousers ornamented at each knee with an inverted V, also in purple ribbon. They were Practicians, men who had attained the fifth to eighth levels in Wing Tsun and so were entitled to teach their art. Eddy bowed low. None of the students so much as glanced in his direction. They were completely absorbed by what was happening in the centre of the circle.

Two men were fighting – more precisely, one man was attacking and the other was defending. The attacker was a ninth-level 'Man of Arrival', with broad yellow trimmings to his uniform, a Wing Tsun boxer in the prime of life and at the height of his physical powers. He was a big man for a Chinese, tall and muscular. The defender was Lim San Feng, robed in yellow like a Buddhist monk, fragile and diminutive. It seemed impossible that Lim could withstand the superbly delivered onslaught of his opponent. Attacks were coming at him from all angles – kicks, chops, straightline punches, complex patterns of feint and double-feint. Yet the old man deflected and countered each assault with movements of his arms and legs that seemed leisurely in comparison with the rapid darts of his attacker, swaying slightly, but never losing his stance, turning as the other circled him, but never abandoning his position. The young man grunted with each new attack, beginning to pant. Lim was silent.

Eddy realized that he was a privileged witness to a unique contest, a display of matter versus mind. Lim's opponent was tiring. The old Master was not simply deflecting and dissipating the younger man's energy, he seemed to absorb it into himself. The end came with extraordinary suddenness. For the first time, Lim gave ground. His opponent, recognizing a feint yet unable to interpret it, lost his rhythm for a fraction of a second, and Lim struck. He used the deadliest of all Wing Tsun techniques, the *biutze* or 'thrusting fingers', for centuries forbidden knowledge to all but the elect. His right arm shot out horizontally, all the accumulated weight of his body travelling along it to explode through his fingertips and catapult his opponent across the room.

Eddy marvelled not at the power Lim released but at the power he held back. In terms of the force he could have unleashed the blow was a flick; the defeated Man of Arrival was winded but unhurt. One of his companions helped him to his feet and, against all the rules, the others applauded. Victor and vanquished exchanged bows. Lim turned to welcome Eddy and introduce him to the students. After a moment a gong sounded from somewhere in the building and the pupils filed out for two hours of prayer and meditation, leaving Eddy and Lim alone.

In front of the students Lim had been grave; now his eyes creased humorously and he gripped Eddy's hand and embraced him.

'So, brother-from-the-West, you are now an American. I have been invited to visit America but I shall not go.'

'Why not, Master? You could teach them so much.'

Lim shook his head. 'They do not want me as a teacher. They want me as a performer – a ninety-year-old man who can break a brick with his fingertips.' He sighed, 'That is what our art has become. A spectacle.'

Eddy looked at the empty space between the two framed photographs on the wall. He had an idea of whose portrait might have hung there. Lim nodded.

'He betrayed himself and his art. He vulgarized our inner mysteries and so he paid the price.'

Eddy glanced at Lim but the old man's face was expressionless. The death of Bruce Lee had been sudden and mysterious, he reflected, and he had given great offence to the Masters.

'At this hour I walk in the Golden Dragon Garden,' Lim was saying. 'Will you accompany me?'

He led Eddy out of the back of the house, through a walled vegetable garden, where all the food for the school was grown, across a banana grove, to a metal gate, which he unlocked with a key. Beyond the gate lay an immense pleasure-garden, a place of delicate waterfalls, lily-pools, roses, and exotic trees. Lim explained that the gardens had been created by a Hong Kong millionaire called Kohr, a cousin of his, and contained the old man's tomb and family shrine. The tomb itself was a marble hemisphere set on a small plateau with a hill rising steeply behind. Below it were the gardens and the green tongue of the Golden Dragon peninsula and, beyond, the sea, with Ma Wan Island in the foreground and the lights of Hong Kong in the distance. It was dusk. Suddenly, as if at a signal, the cicadas came to life, filling the sweet-scented air with a great, mechanical purr.

'Cousin Kohr achieved what every Chinese desires. A place where his soul can rest in peace. You see, he has the mountain at his back and the sea at his feet, with an island as a serving-table for his spirit. Strange to think that when I die I shall be buried here in these gardens, beside Cousin Kohr. I who made the long march to Shensi.'

'You die, Master? I don't believe it will happen.'

'It will happen. I will die at the hands of a man.' Lim shrugged, speaking of the inevitable as if it were unimportant.

'I don't believe such a man exists.'

They had completed a circle and were approaching the front door of the house, where an exterior lamp was lighting up the old wooden board. Lim paused and touched the board.

'There is always such a man. When I was young, the greatest boxer in China was said to be an old Master who lived near Fatshan and had a great school where the sons of the rich went to learn the arts of Wing Tsun. His sign of Mastership – a board like this – had hung by the gates of his school for fifty years and it was said that no one would ever defeat him and take down his board. But one day a young man went to the school and challenged the Master. They fought, and the old man was defeated. His pupils tore down his board and fled, and the young man put up his own board in its place.' Lim was looking out towards the sea and the brilliant, myriad lights of Hong Kong. 'The young man who put up his board will be overtaken by the same fate.'

Eddy ate with the students – a meal of vegetables, wheat meat, ginger, garlic and onion. Afterwards Lim addressed them. He spoke in English in deference to his guest and told tales of the three-hundred-and-fifty-year history of the Wing Tsun school, of its founding by the Buddhist priestess, Ng Mui, of its naming after its first pupil, the beautiful Yim Wing Tsun, who had beaten the bully, Wong, and married the man of her choice, of a civilization that had been old when Europe was in barbarian infancy.

That night Eddy slept in the big dormitory on a bed as hard as concrete. But he slept the profound sleep of one who knows he is utterly secure. It was the sort of sleep he had not enjoyed for a very long time. In the morning, when one of the students woke him, he felt resurrected.

The student said: 'Master want see you.'

Lim was in the gymnasium. The morning sun was slanting through the high windows but Lim was standing in shadow. At his feet were the bodies of two men. They were both Chinese, in their twenties, dressed in jeans and leather jackets. They were breathing but unconscious. Lim turned.

'They were discovered trying to enter the building last night,' he said. 'Happily we keep a watch.' His old eyes asked a question.

'I've had people following me ever since I arrived in Hong Kong,' Eddy answered. 'It's a problem connected with my business. I apologize for bringing my troubles into your house.'

Lim shrugged faintly and smiled. 'That is of small account. But I do not think these men were merely following you.' From a fold in his robe he produced two knives. 'They are Triad killers. I am familiar with the type.'

Eddy stared.

'There is no doubt.' Lim said. 'Do you wish me to inform the police?'

'I'd prefer you not to.'

Lim inclined his head. 'Very well. Do you wish me to release them, then, when they are recovered? Or do you want to question them?'

'I doubt if they'd talk and they probably don't know anything worth hearing.'

'They certainly cannot have known the nature of this place. If they had, they would never have dared to enter it. But they are merely hirelings. There will be others.'

'I think I can handle them, Master.'

Lim shrugged very faintly. 'Once, perhaps,' he said. 'Once you had the makings of a formidable boxer. But you have grown soft in the West. You would be well advised to remain here, brother. Here, I can guarantee your safety.'

'I have to get back to Hong Kong this morning.'

'Very well. I will hold these two men for a few hours and then release them – with a warning. But it will be a small protection.'

Eddy held out his hand. 'I am grateful for everything. You teach me so much.'

'I wish you good joss,' Lim said. Then that almost impish smile lit up his face. 'If you ever find what you are seeking, come to see me again. I shall have something to learn from you.'

9

Eddy phoned Cabererras from a call-box near the entrance to the Star Ferry terminal. The Filipino sounded elated.

'The King wants to see you.'

'Where and when?'

'Where are you calling from?'

'Across the street from your office. Outside the Star Ferry.'

'Have you got company?'

'I don't know. Probably.'

'It doesn't matter. You won't have when they see his car. It's a white Rolls Royce. It'll pick you up in twenty minutes.'

Eddy waited about by the slip road where the taxis pulled in, rejecting the high-pitched advances of the rickshaw drivers and watching the hordes that streamed in and out of the terminal. The white Rolls was driven by a Chinese chauffeur in grey livery. He acknowledged Eddy with a nod but was otherwise uncommunicative. Eddy had half expected to be driven up to The Peak, where the Chinese millionaires had their mansions and villas, but the journey lasted barely five minutes, and Eddy could have walked it in less. Their destination proved to be a big jewellery store in Queen's Road Central. A security guard took him up in an elevator to the sixth floor where another was waiting. He was led through empty corridors, and a series of locked doors, to a large windowless room. The guard said: 'You wait here, please,' and left him alone.

Plump sofas and low tables suggested that this was a reception area attached to the suite of offices, whose doors – all closed – filled one wall. But it was like no reception area Eddy had ever encountered. The other three walls were completely filled with display cases, subtly lit from within, containing some of the most exquisite art objects Eddy had ever seen. There was a group of figurines, over a thousand years old, representing gorgeously robed officials of the court of the T'ang Emperors. There was a display of fans; shelves of carved jade and lapis lazuli; paintings in jewelled frames, masterpieces of the school of Chou Chin-mien. It was the collection of a connoisseur of unlimited wealth and Eddy had seen nothing like it outside the great treasure-houses of Peking where, as a privileged visitor from the Soviet Union, he had wandered for hours, steeping himself in the graces and refinements of China's Imperial past.

Not a sound penetrated the room from the outside world. Eddy moved from cabinet to cabinet, completely absorbed, hardly aware that time was passing. He was admiring a fragile, golden bowl, chased with fretwork, when he sensed another presence in the room. He turned. An old Chinese man was standing in the open door of one of the offices. He had a wispy, drooping moustache and beard and although he was dressed in a point-device suit, he somehow reminded Eddy of the rich silks of the porcelain courtiers in the cabinet. He almost expected to see a Pekinese nestling in the man's cuff.

'You admire my little bowl?' the old man said. His English was mission-school.

'It's wonderful.'

The old man glided over and unlocked the cabinet with a tiny key on a chain. He placed the bowl in Eddy's hands. It was as thin as paper yet heavy.

'It is Ch'in dynasty. In your occidental calendar, two hundred BC.'

'I've seen one like it in the Forbidden City,' Eddy said, handing the bowl back. The old man smiled thinly.

'That would be its twin. One belonged to the Dowager Empress Tz'e Hsi, the other to my great-grandfather. My name is Tan Han Yu.' He offered his hand with the suspicion of a bow. 'Please come this way, Mr Polonski.'

Tan's office was in complete contrast to the reception area, although quite as extraordinary. It was luxuriously modern, with a vast picture window looking out onto a roof garden with waterfall, a lily pond, exotic trees, shrubs, and an aviary full of darting finches. The window was ajar and Eddy could hear the blare of traffic from the street below, but the surrounding high rises were masked by foliage. Remembering that office space in the Central District was worth four thousand dollars a square foot, Eddy was staggered by the size of the garden. The building must have been half demolished to accommodate it. But then Tan was the King, the biggest gold dealer in Asia, and one of the biggest in the world.

Two people had risen when he entered the office. Both were Chinese. One was an over-fed man like a soapstone Buddha, and the other was a wiry old woman in a severe black skirt and white twin-set. Tan introduced the man as Mr Leung of the Sino-Hong Kong International Bank, and the woman as Mrs Kwei. Mrs Kwei seemed to be Tan's personal assistant. As they sat down round a glass-topped coffee table she produced a lacquer tray with a teapot and tiny porcelain cups.

'My friend Cabererras speaks very highly of you, Mr Polonski,' Tan said. 'He tells me that you have some documents to show me.'

Eddy took the letters from his pocket and handed them to Tan. The old man seemed to do little more than glance at them before passing them to Leung. Leung rose and went over to a desk on the far side of the room. He opened a thick, leather-bound ledger, which Eddy guessed was an international register of bank officers' signatures, and compared entries with Eddy's letters. Leung returned to his seat and nodded shortly to Tan. Tan turned to Eddy.

'Forgive us, Mr Polonski. So many people attempt to sell me gold, and so often their gold turns out to be imaginary. Would you like to tell me more about this – remarkable hoard?'

Eddy repeated what he had told Cabererras, again leaving out names and any references that could lead Tan directly to the Greek or Collins.

'An interesting tale,' Tan said when Eddy had finished. 'You have added to my education this afternoon, Mr Polonski.'

'I'd like to add to your stock of bullion, sir.'

'Quite so,' Tan said.

To Eddy's surprise, Tan rose. 'You will forgive me,' he said, 'if I leave you for a moment. I think Mr Leung has some questions to ask you and I have another matter to which I must attend.'

He bowed faintly and left the office. Eddy was puzzled, but he could hardly protest. He turned to Leung.

'How can I help you, Mr Leung?'

'The bars, Mr Polonski,' Leung said. 'What guarantees can you give of their purity?'

'My information is that they are Good London Delivery bars, in other words, with a purity of between 995.0 and 999.9. Naturally, in the event of a transaction, that would be certificated by the vendor's bank, assuming you require physical delivery of the bars.'

Leung nodded. 'Possible to have an independent assay?'

'I would imagine it's possible, yes – but unnecessary. If we're talking about a substantial tranche, a meaningful sampling would involve drilling a lot of bars. If you don't want physical delivery but a transfer by metal account you could assay here in Hong Kong.'

Mrs Kwei was taking shorthand notes of everything he said. As Leung launched into a catechism of banking mechanics, her pencil flew efficiently over the pages of her notebook. When Leung's questions were over, she closed the pad and put it down on the table.

'And now, sir,' she said in a sing-song voice, 'we talk about price.'

Once again Eddy was taken by surprise. But the sudden transformation of Mrs Kwei from stenographer into negotiator was accepted by Mr Leung as perfectly normal. Eddy turned to Mrs Kwei. The blackness of her hair owed a great deal to the dye-pot, he observed, and the mother-of-pearl perfection of her complexion to the expert application of cosmetics, but she must once have been beautiful. He wondered, irrelevantly, whether she had been Tan's mistress.

'The price,' he said, 'would naturally depend on the quantity.'

Mrs Kwei nodded. 'Tell me price, please, on five hundred tons.'

There was something in her manner that suggested to Eddy that she expected him to challenge her right to discuss price and quantity. After all, she was only an underling. But Tan was the King, the principal. For him to haggle over prices with a Western businessman of doubtful status would be an immediate loss of face; a still more disastrous loss would be sustained if he should be seen to have come off worst in the bargaining. And face, to a Chinese of a certain type, was everything. To an occidental the minutiae of face were bewildering. If Eddy did challenge Mrs Kwei's right to conduct negotiations by appealing to Leung, would Mrs Kwei lose face? Or would he himself lose face by betraying his barbarian ignorance of the niceties? If Mrs Kwei felt that she had lost face, she would make every attempt to regain it. Negotiations would be more difficult.

Eddy smiled. 'On five hundred the price would be three dollars under London Gold Market, second fixing.'

'For five hundred,' Mrs Kwei said, 'twenty dollars under is a good price.'

He was in for a long and wearisome session of bid and counter-bid, complicated by the fact that he must ensure that Mrs Kwei suffered no serious loss of face, and at the same time retain enough face of his own to remain credible. His normal method of dealing was to state a fair price and stick to it, but that was no good here. The minimum spread he was prepared to accept was one and a half dollars per ounce, which meant that eight under was the maximum he could concede to Mrs Kwei. He had no hard information about the funds Tan might have at his disposal, nor how anxious he really was to acquire a large amount of bullion, but he had decided, before the meeting, that he should be able to make a deal with Tan at seven under. He decided to concentrate on the figure seven and banish the figure eight from his thoughts.

Half an hour later Mrs Kwei had come down to eight under and Eddy up to six and a half. He decided to stick there, leaving himself a fifty-cent margin in which to manoeuvre, in the last resort.

'That's my best,' he said and Mrs Kwei nodded and smiled faintly.

The door opened and, as if on cue, Tan entered. He spoke briefly with Mrs Kwei and Leung in Cantonese. Mrs Kwei and Leung rose, shook hands with Eddy, and left the room. Tan sat down.

'Mrs Kwei has informed me of your offer,' he said. 'I will consider it and give you an answer tomorrow. There is another matter, however, which I did not think it right to discuss in front of Mr Leung and Mrs Kwei.'

Face again, Eddy thought. But this time my face.

'I mean your personal problem,' Tan said. This was dangerous ground. 'I have made some enquiries, Mr Polonski, and I have discovered that the source of your troubles lies in America, not in South Africa as you suggested to our friend Cabererras.'

'That may only mean that Jan Pienaar is operating through his American company.'

'That is possible, yes.'

Eddy leaned forward, placing his hands on his knees. 'Mr Tan, I want to assure you that pressure from the cartel isn't going to affect my capacity to carry through this transaction. If you decide to buy from me I guarantee you absolute security.'

Tan spread one hand – his version of a shrug.

'I have no doubts about your capacity, Mr Polonski. By impressing Mr Pienaar, you impress me. As to security, I have let it be known that you are not to be troubled further in Hong Kong.'

'Thank you, sir.'

'Please return tomorrow at this time.'

Eddy took Cabererras out to dinner at Hugo's that evening: it was the least he could do. By the time he got back to the hotel, it was late. He took the elevator up to the twelfth floor, and found that Johnny, the house-boy, was not asleep in his truckle-bed behind the service desk. Eddy was exhausted and he fumbled in his pockets for his key. It was that slight delay in unlocking the door which saved him, that and the faint sound he heard coming from within his room. He stood to one side of the door, his back to the wall, and waited, trying to decide what to do. It was a decision he never had to make. There was a sharp explosion, a simultaneous shattering of glass, and a vibration that shook the wall at his back. He fell on the door and flung it open. Smoke billowed out, making him cough, and a shaft of light from the corridor cut through the vapour-filled darkness. He could see that the desk, opposite the bed, had been demolished. On the bed itself, flung there by the blast, was a bundle of blood and clothes that he recognized as Johnny the house-boy. He went back into the corridor. Sleep-furrowed faces, bug-eyed with shock and curiosity, stared at him. People in their night-clothes were creeping out of their rooms and there was a babble of panicky questions in five or six languages. The elevator doors opened and a party of hotel officials poured out. With their arrival the level of noise and panic began to rise. The manager and the house detective pushed into Eddy's room and he followed them. The lights had blown but the detective had a torch.

Johnny was dead. The charge, which must have been placed in the desk, probably in the drawer, had ripped one arm clean off and left the other a stump.

Eddy took advantage of the others' shock to barge through the peering, whispering crowd that had formed in the doorway and stride to the phone on the service desk. He dialled Cabererras's home number.

For the next half hour police, ambulancemen, and firemen swarmed in and surged about shouting contradictory commands. Then Inspector Lau appeared, a capable-looking Chinese officer whose natural authority rapidly established order. Lau was courteous, offering Eddy a cigarette and a drink, both of which he declined. He responded to every answer with: 'Yes. I see.' It was perfectly obvious that he didn't believe a word. At last Cabererras arrived. Lau evidently knew him. They exchanged a few sentences in Cantonese. The inspector reluctantly agreed to some suggestion made by Cabererras. He turned to Eddy.

'Mr Cabererras has vouched for you, sir. You may go with him now. Later today I will ask you please to make a full statement.'

His manner was half contemptuous, half resigned, as if he anticipated that the statement would never be made and that his superiors would quietly insist on a cover-up.

'What did you tell him?' Eddy asked Cabererras when they were in the car, heading up towards The Peak.

'I mentioned a few names. I'd made a call before I came. He's a good guy Lau. Straight. Not like most of the force. I mean straight in all ways.' He laughed. 'Well, you sure are making waves, friend Eddy.'

'Yes.' Eddy longed for a clean bed and a soft pillow.

'Like to tell me what happened?'

'Could it wait until I've had some sleep?'

'Sure, sure.'

Cabererras lived in a $750,000 penthouse apartment in a tower near the Botanic Garden. He showed Eddy into a small guest-room decorated in a flowery wallpaper, with pink furniture and chintz. Eddy sank into a blancmange of a bed, and dawn was edging into the room by the time Lim's deep breathing exercises eased him into sleep.

He awoke around eleven only half refreshed. Cabererras was in his split-level living area, sitting at his desk in his shirtsleeves, talking on the phone. The room was grossly over-furnished and cluttered with Americana. Cabererras's wife bustled in with a tray of coffee and biscuits. She was a surprisingly plain and pudgy Filipino dressed in a cotton-print housecoat that went with the blinding wallpaper. She clearly ruled in matters of interior decoration. She went out again as her husband came off the phone.

'Morning Eddy,' Cabererras said. 'Good sleep?'

'Yes thanks.'

Cabererras sat down and poured two mugs of coffee.

'I've been busy on your behalf, Eddy. Made a few calls, seen a few people. I've managed to get friend Lau off your back. You sign a written statement to be read out at the inquest and that's you clear.'

'How did you fix it?'

Cabererras was evidently pleased with himself. 'Not difficult,' he said. 'I have old friends in Intelligence. I got them to call Lau's boss and tell him it was their baby. Security stuff. Never known it fail.'

Eddy laughed. 'I owe you for this.'

'You'll pay, friend Eddy. The King wants to see you at two.'

'I need a couple more favours. I'm going to have to vanish and to do that I need a passport in a different name. Can you fix it for me?

The Filipino smiled. 'In a city that houses several hundred thousand illegal immigrants the passport business is bigger than the garment industry. And I'm in big business.'

'They'll be watching the airport. Any way you can get me on a flight through the back door?'

Cabererras was enjoying himself. 'Easy. We hire a private jet. You can go in as crew, and hide out in the VIP lounge. Where d'you want to go?'

'Anywhere in Europe.'

Eddy rose and went over to the window. The view, which in the winter would have been spectacular, was obscured by rain-clouds. Another storm was brewing.

'And then what?' Cabererras asked.

'With a new passport I can stay out of sight for a few weeks, get myself organized, then go and negotiate with Pienaar.'

'Negotiate? Are you in a position to negotiate?'

'Certainly. I'm selling the gold on behalf of some very powerful people. They have a vested interest in keeping me alive.'

Over lunch, served by Cabererras's wife with the aid of an old Chinese servant, the Filipino reminisced interminably about the fleet of ore-carriers he had owned before the war; how in 1942 he'd loaded up his flagship with politicians, millionaires, and bullion, and spirited the whole lot out of Manila as the Japanese bombs started falling; how he'd been decorated by Lord Louis Mountbatten in person; how he'd laid the foundations of his fortune by smuggling gold in and out of Red China by hammering it into foil a thousandth of an inch thick and sewing it into clothes.

Tan's car arrived at half-past one to take Eddy down to Queen's Road Central. The storm had broken and heavy rain thrummed on the roof of the Rolls. Tan was alone in his office, standing by the window and staring out at the roof garden where the downpour, now furious, was boiling the lily-pond. He turned and offered his hand.

'I imagine that you expect an apology from me, Mr Polonski,' he said. 'I gave you an assurance and I appear to have failed. Please be seated.'

'I don't expect or want an apology, sir.'

'That is generous of you.' Tan made his graceful hand-spreading gesture. 'But in my own defence I would like to offer you an explanation of last night's events. Mr Polonski, I honoured my commitment and spoke to the leaders of the organization paid to spy on you. They complied with my wishes and withdrew their men. I have no doubt of that, Mr Polonski. What I did not know – what perhaps you did not care to tell me – was that there was a second group who had been hired, not to spy on you but to kill you.'

'A second group?'

'That surprises you?'

'Yes.'

'You were not aware that your life was in danger?'

Eddy looked at Tan. To hell with face, he thought, I need this man. I have to be open with him.

'I was, yes,' he said. 'But I assumed that the South Africans were behind both the surveillance and the murder attempt.'

'It appears that this is not the case,' Tan said. 'As I informed you yesterday, the origin of the surveillance is American. What I discovered this morning is that the origin of last night's violence is South African.'

'And the house-boy? Was he working for Pienaar?'

'Apparently not.' Tan smiled thinly. 'According to my sources in the police the man had been boasting to his friends and relatives that there was a rich gold-dealer in the hotel. It seems that he must have been searching your room, presumably looking for gold, and accidentally set off the device intended for you. The phrase is "the biter bit", is it not?'

Eddy did not answer immediately. He was trying to get the picture into focus. Pienaar had hired Triad A to kill him. That was clear if inexplicable. But who in hell had hired Triad B to keep him under surveillance – and why? He looked at Tan. The old man was still smiling. Johnny's pathetic and unnecessary death evidently amused him.

'In the circumstances I imagine you do not want to proceed

93

with a transaction,' Eddy said.

Tan looked down at his hands, which were lightly clasped in his lap.

'I have been a buyer and a seller of precious metals for many years, Mr Polonski. I am no stranger to the violence and intrigue that so often surround a transaction of great magnitude. What has happened tends to dispel certain doubts I confess to have entertained about the existence of the gold you are attempting to sell.' He looked up suddenly. 'I am prepared to buy 13.36 million *taels*. That is five hundred tons in your metric system. I will buy this quantity at eight dollars under.'

The smile had vanished from Tan's lips but it lingered in his eyes, mocking Eddy. Eddy knew that it was hopeless to negotiate further. Between them, Tan and Cabererras held the key to his safe escape from Hong Kong. Anyway, a two-dollar margin on five hundred tons would make him twenty-four million, less the increased cut Cabererras was now bound to demand. 'Eight under. Agreed.'

Tan let out an almost imperceptible sigh. 'I have made an appointment for you to see Mr Leung at the bank this afternoon. You will deal with him from now on. You and I will not meet again – at least for the time being.'

Eddy took this as a dismissal and began to rise.

'One more thing before you go, Mr Polonski. You have had some experience, I think, in selling gold bullion to private individuals, therefore you appreciate that discretion – absolute discretion – is perhaps the most important element in the transaction. In this case, however, we are not talking of a few thousand *taels* and a few million dollars. As you will discover when you speak to Mr Leung, the banking arrangements I intend to make will be such that the purchase of the gold will never be traceable to any of my accounts. I make such arrangements because it would be extremely dangerous for me – I would go so far as to say that it would be potentially fatal for me – if it was known that I had purchased five hundred metric tons of gold. For example, here in Hong Kong the authorities would be bound to take action, to investigate my affairs. I would be vulnerable not only to political, but also to criminal pressures – blackmail, extortion. Therefore I must demand from you absolute secrecy in this matter.' Tan smiled his thin smile. 'I have formed a very favourable opinion of you, Mr Polonski. I do not think you are the sort of man to betray my trust. For those who might, the consequences are extremely grave.'

'I appreciate that, Mr Tan,' Eddy said.

Tan rose and they shook hands. Tan's touch was dry and faint.

'Goodbye, Mr Polonski. If you succeed in disposing of the balance of the gold you will have achieved a remarkable feat. I wish you joss.'

Eddy spent two hours in the Sino-Hong Kong International building, a pillared colonial pile a block away from the Head Office of its great rival, the Hong Kong Shanghai Bank. In conference with Leung he laid down the technical foundations of the transaction. Leung gave him a coded letter to a bank in Brussels which would furnish the necessary 'buy' letters. Cabererras met him after the meeting and took him to a nearby shopping arcade where there was an automatic machine that dispensed passport photographs. Cabererras pointed to a barber's shop and suggested, half seriously, that Eddy have his beard shaved off.

'Forget it. I'm like Samson. Without my hair I'm powerless.'

He was in high spirits. Not even the presence of two bodyguards, hired by Cabererras, quelled his elation. They dropped off the photographs at a little clothing store near Hennessey Road and drove on to the Filipino's apartment. At dinner Cabererras drank enough to make him incautious. Eddy learned many things, especially about Tan. He was the head of one of the great merchant families of Imperial China, a dynasty that could trace its history back to the era of the first Ming Emperors.

'Isn't he worried about what's going to happen when the lease on the New Territories runs out?' Eddy asked. 'Aren't *you* worried?'

Cabererras laughed and swirled his brandy. 'You know what happened to the Portuguese in Macao? They had a revolution or something back in Portugal – shiny new Socialist government. Didn't approve of colonies. So they go to the Chinese and say, look, you can have Macao back. The Chinese are amazed. "Have it back?" they say. "It's always been ours. You stay right where you are and keep mending the drains." They'll say exactly the same to the British in 1997. This is a Chinese city, Eddy, run for the benefit of Chinese commercial interests. The King's family set up shop here the day after Captain Elliot raised the British flag. The British mend the drains and the Chinese make money.'

'Maybe. But someone like the King can't be very popular in Peking.'

'Don't be naïve, friend Eddy. Do you think all of the gold he's buying from you will stay in Hong Kong?' He laughed nervously. 'Hey, you're pulling my tongue,' he said and seemed grateful for the diversion caused by the arrival of a courier with Eddy's new passport. It was dark blue and bore the Royal Arms of the United Kingdom, in gold, on the front. It was made out in the name of Peter Edwards, a citizen of the British Crown Colony of Hong Kong.

'There you go, Mr Edwards,' Cabererras said as he handed it to Eddy.

'Listen, my friend,' said Eddy. 'You've gone above and beyond the call of duty in the last few days. Let's forget the five million commission and make it six.'

'That's what I like about you, Eddy,' the Filipino said with a quick smile, 'you anticipate.'

Eddy slept well in the garish guest room, confident that the arrangements for his exit the following morning would be foolproof. They were. He was driven to Kai Tak Airport in an anonymous cab, deposited at an entry reserved for air crew, then escorted to a small VIP lounge. He didn't show his face in any of the public areas. The first leg of his journey was by private Lear to Singapore and so his name was not logged into the computers of any airline.

As the Lear circled over the slums of Kowloon, Eddy looked down. It was seven o'clock on a clear, blazing morning, and the roofs of the high-rise blocks were dense with tiny figures performing the *tai-chi* ballet among chicken pens and pig sties. The plane was climbing. To the north the mountains and valleys of China stretched green, immense, and mysterious to the horizon. Eddy ran a finger over the inlaid arms on his passport, and recalling what Cabererras had let slip, he smiled.

10

The same day that Eddy left Hong Kong, Dan Daniels flew out of London on one of the twice-weekly, direct flights to the Emirate of Khatam. He'd spent an unprofitable week chasing a Kuwaiti prince around Paris, trying and failing to compete for His Highness's attention against a string of bejewelled doxies supplied by Madame Claude. After seven days of blind-alley meetings with royal 'cousins', and seven nights of Georges Cinq prices, he'd decided to cut his losses and try his luck with the remote, but paradoxically more accessible, Prince Nasir of Khatam.

The Air Khatam 747 was, as usual, virtually empty. Nobody went to Khatam if he could help it. Somebody had described the country as 'a piece of shit floating on oil' and it was a judgement that, in Dan's view, seriously slandered shit. The place was nasty, brutish, and short of hotels. The old Emir had been taken for some monumental rides by Western bankers and businessmen back in the sixties and had become as isolationist as an Albanian commissar; his policy of Khatamization had more or less sealed off the country.

Dan was the sole occupant of the first class section. In tourist class were a handful of Ugandan Asian businessmen – a breed that seemed to thrive in Khatam – and some heavily veiled Khatami women who'd presumably been doing the rounds of Harley Street consultants.

As they circled over the purple-blue disc of the Arabian Sea and began their descent, Dan peered out of the window. The futuristic glass and steel buildings of Khatam International Airport looked like a cluster of quartz crystals dumped at hazard in the desert. They seemed to bear no relation to the little, white-walled city huddled on the shoreline, or even to the ugly port and refinery beyond. The airport was a billion-dollar folly: it had every facility that technology could provide and limitless money buy; all it lacked were aeroplanes and passengers.

In fact, as Dan strolled into the main terminal building, he was surprised to find that the immigration and customs area was, in Khatami terms, positively humming with activity. There were twenty or thirty passengers from another flight lined up at the passport control. Dan sat down on one of the suede seats to wait for Major Hussin, Prince Nasir's senior aide. Thanks to his special visa he did not have to endure the pettifogging of Khatami bureaucracy; on the other hand he knew he could be in for a wait of anything up to an hour. Major Hussin was the only civilized Khatami he had encountered, apart from the Prince himself. In Europe he was as punctual as a creditor, but on his home ground his ancestral inability to gauge time re-asserted itself completely. Dan sighed and settled back in his seat to observe the piece of theatre developing at the passport desk. A stocky, excitable American was arguing with three grey-uniformed officials about his visa. Voices were beginning to rise. Dan heard the stocky man shout, in pure Brooklynese:

'I wanna see the head man here. Just go get him, would ya. Just fetch him, huh?' He was wearing a sharp, white suit, his hair was black and short-cropped, and in his left ear was a small, silver ring. His temper was fraying fast. 'Are you coons going to fetch me the boss or do I have to fetch him myself?'

The Khatamis were making negative gestures. One of them said loudly: 'Visa no good. Not in order. You go back. Go back.'

Dan's photographic memory for faces suddenly went click and there it was: a corridor in the Warwick Hotel, Houston, a fortnight or so ago. The pro in the blue suit who'd been hanging about outside the Greek's suite.

Dan was digesting this when one of the Khatamis began unholstering his pistol. Collins's man lashed out at him. Then all hell broke loose. Someone hit an alarm siren, soldiers came pounding in out of nowhere. There was a confusion of flying fists and grappling arms and a high-pitched yell.

'I'm an American citizen. I'm a fucking American citizen.'

'Mr Daniels.'

Dan turned. Major Hussin was standing a few feet away, in full dress uniform, smiling and holding out his hand.

'Welcome to Khatam, Mr Daniels.'

Collins's man was being hustled away, invisible in a knot of soldiers and security guards.

'Hi, Major. Listen, there's been some trouble——'

Hussin took his arm. 'I should not concern yourself. If you would come this way.'

'What happens to loud-mouthed tourists?'

'Oh, nothing. He will be sent home on the next available plane.'

They walked rapidly through a series of empty corridors, past saluting guards, through the main concourse, with its fountains and giant ferns, and out into the heat. Dan's bag was being placed in the trunk of a long white Mercedes. Hussin ushered him into the car and they set off down the highway towards the capital. The great road was deserted save for a stray truck or two. It was one o'clock in the afternoon and the place was dead. They passed through the abandoned new town, a wilderness of half-completed hotels, their naked, steel frames corroding in the harsh, salty air. The only buildings that were alive were banks, two American, one British, one Swiss. The Khatamis needed the banks to handle their oil billions but they sure as hell made the bankers sweat for their percentages. There were no facilities, no pools, or clubs, just a couple of apartment buildings, as impersonal as the Lubianka.

They entered the city through the ancient east gate and drove along by the ocean. Since Dan's last visit, nine months before, the authorities had attempted to create an esplanade. There was an avenue of palms, kept alive by copper pipes that dripped water onto the trees day and night; small boys were hosing the grass strip between the road and the beach.

They pulled up at Nasir's newly built guest house, a square, white, windowless structure on the edge of the city. Hussin showed Dan to his suite, overlooking a paved courtyard with a pool and consisting of a bedroom, bathroom, and living room, all furnished in Second Empire Harrods. Ali, the servant who had looked after him on previous trips, was bowing and smiling and Dan shook his hand. He thought of Ali as an Arabian Walter Shipley. His white jacket was always grubby, his black bow tie permanently askew, and he had the ingratiating cunning of a pimp.

'I think you will be comfortable here, Mr Daniels,' said Hussin. 'His Highness holds the afternoon *majlis* at five o'clock. I have arranged that he will receive you at that time. And for the evening——' he smiled knowingly. 'Ali has been instructed to provide any entertainment you desire.'

Dan thought about the little Thai girl who'd spent the night with him last time round – a girl with a lot of tongue, but few words. He thought of Gina.

'What I'm short of, right now, is sleep.'

Hussin raised an eyebrow. 'We meet again in three hours, then.'

When he'd gone Ali said: 'Now, you like some cold tea, yes?' and chuckling, poured Dan a straight Scotch.

Hussin was punctual for a change. He picked Dan up in the white Mercedes at a quarter to five. It was a short drive to Nasir's palace, through blank, narrow streets that hadn't changed in a thousand years. There were a few people about now – half naked urchins squatting in the gutters, and women, swathed in black, hurrying along, masked eyes on the ground. The afternoon light was the colour of old copper with a greenish tinge to it. The silence and the emptiness were eerie. Hussin talked about Paris and his new apartment in the Avenue Foch, and Dan only half listened. His mind was already occupied with the problem of selling Nasir on the concept of gold. His fingers drummed on the lid of the box that contained his gift to the Prince.

The palace was a huge, rambling pile, white like every other building in Khatam. Sentries, armed with sub-machine guns, admitted them into the hall. There was no air-conditioning, only fans, and, instantly, Dan began to sweat in his light blue suit. The *majlis* room was an immense chamber, a hundred feet long, thirty wide, and fifteen high. It was lined with gilt-framed mirrors and ornate sofas. There were thirty or forty armed guards lolling about and various Khatami peasants sitting on their haunches, waiting for a chance to put their grievances to the Prince. At the far end of the room there was a dais, three feet high, on which Nasir sat in a high-backed armchair. Below him, on cushions, were his falconers. Nasir was dressed in traditional *burnous* and robes. He smiled as Dan approached the dais, leaning forward, and offering his hand.

'How very nice to see you again,' he said. His English was Oxford, as quaint as a BBC announcer of thirty years ago. A servant brought a cushion and Dan sat down, placing the card-board box on the floor, and carefully tucked his legs in; a leg, pointed at an Arab, was a profound insult. As he sank into the soft cushion one of the falcons stirred, blinked, and shuffled its wings. It was magnificent White Greenland, a very rare species, with pure white plumage.

'Highness, I have brought a small gift for you.'

Nasir inclined his head. 'How very kind.' He nodded to a

servant who picked up the box and handed it to him.

Nasir naturally expected a gift and it was critical that he should be impressed by, and pleased with it. Impressing and pleasing a man with an income of several million dollars a day posed something of a problem and Dan had devoted a great deal of thought to what he should give. He knew that to a desert dweller, however exalted, something green and living was most desirable and so in London he had gone to a florist off Berkeley Square where he'd bought a *bonzai* miniature garden in a porcelain dish. It had cost a thousand pounds but it was worth every penny. Nasir was instantly entranced. He fingered the tiny, delicate foliage of the trees almost wonderingly.

'Japanese, is it not? *Bonzai*?' Nasir handed the dish to the servant. He beamed. 'It is most delightful. I am grateful to you.'

'It's modest, I'm afraid, Highness. But we have a saying: small is beautiful.'

Nasir laughed quietly and folded his arms, a preliminary, Dan recalled, to small talk.

'I remember your last visit to Khatam with pleasure.'

Dan remembered it with weariness. He'd been acting for a group of Houston industrialists who'd been trying to set up a bank in Luxembourg in partnership with the Khatamis. On the last day of his visit, when the negotiations were complete, Nasir had invited him to watch camel races in the desert. They'd driven for miles through baking sand and rock in a fleet of Land Rovers. They'd halted at last at a dingy oasis – five or six leaning palms and a brackish puddle of water – and then the Land Rovers had departed, tents had been erected, and Nasir and his entourage had settled down for two weeks of hunting with falcons, praying, philosophizing round the fire, roasting sheep, and drinking treacly coffee. Dan had been able neither to protest – it was a privilege to participate in such soul-purifying activities – nor escape, since there was no transport. All he had in the world was a safari suit, which rapidly became infested with lice, an attaché case full of contracts, and a pocket calculator. After two agonizing days he'd bowed to Kismet, donned a *djellabah*, started to grow a beard, and learned to sleep on a mat on the ground. He'd emerged a fortnight later slimmer, fitter, and handsomely bearded, to face a furious Beau Landau.

Nasir reminisced about those two weeks for half an hour. He was the Emir's youngest and favourite son, cultivated and educated, in sole charge of the financial business of the State, yet he had no sense of time at all. It was no good pushing him: he went at his own pace. At last Dan heard the magic words:

'And what can I do for you, Mr Daniels? You have a proposition to put to me, I understand?'

Dan took a sip of sweet tea from the tiny glass in a brass holder that the servants had incessantly topped up. He took a very small sip – he'd known of too many cases where billion-dollar deals had been blown by bursting bladders.

'I have, yes, Highness,' he said. 'I wondered whether you had ever considered investing in precious metals, specifically gold bullion.'

'Gold?' Nasir said, making the word sound like a sigh. 'I am always interested in gold. You have some gold to sell?'

'I have, sir, yes.' Before Nasir could divert him, Dan launched into a general statement about the value of bullion as an investment, its historical role as a store of value and a hedge against inflation. He invited Nasir to compare the steady fall in world stability throughout the seventies with the steady rise in the gold price from $150 in 1976 to the current price of $370. 'It's no coincidence,' he concluded, 'that major private bankers are buying bullion in quantity. They know, better than anyone, that gold is going to go on rising throughout the next decade.'

'If this is true, Mr Daniels, then why are your clients so anxious to sell?'

Dan gave him an edited version of the truth: it seemed to satisfy him.

'Have you yourself seen this gold, Mr Daniels?'

'No, Highness. It is currently in a vault in Zurich.'

'Then how do you know it exists?' Nasir was triumphant in his logic.

Dan produced his Limmatbank letter and a phrase calculated to convince Nasir. 'This document is legal proof that the gold exists.' Handing him Schurch's letter, he added: 'And this gives me the legal right to negotiate a sale.'

The key word was *legal*: it was magic to Nasir. It was the open-sesame to his exchequer.

'Very well, Mr Daniels,' Nasir said, handing the letters back via a servant. 'I am interested in buying some of this gold. I could, perhaps, take three hundred tons – if the price were right.'

'The price would be six dollars under London Gold Market second fixing.'

Nasir smiled. 'You will have to explain that to me.'

102

'It's quite simple, Highness. London is the most important gold market. Effectively, it sets the price of gold for the rest of the world. The price is fixed twice every working day, at ten-thirty in the morning and at three in the afternoon. We agree a date to make the transaction. Say the price at second fixing is four hundred dollars per ounce on that day. You buy your gold at three hundred and ninety four dollars per ounce.'

'I understand. And is that a fair price, Mr Daniels?'

'I think so, Highness.'

Nasir gave him a rare direct look. It was as penetrating and emotionless as the stare of one of his falcons. 'And what commission will you personally be making on this transaction, Mr Daniels?'

It was a question no Western businessman would ever have asked in those terms; it could have come only from an Arab.

'Four dollars an ounce, Highness.'

'I see.' Nasir smiled and looked away, reaching out to fondle a little red and black Shahin falcon, hooded and perched on the arm of his chair. 'Then this is my offer to you,' he said. 'I will buy three hundred tons of gold at seven dollars under. That is the correct expression?'

Dan hid his elation. In just over an hour he had achieved what might have taken months of negotiation through middlemen. During his two-week ordeal in the desert with Nasir he'd often had to boost his sagging morale by telling himself that some day it would all pay off. Well, that day had dawned – the most spectacular sunrise in his career.

'Agreed.' He paused for a moment then went on: 'All that would be required of you at the moment, Highness, is a letter from your bankers in Luxembourg, addressed to Limmatbank in Zurich, confirming that you intend to make the purchase and that you have funds available. May I suggest that you contact Rolf Pradel? He will be able to explain the banking procedures to you.'

Pradel was the President of the Khatami-Texan bank Dan had been instrumental in setting up. Nasir nodded again and held out his hand. Dan rose – sharp pains stabbing through his cramped knees and calves – and shook on the deal.

'A very great pleasure to see you again, Mr Daniels. I hope you will return to Khatam before too long. In the meantime you may be sure that I will speak with Pradel. Goodbye.'

'Goodbye, Highness. And thank you.'

Dan made his way back down the *majlis* room to the far end, where Hussin was waiting, past the incurious stares of the guards, and the blank, down-turned eyes of the eternally squatting, eternally waiting, eternally patient peasants, who could not have understood a word of the billion-dollar conversation he and Nasir had just completed. And if they had? It would have had no meaning for them. Nothing had very much meaning for a Khatami now, except possibly his religion. Every native born Khatami was on the government pay-roll. Nobody had to work if he didn't want to; the poor of less fortunate countries were drafted in. Idleness had been nationalized.

In any other city Dan would have celebrated his coup with a night out on the town. But in Khatam there was no town for a night out – just a couple of sleazy clubs patronized by lower grade technical workers from the refinery, where a bottle of illegal Scotch cost a hundred dollars and one could pick up a dose of crabs by sitting down. Entertainment, it was true, was available in Khatam but at a terrifying price and Dan was worried about money. Gina's credit-card scheme was all very well in theory, but in practice it had a short life. Already, he was dangerously near his limit on his two major cards and unless he found a new source of finance fast – by cutting someone in on the Nasir deal, for instance – he would simply run out of cash.

But far more worrying, now that he had time to think about, was the implication of having been tailed to Khatam by Collins's man. He brooded on this throughout dinner, which was served with very ill grace by Ali, peeved at Dan's refusal of his services as pimp. For the first time, Dan was oppressed with a sense of the loneliness of the task he had undertaken. He tried to think himself into the position of Collins and Maniatos, work out the logic of putting a man on his tail. If only he had someone there with whom he could talk it through. He was used to working in a team. Even Beau Landau had been useful in the past, if only as a stone wall off which to bounce ideas.

At ten, he called Hussin. He thanked him for what he'd done and fished for more information about the incident at the airport. Hussin was bland and evasive. All he would say was: 'It seems he was drunk. He had several litres of bourbon in his luggage. He will be deported.' Then he invited Dan to lunch the next day. Dan accepted, with a sinking heart.

The meal was interminable and indigestible. Hussin pressed course after course on him, to refuse which would have been a serious breach of etiquette. The Major's jet-set tittle-tattle was unendurable. It was nearly six by the time he was released to waddle to the white Mercedes and be driven back to the guest house. He was half asleep when the car suddenly stopped. They were in a dark alley that ran into the main square of the city.

Ahead was a crowd of people – the biggest crowd Dan had ever seen in Khatam. They were pouring into the square, blocking the alley. The driver got out and began to shout. A couple of soldiers appeared and shouted back, gesturing him to reverse the car. Dan stepped out into the heat and stench of the alley and asked the driver what was going on. The driver indicated in graphic mime that a public flogging was about to take place in the square. Dan was seized by a curiosity of which he was instantly ashamed. He would just take a look at the scene, but not witness the flogging itself. He joined the crowd and found himself being borne into the square.

Most of the square was occupied by market stalls but in front of the mosque there was an open space kept clear by soldiers in combat uniform. A murmur ran through the throng and Dan pressed forward to a vantage point on the steps of a fountain. He was aware of sullen, suspicious eyes on him. From behind the mosque a ragged platoon of soldiers appeared. They were followed by police. The police began to assemble the metal triangle to which the prisoner would be strapped. There were shouts and an excited babble from the crowd as more police appeared, dragging the prisoner. He was semi-conscious and stripped to the waist. In the bronze light his skin seemed whiter than milk.

Dan began to fight his way back through the crowd towards the alley. He was pushed and jostled, hemmed in by hot bodies, half choked by rank, spice-laden breath. It was as if the people were determined to make him witness the humiliation of one of his own kind. He was elbowing his way back. He heard the zing and smack of leather slicing into flesh, an animal scream, and jeers from the crowd. Then he was free and staggering towards the Mercedes and its scared driver. He yelled at the man to take him back to the guest house. The car reversed through a flock of grey-white bodies, out of the alley, back into a wider street. It was deserted. Not a human being in sight. Dan thought of calling Hussin again or the American consul – but what was the point? Nobody could do anything. This was Khatam. Only the knowledge that the next flight to London did not leave until the following morning prevented him from ordering the driver to take him directly to the airport.

11

There was a heatwave in Europe. In Luxembourg the temperature was in the eighties and the well-covered housewives of the Continent's most prosperous city stopped and fanned themselves and exchanged complaints about the weather as they puffed from shop to shop along the Grand-Rue. In the Place d'Armes thousands of tourists were slumped at the café tables under the lime trees, panting, chattering, and soaking up beer by the litre.

Eddy had arrived in the morning and set up house in a room in one of the big, anonymous hotels opposite the station. Since leaving Hong Kong he'd visited Brussels, where he'd obtained a letter of commitment from Tan's bankers, and then Zurich, where he'd spent three hours at Limmatbank with Schurch, who had promised to supply a letter from his bank within two days. In Brussels he'd wined and dined an old contact from the early days of Fork Road Metals, a gold dealer called Hooghens who supplied the West German electronics industry. Hooghens had given him a line on a Luxembourg bank controlled by a group of German industrialists who, Hooghens thought, might be interested in buying bullion. 'They're looking over their shoulders, those boys,' Hooghens had said. 'Looking east, you know, where the cold winds come from.' Eddy had promised Hooghens a million-dollar cut in the event of a transaction. He felt confident. The deal with Tan was proceeding smoothly; Hooghens's contact sounded promising; as he walked past the sombre pseudo-Renaissance piles on the Avenue de la Liberté and crossed the Adolphe bridge into the old city, he even felt easy about Jan Pienaar. He hadn't bothered to contact the South African – he had more important things to do – and he calculated that, by continuing to use his Hong Kong passport, it could be several weeks before Pienaar found him.

That was his mood as he entered the white-marbled foyer of the Cravat Hotel for his introductory meeting with Hooghens's man,

Walther. Five minutes later it had radically altered. Eddy had deliberately arrived ten minutes early for his meeting with Walther. He ordered tea and cakes and sat down in a plush arm-chair to contemplate his strategy. A scout-master voice broke brutally into his reverie.

'Eddy! Eddy Polonski! Dammit I've been trying to raise you all over Europe and America, you old buzzard. Must have made twenty calls – and here you walk in off the street and right into my arms.' Bob Hutchinson. Gold broker. Plump and balding. The man from Chicago pumped Eddy's arm, all *bonhomie*. 'This has just gotta be my day out.'

The freelance gold broker is a strange animal; his habitat is the foyers and lounges of five-star hotels, smart restaurants, and night-clubs; his prey, the rich, the greedy, and the gullible; his method of attack, the big deal and the big spiel. While a deal is hot he lives like a lord on someone else's expense account; when it dies, as it frequently does, he goes chasing from capital city to capital city, hunting for another. His life-span is generally short; he dies at forty-five of a coronary, leaving a baffled widow in some desultory suburb to untangle a cat's cradle of debts and commitments.

Bob Hutchinson was typical of the species. He was a man of limitless energy, optimism, and enthusiasm who, if he had chosen any other way of making a living, would have swiftly risen to fame and fortune. But there was a fatal streak of poetry in his nature; he believed in Eldorado, in making millions overnight on a gold deal. He knew it could be done, he knew he would do it one day, and that day was always tomorrow. Eddy stared at him with a hostility he didn't bother to disguise.

'What the hell are you talking about Bob?'

Hutchinson sat down and helped himself to a cake.

'The Greek *Au*,' he said, flakes of *mille feuilles* floating onto the front of his suit. 'You're a sly fox, Eddy. How in hell did you get in on it?'

'How in hell did you get to hear about it?'

Hutchinson shrugged. 'Come on, Eddy. It's mega-bucks. Everybody knows about it.'

Delgado's talked, thought Eddy. He'd known the word would get out but he'd reckoned on at least two months of peace before the stampede of the Bob Hutchinsons.

'The word is it's two thousand tons,' Hutchinson was saying. 'I've got buyers right now, here in this city, for five hundred tons.

Give me a month and I'll sell the rest. Certain sure. I'm not going to be greedy, Eddy. With a whopper like this I don't need to be greedy. Let's talk percentages.'

'Let's talk farewells, Bob. I have a meeting.'

'Sure. Otto Walther. He's standing by the desk. Great guy. Have dinner with me tonight. You like Chinese, don't you? The Mandarin. Eight o'clock.'

Eddy sighed. The only way to get rid of Hutchinson was to agree. 'Okay, Bob,' he said, 'I'll be there.'

Hutchinson left, waving to Walther as he crossed the foyer. Walther and Eddy introduced themselves.

'I see you know Herr Hutchinson,' Walther said icily and Eddy damned Hutchinson to hell.

'One doesn't know Bob Hutchinson, one suffers from him – like an incurable disease.'

Walther laughed. A de-frosting laugh. He was in his early forties, one of those let's-bury-the-past Germans who was as proud of his country's economic achievements as his father had probably been of Hitler's *blitzkrieg*. It took Eddy half an hour to wear down the barriers of suspicion and convince him that he was bona fide. And a further fifteen minutes to get him to agree to a meeting with one of his principals. He felt that he'd handled Walther badly, but his mind had been on another matter: the fact that, with Bob Hutchinson round his neck, and the rest of the gold-broking pack about to start yelping at his heels, it would only be a matter of days before Pienaar picked up his scent. He walked for an hour through the pretty gardens beside the Petrusse, the anaemic little tributary of the Alzette that runs in a concrete bed round the foot of the grey limestone crag where Luxembourg's founder, Count Siegfried, built his stronghold in the tenth century.

It was five o'clock, ten in the morning in Houston. He walked back to his hotel, collected his address book, and proceeded to the main Post Office a little way down the street, opposite the station. He had decided to call Querby at Westmacott but he had to do it in such a way as would not reveal his own whereabouts. That ruled out calling from his hotel, or going through the international operator, and left him with no alternative but to direct dial from a booth in the Post Office – a tedious process that involved waiting in line, paying a deposit, then waiting in line again to collect the change.

Querby's voice boomed uncannily clear and near.

'Eddy! How y'all doing? Where are you calling from?'

'A call-box, Henry. Now listen. I want to talk to Jan.'

'And he sure as hell wants to talk to you, boy. You-all in Europe or what?'

'Henry, I'm going to call you back at this time in two days. I want to know where I can contact Jan.'

'Can do, Eddy, but listen——'

'Just locate him for me, Henry. I'll call you in two days. *Sayonara.*'

Over dinner Eddy listened patiently to Bob Hutchinson's dreams of glory, and because it was useless to give him a no for an answer gave him a string of maybes. After dinner he had to endure an hour of ersatz jazz at Bugatti's before finally shaking off the broker. The next day he left for Zurich.

It was on his first night back in Switzerland that Eddy met Tania.

On previous trips he'd noticed a Polish restaurant, called the Liszt, tucked away in one of the crooked alleys in the old quarter behind St Peter's Church. When he stepped across the threshold of the restaurant, stooping to avoid the low lintel, it was as if he'd taken an eight-hundred-mile stride across Europe into the Kamienne Schodki in Warsaw's Market Square. There were intimate booths and tables, glinting brass sconces on the walls, a smell of roast duck and baked apples. He felt that if he opened a window at the back of the building he'd find himself looking out onto the Stone Steps and the Vistula below. The only difference was that the place was empty – it was early – whereas the Kamienne Schodki was packed at any hour. An old man with a grey walrus moustache emerged from the back regions.

'*Dobry wieczór*,' Eddy said and the old man smiled and replied in Polish. He was talkative. From Warsaw, he had been deported to Germany during the war as a slave-labourer, had escaped to Switzerland, and, like all exiled Poles, talked of his native country with passion and longing. Eddy luxuriated in his mother tongue, cracking the wry jokes so beloved of Poles and so baffling to others. He ordered *chłodnik*, the ice-cold summer soup of cucumber, crayfish, and sour cream, *flaki po warszawsku*, and watery tea flavoured with lemon.

He was eating the *flaki*, highly spiced tripe, when she entered. She stood in the doorway for a moment, her back to the tangerine light of the summer evening. As she advanced into the restaurant she evidently became aware of his eyes on her. She looked in his direction and faltered fractionally, as if startled or afraid. Then she swept past him, and the old man came out of the kitchen and greeted her with kisses on both cheeks. She sat down at a table diagonally opposite and began chatting to the old man in Polish. Her voice was light and musical, full of warmth and humour. Her hair was black and fell in natural curls round the perfect oval of her face. Her skin was finely textured and lightly tanned. She wore a simple cream linen dress embroidered at the hems with a peasant pattern in red and blue. The neckline plunged between her breasts which Eddy imagined to be naked beneath the cloth.

His tripe had gone cold. He forked at it for a moment but his appetite had vanished. The girl and the old man were still talking animatedly. She never looked at him. The old man shuffled back into the kitchen and the girl raised her eyes and looked directly at him for a few seconds, then lowered them as she rummaged in her bag for cigarettes.

A plant. The restaurant pick-up – the hoariest trick in the book. But no sooner had he decided this than he began to tell himself that it was irrational. Nobody knew he was in Zurich; the girl was obviously a regular client of the restaurant, well-known to the waiter. A straight pick-up, then?

The waiter had brought a plate of *flaki* and she was eating, her eyes cast down. He was able to observe her. She was neither a prostitute nor an agent of Pienaar. He had become so paranoid that any human being who showed the remotest interest in him was instantly suspicious. It was crazy; here was a beautiful girl, probably lonely, definitely Polish.

He stood up and walked over to her table.

'*Flaki* tastes much better when eaten in company,' he said. 'That's an old Polish saying.'

She looked up, smiling quizzically. 'Really? I've never heard it before.'

'But how long is it since you were in Poland?'

'Some years.'

'Well there you are.' They smiled. 'I haven't been back myself for a long time.'

'Won't you sit down?'

'My name's Eddy Polonski.'

She held out a hand. 'Tania Larionov – I was married to a Russian,' she explained.

'Was?'

110

She laughed lightly. 'Yes. Was.'

The restaurant began to fill up. It was the sort of place that attracted regular customers. People greeted each other and stood, swopping news, but Eddy and Tania's table remained an island of privacy. They talked – talked as if they'd known each other for years. She told him she was a freelance financial journalist selling articles mainly to the *International Financial Digest* at its editorial base in Zurich. She had worked for the Soviet Embassy in Washington, in the commercial section, and had defected two and a half years ago when her Russian husband had been killed in a car crash. She was evasive about her past and he didn't press her; they talked about gold, which seemed to fascinate her. When she left him for a moment, just before they quitted the restaurant, Eddy paid their bill. The old man, Stefan, took the money.

'That's a wonderful girl. You look after her, huh?' he said.

They strolled through the warm, dimly-lit streets and Eddy suggested a coffee at one of the lakeside cafés.

'I'm rather tired,' she said.

'Okay. I'll take you home.'

'No. I'll get a taxi.'

'Will I see you tomorrow?'

'Of course. Shall we have lunch?'

'Wonderful.'

They arranged a rendezvous and Eddy kissed her lightly on the lips before she got into her taxi. He walked back to his hotel. It was only when he was sitting in the dark in his room, looking out at the lights of Zurich mirrored in the lake, that he wondered about Tania again. A beautiful girl stepping off a street into his life. It was too pat. Things only worked like that when they were arranged. He knew.

When he met Tania the following day he was wary. If she noticed his coolness, she didn't show it.

'To hell with lunch,' she said. 'We have sun and a lake and we're going to go swimming. I've got towels and everything.'

She had a silver Lancia Beta convertible and they drove out along the western shore of the lake and found a beach, screened by pines, that was obviously the property of some millionaire. Eddy muttered something about trespass.

'Who cares?' Tania said. 'It's August and every gnome in Zurich is in the South of France or Mustique or somewhere. Come on Eddy, come swimming.'

111

12

The Greek turned his face away from the open window and the pale evening light played shadow-tricks with the corrugations of his face. The traffic in the Place de la Concorde rumbled and hissed like waves sucking at a beach and the high summer air of Paris, smelling of Gauloises, aniseed, and hot dust, fluttered the curtains.

It had taken Dan a day of international calls to track the vagabond billionaire through the great hotels of Europe and America to the Crillon. Dan had anticipated difficulties in securing an interview with Maniatos: he was protected by a screen of aides. But the Greek had agreed to see him immediately.

'You want make money, be rich man,' the Greek said. 'I understan'. You sell the gold, you be him.'

'I can't proceed until I've had an explanation,' Dan said. 'I was followed to Khatam by one of Mr Collins's people. Why?'

'You fight in the war?' the Greek said. 'No. You too young.' He nodded. 'I fight. Partisan.' Dan said nothing. He was content to allow the Greek to answer the question in his own elliptical way. 'Before the Germans come, just before,' the Greek went on, 'my father take us from Athens to our farm at Yannina – my mother, my brothers. One day we drive up to the mountains, my father and me, alone. We drive many miles, high, high, to a place my father know. Old church there – ruins – you know? In the car he has a box. He tell me, you dig a hole, deep, bury the box. But before we bury box he say to me, you are my first-born, I show the secret. He open the box and there is gold – bars and coins. He say, the Germans come, take everything, kill me. It is hot – sun like fire – my father says here, here, this will be yours, my son.'

The Greek's eyes were staring inwards, 'Four years of war, I am a man. Partisan. We fight in the mountains. I come to the place at night. My father dead. The Germans hang him in the square at Yannina. I dig down, dig with my hands. I feel the box. Then——'

112

he paused and clicked his tongue twice, '*click click*' – I hear a rifle bolt. I am blind – a flashlight in my face. There is voice of a man. I know him. It is Patras, our group leader. He jokes me. "You are a patriot, Gheorgis," he say. "With this gold we buy many guns, kill many Germans."'

It was getting dark in the room and the Greek suddenly leaned forward and snapped on a table lamp. He squinted at Dan.

'They blew away my father's gold in their crazy war,' he said. 'All of it.' He began a slight rocking motion in his chair, staring at the ground. 'The war is over,' he said. 'My father's business, money – all gone. So I go to America. I know people, powerful people. I borrow. I work and I work and I work. And all the time I buy gold, always gold. I sacrifice everything for gold. Gold is power. I look for a mountain of gold. I sacrifice everything. And then I find my mountain.' He was still rocking, like an old man on a porch, and there was a ghastly smile on his face. 'Hendrik Verwoerd, he knew me. Yes, he knew my passion. He want my ships, my refineries. He show me a mountain of gold – it make me mad, blind – I take it.'

He stopped rocking and stared at Dan, his eyes baleful.

'And then, Mist' Daniels,' he said, placing a space between each word, 'I begin to die.'

He was silent for a long time, then he touched his face with his hand. 'Horrible,' he said. 'You think that. Everybody think that. Why? Because I have lay a curse on myself.' He lay back in his chair, as if exhausted. 'You ask me question. I answer you honest. All I care is to sell my gold. Who sell for me make no difference – you, Collins, the devil, I not care. You come to me and say I have the buyers, I want hundred million dollars, I give it you. It is for you to do, not me. I have try for eight years. I am tired.'

Dan cleared his throat. 'I think I understand,' he said.

'I am honest with you. It is for you now.'

Dan stood up and offered his hand but the Greek didn't seem to notice. Dan turned to leave. He took three paces towards the door.

'Wait.'

The Greek bent down and picked up an old, blue airline bag from the floor. He fumbled inside and when his hand came out it was holding a bundle of dollar bills.

'Take,' Maniatos said, 'take.'

In the cab on the way out to Charles de Gaulle Airport Dan counted the bills. They amounted to fifteen thousand dollars.

Dan arrived in Luxembourg late in the evening and took a room at the Rix in the Boulevard Royal. In the morning he called Pradel at the Khatami bank and on his way·to their offices, walking through the Fish Market, he saw the portly figure of Bob Hutchinson hoving into view. He quickly wheeled into a side-street and waited until Hutchinson had gone by. But after his meeting with Pradel, he saw Hutchinson again. He was sitting at a table outside the Maison des Brasseurs, a café in the Grand-Rue, deep in conversation with another man, an odd-looking figure with a crew-cut and a cadaverous face with a nose like a shark's fin. The temperature was high in the seventies, but Hutchinson's friend was wearing a black raincoat.

Dan had lunch with Sayed, a young Iranian who was the personal assistant and emissary of a man called Hofer, a retired Amsterdam bullion dealer who now lived in the Swiss Alps but still dealt extensively in gold. After lunch, strolling back to the hotel, he kept a weather eye open for Hutchinson. Luxembourg was getting to rival Switzerland as a multi-national banking centre, but the city itself was still like a village; after a few hours you began to recognize faces. There was no sign of Hutchinson, which was a relief, but there was a message waiting for him at the desk at the Rix – a verbal message which struck Dan as odd.

The desk-clerk said: 'Mr John called, sir. He asks you to call him at this number.' He scribbled it down.

'John who?' Dan asked.

'He just said Mr John.'

'I don't know any Mr John.'

The clerk shrugged with clerkly indifference and Dan went up to his room and dialled the number. It was answered by a man's voice, a husky Luxembourger voice which slipped easily into English when Dan asked to speak to Mr John. In the background Dan could hear music, the ding of a till, the hiss of a coffee machine.

'Mr John is not here right now. You want to leave a message?'

'Is that a bar or what?'

'You want to leave a message for Mr John?'

'I guess so. Tell him Mr Daniels called.'

'Okay. I tell him.'

Three minutes later Dan's phone rang. The voice on the line was crisp, curt, American.

'Mr Daniels? This is Mr John.'

'Yes?'

'I'd like to talk to you, Mr Daniels.'

'Yeah? Forgive me, but do I know you?'

'Are you free in an hour? If so meet me at the Maison des Brasseurs in Grand-Rue. You know it?'

'Is this some kind of gag?'

'In one hour. Okay?'

'Mr John I don't know who you are or what you want.'

'I don't talk on the phone, Mr Daniels. If you want to sell just be where I said in one hour.' Mr John hung up.

Dan went, out of sheer curiosity. The Maison des Brasseurs was a smartish bar in Luxembourg's most fashionable shopping street. None of the tables outside the café was occupied so Dan went inside. He bought a coffee at the bar and recognized the husky voice of the Luxembourger he'd spoken to on the phone. The place seemed deserted.

'Is Mr John here?'

The bar-tender pointed to the far end of the long, low room. Dan carried his coffee along a line of booths, peering into each one as he passed. In the last booth he found Mr John. He was the shark-like man in the black raincoat Bob Hutchinson had been rapping with earlier in the day. The man looked up but didn't rise.

'Daniels, right? ' he said. 'I'm John.'

'John who – or who John?' Dan sat down opposite him.

'Just John, *kamerad*, just John.'

Dan became aware of a curious smell emanating from John. It was a rank, musty smell, not exactly body odour but something else, something familiar. He got it. A locker-room.

John snapped open a briefcase and took out a document.

'Just take a look at that, *kamerad*.'

It was a letter from a prime bank, signed by two senior officers, confirming to whom it concerned that Mr John was known to the bank and had participated in transactions in excess of nine figures.

'Good enough?' John said. He plucked the letter from Dan's hand and restored it to his briefcase. 'I don't waste time, *kamerad*,' he said. 'I buy gold. You have gold to sell.' He waited, his introduction over.

Dan decided that John was a nut, some kook from Bob Hutchinson's extensive stable of phonies and fantasists.

'What makes you think I have gold to sell, Mr John?' he said.

'I heard.'

'From Bob Hutchinson?'

'Maybe.'

'Did Hutchinson give you my name?'

'Mighta done.'

Obviously Hutchinson had spotted him in the Fish Market, or later in the Grand-Rue, and had told John about him. But how in hell could Hutchinson know that he was selling gold?

'I don't know anything about you, Mr John,' he said. 'Who do you represent?'

'I represent money, *kamerad*. That's all you need to know.'

Dan smiled. 'I guess Bob Hutchinson has been spinning you a yarn, Mr John.' He drained his coffee cup.

'Maybe,' John said. 'Maybe the Greek *Au* is bullshit. Two thousand tons sounds like bullshit. I don't know. You tell me, *kamerad*.'

So that was it. The word was out. There had been a leak, no doubt through Canyon Bank. That *shmuck* Delgado. Or was John mixed up with Collins in some way? He had something of the air of a family man – and anything was possible.

'How well do you know Bob Hutchinson?' he asked.

'Some.'

'That's curious – for a man who says he doesn't like to waste his time. That's what you're doing, Mr John. Good afternoon.'

He thought that would be the last he saw of John, but he was wrong. The next morning, when he came down into the hotel foyer after breakfast, John was there, raincoat buttoned up to his chin and stretching down to his ankles.

'Hi, *kamerad*,' he said. 'Can't talk here. Let's take a walk.'

'Mr John, I have a meeting right now.'

'Okay. This *après-midi*.'

'I told you before. You're wasting your time.'

'I'll call you.'

He did. At four o'clock. In the interim Dan had tried to find Hutchinson, but without success. The broker, so ubiquitous the day before, seemed to have vanished. Dan had called two or three bankers and attorneys but none of them had ever heard of John. Finally he'd thought of calling Hofer's man, Sayed.

'Oh yes,' Sayed had said, 'we know John.'

'Is he genuine?'

Sayed had been guarded. 'He is – unusual. He has no office, not even a telephone number. But, yes, I think he has funds.'

So when Dan took John's call, and John persisted on demanding a meeting, he agreed to see him at Pub-13, a bar on the first floor of a corner building overlooking the Place de Paris. He put the Limmatbank letter, and the letter from Schurch, into his briefcase; but he was resolved that John would have sight of them only after he'd answered some hard questions.

Pub 13 was full of fake oak beams, fake diamond-leaded windows, and fake hunting prints, but empty of people. It seemed that John favoured empty places. He was sitting at a table in the angle of the room where a semi-circular balcony, with open French windows, commanded a view of the *place*. He was drinking Guinness. Dan went up to the table.

'Can see five streets from here. See who's approaching the building. Okay, *kamerad*, let's talk gold,' said John.

Dan had intended to interrogate John, but he found himself immediately on the receiving end of some very searching questions. John seemed to be trying openly to trip him up; at the same time he displayed an impressive knowledge of the gold market. Still more impressive were letters from prime banks identifying John as the principal in three major bullion transactions. It was this evidence that finally persuaded Dan to lay his own letters on the table. John scanned them hungrily, then looked up.

'How long you in Lux?' he said.

'I don't know. A few days.'

'I wanna get back to you, talk prices.'

'Okay. How do I reach you?'

'I'll reach you, *kamerad*.'

'What if I have to leave town suddenly?'

John smiled – or rather he made a grimace that bared his teeth, grey with plaque. 'No sweat. I'll reach you,' he said.

13

Jan Pienaar leaned into the island of light over the green baize billiard table and addressed himself to the cue ball. His eyes flicked round to assess the angles then, with a smooth, professional action, he potted the black.

'Good shot,' Melldrum said.

Pienaar straightened and chalked his cue. They were in the billiard room of the Audley Club, a high yet intimate room, lined with Spy and Beerbohm cartoons of long-dead literary lions – Kipling, Stevenson, Wells.

Mid-August was a time of limbo in London's Clubland, that incestuous world centred on the great St James's clubs – Boodles, Whites, Brooks's. Most of the clubs were closed for the annual holiday and those members who were not touring in Italy or France, or who had no country house to which to retire, were pigging it in lesser establishments, where reciprocal arrangements existed. The majority of such people regarded the August exile as a damned nuisance: unfamiliar food and servants made lunching a tedious and indigestible affair, and the unfamiliar contours of alien armchairs and chesterfields caused back pain and insomnia. Anthony Melldrum, however, always looked forward to his yearly stint in the raffish, entertaining Audley, which was famous for its literary conversation and its late-night bar brawls. His own club was solidly Establishment, which was important from the point of view of status, but was undeniably dull.

A servant came in with tea, buttered toast, and cakes. He was an Italian youth in a pink jacket. A far cry, Melldrum reflected, from the venerable old dodderers who served in his own club. When the boy had gone and Pienaar had attempted, and failed, to put a red into the centre pocket, Melldrum resumed their conversation.

'I assume you know about the Greek gold?' he said.

'Naturally. I have known about it from the beginning. MCI

supplied Pretoria with a major proportion of it back in the sixties.

'And presumably you know that Maniatos and his confrères tried to sell it earlier in the year?'

Pienaar smiled, watching Melldrum attempt a snooker. There was something about the tall Englishman Pienaar didn't like, though he'd never been able to put his finger on what it was.

'There was a mild panic in Jo'burg at the time,' he said.

'Quite. It would have done nasty things to the gold price.'

Pienaar shrugged. 'Such a quantity of bullion in the hands of a man like Maniatos is always dangerous. It gives him immense power. Happily he doesn't know it.'

'Exactly. Correct me if I'm wrong, Jan, but put simply the threat the Greek gold poses to your company, and companies like it, is a massive over-supply to the market?'

'That's one of the dangers, certainly. But it is a situation we can control.'

'Of course. But imagine for a moment that the enormous supply represented by the Greek gold were converted into an equally enormous demand.'

It was Pienaar's turn to play but he remained standing just outside the pool of light over the table, holding his cue like a sentry's pike-staff.

'I don't follow you, Anthony.'

'Put it this way. Suppose there was suddenly a world-wide demand for bullion, equal to the Greek gold? In other words, a demand for two thousand tons.'

'In that case,' Pienaar said after a moment, 'there would be the most spectacular rise in the gold price in the history of the metal.'

'Which would be of benefit to you and the other producers?'

'To a degree, yes.'

'I take your point. In an ideal world, of course you and your colleagues would have prior knowledge of such a rise; you would know exactly when the boom was to start, exactly how high the price would go, and exactly when the bubble would burst.'

Pienaar was staring at the tip of his cue, rubbing it with a little cube of blue chalk.

'In an ideal world, yes. And to a certain extent,' he said, 'such knowledge is always available to us.'

'Quite so. But I am not talking about "a certain extent". I am talking about total market control, temporary but absolute.'

Pienaar pondered a moment. 'Undeniably,' he said, 'that would be valuable.'

Melldrum smiled. 'You really are a master of understatement, Jan.' He poured two cups of tea. 'Sugar?' He handed Pienaar a cup and they sat down, side by side, on one of the raised, padded benches that lined the room.

'That's what I have to offer you, Jan,' Melldrum said abruptly.

Pienaar pursed his lips and sipped his tea. He had spent much of his recent working life manipulating minor gold rushes, using the circulation of bullion from Westmacott in Houston via London to Johannesburg to create small price fluctuations. But what Melldrum was proposing was on a completely different scale.

'I don't see how it would be possible,' he said, 'without breaking the law to an extent which would really be unwise.'

'What I propose is perfectly legal – in its wider aspects at least. The only likely casualties will be a couple of American businessmen – a thoroughly expendable species I think you'd agree.'

Pienaar began to understand – only very dimly. 'Does one of these expendable Americans go by the name of Polonski?'

'As a matter of fact he does. You seem to know rather more than I thought, Jan. How have you come across Polonski?'

'Eddy Polonski used to work for me.'

'I see. Do you know much about him?'

'I know everything about him.'

'What an extraordinarily small and ideal world we live in, Jan,' said Melldrum, genuinely surprised. 'I've been trying to compile a dossier on Mr Polonski for weeks. Perhaps you'd like to fill me in?'

Pienaar set down his tea-cup. 'Before I do that, Anthony, it would be helpful if you would explain exactly what role Polonski is to play in your plans.'

Melldrum explained. Pienaar was not a banker, and much of the technical detail eluded him, but one essential point was clear: if Melldrum was to succeed it was vital that Eddy Polonski should remain healthy and vigorous. Pienaar chose his words carefully.

'Eddy Polonski is a very interesting man,' he said. 'He's a Pole. His father was a professor of physics at Warsaw University, who was liquidated by Stalin in the early fifties. His son Eddy was a child prodigy. His field was metallurgy. The Russians recognized his value, scooped him up, and put him into Shulov's laboratories in Moscow. Shulov was working on a very radical line of research. I won't baffle you with science but it was leading towards a complete revolution in gold extraction. Polonski studied with Shulov. Later he was sent to Kazakstan and then to Peking. Then he went to South Africa.'

'You mean he defected?'

Pienaar was amused that the banker could be so naïve. 'Not at all, he was part of a joint Soviet-South African research venture.'

Melldrum's silence revealed his ignorance.

'You seem surprised.'

'Well——'

'In the field of international politics the Soviet Union and South Africa are at opposite poles. But as the world's two major gold producers they are naturally in partnership – as with diamonds.'

Melldrum was annoyed. This was exactly the sort of thing his father-in-law would be able to talk about knowledgeably.

'If you think about it for a moment, Anthony,' Pienaar was saying, 'it becomes obvious. If it were not so, a price war would have broken out many years ago. Yet the gold market is relatively stable. That is because the Russians are happy to do the mining and refining and to leave the marketing to us. Even so, a healthy rivalry does, of course, exist especially in the area of technology. I could hardly steal Professor Shulov from the Russians, but there was his deputy, Polonski, in South Africa panting to defect. So I arranged matters and Polonski came to work for me, first in Jo'burg, then in America. While he was under my control he was a most valuable man. Unfortunately he decided to branch out on his own. At which point he became dangerous.'

'How dangerous?' Melldrum asked and there was nothing naïve about that particular question.

'Very. You see, he has certain knowledge that even we don't possess. If he had the money to set up a plant he could very rapidly make half the world's gold mines redundant.'

'That sounds like science fiction.'

'It is sober fact.'

Melldrum pondered for a moment. 'After what you have heard this afternoon, Jan, I hope you appreciate that it is in your own short-term interest for Mr Polonski's health to remain good.'

'Yes. I do appreciate that.'

'Good. Shall we resume our game?'

As they played they discussed terms. Melldrum won the financial arguments, Pienaar the game. Melldrum saw the South African into a taxi then went back into the club, to the billiard room. The Italian servant was clearing up the tea things.

'I'm only a visitor to the club,' he said to the boy. 'What's your name?'

'Mario.'

Melldrum laughed. 'All Italian boys seem to be called Mario,' he said. 'You're very handsome, Mario.' Mario blushed and looked a little sly. 'Has anyone told you that?''

'Some people say that, yes.'

'I like your pink jacket,' Melldrum said, reaching out to finger a lapel. His hand rested on Mario's shoulder. 'Do you like working here?'

'It's okay,' Mario said, moving closer to Melldrum. 'But the moncy, it's very bad.'

'Ah yes,' Melldrum said, 'money. That's always such a problem isn't it?'

In his hotel, Pienaar had a leisurely bath, put on a towelling robe, and sat down with a whisky and soda to contemplate the tree-tops of Green Park and decide how to handle the call from Eddy Polonski that Henry Querby had told him was due at seven o'clock. At ten minutes to seven there was a knock at his door. Pienaar tightened the belt of his robe and opened the door, expecting to see a chambermaid. But it was not a chambermaid. It was two nondescript men in business suits. One of them said in a strong Cockney accent, 'Mr Pienaar?', the name coming out as 'Pinnerer'.

'Yes?'

'We'd like to 'ave a word wiv you.'

Pienaar tried to slam the door, but he was too late. And he was too late to twist away from the knee that flashed up into his groin. He doubled up and rolled onto the carpet, nursing himself, blind to everything but the pain. There were three more blows: a boot thudded into the small of his back, straightening him; another boot went into his groin again and as he jerked back into a foetal position, the third blow jarred the base of his spine. Then it was over – it had taken a few seconds – the door slammed, and he was alone.

The pain subsided to a tolerable level quite rapidly. He wanted to retch but controlled himself. He lay on the floor panting, not so much from pain as from shock. After a time he was able to get to his knees and then to his feet. He limped over to the phone to call the management. But as he reached for the receiver the phone rang. He picked it up and heard Eddy Polonski's voice.

'Good evening, Jan.'

Until that moment he had not connected the attack with Polonski. 'You'll pay for this, Polonski. By Christ's blood you'll pay.'

'You'll be fine, Jan. What happened to you was nothing compared with what happened to a Chinese house-boy in the Harbour Hotel, Hong Kong. Still, I'm sorry it had to happen. I have to protect myself.'

'By God you do.'

Eddy's voice was level, unemotional as always. 'After the incident in Hong Kong I asked myself why you wanted to kill me. I concluded that you must have found out about the business transaction I'm currently engaged in. You saw me getting rich. You should have looked a little further. If you had you would have found out that one of the people I'm working for is called Jim Collins of Las Vegas, Nevada. Mr Collins is a bit like you, Jan. He picks up a phone and a few hours later somebody, somewhere dies. Well, Mr Collins is on my side. You should bear that in mind.'

Pienaar was in control of himself now. He even smiled. In a way Polonski had made it easy for him. He no longer had the problem of finding a credible reason for cancelling the contract on the Pole.

'Very well, Eddy. But remember something. Your relationship with your friend in Las Vegas is a business relationship. When the business ends, the friendship ends.'

As Pienaar and Eddy hung up, one in London the other in Zurich, each had a smile on his face. Pienaar went into the bathoom to examine his bruises, Eddy emerged from the cabin in the Post Office and lined up to collect his change. He wasn't thinking of Pienaar – that problem was solved – he was thinking of Tania. How they'd both bathed in the lake that afternoon – as innocent as children. Friendly and happy with each other, but holding back – waiting. He didn't know what he wanted from her, but he did know that he couldn't stop seeing her. He called her.

Tania was at home, a three-roomed apartment in a modern block on the hill behind the university. She was sitting in the living room. The shutters were closed, the blinds were drawn, and a movie camera was purring in the dark. She was looking at a short clip of eight-millimetre film. It showed a little boy with dark hair

123

and very slightly Tartar eyes playing in a garden. The boy was sitting cross-legged on a lawn with a high hedge behind him and a border of roses. He was building a castle out of Lego, frowning with a child's intensity. He looked up suddenly, smiled, and then shyly shielded his face with one arm, having evidently seen the camera. He rolled over and pretended to burrow into the ground. The phone interrupted. It was Eddy.

'Dinner tonight?'

'I don't know, Eddy. I've been working——'

'You sound depressed.'

'No. Not really. Yes. I'd love to come.'

'The Liszt? Round about eight?'

'I'll see you there.'

Old Stefan clucked round them. Two fine Poles he'd brought together.

'This is kind of a farewell dinner,' Eddy said. 'But only temporarily. I have to go away for a few days.'

'Where are you going?'

'Luxembourg. I have to be there for a meeting on Monday afternoon. I thought I'd fly up on Saturday, spend Sunday there. Unless you——'

She shrugged and changed the subject, but as they were sitting over coffee she returned to it.

'As a matter of fact, Eddy, I have to be in Luxembourg on Monday too. I was going to drive – leave tomorrow afternoon and spend the weekend in France.'

'Is that an invitation?'

'Yes,' she said, looking at him directly.

On Friday afternoon she picked him up at his hotel in the silver Lancia. She flicked the little car through the constipated traffic of the city centre with the casual ruthlessness of a cab-driver and once they were on the northern *autoroute* she changed into fifth and wound it up to ninety. They flashed past a police car near the airport exit.

'What's the hurry? You don't want to offend the law-abiding Swiss by breaking the speed limit.'

'I do,' she shouted above the wind-roar. 'I loathe the law-abiding Swiss. I loathe their tidy little cities and their tidy little minds. I want open country.'

She got it when the *autoroute* ended and they took the road to Winterthur. It was a landscape that seemed too wide to belong to Switzerland, a vista of high, green pastures and fields of standing maize and mountains on every horizon. But Tania would have none of it. When Eddy commented on the neat farms dotted about the slopes she said:

'Cuckoo clocks! Here they don't pasteurize the milk, they pasteurize the grass and the rain. The owls are forbidden to hoot between the hours of midnight and six. I'll show you real country, Eddy, and before that I'll show you the most exciting birthplace in Europe.'

They came to Schaffhausen, dropping down into the ancient town under the battlements of the castle. They crossed the river and she pulled over suddenly and parked under some lime trees by a little fountain.

'Here I always stop,' she said, 'to drink a toast to the baby's health.' She led him to a café by the river and bought a cold beer for herself and a *Spa* water for him. They leaned over a rail and watched the river fretting between its banks. 'To the infant Rhine. You see how green and turbulent she is Eddy, like a young creature should be.' She laughed. 'I know what you are thinking.'

'You do?'

'Of course. You are standing by the Rhine, on your way to Luxumbourg to talk with bankers. You are thinking about Wotan and the *Rheingold*.'

Eddy smiled.

She looked away, staring at the river. 'I think gold is your life.'

'Maybe,' he said. 'And what's yours?'

'Like this river,' she said after a moment. 'Only after the falls I never saw the mountains, only the cities of the plain. The polluted plain.' She shrugged and took his arm. 'Come on Wotan, we've got some kilometres to cover. Like to drive?'

'No. I like watching you drive.'

They crossed a tongue of the Black Forest then swooped down, ears popping, into the valley of the Rhine, a place of lazy streams, patchwork water-meadows, and willow trees. A tiny ferry took them across the river and they were in France. The sun was beginning to go down and the poplars along the verges were striping the road with shadows. They traversed the *R.N.* 85 and headed into the dying sun, through flat pastureland. Then, as they rounded a bend, Tania slowed the car.

'There you are, Wotan,' she said. 'Real country.'

Ahead, the sharp peaks of the Vosges seemed to rise sheer from the level fields. By some trick of the fading light they appeared to be painted against the sky.

'I love rivers,' Tania said, 'and I love mountains. You can put away the map, Eddy. Where we're going isn't on it.'

They began to climb through an enchanted land of steep vineyards and cypress trees and absurdly pretty villages of twisted beams and geraniums in hanging baskets. Then the *virage* warning signs began and the road twisted up into the mountains and there was a smell of crushed pine needles and rotting cones. They turned off the road and onto a rough forest track, walled and roofed with conifers, like the nave of a cathedral. They were both silent now. They began to descend, through a maze of logging roads, with straight rides branching off them, and then the trees thinned out and Eddy caught glimpses of green grass and a flash of water. They bumped down a steep gradient and suddenly the world opened up. They were in a valley, hemmed round with high mountains and floored with meadows. At the head of the valley there was a cascade that turned into a busy river which became shallow and lazy as it threaded the meadows. Beside the cascade, on a pink sandstone outcrop, was a pink sandstone château – a squat, square bastion built by some baronial warlord of the twelfth century and later embellished with grey, pepper-pot turrets of the seventeenth century. A tall radio mast rose from its steep, slate roofs. The mast was the only hint of the modern world in the whole place. Below the château was a huddle of cottages and, on an island in the river, a stooping, half-timbered building whose faded signboard declared it to be the Auberge de la Pêche. They parked by the wooden bridge that led to the entrance of the inn.

'Cowbells tinkling in the dusk, a château on the hill,' said Eddy, 'I don't believe any of it.'

'It's a secret place,' Tania said, lifting her bag off the back seat. 'Only a few trout fishermen know about it.'

They ate fresh fish from the river, the soft-crusted bread of the region, and cheese flavoured with cumin. The dining room was full of candle-shadows, and low, mysterious conversations about the psychology of the trout. It was an atmosphere that should have led them to the same bed, but Eddy knew that when dinner was over they would kiss and go to their separate rooms. He didn't know why this was so; it didn't worry him. It was simply right.

The next morning they met at breakfast and set off on a six-hour hike over the mountain behind the château, and back through the forest. Tania was distant and withdrawn; the response of a private, independent person to intimacy, Eddy thought. Sunday passed in the same way – a long walk, a leisurely dinner, and a communion that seemed all the more extraordinary since it owed nothing to sex.

It was sheer instinct that woke Eddy in the early hours of Monday morning, and made him pad along the creaky passage to Tania's room. He opened the door. The room was empty. The doors of the *armoire* were standing open and the hangers were naked. The song of the river was chuckling through the window. Above it, Eddy heard the cough of the Lancia's starter-motor. He looked round to see if there was a note. There was nothing.

Tania had paid the bill, he discovered, when he questioned the house-maid sweeping the hall.

'Did she say anything before she left?' he asked the woman.

She shook her head. 'Do you want breakfast now, *monsieur*?'

'No,' he said. 'I won't take breakfast. Is there somewhere I can phone for a taxi?'

The taxi took him the fifty-odd kilometres into Strasbourg where he hired a car to drive on to Luxembourg. He was ten minutes late for his meeting with Walther and his principal, a dour Düsseldorf steel man of the type that has to have everything spelt out in words of one syllable, three or four times.

At one point Walther remarked confidentially to Eddy: 'You don't seem very anxious to sell the gold, if I may say so, Mr Polonski. Perhaps you are not feeling well?'

By the time Eddy checked into a hotel he was exhausted and listless. He had five or six calls to make but he didn't bother to make any of them. He was hungry but he couldn't summon the energy to go down to the restaurant to eat. When the phone in his room rang at eight o'clock he let it ring. But it persisted. Only the sudden thought that it could be Tania made him pick it up.

'Mr Polonski?' a male, American voice said.

'Yes?'

'My name is John. Mr John. I buy gold. I'd like to make a meeting with you.'

14

The next morning Eddy called Hooghens in Brussels and asked him if he knew a good enquiry agent in Luxembourg. Hooghens laughed.

'The town's full up with them.' He recommended a man called Stephany.

Then Eddy asked him casually about Mr John.

'The American? Face like a corpse?'

'I haven't met him.'

'You get a call – out of nowhere?'

'Yes.'

'That sounds like John. I've had dealings with him. A very strange man. But he has money. *Mon dieu*, such money.'

Stephany was well-groomed, well-spoken, and obviously well-heeled. It was clear that he hadn't pounded pavements or knocked on doors for years. He noted down Tania's name and address.

'She claims to be a freelance journalist,' Eddy said, 'working for the *International Financial Digest* in Zurich. She says she was married to a Russian who died in a car crash. She also says she worked in the Soviet Embassy in Washington and defected in seventy-six. It shouldn't be too hard to check on all that.'

'A fairly simple matter,' Stephany said. 'That's all you require, *monsieur*?'

'Yeah. I just want to know if she's genuine. How long will it take?'

'Perhaps a week. Not more.'

'Okay. Fine. I'll call you in a week. Just one more thing,' he added, 'check if she's got any South African connections.'

As Stephany saw him out of his office, Eddy said: 'I don't suppose you've ever heard of a guy called John, have you?

'John who?'

'It doesn't matter. I'll call you in a week.'

It was only a short walk from Stephany's office to the Maison des Brasseurs in Grand-Rue, where he'd agreed to meet John at eleven o'clock. According to his custom, he arrived ten minutes early; but Mr John was ahead of him. As he paid for his tea at the bar a voice said: 'Polonski, right?'

Eddy turned. An agent – his instant reaction to the lanky figure in the black raincoat. He had that air of not belonging to the human race that some agents acquire through years of isolation and disillusion in government service. And there was another thing: he had a look of Jan Pienaar about him.

'Quiet up the far end,' John said. 'Follow me, *kamerad*.'

They sat down, facing each other. John placed his briefcase on the table and snapped the catches open.

'Like I told you on the phone, I'm a buyer,' John said.

He produced a letter from the briefcase and handed it to Eddy. Eddy read it through. It was from a prime bank and it stated that John represented a client with a bank capability in ten figures.

'This is a conditional letter.'

'Sure,' John replied quickly. 'Think I want people checking with my bankers and lousing up my credibility?'

That made sense to Eddy, but even so his instincts warned him to proceed warily.

'I'd like to see your own documentation, Mr Polonski.'

Eddy temporized.

'I'd like to know how you got my name. And how you found me.'

'I buy gold, Mr Polonski,' John said. 'If there's gold for sale I hear about it. Finding people is easy.'

'It shouldn't be – not the way I operate.'

'Globe's loused up with guys like Bob Hutchinson, *kamerad*.'

Eddy nodded. 'I get the picture. Mr John, I guess we can talk business.'

From his inside pocket he drew out his Limmatbank letter and Schurch's letter of authority. John took them and leaned back in his seat, holding the letters close to his chest. He began reading them. He read very slowly, suspiciously slowly, Eddy began to think. As if he were playing for time. Eddy was about to say something when a movement behind him made him glance round. There was a man hovering near their table, staring curiously at him. John looked up, with a grey grin. 'Ah. Mr Daniels. Hi, *kamerad*. Won't you join us?'

Dan stood still. 'I don't know,' he said. 'Is this gentleman an associate of yours?'

Eddy suddenly knew that this was a dangerous situation.

Very quietly he said: 'I'd be glad if you'd hand my documents back to me, Mr John.'

In a movement too quick for Eddy to block, John slid across his seat and held the letters out to Dan. Dan made no attempt to take them but he could not help seeing the Limmatbank logo and Schurch's flamboyant signature.

'Snap, *kamerad*,' John said. 'That's the name of the game, huh? Or is it —— con?'

Dan took the letters. At a glance he established that they were identical to his own.

'Your partner's suddenly a silent partner,' John was saying to Eddy.

Eddy stared. 'I've never set eyes on this gentleman in my life,' he said. He turned to Dan. 'Those documents are my property.'

Dan nodded and handed the letters to Eddy.

'You think I'm stupid?' John said. He looked at Dan. 'You think I didn't see you recognize him? You should bone up on your acting, Daniels. Might get as good as your partner.'

Dan ignored John. He was looking at Eddy. 'I think you and I should talk,' he said.

'I think so,' Eddy said.

'Not so fast,' John said. 'I wanna know what goes on here. There are laws in this country. Nobody takes me for a sucker. You stay right where you are.'

Eddy had replaced his letters in his pocket. Now he rose and said very quietly: 'Do you have jurisdiction in Luxembourg, Mr John?'

John squinted at him. 'What's that supposed to mean?'

'Is your badge valid here?'

The effect on John was curious. For a moment he looked as if he were going to lash out at Eddy. Then an expression of strange satisfaction spread across his face.

'Smart, huh?' he said, and made no attempt to prevent Eddy and Dan from walking out of the café together.

They walked side by side down the Rue des Capucins and Dan was the first to break the silence.

'We seem to have a problem.'

'I assume you have letters from Limmatbank that are identical to mine?' Dan nodded. 'Am I also correct in deducing that you know Jim Collins and Paul Delgado?'

'I do.'

130

They had reached the Place D'Armes.

'Would you care for a drink?' Eddy asked.

'I think I need one.'

They sat down and Dan ordered Scotch, Eddy tea.

'John was right about one thing,' Eddy said. 'I think you did recognize me.'

'I know you from somewhere. I'm sure of it. I saw you a few weeks ago coming out of the Hairless Wonder's office in Zurich and I knew I knew you from somewhere.'

'From your voice,' Eddy said, 'I'd guess you were from Houston. I'm from Houston too.'

Dan smiled. 'Maybe it would help if I knew your name.'

'Polonski. Eddy Polonski.'

'Doesn't make any connections. Oh, Dan Daniels.'

They shook hands self-consciously.

At that point they both saw John striding out of the square.

'This town's a goldfish bowl,' Dan said. 'Maybe we should talk some place else.'

'Okay. I have a car. Shall we take a run in the country?'

'Fine.'

It was during the short walk to Eddy's hotel, where his hired car was garaged, that Dan's memory responded. What tripped it was a photographer's window full of specimen shots of brides and grooms smiling plastically and cherubic children of the type that should have been strangled at birth.

Dan flipped his fingers. 'I've got it. Connie Schumacher!'

'Connie Schumacher?'

'Connie. Former wife of Zak, premier closet queen of Houston? She has a photograph of you by her bed.'

Eddy stared for a moment.

'I never even knew her name was Schumacher. What the hell were you doing in her bedroom?'

'What the hell do you think I was doing? The same as you, I guess.'

'We always used a motel.' He looked puzzled. 'Why would she have a picture of me by her bed? I don't remember her taking one.'

'Well it's there – right between Zak and her mother. She calls you Paderewski, right? She talks about you almost as much as she talks about Zak.'

Dan noticed Eddy smile – for the first time. It was reassuring. In the bar he'd seemed as stony as John.

131

'My God,' Eddy said. 'Does she have psychological theories about me too?'

'Plenty, my friend. Plenty.'

As they resumed their walk, Dan glanced sidelong at Eddy. When he had seen him sitting opposite John in the Maison des Brasseurs he had instinctively thought of him as an ally. The production of the letters, which should have put him on the defensive immediately, had somehow failed to do so. Now, the Schumacher connection, which placed Polonski in his own world, made him want to confide in him. Eddy was by nature more circumspect. Logically, there was everything to mistrust about Daniels; his gut told him, however, that he was a man to be trusted.

The result was that once they were in the car, and heading out east towards the Eisch Valley, both men were predisposed to talk frankly and Dan in particular, at length. It was a short journey in terms of kilometres but a world tour in terms of the ground they covered between them, from their first contacts with Collins and Delgado, to their meeting with John. The conversation produced more than information. In the intimate atmosphere of a closed car each was able to assess the other in personal terms. Eddy was impressed by Dan's legal expertise and professional approach; Dan recognized Eddy's drive and absolute determination to succeed.

By the time they found a hotel, and sat down to lunch in an empty restaurant, the only area of reserve between them was the identity of their buyers.

'I'm beginning to get the picture,' Dan said. 'The turkey who tailed me to Khatam, the people who had you under surveillance in Hong Kong – obviously Collins's plan was to have both of us watched, find out who our contacts were, and then do a direct deal, under-cutting us on the price. We do the brainwork and the legwork, they make the deal.'

'And the Greek knew?'

'Sure.'

'What kind of relationship do you have with him?'

Dan shrugged. 'I guess the Greek's got beyond being able to have a relationship with anyone. He's a little crazy you know. Only one thing really motivates him – the desire to dispose of his gold.'

'That could be our edge. How deep is he in with Collins?'

'Up to his eyeballs, I'd guess. God knows what he owes them –

but it must be plenty. The difference is that he's desperate.'

Eddy was toying with a salad. He looked up. 'A couple of times we've said "we" and "our". Do you feel like making that a formal arrangement?'

'A partnership? Frankly I don't see any other solution to our problem,' Dan said. 'And I'll admit I've been getting mighty lonely out there on my own.'

'I think we could make an effective combination.'

'I think we could.'

Eddy raised his cup of tea, Dan his wine, and they drank.

'I want to be open with you,' Eddy said after a moment. 'There is an additional problem on my side.' He told Dan about the sabotage of his refinery and the threat posed by Jan Pienaar.

'Since it's confession time, I may as well tell you that you've picked up a pauper for a partner.' Dan talked about Landau and the two-hundred-thousand-dollar debt. 'On top of which the digits on my credit card are getting kinda worn. If the Greek hadn't come through with that fifteen grand——I still can't figure out why he did it.'

Eddy shrugged. 'It seems we both have a powerful motive to make this work.'

'Motive we have. What we lack is method.'

By the time the black looks of the waiter finally forced them out of the restaurant, a friendship had been established. And friendship, Eddy reflected as they drove back to the city, was a rarer and more valuable commodity even than gold.

The next morning they met again in Dan's hotel room, having agreed to sleep on their problems.

'I'll need tea,' Eddy said. 'An endless supply.'

'I'd rather take Scotch for inspiration.'

'Have you had any inspiration?'

'Some. What about you?'

'Maybe. But you're the lawyer. Go ahead.'

'It's no help being a lawyer to unscramble this situation – you need to be Machiavelli. But the bottom line is this. We're both of us acting as agents for clients who have no intention of paying any commission. In that situation the rational thing to do is admit error, cut our losses, and vanish. The crazy thing to do – and what I suggest we do – is forget about acting as agents and become – principals.'

Eddy nodded. 'I'm all for craziness. But how?'

'Whatever we do, we're still committed to using the banking system – so let's use it. Say we had control of a bank – call it a fiduciary bank. We instruct Limmatbank to address the selling letters to the fiduciary bank. On the other side, we instruct our buyers' banks to address buy letters to the same fiduciary bank. The whole transaction takes place within a bank we control. We take our cut at the point of exchange. Hey presto. Only one problem. I'm not a magician. Are you a magician?'

'I seem to be a mind reader.'

Eddy fumbled in his inside pocket and drew out a sheet of paper covered in his scrawl. Dan took the paper. It was headed: 'Screen Bank: Criteria.' He read:

1   *Size*: Minimum capitalization 50 million dollars. Minimum deposits of 3 billion dollars.

2   *Credibility*: The bank must have an established reputation internationally. Valid history and track record. The chief executive officer should have a sound reputation.

3   *Security*: Vital to ensure that junior personnel, i.e. telex operators in particular, are not vulnerable to external pressure.

4   *Location*: The prime consideration is that the bank should be located in a country with a viable banking system and a credible political situation, preferably in a jurisdiction where the transaction would not be subject to taxation. Possible locations are thus:

   (a)   *Switzerland*: A poor option for two reasons: taxation; pool banks located there.

   (b)   *Liechtenstein*: Controlled by Swiss.

   (c)   *Benelux countries*: Belgium is a good option. Holland is doubtful – socialist government. Luxembourg ideal. No restrictions.

Dan put the paper down. 'You thought all this up on tea?'

'Does it make sense?'

'Except that it doesn't say how a busted lawyer and the gold cartel's public enemy number one go out and get themselves a tame bank, it's brilliant.'

'Do you have any ideas?'

'As a matter of fact I do. But they're far out.'

'Try me.'

'Okay. We buy a bank.'

'Buy a bank?'

'Well, okay, buy a banker.'

'With what? American Express?'

'Touché. I'll come to that in a minute. First up, in the past five years I've represented corporations and investment groups who've bought and sold several medium-sized banks – the type we're looking for. As long as nobody runs a credit check on me I'm credible as an attorney making researches on behalf of Texan investors. I'm familiar with the documentation and I have the contacts in Europe.'

'Great. But money. We're talking about suborning the chief executive of a bank. He'll want up-front money. Plenty. Assuming we can find someone who's interested.'

'Eddy – we're in the middle of the biggest depression since the Wall Street crash. Europe's rotten with bankers about to jump out of high windows.'

'Because of money.'

'Okay. Money. We need a third partner. A money man.'

Eddy didn't like the suggestion. 'And obviously you have someone in mind.'

'Ever heard of a man called Harvey Ravenscroft?'

'I'm in gold. Of course I've heard of Ravenscroft. Heard of him – but never met him. Nobody's ever met him.'

'I have.'

Eddy looked at him. 'I'm impressed. Go on.'

'I have a little place in the Davis Mountains. Harvey has a big place – on the other side of the mountain. We're neighbours.'

Eddy was staring into his tea. 'I don't know.'

'We can't afford to be too exclusive about this. We need fresh capital. Expenses are going to be frightening. We can't go to an institution – obviously. The only alternative is an individual. Can you think of anyone better than Harvey Ravenscroft? I mean, he's travelled this road before.'

'Can we trust Ravenscroft?'

'We trust each other.'

Eddy nodded. 'But won't Ravenscroft want collateral?'

'We have collateral. It's not much – but it means a lot to neighbour Harvey. Like the man in the Bible who coveted Naboth's vineyard, Harvey covets my little piece of the mountains.'

'You think it'll swing him?'

'I'm certain. Do I call the airport?'

'I suppose so.'

Dan reached out for the phone, then paused. 'Oh, just one thing. I had a call from my girl friend in Houston last night. It seems that Beauregard Johnson Landau is getting vindictive. He's cooked up an embezzlement charge against me. What you might call a Federal rap. I show up at any airport in America and I go straight into the can. You're the great defector. Any ideas?'

Eddy smiled. 'I think I might be able to come up with something.'

15

When the Pilgrim Fathers entered America they had only the elements and the Indians to contend with; when the twentieth-century air-traveller enters America he has to face the twentieth-century American immigration officer, a man more ferocious that a Pequot, more suspicious than a Mohawk, and very, very efficient. Eddy had advised Dan that the only feasible back-door into the country was by road. Accordingly, he flew to Vancouver, kicked around the city for a day, then bought a reduced tariff ticket on the last bus across the border to Seattle. As he'd hoped, the bus was full of students and drop-outs eager to enjoy the fleshpots of San Francisco and Los Angeles on a shoestring. The bus reeked of pot.

When the bus reached the border, they were all herded out to go through Immigration. Dan saw that the officials were hardly bothering to glance at American passports held by reasonably respectable looking people, but were concentrating on keeping undesirables out of God's Own Country and scrutinizing visas with the officiousness of Khatamis. When it came to his turn he held up his passport, unopened, and the man waved him through.

He snatched some sleep in a motel in Seattle then took the first flight to Los Angeles, where he changed planes for Phoenix and San Antonio. In San Antonio he chartered a two-seater plane and a pilot to fly him up to the strip near Hoke's Lake. He paid cash and used a false name. It was mid-afternoon by the time he reached the lake. The canoe was there, but there was no sign of Gina. He examined the canoe and when he saw that it had been made fast with a wonderful granny knot in place of his own neat round turn and two half hitches, he set off in search of her. He found her a few hundred yards away in a clearing by the shore, lying on her back in the sun, fast asleep, and stark naked. A black bug was making slow progress along the inside of her thigh. He flicked the bug off but it didn't wake her. He knelt by her, simply looking. Her eyes were closed and there were delicate beads of moisture on her upper lip.

'Hi, Daniels,' she said without opening her eyes.

'When did you wake?' he said.

'I was never asleep.'

'It could have been anybody.'

'Yeah. But best of all it was you.' She grinned and opened her eyes, then reached for him.

'Hadn't you better get some clothes on?'

'Why? What's wrong with here? Or has Europe slowed you down?'

Half an hour later, Dan paddled them across the lake. 'How did you get here?' he asked.

'Drove to Jeffstown and walked.'

'Walked? It's five miles. Why didn't you get a plane like I said?'

'Because you can't afford it. And I sure as hell can't. Anyway I love to walk. Though I hate to carry.' She pointed to her bag. 'Steaks and wine.'

'Gina, you're a ——'

'I know. Now tell me about Europe. Not banking and gold and all that bullshit, I want tourist stuff. I've never been to Europe.'

'Okay. But just one thing before I start. Has anyone been watching you – following you around?'

'Apart from men?'

'Gina——'

'Well, you are getting paranoid.'

'Okay. But Landau could have had you tailed. I don't think he knows about you but he might.'

'Enough. Now, start with Paris. Did you see Notre Dame?'

They had the night, a whole day, and another night together and then they walked the five miles into Jeffstown, picked up Gina's hired car and she dropped him off in Fort Davis, at the motel where he'd arranged to meet Eddy.

Eddy seemed subtly more cheerful. As they drove out on State Highway 118 towards the Blackwind Ranch, he mentioned that he'd called Stephany in Luxembourg. Tania's story had checked out. She was clean.

There were two ranch-hands, both armed with rifles, at the gates of Blackwind. One of them recognized Dan.

'How you doin' Mr Daniels? Drive right on up. The boss is expecting you.'

They bumped up a dirt track through neat corrals of grazing horses and halted by a group of white adobe buildings, like an overgrown pueblo. In the noon sunshine the white paintwork made the eyes ache. There was an old man standing in the yard, leaning on a stick. He had thick, grey hair and a sharp, narrow nose. He was dressed in old jeans, a white shirt, and a string tie.

'Well, Dan,' he said. 'Good to see you.' His voice had the faintest trace of a Central European accent. He looked at Eddy. 'Mr Polonski? Welcome to Blackwind. Come on in – this sun's too fierce.'

They sat down in a vast, low living room that was spartan in the simplicity of its furnishings, except that on the walls were two glowing Sisleys and a Cézanne study of the Mont Sainte Victoire. Ravenscroft listened to them without interrupting. He nodded from time to time, and ceaselessly rubbed his left knee with a scaly, brown-blotched hand. Dan summed up.

'Well there it is, Harvey. We need a million. We undertake to pay it back, with five on top, in six months. The only collateral we can offer is Hoke's Place.'

Ravenscroft was silent for some moments. Then he seemed to decide something.

'Come with me, both of you. I have something I want to show you.'

They followed him to the far end of the room. There was a round-topped, rough timber door to the left of the massive fireplace, and by the door was a small, digital keyboard, recessed into the wall. Ravenscroft tapped out a combination, then opened the door, snapping on powerful overhead lamps.

Dan and Eddy followed him into a square strong-room. Apart from a massive safe there was only one object in the room. It was a small golden statue on a pedestal. Part of one leg and one arm were damaged – the gold covering had been worn or torn away, revealing pitted wood underneath – but the rest of the statue looked as if it had been made five minutes before, so purely had the gold retained every nuance of the sculptor's art.

'This', Ravenscroft said, 'is an Inca sun god. He's five hundred years old.' He reached out and touched the statue, his bony fingers caressing its contours. 'The ancients were wise,' he went on. 'They looked at their world and saw that the sun was the source of all life. They looked at gold and recognized that in its rarity, its purity, its immutability, in its mysterious weight, in the way it glowed, it was the essence of sunlight itself. They called

139

gold the flesh of the gods. They believed that it was the very tissue of the sun itself. So, when they made their graven images, they covered them with gold.'

Dan and Eddy followed him back into the living room.

'Gold was the first object of worship of civilized man,' Ravenscroft said when they were once again sitting under the Sisleys. 'The origin of its value and its power is mystical. Have you any idea how many human lives were sacrificed on the altar of my little god in there? No more have I. Many hundreds, maybe thousands.' His hand resumed its ceaseless rubbing of his knee. 'Gold is at the root of all human history. Why did man begin to explore his planet? Why did he risk his life in papyrus boats? Because he was curious? No. Because he was in search of gold.' He smiled. 'Why should I remind you of these things? Because what you have undertaken is bigger than anything even I have ever heard of. In theory there is no reason why you should not succeed. Your strategy is brilliant. I'll give you your million. But before you take it, think. Think what men have done for gold in the past. Think of the scale on which you propose to operate. Forget about the rewards success would bring for a moment and consider the consequences of failure. Think very carefully.'

He picked up his stick and tapped it against his left leg. It made a hollow, metallic sound.

'In 1946,' he said, 'I was in Buenos Aires. I was approached by an Argentine banker. He said he had clients who wished to dispose of a large quantity of gold bullion. When I eventually met his clients I recognized who they were. What they did not know was that I was not born Harvey Ravenscroft but Herschel Rabenstein.' He smiled again. 'I sold their gold for them, but they never received their money. Part of it I kept for myself, the bulk of it I returned to the people from whom it had been stolen – in Auschwitz, Dachau, and Belsen. One day I'll tell you how I did it. It's a story you'd appreciate. Unfortunately, one of my – can I say victims? – remained alive. He found me a few years later – ' he tapped his artificial leg again '– and, well I won't worry you with the details. My point is that I made a fortune and lost a limb. You two want to make a fortune. The question is what are you prepared to lose?'

After a moment Eddy answered. 'I think we're both aware of the realities.'

Ravenscroft nodded. 'Very well. You can have the money. I accept Dan's offer of his land as collateral. But I require one further condition.' He looked at Eddy. 'I have heard of you, Mr Polonski. We have a common friend in Mike Mulligan. I know a little of your past. I believe you have certain knowledge. If you should fail in your present enterprise and be unable to return my money to me, assuming that you are still alive, I want you to work for me. I want you to share your knowledge with me. If Dan draws up an agreement to that effect, would you be prepared to sign it?'

Eddy was staring at one of the Sisleys. It was a view of an island in the Seine just before dusk, a study of quiet waters and muted light.

'That knowledge is worth more than a million dollars,' he said at last.

'It isn't the money,' Ravenscroft said. 'I'm an old man. I haven't got many years. I don't need money. It's simply that I'd like to know – *know* before I die.'

Eddy turned away from the picture and looked at him.

'Very well,' he said. 'I agree.'

Ravenscroft nodded. 'It would be nice if and when you return my stake to me you could return part of it in bullion.'

Twenty-four hours later, when the agreements had been drafted, agreed, and signed, Eddy and Dan set off together on the first leg of their separate journeys back to Europe. Eddy drove Dan down to the Mexican border, where he would leave America by one of the busy tourist routes.

'As far as I can see,' Dan said, 'we have only one further major problem – Collins. I can't see him being overjoyed at our partnership.'

'He mustn't find out, certainly not until we've got the fiduciary bank wrapped up and the transaction's ready to go through. At that point we can present him with a *fait accompli*.'

'And until that happy moment?'

'We have to keep our relationship discreet.'

'Well, I'm getting kinda used to that – but it's wearing. Strange, too, creeping about your own home State using false names.'

'We're going to have to be tight on security,' Eddy said. 'When we talk on the phone we use public lines from main Post Offices, and we always direct dial. That kind of thing eats into your time, but it's the only way. There are some other rules we should observe anyway, to protect the transaction from the Bob

Hutchinsons. You never send any documents out for copy unless you accompany them. You should take your own copy paper – you know, with the metal threads – so no one can copy your copy. Never throw documents in the trash –.always shred them. Keep all sensitive documents on your person – the really sensitive ones should be notarized. Always take your hotel key with you, never leave it at the desk. We should work out some kind of code to use between us. Schurch, for instance, is The Hairless Wonder, Luxembourg is The Little Place.'

'Okay. Test question. Who's Jaws?'

'Easy. John.'

'Right. More difficult. Who's The Alchemist?'

Eddy thought then shrugged.

'You – you genius,' Dan laughed.

Eddy smiled and said: 'Might be worth going to an electronics supply house and buying a couple of portable scramblers. Maybe a bug detector, too.'

'Are you kidding?'

They were approaching El Paso, and Eddy was slowing down.

'I'm a hundred per cent serious,' he said. 'Ravenscroft is right. A lot of unhealthy emotions have already been generated by the Greek gold. What we propose to do is going to cause an epidemic. Okay, here's the bus station. I'll see you in Zurich in three days. The station at four. Okay?'

'Okay. Take it easy.'

'And you.'

Eddy flew first to Geneva, to arrange the distribution of Ravenscroft's million in various accounts, then he went on to Zurich. Old Stefan at the Liszt seemed pleased to see him.

'Would you do me a favour, Stefan? Tell Tania I'm back in town. This is a number she can call me at.'

The call came that evening.

'Hello Wotan.' She sounded tired.

'Tania. Are you okay?'

'Will you come out to the apartment?'

'Now?'

'Yes. Now.'

What Eddy liked about Tania's place was that it reminded him of his own – it was all books and comfortable, modern furniture and he felt at home there.

She kissed him when he arrived, and held him fiercely.

'I'm sorry, Eddy,' she said when they were sitting in the living room. 'I woke up that morning and I knew I had to—— All I could think about was getting in the car, feeling the wind on my face, seeing an empty road ahead of me. I thought you'd understand.'

'I did.'

She looked away. She said very quietly: 'Did you? I wonder.'

'You have to be separate. I understand that. I have to be separate too.'

She smiled. 'Maybe it won't always be like that.'

'Maybe. But I'm happy with things as they are. We can be separate – and together.'

'I'm glad you don't want to make love to me. But I hope you love me. You do, don't you?'

'Do you want me to answer that question?'

She was quiet for a long time. Then she smiled again.

'No.'

16

By the beginning of October the leaves were falling in Europe, the first frosts crisping them, and the first mists were cloaking the naked fields at dusk. But at the Château of Montillac, five hundred kilometres south of Paris, and twenty east of Cognac, it was still possible to sit out on the terrace before lunch and drink a glass of wine.

'It's a paradox, Anthony,' Lord Ilminster said, 'but the one thing I miss about England is the winter. Come February the majority of the English are dreaming about Benidorm and the Algarve and other such frightful places, and, if they can afford it, paying through the nose to snatch a little sunshine in the Canaries or Bermuda. They think of winter in terms of slush on the pavements and central-heating bills. I think of it in terms of pheasant and burgundy and mornings as cold and fresh and cleansing as this wine.' He took a sip, and sighed.

'Come to Hamcary for Christmas and stay on for some shooting,' Melldrum said.

Ilminster shook his head. 'Alas, my dear boy, I have responsibilities here.' He waved his hand in a gesture that seemed to encompass half the countryside, and indeed most of the land that could be seen from the terrace was his property. Below the terrace, park-like meadows, studded with old trees, sloped gently down to the River Charente, and beyond the river the vineyards of the Montillac estate rose in steep terraces up to the village, walled like a fortress, and the ruins of Count Guillaume de Montillac's castle. 'Monsieur le Curé and Monsieur le Maire would never forgive me if I failed to open my doors, and my cellar, to the community on Christmas Eve,' Ilminster said.

'Come after Christmas, then. A lot of old friends would be glad to see you. And Frances and the children, of course.'

Ilminster smiled. 'I must come clean, as they say; my old friends bore me, Anthony. I no longer have any taste for County society. I prefer the company of realistic peasants and *petits bourgeois*. I prefer to talk about the *vendange* rather than the prospects for the shooting season. It is better to grow good brandy than to rear pheasants.'

'Frances will be disappointed.'

'No she won't,' said Ilminster abruptly. He topped up his glass. 'I fell in love with this countryside a long time ago. The landscape of the vine never changes. Horace and Virgil would recognize these hills. I like the Europe of the Roman Empire – and Britain was never really part of it, you know. Besides, provincial France is a traditional refuge for the very rich, owing to the peculiarity of the French system which confines all active politics to Paris and allows rich men to make whatever arrangements that suit them in their local spheres of influence. It is an admirable system. But you haven't flown out to listen to my complacent *pensées*. What do you have to report?'

Melldrum masked his annoyance by leaning forward to take the bottle of wine out of the ice-bucket and fill up his glass. What did he have to report? As if Ilminster was the grand strategist and he the aide-de-camp. However, one had to play the game – until one was in a position to change the rules.

'As you foresaw,' he said, 'Daniels and Polonski ran across each other in Luxembourg. They compared notes and – rather intelligently – decided to form a partnership. They appear to have found a source of finance and are now looking round for a medium-sized European bank to take over.'

'What?'

Melldrum smiled. 'What I mean is that Daniels is going round posing as a representative of some mythical Texan oil men. They have no intention of actually taking over a bank.' He explained the strategy of the fiduciary bank.

'Ingenious,' Ilminster said when he finished. 'This bodes well, Anthony. By the way, you seem very well-informed.'

Melldrum shrugged. 'We live in an age of advanced electronics. And nowhere is more advanced than Luxembourg.'

'Quite so. In my day, of course, it was the gossiping lady's maid and the homosexual clerk. I hope your – bugger is discreet?'

Bugger? Melldrum winced. Was this the hint of a threat? Or just one of Ilminster's donnish jokes?

'Absolutely discreet,' he said. 'You should know. It was you who recruited Zwingler in the first place.'

'Ah – Zwingler. When I was at school bugs were things hunted

by a certain type of boy who belonged to the Natural History
Society, wore wire-rimmed glasses, and was invariably bullied.
And do our two Americans make progress?'

'Not particularly.'

'And you think they require a helping hand? Is that it?'

'It had occurred to me.'

Ilminster pondered for a moment. Then he said: 'Stoffel. Rolf
Stoffel. Euro-resource Bank. That's your man.'

'Stoffel – an excellent suggestion. In fact I can't think why
Daniels and Polonski haven't latched onto him.'

'Probably because Euro-resource is in such very deep trouble
that Stoffel has taken care to cover it up. Our Rolf is a very
bribeable man, all the same, as we both know.' Melldrum nodded, deep in thought. 'You must tread softly, Anthony,' Ilminster
said. 'A hint here, a word dropped there – all through
intermediaries.'

Melldrum hid his irritation. 'Naturally,' he said. 'This sim-
plifies matters. If Stoffel bites I calculate that Daniels and
Polonski will be ready to move before Christmas.'

Ilminster smiled and drained his glass. 'In that case we can all
look forward to a handsome Christmas present, can we not?
Now. Shall we go in to lunch?'

The Grande Place in Brussels is one of the architectural wonders
of Europe; but unlike the majority of Continental set-pieces it was
raised neither to the glory of God nor to a monarch: it was a
monument to commerce. Its perfectly preserved Flemish Baroque
buildings housed the great trade guilds, and the gold leaf that still
glows richly on their ornate gables is an enduring symbol of the
power of the shrewd burghers who created a market-place at a
crossroads, and then invented the banking system to make their
power absolute. A café, appropriately called *La Chaloupe D'Or* –
the Golden Boat – in the eastern corner of the square, was one of
three designated rendezvous for Eddy and Dan. On a raw night in
mid-October they met there to review progress. Eddy had come
from Paris, Dan from Luxembourg. Eddy, who had taken charge
of the selling, made his report first.

He calculated that he had fourteen hundred of the two
thousand tons sold for sure. There was Tan in Hong Kong solid for
five hundred tons; the paperwork was filtering through a Swiss
bank at two removes from the Brussels bank to which Leung had

146

originally directed him, but progress was steady, if slow. Then there was Nasir, good for three hundred tons; Dan had introduced Eddy to the Prince's Luxembourg bankers and Eddy had taken over the negotiations which had proved straightforward in comparison with Tan's oriental subtleties. The deal with Walther and the West German steel men had died; but Hooghens had come up with a red-hot contact to replace them.

'It's a sub-culture I haven't come across before,' Eddy told Dan. 'A group of big arms dealers with a heap of off-shore cash.'

'Arms dealers?'

'They buy from Eastern bloc countries, Czechoslovakia mainly, and pay in bullion. It enables them to beat the price right down and the Czechs are happy because they get gold which is harder and more discreet than the hardest currencies and easier to trade for wheat and oil.'

'How much can these guys take?'

'Two hundred tons.'

'They really have that kind of money?'

'One man alone turns over three billion a year.'

'He must be one sharp shooter.'

'He's quite a character. He told me he got big when the Arab countries started hating each other. He says what he really needs is a full-scale Middle East war.'

'Are we in the right business?'

'Then there's Hofer,' Eddy said.

'He's coming through?'

'He's coming.'

'How much?'

'Four hundred.'

Dan whistled. 'I thought Hofer was semi-retired.'

'I don't know. I figure he's acting on behalf of a government, maybe several governments – France, Spain. They're probably trying to top up their gold reserves – and they have to do it covertly. A lot of central banks shed a lot of gold during the sixties. The Bank of England, for instance.' He paused and sighed. 'And then, of course, there's Jaws.'

'And God alone knows who he's buying for.'

For the past month and a half John had been the bane of both their lives. He was everywhere – Paris, Zurich, Amsterdam, even Brussels. Careful as they both were to cover their tracks, and lead separate lives, John seemed to know their every move. His cryptic messages awaited them in hotel foyers and banks; they had lost count of the number of empty bars in which they had to endure his hostility and mania for secrecy.

'John isn't rational,' Eddy said. 'I saw him in Paris last week. He started asking me what I thought was the most effective way of killing a man. I told him sitting around in draughty cafés listening to garbage. Then he took a length of piano-wire out of his pocket and started telling me how you can garotte a man in five seconds with two feet of it.'

Dan laughed. 'One time I tried to get alongside him and draw him out – you know, talk about ordinary things. I wanted to see if there was any kind of human being under that raincoat. For about half a minute he was actually opening up, started talking about the farm in Iowa where he was raised. But then: "We don't have a social relationship, *kamerad*." He clammed up like a pro.'

'Well, I've issued an ultimatum. I've told him that unless he comes up with a letter, that's it. Anyway. How've you made out?'

'I think I may have found our man', Dan said. 'I had a meeting with him yesterday – a guy called Rolf Stoffel. He's President of an outfit called Euro-resource Bank. Take a look at the documentation.' He handed Eddy a bulky file containing the annual reports, lists of shareholders, divisions of shares and financial statements of Euro-resource Bank. 'As you can see, it's jointly owned by Arabs and West Germans and they've fallen out. Stoffel is sitting in the middle and he's sweating. I think you should meet him.'

'The Little Place?'

'Yes. Tomorrow, if that's possible.'

'Great, Dan. It's coming together. Anything from Collins?'

'Not even a postcard. You?'

Eddy shook his head. 'But it can only be a matter of time.'

Rolf Stoffel was as mysterious as John, though in a completely different way. He was a very clean man. Even in the evening after a day of meetings, he looked scrubbed and wholesome, and smelt of Roger & Gallet soap. His hair, his eyes, his clothes, were all colourless. He spoke five languages – Luxembourgeois, German, French, English, and Dutch – with equal fluency, and equal lack of expression. Dan called him the Esperanto Man. He was a creature manufactured in the automated factory of the new Europe, a bland compromise of a man – and cautious. His constant refrain was that a transaction of the magnitude Dan and

Eddy were proposing could wipe out his bank overnight if anything went wrong. It took a payment of two hundred and fifty thousand dollars into his private account and the promise of a personal commission of ten cents an ounce on the gold to convince him, finally, that he should place the facilities of his bank at the disposal of the partnership.

All through the negotiations in Luxembourg, John hovered like a pestilential fly. At yet another meeting in the back regions of the Maison des Brasseurs, during which John claimed to be able to buy the whole amount of the Greek gold, Eddy gave him a final warning.

'Most of the gold is sold, John,' he said. 'Give Rolf Stoffel, at Euro-resource Bank, a sight of a letter, and you might be able to pick up the tailings. But you should hurry.'

In the next two weeks Dan and Eddy were busy flying round Europe, re-structuring the transaction. They had to persuade the buyers' banks to issue new letters, addressed to Euro-resource Bank, and they had to explain the new order to Schurch at Limmatbank. When they returned to Luxembourg, Stoffel had some news for them. John had been in contact with him and had told him to expect a letter, for his eyes only, to be delivered by courier from a bank in America.

At the hotel there was the inevitable message from John. He wanted to see them both at Pub 13 the following morning. They went.

They arrived punctually, but John wasn't there. They had waited ten minutes and were about to go, when he came in. Now that it was winter he had added a black, woollen scarf and a black, peaked cap to his costume. He sat down and placed his attaché case on the table. He opened it with the air of a conjuror.

'Well, *kamerads*,' he said, 'you wanted, you get.' He was panting slightly, as if he had been running. He took out a white envelope which had been sealed with a banker's signature across the flap. The seal had been broken. 'You need a letter, right? Here's a letter.'

Neither Dan nor Eddy made a move to take the letter. Eddy said: 'We don't have to have a sight of it, John. It's only necessary for Stoffel to see it and verify it.'

'Take a look, *kamerad*,' John said. 'You've been telling me I'm bullshit for the past three months, now you take a look.'

Eddy shrugged, took the letter, read it, and passed it to Dan. The letter was from a wholly owned subsidiary of the Unity Trust

Bank of California, addressed to Euro-resource Bank. It stated, with the bank's full responsibility, that the bank held funds on behalf of its client, Mr John, to purchase two thousand metric tons of gold bullion at ten dollars under current market price.

'Is that bullshit, *kamerad*?' John said. 'Is that fucking bullshit?'

Dan said: 'Until our bankers have verified the signatures and the status of your bank, it could be, John.'

John snatched the letter back. He bared his teeth.

Eddy said: 'I've already told you, John, that the bulk of the merchandise is committed.'

'Crap, *kamerad*,' John said. 'How does six under on the whole amount sing to you?'

Eddy shrugged. 'The maximum you can buy, right now, is six hundred tons. And the price would be four under.'

It took an hour to persuade John, and they had to compromise on the price, finally agreeing five under on the six hundred tons.

'Produce a letter of full commitment to that effect to our bankers, John, and you have a deal,' Eddy said.

John locked his attaché case and rose.

'No need to remind you two gentlemen about security. Lips buttoned, *kamerads*, or——'

'Yeah, yeah,' Dan said, 'we know. Two feet of piano wire.'

John grinned again. 'Why not, *kamerad*,' he said, 'why not?'

'If he's so paranoid why show us the letter?' Eddy said when John had gone.

'I guess he's so proud of coming up with something real at last, he wanted to brag.'

'Well, it's the first human reaction I've ever seen in him. If the letter *is* real.'

'His language certainly was,' said Dan.

So was the letter. Stoffel confirmed that to them in the afternoon. But he didn't know anything about the Unity Trust Bank of California beyond the fact that it was good for its commitments. Dan was curious, so curious that he called Harvey Ravenscroft in Texas. Ravenscroft had the answer.

'Unity Trust? Assuredly I have heard of it. It's a CIA front bank. One of several. About twenty per cent of its business is bona fide commercial – but that's just cosmetics. I've had dealings with Unity Trust in South America and other places. Devious people.'

Eddy shrugged when Dan conveyed the information to him.

150

'First time I saw John,' he said, 'I put him down as an agent.'

'It explains the piano wire and the paranoia. What it doesn't explain is why Uncle Sam wants to buy six hundred tons of bullion.'

'Or originally two thousand tons.'

'That's right. Why?'

'Evidently they think the time is right to start putting some of the gold back into Fort Knox.'

'Come on, Eddy. That Fort Knox thing was just rumour.'

Eddy shrugged. 'John's letter's no rumour. It's fact. The United States Government wants two thousand tons.' He shrugged again.

Dan was not completely convinced but he was curious. He had to go to London the next day and he extended his visit to include a trip to the Newspaper Library at Colindale. He took the tube out to the northern suburbs and, as the train emerged into the grey light of a November morning at Golders Green, he stared out of the rain-flecked window at an endless vista of smug, red rooftops, rummaging in his memory.

There was an academic hush, and a faint smell of post-graduate armpits in the library. Dan filled out a request for micro-film copies of the *Washington Post* for the year 1974 and eventually a porter brought them. He found what he was looking for in a small column towards the bottom of a page in the edition for Friday 12 July 1974. It was a report that the Treasury Secretary, William E. Simon, had agreed to allow a delegation of Congressmen to in-spect the gold in Fort Knox in response to a request by Representative Philip M. Crane, who was agitated about the rumours, spreading like wildfire, that Fort Knox was empty. Dan continued turning through the reels of micro-film until he came to the edition of Tuesday 24 September. There was a picture of Mrs Mary Brooks, the director of the Federal Mint, standing in front of a stack of gold bars and grinning. The report, beneath the picture, quoted Representative Crane as having said: 'The gold is safe. The gold is here.' It also stated that the US Treasurer, Francine Neff, had announced that the bullion would be audited.

'It never was, so far as I know,' Eddy told him when they met in Zurich two days later. 'According to what I've heard the whole Congressional trip was a pantomime. You know, they load up a plane with Congressmen and reporters, fill them full of booze, put them through security – guards, passwords, electronics – and finally open up a small vault and show them a couple of hundred tons. The suckers reel home fully believing that Knox is stacked to the rafters with gold.'

'Okay, Eddy,' Dan said, 'I'll buy it. If Knox is half empty where is the gold?'

Eddy smiled. 'I could make an intelligent guess. I should imagine a lot of it is right here in Zurich. Reconstruct what happened. For years Washington controlled the gold price. Kept it at thirty-two dollars an ounce by selling it at that price to anyone who wanted to buy – except their own citizens, of course, who were forbidden to own gold.'

'In defiance of their rights under the constitution.'

'Very possibly. Meanwhile some dupes in the Treasury Department start listening to the big bankers. The bankers convince them that the gold is strangling the US economy. It sits in Knox earning no interest and with the price stable at thirty-two dollars. Bad business, the bankers say. They offer to exchange cash or credits for the gold and the Government agrees. Then Gerry Ford stumbles onto the scene. He lifts the restriction on American citizens' owning gold, the price hesitates momentarily, then goes up like a zipper. The bankers clean up.'

Dan laughed. 'Okay so it makes sense. But why should the Government, in the guise of a freak like John, want to buy back now?'

'Because they're considering putting America back on the gold standard.'

'They're talking about it, sure, but do you really think it's serious?'

'The historical argument is quite convincing. Whenever America has been on the gold standard the economy has been in boom and the rate of inflation has been low. But I don't believe that's the real reason.'

'No?'

'Listen to this for a theory. Go back to basic economics. Governments have created a massive problem of inflation by printing too much money. The only way out of the problem is to devalue the dollar and, realistically, you'd have to do it by a factor of five to one. But that would be political suicide for any administration. So. At current prices four hundred dollars buys one ounce of gold. The Government arranges for the discreet purchase of say ten thousand tons of gold. In collaboration with the banks they manipulate a price rise – they have the capability to control the price after all. They pegged it at thirty-two for over

152

forty years. The price shoots up to two thousand dollars an ounce and the price of every other commodity rises in proportion. They then announce that America is back on the gold standard. One US dollar buys one two-thousandth of an ounce of gold. Effectively they've devalued the dollar by that factor of five. The standard of living drops drastically, of course, but so does the inflation rate. And the administration doesn't get crucified at the polls because there has been no official devaluation.'

Dan smiled and glanced at his watch. 'I hate to have to bring you back to earth, Eddy, but we have a meeting with The Hairless Wonder.'

They'd been talking in a small restaurant off Pelikan Strasse and they walked the block or two to Limmatbank through light snow. When they arrived at the Limmatbank building they were escorted not to the reception area nor direct to Schurch's office, but into another office on the first floor. 'Monsieur Schurch will be with you in five minutes,' they were told.

But when the door of the office opened a few moments later it was not The Hairless Wonder. It was Jim Collins.

Both Dan and Eddy agreed, later, that Collins had aged. He seemed greyer and thinner. He said: 'I thought it was time we had a talk. I heard that you two gentlemen had got acquainted.'

'Word does get around,' said Dan.

Collins sat down. 'You seem to have changed the rules of the game.'

Eddy smiled. 'That's the nature of the game, Jim. You should know.'

Collins thought for a moment. 'I did you a favour a couple of months back, Eddy. It was no trouble to me. I'm used to doing favours like that. Have you two thought about the consequences of what you're trying to pull?'

'We're just carrying out our instructions,' Eddy said. 'You asked us to sell the gold. We've sold it. We can complete the transaction in approximately one month. All we require is for you and Mr Maniatos to instruct Limmatbank to issue the final sell letter.'

Collins leaned back in his chair and tapped out a tattoo with his fingers on the desk. 'I've come to Europe to offer you a deal,' he said. 'One million dollars each when the transaction is completed. One million. No questions, no come-back. Think about it.'

Eddy glanced at Dan, who indicated that he should speak for them both. 'Let us be straight,' Eddy said. 'We know that you and the Greek *have* to sell the gold, and sell it fast. We also know that, from the start, you never had any intention that Dan or I should make a nickel. Close surveillance, then a direct approach by you to our buyers, that was it, right? I don't resent it. It was a nice try but it didn't work. So what? You're going to get what you want. We don't intend to circumvent you. We'll protect your fifty cent spread as agreed. But at the same time we'll get what we want. It's as I said from the beginning – market forces.'

Collins frowned. 'I'm not going to be subtle. I want to sell the gold. You can take your money – I can't prevent that – but then you'd better run, buster, and you'd better run fast. I'll make a last offer: two million each. You can take that and sleep easy.' When there was no response he shrugged faintly. 'Have it your way,' he said. He rose. 'I'll arrange the necessary instruction to Schurch.'

At the door he paused. 'Just one final word. I made it my business to find out how you two met. You met because people didn't keep their mouths shut. When you're next in Vegas you might care to discuss the subject of indiscretion with Paul Delgado. You'll need a first-class medium to conduct the conversation, and if you have any respect for the dead you'll take along some flowers. If you want to call me, you know my number.'

When the door had closed behind Collins, Eddy said: 'He's a bad poker-player.'

'I don't know. I get an edgy feeling that he wasn't bluffing about Delgado.'

'No. Delgado talked. He probably wanted to cut himself in on the deal. He gave our names to somebody and then the whole gold world got talking. John picks up the rumour from Bob Hutchinson, assumes it's some kind of set-up, and engineers a confrontation between us. We get together and it instantly costs Collins a hundred and fifty million dollars – our commission on the deal. If we'd never met, Collins would have had both of us screwed.'

'He may still have us screwed.'

'Don't be a pessimist, Dan. With a hundred and fifty million behind us we're invulnerable. Collins would have to go to war to get us and he won't do that. It was a poor attempt at bluff. I guess Collins himself is none too popular with his own people right now. He had to try something.'

'You're a great comfort to me, Eddy. Now where in hell is Schurch?'

It transpired that Schurch was out of the office. They didn't see him until three days later, by which time he had received instructions from Collins and Maniatos.

'I am ready to issue the final letters on two conditions, gentlemen,' he said. 'The first is that we have sight of your buyers' letters. The second is that we make this an arm's-length transaction, through the Banque D'Arve in Geneva. If you would instruct Euro-resource to send the letters, by courier, to the Banque D'Arve – I have the codes here – we can proceed.'

Eddy glanced at Dan, sensing that the same thought was in his mind: that Schurch's conditions were curious. On the other hand they were perfectly justifiable banking procedures in the circumstances. He waited a moment, in case Dan wanted to query the demands. Then said to Schurch:

'Agreed.'

'It may take a week or two to synchronize the buyers' letters,' Dan said. 'How long will you require possession of them for?'

Schurch shrugged. 'A few days, no more.'

'Could you be specific?' Eddy said.

'Three days,' Schurch said. 'No longer, I assure you.'

'The Banque D'Arve, Geneva?' Dan said, noting it down.

'If you would be so kind.'

Schurch shook hands first with Dan, then with Eddy.

When they'd gone, Schurch dialled London, and made sure he tripped the scrambler on the phone. His conversation with Anthony Melldrum was very brief. When it was over he went to the drinks cabinet and poured himself a large vodka. He drank it quickly and then he poured himself another.

In London, Anthony Melldrum placed several calls to Zurich and Liechtenstein. They were purely personal calls, to various lawyers who handled his own and his wife's overseas money. He arranged to buy some twenty-five thousand ounces of gold bullion in various markets over the next few days, at an average price of $400 per ounce.

Dan and Eddy spent the next fortnight in a bewildering variety of airports and banks. Since there was no longer any necessity to operate clandestinely they travelled openly together. By 28 November all the buyers' letters were in and on the next day they were sent by specially selected courier to Geneva. On the thirtieth the Banque D'Arve acknowledged their receipt by coded key-test telex.

For the first time for many months Eddy and Dan had nothing to do but relax and wait. It was the weekend and Luxembourg already had a Christmas air, with tinsel and fairy lights in the shop windows, and even a slight fall of snow to complete the picture. Eddy and Dan went Christmas shopping.

In Johannesburg it was high summer; there was not a hint of snow unless you could imagine that the mine dumps, rising like whale-humps among the sprawling suburbs, were old drifts, stained with ochre and green. Jan Pienaar had no such gifts of imagination. To him, as to the majority of Johannesburgers, the dumps were a reminder that the foundations of the great city were laid in the rich, gold-bearing strata of the Rand, and that the high rises of the centre had soared as the price of gold had soared. The terrace by the pool of Pienaar's house in Parktown commanded a magnificent view of the gold city and Pienaar was relaxing by the pool, contemplating the view, when the call from London came. He listened, and then started to make a few calls of his own, organizing an impromptu drinks party for noon of the following day.

The men who gathered by his pool on Sunday all wore a standard weekend rig of short-sleeved cotton shirts and slacks. They drank Buck's Fizz and nibbled little delicacies handed round by an army of black servants. From time to time they stepped aside with their host to talk in undertones. An outsider would have seen nothing more interesting than a dozen or so rich South Africans enjoying the privileges of the white man. But an observer who had inside knowledge of South Africa's gold community would have seen a gathering of the elect.

In Paris that same Sunday, Lord Ilminster entertained an even more select group of men at a lunch in his apartment in the Boulevard Lannes. Lord Ilminster had also received a telephone call from England and he discussed it briefly with his guests before inviting them to sit down to traditional roast beef. He apologized to them for the beef, explaining that it was a fad of his. It was a short lunch, concluded with a bottle of the host's own Montillac brandy, and after it his guests departed for Rome and Zurich and New York. They had all travelled a long way, in deplorable weather, for a simple lunch. But it had been worth the journey.

17

Monday 3 December, dawned grey and blustery over London. At a little before half past ten five men assembled in the Fixing Room at the offices of N. M. Rothschild & Sons Limited, in New Court, St Swithin's Lane. They were the representatives of the five banks which constitute the London Gold Market: Mocatta and Goldsmid; Sharps, Pixley & Co., a wholly-owned subsidiary of Kleinwort, Benson; N. M. Rothschild; Johnson Matthey; Samuel Montagu & Co., a wholly-owned subsidiary of the Midland Bank.

Each man had his appointed place at the table, the representative of N. M. Rothschild, by tradition, taking the chair. Each had a row of telephones by which he could communicate directly to the dealing room in his own bank; each was provided with a miniature British flag on a stand. The flags were another tradition, and a particularly British one. If at any stage in the day's business any representative wished to drop out of the dealing, or to switch from buying to selling, or vice versa, he could call 'Flag!' and place his flag in the upright position. While any of the five flags was up, all dealing was suspended. Only when all the flags were down could the price of gold bullion be fixed.

In an office only a short walk from St Swithin's Lane, an office on the thirtieth floor of the Central and Shires building, Anthony Melldrum sat down at his desk, lit his first cigar of the day, and stared out of the window, gathering himself. The window framed a panoramic vista of London, with St Paul's in the foreground. His father-in-law had once remarked that the view of the cathedral was such as Sir Christopher Wren must have seen on his way to Heaven.

His office was a large room, yet it contained nothing but a desk, with an array of telephones, a computer terminal, and a few comfortable chairs. Melldrum had more ordinary quarters next door, with panelling, portraits, and other conventional trappings, and he used them for conventional business. Anyone was welcome to walk in. But the bare, inner sanctum was closed to all but a few members of the Board and his personal asistant, Mark Price-Smith.

Melldrum pressed his intercom.

'Morning, Mark, would you make sure that Mrs Brandon doesn't put any calls through to me until after four? I don't want to be disturbed – by anyone. My diary's fairly clear for the next month or so? Don't arrange any appointments. Do your mother-tigress act.'

He sat back in his chair for a moment. 'Ah well – *attaquons*,' he muttered to himself. He picked up a phone, tripped the scrambler, and dialled the Banque D'Arve in Geneva.

In another room, on the same floor – a much more homely room than Melldrum's – Mark Price-Smith relayed the International Treasurer's instructions to his secretary, Mrs Brandon.

'He's going incommunicado again,' he said.

'Oh Lord.' Mrs Brandon's voice on the phone was peevish. 'How long for this time?'

'Don't ask me, Beth. Ours not to reason why.'

Mark put the phone down and sighed. He was twenty-eight and handsome almost to the point of prettiness – blond and blue eyed. Indeed, he was known throughout the bank as 'the blue-eyed boy': he was Anthony Melldrum's favourite, protégé, and confidant. Many people spoke of him as Melldrum's eventual successor; those who knew the inner workings of the organization discounted the possibility: Mark Price-Smith wasn't family.

Eddy and Dan experienced their first feelings of disquiet on Wednesday, when the letters that had been sent to the Banque D'Arve in Geneva were due to be returned. They were not returned. On the previous day, the price of gold in London had suddenly risen to $432.25 an ounce but neither of the partners saw any particular significance in the fact. Stoffel had allocated them an office in the Euro-resource building and they spent most of the day there. On Thursday they called Schurch in Zurich and were told that he had gone away for a long weekend. They called the Banque D'Arve but couldn't find any officer who knew about their business.

'Goddam bankers,' Dan said as he put down the phone. 'Delay, delay, delay. Nobody knows anything. How the hell can The Hairless Wonder go off on a weekend at a time like this?'

'Relax, Dan. The banks are bound to move cautiously.'

Dan rattled a newspaper. 'Yeah – but look at the gold price. Still rising. It's costing our buyers. If it goes on we're going to start getting retractions. We don't have irrevocable commitment.'

'I'm not too concerned. The price'll come down. If it doesn't and we see a steady rise, then our people will just be keener to buy.'

They passed an anxious weekend all the same and first thing on Monday they called Schurch.

He was apologetic and reassuring. 'I have spoken with Geneva. Everything is perfectly in order, except for an internal mix-up for which I apologize most profoundly. The letters will be returned within twenty-four hours and we can proceed.'

But by Wednesday there was still no sign of the letters, gold was still rising steadily, and Eddy and Dan decided to fly to Zurich. They sat in Schurch's office and listened while he spoke to Geneva. He spoke in rapid French, which neither could follow completely, but his tone was by turns cold, curt, and finally exasperated. As he put down the phone he said:

'I am covered with embarrassment, gentlemen. The documents were directed here in error. I have arranged for them to be redirected.'

Dan said: 'I thought prime banks didn't make errors, Pierre.'

Schurch shrugged helplessly. 'Have pity on me, gentlemen. I have had a call from Mr Maniatos this morning.' He made an eloquent gesture. 'I am as anxious as you to proceed. I have the final document drafted. Here.' He showed them the letter. 'All I want is to be able to sign it.'

'Jesus,' Dan said as they sloshed down Tal Strasse later, 'that guy should be behind a counter changing travellers' cheques for tourists.'

'I don't know,' Eddy said quietly. 'Either he's inefficient or he's stalling. And I don't think he's inefficient.'

They sat down in a café and Dan tipped a measure of brandy into his coffee.

'He's acting under instructions, remember,' Eddy said. 'Instructions from the Greek and Collins. They see gold rising. Naturally they want to stall the deal for as long as possible.'

'If they stall too long, they'll blow it. Don't they know that?'

'If they don't, we'll tell them.'

On Monday 17 December the gold price stood at $461, and still the letters had not been returned by the Banque D'Arve. Eddy and

Dan drafted an urgent telex to Schurch. But when they tried to send it they were told that the machine was out of order.

They found Stoffel in his room, talking heatedly on the phone, while his office manager and various minor employees shuffled their feet and looked scared. And well might they look scared: the imperturbable Stoffel was seriously rattled, actually shouting into the receiver at one point. Eventually he slammed the phone down and said:

'Incredible! All three telexes dead and they say they don't know anything about it.'

'All *three*?' Dan said.

Stoffel threw up his arms. 'Friday night the men come to service them. It's standard procedure – we have a contract with the company. Service them! They took the guts out of them – the whole works – just took them away. And now the company says they never sent any men.'

Dan and Eddy exchanged looks. To take away telex facilities from a bank was to cut its throat. Someone was playing very serious games. They went back to their own office and called Schurch. They were told that he was in Berne. They called Berne and were told he was on his way back to Zurich.

'This is crazy,' Dan said. 'They're giving us the run-around. D'you think Schurch hired some jokers to take out the telexes?'

'Dan, we're dealing with a prime bank, not gangsters. What we have to do now is find the Greek.'

It took them a whole day to track Maniatos down to the Connaught in London. They decided that a phone call would not have enough impact and flew to Heathrow on the nineteenth.

Maniatos had taken two adjoining suites at the Connaught. The outer suite housed his three bodyguards, two personal aides, and two secretaries, and it took the combined personalities of Eddy and Dan to breach this outer wall of defence. Eventually Dan managed to persuade the Greek's people to let him talk to Maniatos directly on the phone and Maniatos agreed to see them alone.

They were shown into the inner suite, accompanied by two of the bodyguards. The Greek was sitting in a dark and pokey sitting-room, whose windows looked out onto grey brick walls and drain-pipes. It was the first time that Eddy had set eyes on the Greek and he was fascinated. He was happy to let Dan do the talking while he observed the Greek's reactions. Ostensibly there was little to see. Maniatos sat extremely still, and his eyes, which

160

Dan had described as so compelling, were as dead and expressionless as a haddock's; but small, involuntary jerks of his hands, and tiny spasms in the muscles beneath the ruined skin of his face, betrayed his tension.

When Dan had finished Maniatos remained silent for a moment. Then he said, in a voice pitched lower than normal and less *staccato*:

'You think I lie to you? You think with sale of gold few days away I make delay?'

'What else can we think, sir?' Dan said.

The Greek turned towards Eddy. He stared at him for a long time.

'Why you think I live like this?' he said eventually. 'Alone – in the dark – like a prisoner. Why you think I never go home to Athens? Why you think I have no wife, no son? Why you think Collins has me by the throat? Me. Maniatos.' He put up a hand as if to shade his eyes from a bright light – yet the room was as gloomy as a crypt. 'I tell you why. Hendrik Verwoerd's gold has done this to me. I had wife, I had son. But people know about my gold. They take my family and they demand gold in ransom. Do I give them the gold? Oh no. I am Maniatos. With my gold I am all powerful. I can fight them.' He paused. 'Both die – both.' He reported this as fact, without emotion. 'And then I have to guard myself. I cannot go to my own country because Government, they too know about my gold and they want it. Think, think what the gold could do for Greece. I have to go to Collins because I need cash for my business. My gold is a dead thing – lies in a vault – produces nothing. You see? You see how I have been destroyed by it? You think I want delay?'

After they left Maniatos they booked into a hotel and put a call through to Collins in Las Vegas. Like Maniatos he denied any desire to delay the transaction.

'Don't ask me what's happening,' he said. 'Banking expertise is what you're selling *me*. You said the deal would go through before the end of the year and I'm holding you to that. Limmatbank has our instructions. If there's a screw-up, right or wrong it's you I'm coming after.'

'Okay, okay. But remember this: you hold out for too long and you have a dead deal,' said Dan.

'I'm not holding out, Mr Daniels. I don't want a dead deal and, if I may remind *you* of something, you want one even less.'

'Do you believe him?' Dan asked Eddy when the call was over.

'I don't know. I just don't know. The Greek's genuine. Dammit, the guy's haunted. But Collins. Collins is not only smart, he's in trouble. He has a hundred and fifty million to recoup. Maybe he's trying to recoup it. But I don't know.'

They returned to Luxembourg to find that the deal was not dead, but dying. They had calls from bankers and lawyers representing all their buyers. The calls were polite and friendly, but each one contained a threat. The one exception was John's call. It was not friendly, nor polite, nor subtle.

'Don't give me any crap,' John said. 'You're jewing me on the price, right? Well get this and get it good, I don't get jewed. Not by anybody.'

Dan, who had lost the toss and taken the call, wished John a Merry Christmas.

The advent of Christmas compounded their problems. It fell on a Tuesday that year which meant that from the twenty-first to the twenty-sixth the European banking system to all intents and purposes closed down.

'There's nothing we can do until after Christmas,' Eddy said, 'so I suggest we put the whole thing out of our minds and try to live like ordinary mortals for a few days. Let's pick up Tania in Zurich and go to the mountains.'

'I don't want to play gooseberry——'

'You won't, I promise you.'

They flew to Zurich. On the plane they overheard at least three conversations about the rise in gold. There were other reminders – marker boards in the windows of banks and precious metal dealers. When Dan went into a jewellers to look for something to mail to Gina, there was an old woman in a fur coat trying to sell a bundle of gold bracelets, and arguing about the price.

'I am not an idiot,' she was telling the manager. 'I can read a newspaper. I know the price of gold.'

The manager patiently tried to make her understand the difference between jewellery gold, which, at eighteen carats, was only seventy-five per cent pure, and the 999.9 fine bullion in which the market traded. But the old lady would not be persuaded.

'Don't tell me my grandmother's bracelets are not pure gold, young man,' she said. 'My grandmother never had anything but the very best.' Angrily, she collected up her trinkets and stuffed them in her bag. 'If you think you can swindle me,' she said, 'you are very much mistaken. I've a good mind to report you.'

As she stalked out Dan caught the manager's eye. The manager shrugged wearily. 'It's always the same. They see gold rise and they come in here thinking I am going to give them a fortune for their old rings and bracelets. *C'est vraiment affreux.* At this season too.'

'Have you had many in?'

'Too many, *monsieur.* Why can't they go to the banks or the metal dealers. Why do they have to come to me? Every time it happens I lose good customers because they think I try to cheat them.'

'The price'll level out.'

The manager shrugged. 'I don't know, *monsieur.* There is something in the air. If it goes on rising there will be a stampede.'

Dan looked at some necklaces and watches but couldn't make up his mind on any of them. He was uneasy. He had a feeling that the incident with the old woman and her bracelets was a bad omen.

The next morning he joined Eddy and Tania and they drove east, on the same route that Eddy and Tania had taken back in the summer, through the Black Forest and down into the valley of the Rhine. They reached the Auberge de la Pêche in a pure, coral dusk and the beauty of the place succeeded in banishing Dan's worries. It also made him wish that Gina was there.

On Christmas Eve they drove to the nearby village for Midnight Mass. Tania held Eddy's hand as they knelt side by side in the pew with the murmur of the Latin ritual rising and falling around them.

Later, when Dan had gone to his room, they talked for a little while in the deserted bar, by the vermilion embers of the fire.

'I'd forgotten how deep it goes – our Faith,' Tania said. 'When I hear the Mass all I have to do is close my eyes and I am home, in Poland.' She laughed, and touched him lightly. 'Ah – I know it means nothing to you, you unbeliever.'

'Sometimes it does. Tonight it did.'

'Will you wake me in the morning?'

'What time? It already is morning.'

'Any time. Whenever you wake.'

But when, six hours later, he went to her room, she was sitting up in bed. She fumbled in the drawer of the bedside table and brought out a box.

'Happy Christmas, Eddy.' She offered him the box tentatively, almost as if she expected him to reject it.

163

He opened it. Inside was a gold medallion on a chain. Each side of the medallion bore the face of a venerably bearded man, sculpted in relief. He waited for her to say something; but she said nothing.

'Copernicus,' he said. 'The first man who had the humility to see that the earth went round the sun and not the other way around.'

'And a Pole.'

'It's beautiful, Tania, really beautiful.' He weighed it in his hand. 'Heavy too. Hope you bought it before the price went up.'

She didn't laugh. 'I'll put it on for you.'

He bent his head and she helped him to fasten the catch.

Christmas Day in the Vosges had a special flavour. The inn was the focal point for a scattered neighbourhood: people from nearby farms came crowding in and there was singing and a prodigious amount of drinking. At odd moments Dan glanced across the table at Eddy and, too often for his own peace of mind, he saw him looking preoccupied.

They spent the next day skiing and tobogganing, and on Thursday they drove back to Zurich. At the first opportunity Dan bought a paper. He didn't need to turn to the financial pages to find the gold price. It was on the front page. For the first time in history gold had broken through the $500 barrier.

18

It got worse.

The International Monetary Fund, announcing its monthly gold auction, reported bids for 1.3 million ounces at a record price of $562.5 an ounce. But that record was swiftly broken: on 4 January the gold price went to $630; by 18 January it was $760 in London, $805 in New York. On 22 January the Chicago futures market reported a price of $1,000.

And then the bubble burst. On 24 January dealing was suspended in London and the price began to plummet – by $135 in one, unforgettable day. But by that time Eddy and Dan's deal was as dead, as Dan put it, as a shredded telex.

Panic calls from their buyers' representatives had started right after the New Year. The message had been conveyed differently in each case, according to nationality and temperament, but it was the same message every time: transaction cancelled. Collins had called them on 17 January, the day Western Finance Ministers met in Washington. His message, too, had been very clear.

'I don't know what you've done, or how you've done it – I'm not that smart – and I don't know how much money you've made. But if it's a billion it won't be enough. People like you don't double-cross people like me. Ever. We have long memories, Polonski. We never forget and we never forgive. We will wait. We can wait for years. I could die; it wouldn't make any difference. Your names are marked – permanently.'

Eddy and Dan saw very little of each other during those days. Eddy was in Zurich, laying siege to Limmatbank and trying to track down Schurch. The story on Schurch was that he was seriously ill, in a private clinic, and could not be contacted. Dan alternated between Luxembourg, where Stoffel grew daily yellower around the eyes, and Geneva, where the directors of the Banque D'Arve consistently refused to see him.

With a growing sense of impotence and futility, Eddy and Dan instructed a Zurich lawyer to start proceedings against Limmatbank and the Banque D'Arve for the return of their documents. The man they hired was distinctly second-rate but the three or four top attorneys Dan approached – one of them an old friend – all refused to act, pleading pressure of work and other transparent excuses. Dan began to feel like a pariah, Eddy to sense a conspiracy.

Meanwhile the prophecy of the Zurich jeweller was being fulfilled all over the world. It was a stampede on a hitherto unimagined scale, a global frenzy to buy and sell gold. The meanest bazaars in the Middle East resounded with the cracks of the dealer's hammers as they smashed up cherished keepsakes, religious trinkets, pens, cigarette lighters, any object that contained gold. The grandest bullion dealers and the most prestigious brokerage houses in Europe and America were openly accused by the press of scandalous profiteering. In reply, their spokesmen produced masterpieces of suave nonsense.

There was something apocalyptic about it. It was as if the human race had collectively sensed an impending catastrophe, one half of it deciding to turn its gold into cash, and spend before it was too late, the other half deciding to bury its cash, hoard it, protect it, in the most ancient way of all.

That was how the press reported it, as a universal event to be compared with the Wall Street Crash. Every day Dan would buy a stack of papers and wade through articles about East-West tension, Afghanistan, the Ayatollah, the fear of inflation, OPEC petro-dollars chasing bullion. He listened to hundreds of conversations in airport lounges, hotel foyers, bars, and restaurants, as he jetted between the great financial centres of Europe in desperate and increasingly vain attempts to restore life to the transaction. He heard every kind of theory and explanation being discussed, from the apparently sound and reasonable, to the preposterous and the bizarre. In the light of what he knew, none of them made any sense. But then he himself could make no sense out of what was happening to him.

After Collins's call and threat he was forced to go back to using his dummy passport, avoiding big hotels, making his calls from Post Offices, meeting Eddy covertly. When the gold price crashed, it made no difference. Every door that mattered in Luxembourg, Zurich, Geneva, and Brussels was closed to him – and it was the same for Eddy.

Towards the end of January the partners met in a small hotel in

Geneva to review the disaster and assess their prospects. It was a grim day outside: the lake looked like a slab of grey slate; a fine, freezing rain filled the streets; every face seemed to be pinched with cold.

'What seems like a long time ago,' Eddy said, 'I made a statement. You suggested that Schurch might have been responsible for ripping out the telexes at Euro-resource and I said we were dealing with a prime bank not gangsters. I now retract that statement, with apologies.'

'They fixed more than a few telexes,' Dan said. 'What I can't figure out is how. By the way I called the lawyer in Zurich. The letters have been returned to him.'

'Not surprising. They've served their purpose.'

'Obviously it was the letters. It must have been. I mean, the price of gold doubles in less than three weeks at exactly the time when our letters are out of our control. It can't be a coincidence. But I'm damned if I can see what they did with them.'

'I've thought about nothing else for the past week,' Eddy said, 'and I've come up with a theory. It's outlandish but I think it fits the facts. Maybe you can find some holes in it.'

'Go on.'

'Okay. Let's start at the beginning. We went out and we found private buyers for two thousand tons of gold. In doing that we generated letters from various prime banks fronting for our clients, letters stating that our clients would buy gold and had the financial capability, letters addressed to Euro-resource, bank-to-bank letters. I remember warning Collins and Delgado about those kinds of letters. I told them that getting letters like that out of banks was a major operation.'

'You're darned right it is. Dammit, it took us three months and everything we knew to get those letters.'

'Exactly. And when we did get them we kept them next to the skin. Why? Because if a broker or somebody got hold of them it would be fatal. What never occurred to me was that any bank that had physical possession of the letters could use them to back orders to buy on the gold market. I mean *legally* use them.'

'Because they're bank-to-bank letters. My God, you're right.'

'It's so simple,' Eddy said bitterly. 'Go right back to the start. Why couldn't Maniatos sell his gold? Because it represented a massive over-supply on the market and the market naturally refused to handle it. But by taking our letters the bank converts a *supply* of two thousand tons into a *demand* for two thousand tons.'

Dan held up his hand and said: 'Slow down, slow down. Okay, the bank has our letters. It can place orders on the market. But how does that affect the price?'

Eddy took a sip of tea and leaned forward, his shoulders hunched. 'How does the Gold Market function? What do they base their fix on? A balance between buying and selling, right? Those five guys with their little flags in London are in permanent contact with the dealing rooms of the banks they represent. At the start of the day's business the chairman states an opening price. This is relayed back to the dealing rooms and then on to clients – the speculators, central banks, institutional investors. Each representative then declares himself a buyer or a seller. Now. Limmatbank has our letters. They feed in orders to buy into the dealing rooms, probably in small tranches, through subsidiary banks under their control. They create demand. Then what happens? The market, sensing a strong demand, casts about for sellers. But the sellers can also smell a demand and naturally hold out for a higher price. At the end of the day's trading, the fix is at a price considerably higher than at the beginning of the day. Now get this. What does Limmatbank have in addition to our buy letters? It has the sell letter on the Greek gold. Again through subsidiaries it can go into the market posing as a seller. It can buy and sell to itself. And on the basis of two thousand tons, my friend, something like half the total quantity of metal available for sale or purchase in the world, it can manipulate the price up, down, or sideways.'

Dan was running his fingers through his hair, so fascinated by the stratagem being described that he had almost forgotten that it related very directly and very painfully to himself. 'Hold up, Eddy, Limmatbank can only pose as buyers and sellers. They only have paper. They don't have either metal or money. Any transactions that appeared to take place would be phoney transactions. The audit would reveal that.'

Eddy sat back in his chair and smiled. He said, quietly: 'There is no audit on the gold market, Dan.'

Dan stared at him. 'No audit? But, godammit, someone must monitor the fix.'

Eddy shook his head. 'The market is completely autonomous. It is not required by any authority to reveal a record of transactions or volume of sales.'

'You're telling me that private enterprise is permitted to fix the price of gold every day without any form of official policing?

How in God's name did they swing that one?'

Eddy shrugged. 'The right was granted by the Bank of England sometime back in the nineteenth century. That was a buccaneering age when the Rothschilds were gold smugglers, the Barings financed revolutions, and the British Government went to war on the side of the dope trade in China.'

Dan was only half listening. 'They only have to use the dummy transactions a few times – to get the price moving up,' he said. 'Then genuine buyers and sellers go roaring in and create market panic. Result – A Gold Rush. Eddy, my friend, we've been hornswaggled.'

They both laughed – but not for long.

'We were set up,' said Eddy. 'My guess is we were set up from the start.'

Dan was frowning, trying to remember.

'God Almighty, you're right,' he said after a moment. 'The first time I saw Schurch. It was the same day as you. We coincided at Limmatbank, remember? I asked Schurch who you were and he said you were Russian or something. Already he was lying.' He hesitated. 'But are we saying The Hairless Wonder thought this scam up? I can't believe it.'

'Neither can I.'

'Who?'

'Call him Mr X for now. Let's try and analyse the sort of person he must be. He manipulates Schurch. He manipulates the Banque D'Arve. He manipulates a string of other banks as well. He must work in a bank with numerous subsidiaries. He has to have a position at main-board level.' Eddy pulled some documents out of his briefcase. 'This is the Annual Report of Limmatbank for last year. Look at the list of directors, then look at the list in the Banque D'Arve's report – here. You see the common denominator?'

Dan studied the lists. 'Melldrum.'

'Exactly. Melldrum. By a simple algebraic process we deduce X equals Melldrum.'

'That's the hell of a deduction, Eddy.'

'It is – until you look at the man himself. I've had Stephany run a simple check on him. Anthony Melldrum is International Treasurer of Central and Shires Bank, the bank that owns Limmatbank, the Banque D'Arve, and God knows how many others. It's a British High Street bank. Okay, not one of the Big Four – smaller than that – but heavy, especially off-shore. As

International Treasurer, Melldrum is in sole and absolute charge of the bank's overseas operations. He doesn't report to anyone on the Board. So long as nothing goes wrong, he's virtually autonomous. He has to be our man.'

Dan nodded slowly. 'Melldrum,' he said. 'Anthony Melldrum. Okay, how are we going to get him?'

'I don't know. Before we consider any action we should take a look at our own position.'

Dan grimaced.

'I agree,' Eddy said. 'All our old problems are back with us. In my case, there's Jan Pienaar out gunning for me. In your case you have Landau. And we both have a problem with Jim Collins. What's Collins's attitude? He thinks we doublecrossed him, manipulated the gold rush, and made a fortune. He'll watch and wait before he puts out a contract on us. What's he going to learn? That we don't have the kind of money we need to protect ourselves. When he finds that out he won't hesitate.'

Dan nodded. 'On the plus side we do have some money left out of Harvey's investment – about four hundred grand. But there's another problem. How do we pay Harvey back?'

'By doing what we set out to do – selling the Greek gold.'

'Fight Melldrum? Beat him? Impossible. We may make great Davids, but we don't have a sling.'

'We have four hundred thousand dollars and the most powerful force in the world.'

'Oh yes? I wish you'd tell me what that is.'

'The necessity to survive.'

19

'Child Rowland to the dark tower came,' Dan said.

Eddy said nothing. He had remained silent throughout the cab ride from the hotel, preparing himself for the meeting with Melldrum. Eddy needed to create tension inside himself to handle important meetings; Dan, by contrast, had to find a way of relieving it.

They were standing on the pavement outside the Central and Shires Head Office in the heart of the City of London, and Dan was looking up at the giant wrought-iron tiger – the symbol of the bank – that was mounted over the main entrance. The street was like a defile between vertical cliffs, the result of twentieth-century high-rise architecture having been imposed on a medieval topography. It was a part of the City that had been completely re-developed in a bland, universal way but there was no mistaking the high-rumped, black taxis crawling past with a dry rattle of diesel, or a bill-broker from one of the Discount Houses, wearing a top hat, and marching past like a Guardsman, or the raw, sandy tang in the air that was peculiar to London in winter.

Eddy and Dan passed under the wrought-iron tiger into the busy banking hall on the ground floor. They mounted wide, marble stairs up to the main reception area. Neon lit and open-plan, it was entirely modern in feel except for a long line of ornately framed portraits. The portraits were of past chairmen of the bank, and some of them dated back to the late eighteenth century. At the end of the row hung a painting of Lord Ilminster, dressed in the robes of a City Livery company.

Dan glanced cursorily at the portraits as Eddy asked the girl at the desk if they could see Mr Melldrum.

'What time is your appointment?' the girl asked pleasantly.

'We don't have an appointment,' Eddy said, and there was an edge in his voice that visibly disconcerted the girl.

'Well, I'm afraid——' she began.

Eddy handed her his card. 'If you'd just send our names up.'

'I'd better speak to his secretary. Would you wait a moment?'

Melldrum fingered the two cards Mark Price-Smith had handed to him.

'My dear boy, you look positively rattled,' he said.

Mark smiled nervously. 'Honestly. They look like a couple of bloody undertakers,' he said. 'They absolutely insisted on seeing me and now they're insisting on seeing you. I've told them that you don't see anyone without an appointment but——' the sentence trailed away into a shrug.

Melldrum pondered for a moment. 'You'd better show them through,' he said.

Mark looked surprised. 'In here?'

'Yes. If you would. And you'd better make sure we're not disturbed.'

'But who on earth are they? I've never heard of them.'

'Just wheel them in, Mark. Thank you.' Melldrum's tone was sharp and Mark blushed.

While he waited for Mark to usher the two Americans into the office, Melldrum rubbed one of the cards slowly back and forth across his lower lip, debating with himself how to handle them. When they appeared he saw immediately what had so dismayed his personal assistant. There was undeniably a bleak, implacable air about them and they seemed a great deal more formidable in the flesh than they had appeared on Pierre Schurch's video screen. Distinctly formidable, in fact. But the cup had been rather rudely snatched from their lips.

'Do sit down, gentlemen,' he said smoothly when the door had closed on Mark.

Dan and Eddy each took a seat facing him. Before either of them could say a word Melldrum clapped his hands lightly, as if applauding a performance. It was partly sheer brag, but mainly to show them how completely secure he was. City arrogance. What could a couple of underbred cowboys do against the International Treasurer of the Central and Shires Bank?

'Congratulations,' he said. 'I've been wondering for some weeks whether you'd work it out. But I wouldn't get too excited about hearing a full confession from me. If you do happen to have any gadgets concealed about your persons, as they say, the security people will find them when you're searched on leaving the building. Banks, you know, are temples of security.'

'We don't need your confession,' Eddy said quietly. 'We know the facts.'

Melldrum smiled. 'Quite,' he said. 'And I don't see that we need make our discussion a long one. There isn't a single newspaper, magazine, or television company in the world that would believe your story. Even if you had proof, which you haven't, they probably wouldn't understand a word of it – it is rather technical after all – and even if they did believe it their legal advisers would very quickly tell them to drop it.'

'We have our own legal advisers, Mr Melldrum,' Dan said. 'They take the view that we have a good case against Pierre Schurch and Limmatbank.'

Melldrum smiled again. 'A lawyer will always tell you that you have a case, Mr Daniels, especially a Swiss one. You should know that – you're a lawyer yourself. Of course you may well be right. You are at perfect liberty to sue Limmatbank if you want to. You may be interested to learn that Monsieur Schurch is no longer president of the bank. He has retired – on health grounds, naturally. And you might also bear in mind that between Limmatbank and this office there is a great gulf fixed. I don't see how you're going to bridge that gulf, I really don't.'

Eddy said very quietly to Dan: 'Maybe you'd better explain,' and something in the tone of his voice gave Melldrum a faint feeling of disquiet.

Dan said: 'As you've pointed out yourself, Mr Melldrum, I am an attorney – an American attorney. Any American attorney has the right, under Federal law, to bring what is called a class action. A class action is a lawsuit taken against a large organization – a bank or a corporation with assets or subsidiaries in the US – on behalf of the American people where there is a prima-facie case that a significant proportion of the American people has suffered damage or loss as a result of the actions of that organization. It's our view that manipulating the gold market and taking millions of people for a multi-billion-dollar ride constitutes grounds for a class action. Such actions are, of course, quite rare, with the result that they attract a great deal of publicity.'

Melldrum was silent for a moment, then he smiled again, but with very slightly less assurance.

'I am not a lawyer, Mr Daniels,' he said, 'but I was under the impression that any legal action, however quaint, required a little something called evidence. You simply haven't got any evidence.'

'That's your view is it?' Dan said.

'It is.'

'But as you say, you're not a lawyer.'

There was another silence, which Melldrum eventually broke. He had expected accusations, threats, and aggression from the Americans and their outward calm, especially Polonski's softly spoken contributions, was disconcerting.

'I'm not going to bandy words with you about the feasibility of this or that legal action. You're intelligent. You know what you're up against. To borrow some of your own jargon – you can't fight City Hall.'

'Says City Hall,' Eddy said very softly.

Melldrum looked down his nose at him. 'You have certainly tried in the past, Mr Polonski,' he said. 'With singular lack of success if I may say so. Not that I don't admire your fighting spirit – I do. But even you cannot fight with your hands tied behind your back. Do you think I don't know about your friend Mr Collins? My advice to you, gentlemen, is to disappear as rapidly and as completely as possible.'

'I'm afraid we're not prepared to do that,' Eddy said.

Melldrum shrugged. 'That's up to you,' he said.

'Mr Melldrum,' Dan said, 'by your actions you have aborted a transaction in which my partner and I stood to make a great deal of money. We wish to be compensated for our losses so that we can revive the transaction. It's a perfectly reasonable request. I suggest you think about it very carefully before you reject it. And think about this too: we have the capability to expose the financial scandal of the century and you and your bank will be right in the middle of it.'

Melldrum said nothing for a moment. Then: 'Is that all you have to say?' Dan nodded. 'Fine,' Melldrum went on. 'Well I think I understand your position, gentlemen, and I'm sure you understand mine, so, if you'll forgive me——' he leaned forward and pressed his intercom. 'I am rather pressed this morning. Oh, Mark, would you show Mr Polonski and Mr Daniels out?'

When Eddy and Dan had gone Melldrum lit a cigar, inhaling the rich, heavy smoke where normally he would let it trickle slowly from his mouth and wreathe his nostrils. His instinctive reaction was to dial Ilminster's number in France, but he stopped himself. It was premature; perhaps not even necessary. Instead he spoke to his secretary through the intercom.

'Oh, Mrs Brandon – would you get me Peter Naylor's chambers

174

on the phone. I want to talk to Mr Naylor himself.'

Mark Price-Smith escorted Dan and Eddy to the elevators via the security desk. Two uniformed officers searched their briefcases and ran metal-detectors over their bodies. Mark apologized as they took the elevator down to the first floor.

'I'm afraid with all the bomb scares, and all that, the powers that be insist on it,' he said.

Neither Eddy nor Dan replied and Mark was relieved to see them disappear down the stairs into the banking hall. He felt there was something mysterious, almost inhuman about them.

When he returned to his office he found Melldrum sitting on the edge of his desk, swinging a long leg. He knew every gradation of Anthony's moods and thought he detected a shadow of anxiety in his eyes. His voice seemed cheerful enough.

'Look, about lunch,' he said. 'Sorry. I shan't be able to make it today.'

'Oh,' Mark said, failing to disguise his disappointment.

Melldrum was irritated. 'For God's sake don't be *difficile*, Mark.'

Mark flushed. 'We haven't had lunch together for weeks.'

'You're being a bore, Mark,' Melldrum said. Mark shrivelled at the patronizing coldness of his tone.

'That's always your first line of defence, isn't it?' he said. He aped Melldrum's languid voice: ''You're being a bore''.'

'And rather childish,' said Melldrum with an air of finality. 'This is the office. Try to pull yourself together.'

He stalked out. Mark sat down at his desk, twisting a paper clip into spirals. He stared sulkily at a gaudy map of the world which was pasted on the wall facing his desk. It had been put there by his predecessor in the job and had proved irremovable except at the risk of ruining the wallpaper. Mark had met his predecessor briefly – a rather common, ambitious youth. Pretty. Another blue-eyed boy. He'd got a plum job in the Sao Paolo branch. Mark disliked the map intensely. It offended his taste. It was like something out of a classroom in a State school. He felt like ripping it off the wall and to hell with the wallpaper. But he didn't. That really would be childish. Instead he rose, and left the building in search of something to eat. Standing alone at the bar of a noisy City pub, he remembered the two Americans. Something had obviously happened between them and Anthony to make him so peevish. But what?

With a plate of shepherd's pie in one hand and a pint of bitter in the other, Dan elbowed his way through the dense lunchtime crowd of a pub in High Holborn, to the corner where Eddy had secured a table. Someone jogged his arm and beer slopped onto the toe of his shoe. He sat down and took a pull at his beer.

'Sure you don't want anything?' he asked Eddy. Eddy shook his head. 'Well?'

Eddy shrugged. 'The more I think about it the more I get the feeling that the threat of the class action hurt him.'

'I'm darned sure it did. Question is – how will he react?'

'I don't know. He has everything to gain by doing nothing. Time is on his side. There's a good chance he'll try to put us under surveillance – we've got to be more careful than ever.'

'Did you see the computer terminal in his office?'

Eddy nodded.

'That's how he did it – with a computer. I mean a manipulation on that scale must have been incredibly complex. He was placing orders to buy and sell all over the world, through God knows how many subsidiaries. He had to have a record of every move he made.'

'Correct,' Eddy said, 'but I think it could be bigger than that.' Out of habit he lowered his voice but it was unnecessary – the general noise level in the bar effectively scrambled individual conversations. 'Obviously Melldrum personally made a fortune out of the rush,' he went on. 'And obviously he made a fortune for his bank. But think about the other people who stood to gain – the cartel, the gold owners. Melldrum would have been crazy not to have tried to cut them in. If he did, then he used the computer to monitor the deal from start to finish. There'd be no other way to calculate what his partners owe him. If I'm right – you see what that means?'

Dan stared at him. 'He can't erase the program until he's been paid.'

'Exactly. It's better than evens that the whole blueprint of the scam is stored somewhere in the bank's computer. It's logical. Melldrum has his own programs – and the only access to them is by a code-word only he possesses, right? The information is a hundred per cent secure.'

'Is there any way, any way at all we could tap into that program?'

'That's what we have to find out.'

Eddy was staring abstractedly at the pools and rings of spilt beer on the table, making liquid patterns with his finger.

'There's one more thing,' he said after a moment. 'It may or may not relate to our problem but I think it's interesting. Melldrum's personal assistant is gay.'

Anthony Melldrum's club in St James's was as far removed from the world of spilt beer and shepherd's pie as it was possible to be. There, behind a plain, discreet Georgian façade, the ruling class who owned England's acres and who controlled her banks, her insurance companies, her industries, and her all-powerful Civil Service lunched and dined, played snooker, bridge, and back-gammon, read *Country Life* and the *Financial Times* in the comfortable certainty that they had survived thirty years of diluted socialism and would go on surviving.

When the hall porter came up to Melldrum in the Members' Bar and told him that his guest had arrived, he nodded to the former Cabinet Minister with whom he'd been discussing the situation in Iran and went out into the hall. Peter Naylor was standing by the ticker-tape idly scanning the news-sheets that had been pinned to the green baize board on the wall.

'Hello Peter. Sorry it was such short notice. Shall we go straight in?'

Naylor had been a contemporary of Melldrum's at Winchester and was now a barrister, specializing in international law. He was a lean, willowy, sarcastic individual whose reputation as an after-dinner speaker was beginning to be legendary. Melldrum had persuaded the steward to reserve the table for two by the fire and they sat down under a portrait of Lord Salisbury. During lunch they talked mainly of common friends and farming. Naylor had recently inherited a small estate not far from Melldrum's own place in Somerset. But after lunch, when they were sitting in the bay window of the coffee room upstairs with glasses of port and cigars, Naylor said:

'Come on, Ants, out with it. Pheasant, burgundy, and fresh strawberries in February always mean free legal advice. What have you done? Got caught with your trousers down in some revolting banana republic?'

Melldrum grinned. 'Nothing like that I'm afraid. Nothing that'll keep you in your old age. I just want some information. Have you ever heard of a thing called a class action – in the States?'

'Indeed I have. It's a bit of a rarity. The best-known example is probably the case against the Ford Motor company. There was a fault on one of their models and a group of consumers took them on – beat them hollow too. There was another case involving a telephone company. Democracy rampant. Very nasty.'

Naylor's exposition accorded exactly with what Melldrum had been told by Dan Daniels.

'And you say that a multi-national would be as vulnerable to an action as an American company?' he asked when Naylor had finished.

'If it had assets or subsidiaries in America, certainly. Don't tell me that dear old C and S——?'

'Good Lord no.'

'Of course not.' Naylor smiled into his port. 'I've never had to advise in a class action but if the situation did arise I should certainly tell my client to settle if he could. Awful lot of mud tends to get stirred in a class action.'

Melldrum was pensive as his chauffeur drove him back to the City. He went into his inner sanctum and dialled Ilminster's number. He spoke briefly with his father-in-law and then pressed the intercom to summon Mrs Brandon.

'Would you get onto the charter people? I want to fly to Cognac. This afternoon.'

He arrived at the little airport at Cognac at half-past nine that night. South-western France was appreciably warmer than England, but still chilly. The road to Montillac was slick with rain and Lord Ilminster's Irish chauffeur was as maddeningly talkative as ever. He arrived at the Chateau after ten and was told that milord was in the octagonal dining room. He found his father-in-law sitting alone over the remains of dinner.

'Sorry, Anthony,' he said. 'Hunger overcame me. But I've ordered something for you. Have some brandy. You look cold.'

'I am cold.' He stood by the fire and put out his hands towards the flaming logs. 'Thanks.' He took a balloon of brandy from Ilminster and sipped it.

The servants came in with covered dishes and Melldrum and Ilminster invented conversation about family matters until they had gone.

'Eat up,' Ilminster said. 'I'll keep you company with a little cheese.'

Melldrum talked as he ate and, as he described his meeting with Eddy and Dan and explained the implications of the class action and Peter Naylor's views on it, he felt the atmosphere subtly change.

Ilminster listened with a frown on his face, and his cheese remained untasted on his plate. When he spoke there was an edge to his voice that was unfamiliar to Melldrum.

'I don't like the sound of this,' he said. 'Why the hell didn't you mention this possibility to me before?'

'I did not foresee it.'

'What else haven't you foreseen, I'd like to know?'

The remark and the tone in which it had been said were so completely out of character that it didn't occur to Melldrum to resent them. There was a faint flush on Ilminster's waxy cheek, which was certainly not to be attributed to brandy. It was almost as if Ilminster had something to fear – or somebody.

After a moment Melldrum said: 'I really don't think there's any need to over-react. My own view is that Polonski and Daniels are bluffing.'

'And what if they're not? We simply can't take the risk.'

'But I don't see where the risk lies. According to Peter these class actions take years to prepare and cost the earth. Daniels and Polonski (a) haven't got any time and (b) haven't got any money. From the word 'go' I said that we would be able to rely on Mr Collins of Las Vegas to settle their hash and I'm certain that's what will happen.'

'Are you?' Ilminster snapped. 'Then what are you doing here? Jumping onto a plane at a moment's notice, turning up in the middle of the night——'

Melldrum raised an eyebrow and sipped his wine. Yes. There was no doubt of it. Ilminster was a frightened man. Ilminster!

He said mildly: 'There's nothing very extraordinary in that. I spend my life jumping on and off planes and turning up in the middle of the night. The days of the *Queen Mary* and the *Orient Express* are over, you know. I came here to do precisely what I am doing. To talk the situation over with you.'

Ilminster glared at him. *Queen Mary* indeed! Insolent puppy! He was about to speak, but his innate tactical sense stopped him. No, no. The days when he could give Anthony Melldrum a dressing-down were over. The boy had too much power – he had given him that power.

Almost casually, Melldrum said: 'What are you so afraid of?'

The question hung in the air like smoke after an explosion. Eventually Ilminster replied, but not angrily.

'What on earth are you talking about?'

'You're afraid of something or somebody.'

'You're talking nonsense, Anthony.'

'Am I?' He rose from his seat and walked towards the fire, but stopped by Ilminster's chair, forcing his father-in-law to look up at him. 'I think it's time you were more open with me,' he said. 'I think I've earned the right to share more of your confidence. Yes, earned. It was I who thought of using the letters on the Greek gold to engineer a boom. It was I who sweated blood to carry it through. I've more than doubled the bank's off-shore funds – to say nothing of the Rawlins family holdings. I've made you head of what must be one of the richest families in Europe. Don't think I'm complaining. I've made sure that *I'll* never be dependent on Rawlins money or the bank's money or anybody's money. At the same time I'm perfectly well aware that what we've made, and even what the South Africans have made, is a fraction of what' – he paused – 'of what your other people have made.'

Now he did move towards the fire and stood by it, his elbow hitched onto the high marble mantel, his eyes staring at the flames. 'I don't suppose you realize this,' he went on, 'but it took three weeks out of my life. Night after night I used to sit up there, playing ducks and drakes with the most sensitive commodity market in the world. Sometimes I'd stand by the window, looking out at the lights of London, and I'd laugh at myself. I'd tell myself – here you are, playing God with gold, and you don't even know who you're working for.' He raised his head and turned, looking directly at Ilminster. 'Who are we working for? And why do they frighten you?'

Ilminster was toying with a pair of silver grape scissors.

He said quietly: 'Let me answer your second question first. I am not frightened of anyone in the sense I think you mean. But I confess that I am apprehensive about the possible consequences of a highly publicized legal action in the United States. In most circumstances capital and government, in partnership, can control the free press. But there are certain scandals that throw the most sophisticated system of checks and balances out of kilter – scandals that nobody, however powerful, can stop. Which is why they must never, never be allowed to start. People like you and I, Anthony, who operate multi-nationally, beyond the reach of any legal system that we don't control ourselves, tend to underestimate the power of public opinion in the democracies. But it's still the one force that can destroy us.'

'What do you want me to do?' Melldrum said. 'Reach a settlement with Daniels and Polonski? Buy them off?'

Ilminster shook his head. 'Only as a last resort. If you make them rich, you make them powerful.'

'Exactly.' He cleared his throat. 'There is the other obvious solution. It must have been done before and I know of a way it could be arranged.'

Again Ilminster shook his head. 'It's too drastic at this stage – and fraught with imponderables. Besides, this man Polonski—— Apparently he is a valuable man, well worth keeping alive. What we have to do is try to divide them – divide and conquer – it's always a sound principle. I don't think Daniels has anything like Polonski's experience of the – seamier side of life. I think he could be frightened off. Destroy the loyalty that evidently exists between the two of them and you solve the problem, I think.' He smiled. 'Loyalty is a commodity that is easily destroyed.'

'Yes,' Melldrum said. 'I see what you mean.'

Ilminster stood up and joined him by the fire. 'I'm sure you do,' he said.

Melldrum said, after a moment: 'You haven't answered my first question.'

Ilminster was kicking at a log in the grate, creating bursts of red sparks.

'For many years,' he said very quietly, 'it was my bitterest regret that Margaret and I had no son.' He paused and looked directly up at Melldrum. 'If I said that I do not regret it now, would that begin at least to answer your question?'

Melldrum met his gaze. It was nothing in itself – that brief moment when their eyes met and held, before each turned away – but for Anthony Melldrum it was without question the most exciting moment of his life.

Melldrum sat up until the small hours, poring over the dossier Zwingler had compiled on Dan Daniels. In the morning the chauffeur drove him to Angoulême where he caught the express to Paris. Zwingler met him in Paris that evening. They talked for ten minutes in one of the bars at Charles de Gaulle airport and then Melldrum flew home to London.

20

By coincidence, Eddy and Dan were also in Paris that evening, staying at separate hotels. Their main purpose in visiting the French capital was to see their Zurich lawyer. It was not safe for either of them to enter Switzerland in the circumstances. Swiss law, formed by a legislature in which ninety per cent of the members were directors of major corporations and banks, gave the police the power to arrest anybody on suspicion of activities 'prejudicial to the Swiss economy', and hold him without charge for fourteen days. In Dan's judgement their action against Limmatbank could qualify as 'prejudicial'.

Dan had other business in Paris. The most important was to obtain a passport in a new name. The simplest and cheapest method of so doing was to pay a call at the Paraguayan Consulate where, for the modest sum of two thousand dollars and with the right introduction (supplied by Harvey Ravenscroft), one could obtain a Diplomatic Passport with a business classification in the name of one's choice valid for a year in all non-Communist countries. It was not a document on which the bearer could build a new identity – by using it to get a driving licence or a Social Security number – but it did enable him to cross borders safely under an assumed name. Dan paid an extra thousand dollars for his passport because it was already visa-ed for the United States. Right after collecting it he went along to pick up his mail from the *Poste Restante*. There was a letter from Gina. It was a breathless letter, written in her harum-scarum scrawl, full of gossip, love, and her plans for a weekend trip to Hoke's Place.

The partners spent a week in Paris, and then the plan was for Dan to fly to New York incognito to start the legal ball rolling, and for Eddy to return to London where an enquiry agent, recommended by Stephany, was compiling a dossier on Mark Price-Smith. But on the afternoon of the day they were set to leave something happened that knocked their plans sideways. Eddy received a call from the Zurich lawyer. He had been contacted by an anonymous telephone voice who asked him to convey a message to his client, Mr Daniels. The message was cryptic, so cryptic that Eddy wrote it down.

This time it is only a matter of Fire Insurance. Next time it will be a matter of Life Insurance.

Dan's immediate thought was for his Houston apartment, into which Gina had moved soon after Christmas. He called the number and it rang, which suggested that the place was intact, but there was no answer. His next thought was the house in Hedwig Village. He called there and was subjected to a ten-minute moan from Elizabeth. Only then did he think of Hoke's Place. He called Ravenscroft.

'It happened some time over the weekend,' Ravenscroft said. 'I had no means of contacting you. Somebody soaked the walls with gasoline and then set light to the place. They burned the forest too. If there hadn't been a storm, God knows what would have happened. We've had a mild winter.'

Dan spent the night calling his Houston apartment – every half hour. There was no reply. He called Gina's old number and dragged her erstwhile room-mate out of bed. The girl didn't know anything. He called the restaurant where Gina worked.

'She took a week's vacation – she was owed some extra days,' they told him. 'We don't expect her back until next week.'

The first direct flight to Houston was from Heathrow. Dan caught it with five minutes to spare. At Houston he changed to a local flight to San Antonio, where Ravenscroft's plane was waiting for him. Ravenscroft's pilot flew him directly up to Hoke's Lake. The plane was equipped with floats and they touched down right on the water. It was mid-afternoon and there was a sickly sun in a powder-blue sky.

Where the shack had stood very little remained. The winds had scattered most of the ashes, leaving a few heaps of buckled corrugated iron and charred timbers. For five hundred yards all round the forest was a blackened wilderness. But Dan wasn't looking at the ruin of the shack, or the burned-out forest; he was looking at the inlet where he always moored the canoe, trying to believe that his eyes were betraying him and that he could not see its shape behind the thick tangle of bare branches and high grass. The pilot helped him to inflate the dinghy and he paddled ashore. The canoe was there, made fast to a stake with convoluted granny knots.

Dan walked over to the ruins of the shack. He began to sift through the ashes and rubbish and black sludge. He found what he'd prayed he wouldn't. There was no mistaking calcinated bones.

'It was intended as a warning,' Ravenscroft said. It was two hours later and Dan was drinking hot coffee by the fire in the living room at Blackwind. 'They must have assumed that the shack was empty. But I'm surprised they didn't wake her.'

Dan didn't answer immediately. Eventually, he said: 'The first time I ever took her there she told me she slept like the dead. It was the air. Anyway, if it was local boys, they'd have done it quietly, so as not to alert the Rangers.' He was silent again, for a long time, and then he laughed shortly. 'I don't even know the name of her next of kin,' he said. 'I think she had a sister in New York. Her mother died, I know, and her father was divorced. He's probably still alive.' He laughed again. 'It seems crazy to know so little about someone you loved.'

'Somebody'll have the information,' Ravenscroft said. 'You'll have to tell the police. I can do it for you if you like. I know the Chief in Fort Davis.'

'Harvey, you're going to have to handle the whole thing for me. I'm here on a phoney passport.'

'That's no problem, Dan. I can do that.'

'She was beautiful, Harvey.' Suddenly he wanted to talk about Gina.

Ravenscroft let him talk, deliberately asking him questions about her. By dinner-time they both felt able to talk of other matters.

'You probably haven't heard about our neighbour, Miss Barraclough?' Ravenscroft said during the meal. 'She died a few weeks back. Ninety-six, she was.' He laughed. 'She left her entire estate to some convent in Dallas. Her funeral was attended by hundreds of nuns. I didn't know there were so many nuns in America. You know, I never realized that the old lady was a religious woman. Extraordinary.'

'What's going to happen to the place?'

'The Sisters intend to sell it. You used to dream about buying Barraclough didn't you Dan?'

Dan shrugged. 'I used to have all sorts of dreams, Harvey.'

He woke in the middle of the night. As he went into the

bathroom to get a glass of water he saw that there were lights on downstairs. He went down into the living room. Harvey was not there, but the door to the strong-room was open. Harvey was standing, in his night-clothes, in front of the Inca sun god. Dan waited a moment, then went quietly back up to his room.

He lay on his back, his hands clasped behind his head, and stared up at the ceiling. For the first time he began to apply his mind exclusively to the problem of destroying Anthony Melldrum. They had tried a bold, frontal approach, a crude threat. Melldrum had responded with even greater crudeness – and had made a serious error. Intending to fire a warning shot, he had been responsible for a death. There had to be a way, a subtle way, not a crude way, of exploiting that error.

He flew back to London the next day and met Eddy in an obscure Bayswater hotel. They talked for most of the night and slowly a plan began to emerge. The following day Eddy made an appointment to see Melldrum alone, and the day after that he and Dan met again in the Bayswater hotel.

Eddy wasn't alone in his room. There was another man packing up electrical equipment. When the stranger had gone, Dan said:

'The bug expert?' Eddy nodded. 'Everything okay?' Dan said.

'A okay.' Eddy stared at Dan, smiling.

Dan sat down. 'Lousy weather.' He responded to Eddy's smiling stare nervously. Sleet was driving against the window, which commanded a dismal prospect of gardens and patios, abandoned for the winter. 'Well, did you talk to Melldrum?' Eddy nodded again. 'And?'

Eddy didn't answer for a moment. Then he said: 'He took a hard line, Dan.'

'So did you, I hope.'

'So hard,' Eddy went on, 'it must mean he's scared. I think he'd settle.'

'He may want to settle but there's no way we're going to. I hope you told him that.'

'Hear me out, Dan. His basic strategy isn't difficult to read. He wants to divide us. He kept dropping hints. The message was that he's prepared to do a deal with me, but that you're too dangerous.'

'He's damned right about that.'

'Let me finish. I couldn't figure out why I was suddenly so

185

popular and then something he said tripped a switch.' He laughed. 'My past keeps catching up with me, Dan. You know what Melldrum wants? What Jan Pienaar and Harvey Ravenscroft want.'

'The Philosopher's Stone?'

'You've got it.'

They were both silent for a moment. Then Dan said: 'So?'

'So I think we can do a deal. Melldrum must know enough about the line of research I was working on to know what it's worth. So I make him an offer. He pays off Ravenscroft. He pays off Landau and all your other creditors. He buys us both foolproof new identities so that Collins can't find us. He gives you whatever you want – a million, two – and undertakes to get off your back. In return, I go to work for him, and you abort the class action.'

Dan's reply came quickly. 'It's terrific, Eddy – right up to the last bit. There's no way I'm going to abort the action. As far as I'm concerned it's war. I'm going to nail that son-of-a-bitch and his bank and the zombies who killed Gina. Now you devise a way for me to do that and I'll listen. But don't give me any crap about making a deal.'

Eddy spoke calmly.

'Dan, we've spent the last three days busting our brains trying to think of a way to nail Melldrum. But there is no way.'

'Sure there is. The action. You're great on alchemy and security and surveillance and hiding out and Wing Tsun boxing, Eddy, and that's wonderful. But I know the law. I can blow the Central and Shires Bank and Anthony Melldrum so high they'll be picking pieces of them off the moon.'

'Dan, you won't live that long. Face up to it. Think what Melldrum has at stake. You think he'll hesitate?'

'Once the action's filed, I'm safe. He can't touch me then.'

'Safe? You're dead, Dan. It takes time to file an action. Melldrum won't give you the time.'

'That's my problem.'

'It's my problem too.'

Dan seemed to address the wall. 'It needn't be. We can dissolve the partnership, right here, right now.'

'Come on, Dan.'

'I mean it, Eddy. If you can do a deal with Melldrum, do a deal. I have no right to stop you. If I want to take him on alone, that's my affair.'

'How can you take him on?'

'By vanishing for a start.'

Eddy sounded emotional for the first time. 'You don't stand a chance on your own. All Melldrum has to do is pick up a phone and he can have every airport, railway station, bus terminal, and port watched. Dammit, the guy's got unlimited money – unlimited.'

Dan smiled and nodded. 'Thanks for the seminar, teacher,' he said. 'I know I didn't spend half my life dodging the KGB through the back streets of Moscow, but I'm not a total dumb-cluck. I did seven years in the US Navy, and two of them in Intelligence, and I still carry my TS clearance. I can take care of myself.'

'It's absolutely insane, Dan.'

'I'm a lawyer, my friend. When you get right down to it I'm just a dull, honest lawyer. And dull, honest lawyers have a dull, honest belief in the law. When a girl gets killed, somebody goes out and finds who killed her. Then they give him a fair trial, twelve good men and true pronounce him guilty, and a dull, honest judge gives him a life sentence or the electric chair. That's the way it works in my world, Eddy.'

'But dammit you're not in your world.'

Dan looked at him. This time he couldn't keep the contempt out of his eyes. 'Your world, I suppose.'

'If you want to put it that way, yes.'

'And you're prepared to compromise?'

'I'm prepared to survive.'

'I get it. Survival. Well I know something about that game, Eddy – it's a game people play strictly solo. If you're prepared to see Gina blown away and do nothing about it – in the name of survival – you'll eventually sit back and watch me blown away in the same cause. So I think I'm safer out of this partnership.'

'Now listen to me, Dan——'

'That's the logic of your position, Eddy.' He rose. 'Our partnership ends right here.' He picked up his attaché case.

'You can't just walk out of here,' Eddy said. Dan moved towards the door. 'How far do you think you're going to get?'

Dan didn't answer. But at the door he paused. 'You're a cold-blooded bastard, you know that, Eddy?' he said. 'A cold-blooded bastard.' Curiously enough, he smiled. Then he left.

Dan walked briskly along the Bayswater Road to Marble Arch

underground station. He spent three-quarters of an hour dodging from the Central Line to the Bakerloo Line and finally to the Northern Line, surfacing at last at Leicester Square. He spent fifteen minutes in a travel agent, then dived back into Leicester Square station and took the Piccadilly Line out to Heathrow.

He sat among yattering schoolchildren and stolid black women with shopping bags and, as the train rattled through the western suburbs, he went over the plan in detail, trying to find a flaw. Then he put it out of his mind and thought about the conversation with Eddy. As he did so, he shook with silent laughter.

When he arrived at Heathrow Central he took the moving walkway to Terminal One. He went openly up to the British Airways counter, placing pound notes on the desk, and asked for a ticket to Copenhagen on the afternoon flight.

'But they're boarding now,' the girl said, flustered.

'Just give me the ticket,' Dan said. 'I have to get on that flight.'

She issued the ticket and he didn't bother to wait for his change. He ran for the departure lounge. He used his own American passort to go through Immigration – he didn't want any problems – passed through the security check and walked swiftly through the lounge, past the Duty Free shop. He glanced up at a TV monitor which indicated that the Copenhagen flight was still boarding. But he did not proceed to the designated departure gate. He took the transit walkway to Terminal Two. In the main concourse he checked a monitor. The Air France flight to Paris was not boarding yet. He went to the bar and bought a drink, keeping his eyes on the monitor. When the light began flashing to indicate that Air France was boarding, he bought another drink, and sipped it slowly. He finished his drink as the tannoy announced that the flight to Paris was closing. Then he ran.

He arrived at the departure gate breathless and sweating, and inwardly sighing with relief that the man on the gate was French. He pulled his British Airways ticket out of his pocket.

'I have to get to Paris tonight. It's urgent.'

The Frenchman looked at him superciliously.

'It's all right, sir,' he said. 'There is a few moment yet. Your ticket, please.' Dan handed him the ticket. The Frenchman looked at it and raised an eyebrow. 'This is the wrong ticket,' he said.

'I know – but BA tickets and Air France tickets are interchangeable, right?'

'Yes. But this is a ticket to Copenhagen. More expensive than to Paris.'

'Don't remind me.'

'You must go back to the ticket counter and change it, sir.'

'I haven't got time.'

'But if I take this ticket you——'

'I lose my money. Right. Like I said, don't remind me.'

The Frenchman shrugged faintly and tore the ticket, with thinly disguised pleasure. Dan boarded the plane silently blessing the least attractive characteristics of French officialdom. As the plane took off he wondered whether Eddy had been right, whether Melldrum's people had been watching the airport. If they had, there would be someone waiting at Copenhagen. When no Dan Daniels emerged from the London flight, they'd start checking back through the airlines' computers and discover his name on the captain's manifest of the Air France flight to Paris. But by then it would be too late. London to Paris was a forty-minute hop, London to Copenhagen a three-hour haul. It would be three, maybe four hours before they picked up his trail, by which time, using his Paraguayan passort, he could be anywhere in the world.

He had done what he'd told Eddy he would do. He'd vanished.

21

'You must see,' Melldrum said, 'that it is in the interests of both of us to find Mr Daniels as soon as possible.'

Eddy had his back turned to Melldrum. He was staring out of the office window at the spires and roofs of London. A high wind was shunting grey masses of cloud across the sky but the triple glazing of the window blocked off all sound from the outside. He could hear Melldrum's fingers beating a light, irregular tattoo on the leather surface of his desk.

'I can see that it's in your interest,' he said after a moment, 'but why should it be in mine?'

'It's a matter of your——survival, Mr Polonski.'

Eddy looked round at that word. Melldrum had said it as if he intended it to be taken as an echo.

'How do you figure that?'

'Let me make my position perfectly plain, Mr Polonski. Mr Daniels is bent on a course of action which is entirely against my interests. Frankly there is only one way to stop him. If you associate yourself with him——' he shrugged.

'I do associate myself with him.'

'Do you?' Melldrum smiled. 'Have you suddenly been converted to a dull, honest belief in the law?'

Eddy stared at him, then moved to a chair and sat down.

'I had that room screened by an expert.'

Melldrum shrugged again. 'There are experts and experts. I don't pretend to know anything about these matters except that my own bank spends a great deal of money every year in keeping ahead of technological advances.' Eddy was silent. 'Take as long as you like to think about it, Mr Polonski.'

'What exactly are you proposing?' Eddy said after a moment.

'You said most of it for me,' Melldrum replied. 'Come and work for me and I am prepared to settle what debts you have contracted. I will also protect you from Collins and the South Africans.'

'I said more than that. I included Dan in the deal.'

'Yes. But that was before his unfortunate outburst. I'm afraid there is only one arrangement I can make about Mr Daniels.'

'I can't agree to that.'

'You can't do anything else. By his attitude Mr Daniels has made it certain that if you continue to side with him you go down with him.'

'Give me a chance to find him. Let me talk to him some more.'

Melldrum shook his head. 'It's out of the question,' he said. 'One doesn't argue with an idealist. Your loyalty is admirable, Mr Polonski, but misplaced. Mr Daniels himself broke off your partnership. He himself advised you to make the best accommodation you could with me. You are quite absolved.'

Again Eddy was silent, thinking. He said: 'You're very confident that you'll be able to find him. Dan's a smart operator. Maybe you won't find it so easy.'

Melldrum sniffed. 'I'm afraid I must deny your conscience even that small sop,' he said. 'The last of my conditions is that you help me to find Mr Daniels.'

'Why do you think I'll be able to do that any better than you?'

Melldrum shrugged again. 'You seemed fairly confident that you could do it a moment ago when you asked me for more time.'

'I could have been speaking rhetorically.'

'I don't think you were.'

Eddy stood up and paced restlessly to the window.

'This protection you talk about,' he said. 'What sort of protection?'

'As far as Jan Plenaar is concerned,' Melldrum said, 'one telephone call from me will solve your problem. Mr Collins is a different matter. I can provide you with accommodation – a bank flat – and round-the-clock bodyguards.'

'Round-the-clock bodyguards means round-the-clock surveillance. I don't need or want that. I'm not worried about Collins in the short term. And the job?

'That will be for others to decide in detail – but, broadly, you will be given your own laboratories and a virtually unlimited research budget.'

'And you pay off Ravenscroft?'

'Yes.'

'Okay,' Eddy said. 'You have a deal.'

'Good. Now – where is Mr Daniels?'

'I don't know.' He sighed heavily. 'But I can find out.'

'Would you like to tell me how?'

'Sure. Through his bank account.'

'That doesn't sound very convincing, Mr Polonski. If he's fool enough to start telexing for money I can find him myself.'

'Of course he won't telex for money. We're not dealing with an idiot. His bank account is in Vienna.'

Melldrum nodded. 'I see. One of those. He rings them up, gives them a code-word, and they transfer the funds. All verbal – no records – very convenient. Unless, of course, someone else happens to know the code-word.'

'Exactly.'

'Would you like to give it to me?'

Eddy smiled. 'What do you think?'

Melldrum responded to the smile. 'No. Quite. Well, I leave it in your hands, Mr Polonski. How long do you think it will take?'

'It depends what funds he was carrying when he left. A week, maybe two.'

'Very well. The facilities of the bank are at your disposal. Do you want to move into your new quarters straight away?'

'Why not?'

'Good. I'll arrange that.'

He rose and began to extend his hand towards Eddy. Then he saw the expression on the Pole's face and stopped himself with a little smile. 'I'm so sorry,' he said. 'Force of habit.'

Eddy's 'new quarters' was a one-bedroom flat in a mansion block off Sloane Square, a stuffy Edwardian pile of blood-red brick. He fixed himself a light supper from the stores in the freezer, then called Tania in Zurich and spoke to her for an hour. He went to bed early and set his alarm for five in the morning.

Dan flew into Hong Kong at eleven o'clock on a blazing morning. He hadn't visited Hong Kong since his Navy days and he hardly recognized the skyline from the air. The city had expanded both laterally and vertically and on the Kowloon side, where the airport was, a whole new conurbation had mushroomed. But once he was in a cab in the dense traffic of central Kowloon, it all came back: the heat, the noise, thousands of shop signs hanging over the streets as though an oriental flag day had gone mad, and the people – the inexhaustible throngs of people. On impulse he asked the driver to take him to a tea house. The place the driver recommended – 'Best, mister, good *dim sum*' – was packed to the

192

rafters. Ancient women with the faces of wise monkeys were wheeling trolleys of *dim sum* round and round the room in a perpetual cycle, crooning their wares in a plaintive sing-song. From behind a screen in one corner came the inevitable *clack-clack* of mah-jong tiles, and from the two or three hundred Chinese families who were eating, arguing, gossiping, and laughing, came a racket that made a Houston diner sound like an empty church at night.

Dan ate his way through ten or twelve delectable little dishes and wondered how in hell the Chinese people had ever come to be stereotyped as silent and inscrutable. He remembered the old days of hauling drugged GIs out of bars and brothels, and of receptions at the Governor's Mansion, with the men in white uniforms and the women in long dresses and a feeling that the sun had not quite set on the British Empire. He finished his meal, paid, picked up another cab, and asked the driver to take him to Sham Tseng.

Eddy's directions turned out to have been precise. As they drove through Sham Tseng he sniffed the malty smell of the brewery and noticed the lines of plucked chickens, strung on lines by the roadside, that Eddy had described. A mile or two down the road were the gates, with their golden dragons, and beyond, on the right, the turning up into the hills. He paid off the cab and began to walk up the steep path. He felt lonely, cut off.

The confrontation between himself and Eddy, triggered by the code-words 'A okay' and 'Lousy weather', had been staged for the benefit of Melldrum's long-range bugging device. Dan could now only wonder impotently: had it achieved the desired effect? Was Eddy, incontrovertibly established as Judas Iscariot, now operating inside the enemy's camp?

He mounted higher, beginning to sweat a little in the unfamiliar heat, and caught a glimpse of the house. Like the superstructure of an old liner, Eddy had said. It was a good description. He wondered what kind of weird life he was in for. A Martial Arts school! Still, he was prepared for anything now.

He came to the garden gate and then he paused, his hand on the latch. Something was wrong. They'd rehearsed the plan in minute detail, over and over again. All that detail was stored in his subconscious memory and somehow an alarm signal was telling him that something was wrong. What? He waited, his eyes flicking from the door of the house, to the windows, to the trees in the garden. The door. It was the door. But what about the door? Something missing, something that should be there and wasn't.

The board. The carved board. The badge of office or whatever Eddy had told him. What *had* Eddy told him? Some hocus-pocus he hadn't taken very seriously.

He let the latch drop. It was probably nothing, he decided. Only three people on earth knew his destination: himself, Eddy, and Master Lim. And only he and Eddy knew his precise time of arrival. But there was no point in taking an unnecessary risk. He'd walk back to the village and find a phone; he had Lim's number.

As he turned he simultaneously heard the shot and felt fire in his left shoulder. He dropped flat, crawled fast to the cover of some bushes, and, as a volley of shots stuttered out, jumped a ten-foot bank into a banana grove and ran. As he ran, sharp-edged leaves slashing at his face, he tried to remember what Eddy had told him about the lay-out. He came to a high wall. The Golden Dragon Garden. He turned left and pounded up a rise. He saw a gate ahead and vaulted it. He heard sounds of pursuit from behind, in the banana plantation. He sprinted down narrow, twisting paths past waterfalls and pools. He could see pagoda-like rooftops below. The summer house. Maybe there'd be somebody there. There wasn't. The place was shuttered and silent. He crashed on down through the gardens, past a huge swimming pool, and some sort of gaudy shrine – all dragons and tigers and images of the Buddha. Then he heard a car and a couple of trucks and knew he was near the road. He stopped, crouched, and listened. There were no sounds of pursuit from up the hill. Gingerly he eased his jacket off and twisted his head to look at his left shoulder. It was okay – messy, painful, but superficial. The blood was already clotting. He closed his eyes and tried to picture the geography of the area as Eddy had described it. There was only one road, Castle Peak Road. Opposite the main entrance to the gardens there were a few beach houses. Behind the gardens was nothing – wild hill country. The road was obviously out – they'd have it watched. Similarly, the hills. The only hope was to try to make it across the road to one of the houses, try to find a phone, or failing that maybe make a swim for it. He waited a few minutes longer to get his breath back before trying to find a place to scale the wall by the road.

Even here. Even after the planning, the subterfuge, they'd tracked him down. Hopelessness washed over him, but he tried to think logically. It looked as if Eddy's venerable Martial Arts Master had worked a double-cross. But no, he remembered what Eddy had said about the board. The board only came down when the Master was defeated or dead. Eliminate Lim and you were left with — you were left with Eddy Judas Iscariot Polonski, the man who preached friendship, and behind him Anthony Melldrum Esquire, the man with unlimited money.

Dan rose and made his way cautiously along the wall. It was fully twelve feet high, sheer, and in good condition. He came to the gates and saw that he could climb up one of the elaborate wrought-iron pillars, step onto the top of the wall, and maybe jump from there. It was easier than he'd expected. There was a steep bank on the other side of the wall and he only had to jump a few feet. Again he waited, crouched under the cover of dusty bushes. There was no traffic, and no obvious sign of gunmen. He counted to three and ran across the road, into a driveway. He walked down the edge of the driveway towards the sea. There was a little house, built in the same style as Lim's, and overlooking the beach. He halted again to rehearse his story and then pushed open the back gate.

What seemed like ten thousand dogs spewed out of nowhere, barking and yelping like a pack of hounds. The dogs, which ranged in size from a pair of Pekinese to a fat Alsatian, swirled and leaped round him, friendly but deafening. He saw a woman's face peering out of a window and then the back door opened and she emerged. She was thin and elderly and wore a loose housecoat and sandals. She had American ex-patriate written all over her. She yelled something at the dogs in Chinese and the barking instantly ceased. The dogs abandoned Dan and crowded round their mistress, licking and nuzzling her.

'Sorry about the dogs,' she said. 'Can I help you?'

'You seem to have quite a menagerie.'

She sighed. 'Twenty-three. The village people bring me all the strays. You know what happens to them otherwise? The Chinese collect them and ship them to Bangkok. The Thais like eating dogs. It's an obscenity. Anyway, what can I do for you?'

'I've had an accident. Turned my car over. I wondered if you had a phone?'

'You look as if you hurt yourself. You'd better come in.'

He followed her through a chaotic kitchen into a living room full of tubular furniture, books, and startling abstract paintings.

'I'll get the police and the breakdown people for you, if you like,' she said. 'I speak the language.'

'Before you do that, could I make an overseas call? It sounds stupid, but you see I'm in business and I have to make a very urgent call. That's why I was driving so fast – to get to Sham Tseng to make the call. I'll pay for it, of course.'

Dan waited apprehensively for her reaction. She might be a crazy old lady but she was nobody's fool. She looked puzzled and suspicious, but she said:

'I don't see any reason why not. But I only have an internal phone. You have to go through the exchange, and believe me, it can take for ever.'

'Thanks.'

'Where are you calling?'

'London.'

He glanced at his watch. It was two forty-five – six forty-five in London. He had arranged with Eddy that he'd call him from Lim's place at seven in the morning London time. Whether Eddy had really made a deal with Melldrum or whether Eddy was still loyal, Eddy was his only hope.

He picked up the phone.

Eddy had left the apartment at five-thirty to give himself plenty of time to lose any tail that Melldrum might still have on him. He got to the call-box at Charing Cross Station at half-past six, confident that he didn't have company. He bought a paper from a frighteningly cheerful Cockney newsvendor and hung about outside the box to await Dan's call. Seven o'clock went by and no call came. The station was coming alive, the early commuter trains pulling in and disgorging puff-eyed office workers. He had to step inside the box and pretend to be talking into the receiver while keeping his hand pressed on the hook. By quarter-past seven a small queue had formed outside the box and someone tapped a coin on the glass impatiently. The phone rang at last, at seventeen minutes past. Eddy heard a hollow booming, and very faint Chinese voices, and then the mangled English of a Hong Kong operator. He was instantly alarmed. Lim had an external line. Dan could have dialled direct. When he heard Dan's 'Eddy?' he replied quickly: 'Everything okay?'

'No. It's a disaster.'

Eddy listened to Dan's urgent account of what had happened, oblivious to the angry tappings on the glass.

'How long can you stay where you are?'

'I don't know. It's somebody's house.'

'Try not to move from there. They'll have the whole area

196

covered, but they won't try anything in a private house. Persuade the people to let you stay by the phone. Pay them, force them if necessary. Give me the number. Right. Got it. I'll get back to you Dan. But stay where you are. It's critical.'

'This is a public telephone,' a furious, upper-crust voice blared in his ear.

'I'll get back to you, Dan,' Eddy said and put the phone down.

'Are you sure you've quite finished?' the voice said with heavy sarcasm. It belonged to a man in a camel-hair coat.

'Almost,' Eddy said and began to dial a number.

'This is outrageous,' the camel-hair coat said.

Eddy pressed a ten-penny piece into the slot as the pips started. A husky, early-morning voice said: 'Melldrum.'

'I don't require money, Mr Daniels,' Mrs Pearson said. 'I would much prefer the truth.' She was knifing dog-meat out of cans onto metal plates.

'The truth is, Mrs Pearson, that I'm in trouble. Someone took a shot at me.'

'Ah – I thought so. I thought that the minute I saw your shoulder. I thought your tale of an automobile crash was all poppycock. My late husband worked for the government – in the Central Intelligence Agency. What do you think of that, young man?'

Dan shrugged. 'The point is, Mrs Pearson, that if I can just stay here until my partner calls back, I'll be okay.'

'And what would you do if I went right over to the phone and called the police?'

'I don't know, ma'am. I really don't know.'

She held up the knife. Its blade was smeared with dog-meat. 'Attack me?'

Dan smiled. 'No. I wouldn't do that. I guess I'd have to run.'

'Your friend in London advised you to use force if necessary. I heard him. I've sharp ears, you know. Why would you run from the police? Are you a criminal?'

'No. I'm not. It's kinda hard to explain – but once the police are involved I'm sort of, well, blown.'

Mrs Pearson shouted: '*Loi sek, loi sek*,' and the dogs streamed into the kitchen and buried their noses in the plates of meat.

'This happened to me once before,' Mrs Pearson said. 'Oh yes. When I was a girl. We lived out on the Main Line. You know

Pennsylvania? Our house was right out in the country. One afternoon I was alone in the house and this man broke in and threatened me with a knife. He told me he was on the run from the police and demanded food and money.'

'What did you do?'

'Why I cooked him some grits and eggs and made him some coffee. Then I packed some cans in a sack for him and gave him all the money I had. We got friendly and he put the knife away. I told him what roads he should avoid and how to get to the railroad station.'

'I don't know if I'd have done that,' Dan said.

Mrs Pearson laughed. 'It was a practical joke. The man was my cousin William, got up in disguise. In those days people played all kinds of fool jokes like that.'

'I wish this was a joke, Mrs Pearson,' Dan said. 'I wish I was your cousin William.'

'Oh, I know you're serious, Mr Daniels. I know all about the kind of things that happen. My late husband——Would you like a drink, Mr Daniels? I usually take a drink at about this time.'

'I'd love one.'

They went into the living room and she poured him a whisky and a vodka for herself.

'William Crosbie – my cousin – drank himself to death at the age of forty,' she said. 'A lot of people do that in Pennsylvania.'

'Is that all, sir?' the telex operator asked.

He was puzzled and rather peeved. A telephone call from the International Treasurer himself had interrupted his breakfast. Mr Melldrum had asked him to get to the bank as quickly as possible to send some urgent telexes. At the bank he'd found not Mr Melldrum but some man with a beard he'd never seen before. And all he'd had to do was telex a bank in Vienna instructing them to wire some money to Hong Kong, and then wait for their confirmation. A lot of fuss about nothing.

'That's great. Thanks –' Eddy said. He looked at his watch. It was half-past eight. Four-thirty in the afternoon in Hong Kong. Could he risk making a call from inside the bank? It was standard procedure to record calls in many banks. He left the bank and made his way through the now crowded streets to the big Victorian hotel adjoining Liverpool Street Station. He left a small package with the desk clerk then went over to the phones. It took several minutes for the operator to connect him with Cabererras's number. The Filipino's voice came over crisp and clear.

'Listen,' Eddy said. 'I haven't got much time. Call your bank. You'll find that fifty thousand dollars was credited to your account a few minutes ago. If the money hasn't arrived, telex the Auger Bank in Vienna and they'll confirm the transfer. I need you to do something for me. If you can do it I'll telex you a further fifty grand. Okay? Now listen carefully.'

He spoke for two minutes and when he finished Cabererras said: 'I've got you, Eddy. Don't worry, friend, I can handle it.'

'I'll call you back in two hours, okay?'

'Okay, Eddy.'

He put the phone down and went to the reception desk to reclaim his package. The hotel lobby was huge and almost deserted. He found a chair in a dim corner and sat down wearily. Slowly he lowered his head until his forehead was resting on the cold surface of a low table. He remained in that position for several minutes, straightened at last, opened the package, and looked down at the gold medallion with the head of Copernicus that lay glinting in its nest of tissue paper.

He had removed the medallion from his neck before making the call to Cabererras, and before giving the instructions to the telex operator, because during the short journey from Charing Cross Station to the bank he'd worked out the only logical explanation of how the arrangements he had made with Master Lim had been eavesdropped. He'd made the call to Lim from an untappable public phone in a Post Office noisy enough to baffle the most advanced directional bugs. Therefore there had to have been a bug planted directly on him.

He hefted the medallion in his hand. There was moisture in his eyes and he wiped them with the back of his free hand.

Tania.

He slipped the medallion into his pocket and walked quickly out of the hotel. By the time he got to Hatton Garden through the rush-hour traffic several of the jewellers were opening up. He chose a small establishment called Duchinsky. Mr Duchinsky turned the medallion over and over in his hand.

'Beautiful piece of workmanship,' he said. 'Swiss, is it? It seems a crime.'

'If you could just cut it – right down the middle.'

Mr Duchinsky sighed sadly and Eddy looked away and tried not to listen to the whine of the electric saw.

'Well, bless my soul,' he heard Mr Duchinsky say. 'There's some sort of electrical——'

'Thank you, Mr Duchinsky,' Eddy said. 'How much do I owe you?'

'What? Oh, well, I can hardly – shall we say two quid?'

'I tell you what,' Eddy said. 'Keep the medallion.'

Mr Duchinsky blinked. 'But there's a thousand pounds' worth of gold here. Are you having me on?'

'You've got a nice face, Mr Duchinsky. Keep it.'

He walked out of the shop, through the heartland of the London bullion trade. Window after window he passed was full of spotlit trays of bars and Krugerrands – winking at him, mocking him.

He picked up a cab which deposited him at the big Post Office in William IV Street, behind Trafalgar Square. He called Cabererras.

'The money arrived okay, friend Eddy.'

Eddy listened as Cabererras, rather breathlessly, outlined a plan for getting Dan out.

'How long will it take you to organize it?'

'It's already organized, friend. I'll need another hour, maybe an hour and a half, to make the final arrangements then it's lift-off.'

'Okay. I'll call Dan and give him his instructions. You'd better give me a number where I can call you later. Say ten in the evening your time. Right after I call Dan, I'll telex the balance of the money. I'll speak to you.'

He hung up and asked the operator to get him Dan's number. He relayed Cabererras's instructions as succinctly as he could and made Dan repeat them.

'It sounds far out,' Dan said. 'Are you sure it'll work?'

'I guarantee it. I'll be in contact later. I have to go. Good luck.'

'It's truly very exciting,' Mrs Pearson said.

It was an hour after Eddy's call and Dan had been looking at his watch more and more frequently. Now it was time to make a move.

'I know,' Dan said. 'But really I think you'd better stay in the house.'

'Cruel young man,' Mrs Pearson said, with a pout. 'You want to deny a bored old woman the chance of seeing a real life adventure?'

Dan smiled. 'Look, if anything went wrong – well, there could be shooting and you wouldn't want anything to happen to the dogs, would you?'

Mrs Pearson looked at him quizzically. 'Diplomat,' she said.

'I don't know how to thank you,' Dan said, with yet another glance at his watch. 'You've been wonderful.'

'I've done nothing but sit and bend your ear. I've enjoyed your company.'

Dan stepped towards her and kissed her on each cheek. 'When all this is over I'll give you a call,' he said.

'Come and see me.'

'I will, I promise. I must go now. Thank you again.'

It was getting on for dusk. The shadows at the end of Mrs Pearson's driveway hid him. He waited. After a few moments he heard a truck coming from the direction of Sham Tseng. It rounded the bend and he saw that it was an open truck, crowded with *hukka* women, in flat, circular straw hats. The women carried sickles, scythes and spades. The truck pulled into the driveway, the women jumped out and started to cut at the weeds and grass in the mouth of the drive. Dan waited, sweating. So far everything was happening as Eddy had said it would. Some while later the women climbed back into the truck and, keeping low, Dan climbed in with them.

He sat on the floor of the truck as it jolted off. The women ignored him, jabbering amongst themselves. So far, so good. Twenty minutes later the truck trundled into some town, turned left and right and left, and pulled up in a yard. One of the women nodded for him to get out. It was almost dark now. There was a car parked in the yard – the Mercedes that Eddy had told him to look for. The passenger door opened and a light sprang on inside. Dan saw a spruce, little man. The man smiled and beckoned. Dan walked across the shadowy yard. Anything could happen now. He got into the car. This was the final test of Eddy's loyalty. The little man held out his hand.

'Greetings from The Alchemist,' he said, and Dan laughed, letting out his breath in a long sigh.

'Boy, am I glad to see you, Mr Cabererras.'

An hour later Dan was sitting in the sparsely furnished living room of a small, concrete farm-house somewhere up country and Cabererras was pouring him a drink.

'Listen, you don't think they'll bother the old lady?' he asked the Filipino. Cabererras shook his head.

'Not a chance. They'll wait and watch. This is how they'll figure it: you're a foreigner, you have no family here, sooner or later you'll have to seek help, or come out into the open, and then there'll be a whisper. And they're darned right. There's always a whisper in Hong Kong. Which is why you're going over the border, Mr Daniels.'

'The border? You mean the Chinese border? Wait a minute——'

'It's the only way. Discussed it with friend Eddy and he agrees. Don't worry. Getting people over the border is my business.' He smiled. 'One of my businesses. Of course, usually I'm bringing them out not taking them in. But——' he shrugged.

'But what happens once I'm in Red China? I mean——'

'There's a place. Don't worry. You'll be comfortable. And completely safe, of course. Tell me, were you at Harvard?'

'What?'

'Did you study at Harvard?'

'No. The University of Texas at Austin.'

Cabererras seemed pleased. 'All three of my boys studied at Harvard,' he said with an air of triumph. 'One in the law, one in business studies, one in chemistry.'

'Look, I'm not too sure about this Red China thing,' Dan began.

'I'll explain,' Cabererras said. 'That border's like a sieve. You know how many unmanned gates there are in the fence? One hundred and sixty.' He paused for effect. 'They're for the shepherds. You can draw lines on the map but you can't change ancestral grazing grounds.' He leaned forward, clasping his hands together. 'Last year they had two thousand II's climb the fence in one single night. Chaos. So the border patrols are looking at China. Their job is to keep the fat snakes and the thin snakes out of the Crown Colony.'

'What kind of reptiles are those?'

'The fat snakes are the lucky ones, the ones with family in Hong Kong to protect them and set them up. The thin snakes are the ones with no family. They don't survive very long.'

'What sort of snake am I?'

'You don't qualify. You're going the other way. Even so, we have to be careful. This is what we do. At Lok Ma Chau you have the guard-post and the fence. Okay? But beyond, between the fence and the river, is a strip of land we call the Closed Area. It's

Crown territory but it's beyond the fence. It's all pig-farms – you know – pork. Every day you have trucks delivering sacks of pig-meal to the farms.' He winked. 'That's another of my businesses. The guards all know the drivers,' he continued. 'They never search the trucks. So we get a pig-cage – that's like a big metal tube, only it's a cage – and you go in the cage. We pile the sacks of meal over you and you go through the border post under the sacks. Then all you have to do is cross the river there'll be a boat – and you're in China. One of my guys will meet you in the paddies down by the river and – abracadabra!'

'You're not kidding me are you, Mr Cabererras,' Dan stalled despondently. 'I go in a pig-cage, under a ton of pig-meal, to a pig-farm. That's just the kind of cockamamie idea my partner would think was terrific. Why can't I just hide out here?'

'Because, Mr Daniels, the Chinese have three eyes, two noses, and twenty tongues. But over the other side – well, I shouldn't say this – but over there you'll be under the protection of the Government of the People's Republic.'

A few minutes later a doctor arrived to dress and bandage Dan's shoulder and at ten o'clock the phone rang. Cabererras smiled.

'It's your partner, I think. You'd better answer.'

Dan snatched the phone. 'Eddy?'

'You okay?'

'Like a pig in shit. Literally.'

'What?'

'It doesn't matter. Eddy I don't know how you did it but——'

'Tell me one thing, Dan. When they sprung the ambush, did you wonder? About me?'

'For a moment there, I confess I did wonder.' There was a silence. 'Eddy, are you there?'

'Yeah. I have figured it out. They bugged my Christmas gift.'

Neither of them spoke.

One of Cabererras's men had come in and was whispering to the Filipino. Cabererras nodded and came over to the phone. Dan handed him the receiver.

'Eddy?' Cabererras said. 'I'm sorry, Eddy, I have bad news. I've just heard. They shot Master Lim. He was working in his garden this morning and the bastards took him with a high velocity sniper's rifle. His students took off – you know how they are. I'm really sorry, Eddy.' He handed the receiver back.

'Eddy, it's Dan.'

'Dan, listen. I'm making progress this end, okay? There's

203

nothing you can do but sit it out. Cabererras will take care of you. I'll try to get a message through when I have news, but it could be tough. I have to go now. Take it easy, huh?'

'And you, Eddy.'

They hung up.

'He's a good man, your partner,' Cabererras said.

'He is,' Dan said.

The pig truck came next morning at ten. The cage looked alarmingly flimsy and the pig-meal smelt of manure. Dan lay in the dark as the truck bounced and bumped along, and, to his amazement later, he went to sleep. He spent the day in a tin shack listening to the grunting and snorting of pigs, drinking cups of tea, and trying to conduct a conversation in mime with the toothless old man who had charge of him. When it was dark, the old man led him down to the river and a small boy ferried him across the short stretch of water in a flat-bottomed boat like a punt. On the other side a figure in some kind of dingy uniform rose out of the rice-paddy and whispered:

'You come me, thank you.'

He followed his guide along a soggy path, stumbling from time to time, because the moonlight was dim. They came to a rough unmetalled road where a jeep of sorts was waiting. Then there was an hour's drive up into hills, a squat, breeze-block house with no lights showing, a squat little woman in a black tunic and trousers, who bowed unsmilingly, and finally a square, bare room with an iron bedstead, a basin with one cold tap, a table, and a chair. The woman indicated a door and when she'd gone Dan opened it. There was a shower made out of a perforated can, and a lavatory that was nothing but a hole in the ground.

A few minutes later the woman came in with some hot food – rice and fish. Dan smiled at her.

'It's just like home.'

She nodded, her face completely expressionless, and left. It was close and airless in the room and Dan went over to the window and was mildly surprised when it opened easily. He looked out and listened. Apart from the night percussion of the insects, there was silence. The sky was partly overcast and in the far distance there was a curious cloud formation which appeared to be lit from below by some powerful source of light hidden beyond the hills. The clouds had a glow of pure gold.

22

At seven o'clock of a winter's evening the Bunch of Grapes in the Brompton Road was filling up with strangers, attracted by the reputation the pub had built up in the Swinging Sixties as a watering-hole for trend-setters, and by the regulars, most of whom looked like burned-out caricatures from that ephemeral era. The strangers were there to admire the High Victorian decor – ornate acid-etched glass, mahogany, and brass – and to spot famous faces; the regulars were there to get smashed, loudly or quietly, according to temperament.

When Mark Price-Smith walked in and hovered timidly in the door, surveying the crowded bar, Eddy noticed that two over-dressed men, who had been eyeing each other with mild hostility for the past ten minutes, simultaneously turned to appraise Mark. Their mournful eyes followed him as he made his way to the bar.

The bar-tender said: 'Evening, Mark. Usual?' and Mark nodded.

He was a regular. That was one of the pieces of information contained in the dossier Stephany's London agent had compiled on Mark Price-Smith. It was a highly professional bit of work, that dossier, an A to Z of Price-Smith's life from birth to the present day: his widowed mother, his education at a minor public school, his career at Oxford, his recruitment by Central and Shires Bank. From Eddy's point of view the most interesting section of the dossier was the character analysis. This revealed that Price-Smith had lived with a girl for two years during his time at Oxford, but had showed very little interest in the opposite sex since going to work for Anthony Melldrum. It also stated that soon after joining Central and Shires Price-Smith had apparently attempted suicide. Finally, there was the fact that Price-Smith had no money of his own apart from his salary, and that his account was consistently in overdraft.

Eddy made his way over to the bar. Mark was sitting on a high stool, his back turned to Eddy. Eddy touched him on the shoulder.

'Hi – it's Mark isn't it? Mark Price-Smith?'

Mark turned round, startled. When he saw who it was he was flustered.

'You're, er——'

'Eddy Polonski. We met at the bank. You're Anthony Melldrum's right-hand man? I thought I recognized you. Can I buy you a drink?'

For a second Mark had the wild idea that the bearded American was trying to pick him up. No; that wasn't possible. All the same – it was very odd.

'Oh – thanks,' he said. 'Eı, gin and lime.'

Eddy ordered the drink and paid for it.

'How do you, er, happen to be here?' Mark said.

'Why don't we go over there where it's quieter?'

Mark followed Eddy over to a corner table and sat down.

'It's a small world, isn't it?' he said nervously.

Eddy grinned. 'It is – but not that small. You're right. I'm here because I wanted to have a talk with you.'

'Look here. Have you been following me about?' Mark said crossly.

'Not exactly. I have a proposition I want to put to you and I wanted to approach you discreetly.'

'Is this some sort of practical joke?'

'No.' He paused and shrugged. 'I can't think of any other way of saying this but straight out. I want to know whether you'd be interested in making a lot of money?'

Mark stared at him. 'Who are you, Mr Polonski?' he said.

'I'll explain that later. First I'd like to establish whether you're interested.'

Mark looked down. He was flustered; he said the first thing that came into his head.

'How much money?'

'For what I want,' Eddy said, 'I'd be prepared to pay a hundred thousand pounds in any currency, in any country.'

Mark gaped at him. 'A hundred thousand pounds?' He laughed nervously. 'What – what on earth is it that you want?'

'Perhaps we could discuss that somewhere quieter?'

'My flat's just round the corner. But I suppose you know that.' Eddy shrugged. 'How much do you know about me, Mr Polonski?'

'Can we discuss that at your place?'

Mark hesitated. Then he said: 'Very well.'

Mark's flat was in a block behind Harrods. It was cramped and full of rather good Georgian furniture. There was a Hockney over the mantlepiece. Eddy was surprised that Mark could afford such an expensive painting, and that he should have chosen it, clashing as it did with his other pictures, which were rather spinsterly watercolours and prints.

'It isn't mine. It's on loan – from Melldrum.'

'I'm sure he wouldn't mind us calling him Anthony,' said Eddy.

There was a silence.

'Can I get you a drink?'

'No. I won't have anything, thank you.'

'Well I will.' Mark mixed himself a sizeable gin and tonic. He sat down. 'Well?'

'Tell me,' Eddy said, 'have you noticed anything different – strange about your boss's behaviour recently?'

'Strange?'

'Yes – something out of character. Around Christmas time, perhaps.'

Mark frowned. 'Well – no, I don't think so. He did go into *purdah* rather for a few weeks, but he does that from time to time.'

'I'm sorry – into *purdah*?'

'I mean he shut himself up in his office for hours at a time. Worked late into the night. Cancelled all his usual appointments.'

'I see. And that was just before and after Christmas, right?'

'Yes. I suppose so.'

'Can you think of anything else that was going on at that time – in the world, I mean? Any headlines?'

Mark was bewildered. 'Well, there were the American hostages——'

'I should have said in the financial world.'

'You mean all that fuss about gold?'

'Exactly.'

Mark laughed. 'Are you suggesting——?'

'I'm not suggesting anything. Anthony is an expert in computers, isn't he?'

'Yes. As a matter of fact he's always driving our computer chaps mad. He knows more about them than they do.'

'Has his own programs, I suppose.'

'He has his own private account on the computer, if that's what you mean.'

'That's exactly what I mean. Do you know if he keeps any kind of written record of the passwords or code-words that give him access to his programs?'

Mark stared curiously at Eddy. Very dimly, he was beginning to understand.

'Anthony keeps a record of *everything*,' he said.

'Where does he keep his most sensitive documents? Does he have a private safe in the office?'

'Yes – yes he does.'

'And do you happen to know the combination of the safe?'

Mark was aware of a tight feeling in his belly. He swallowed and said: 'As a matter of fact I do.'

'Did Anthony tell you the combination?'

'Yes. He's abroad so much – he rings me up and asks me to get various papers out of the safe.'

Eddy leaned forward, his hands on his knees. 'If, in that safe,' he said, 'there is a list of computer code-words, and if you bring a copy of that list to me, I will pay you one hundred thousand pounds.'

'I – I couldn't.'

'Why not?'

'I just – couldn't.'

'Out of loyalty to Anthony?'

'No – well, yes. I mean what if he found out?'

'If he found out he'd fire you. But if you had a hundred grand that wouldn't matter very much.'

Mark was twisting a lock of his hair into a tight ball.

'You don't know how vindictive he can be,' he said.

Eddy smiled. 'I think I do.'

But Mark was hardly listening to him. He went on: 'He has tremendous power. I mean I don't know half the things that go on, of course——but I know he's done some dodgy things, some very dodgy things. He's boasted about them to me. He can be frightening at times.'

'Well it's up to you. You have my offer. Just one thing. Don't mention this conversation to Anthony.' He paused for a second. 'If you're discreet about me – I'll stay discreet about you.' Mark's reaction was undisguised in his eyes. Hatred – and fear – blazed in them. He said nothing. 'If you decide to go ahead and take the hundred grand,' Eddy went on, 'let me know. I'll call you

208

tomorrow night. At seven. Don't think you have to decide by then. I'll call you every night at that time. But don't take too long.'

'You sa~ you could pay the money anywhere in the world?'

'Anywhere.'

'I mean in Switzerland or somewhere?'

'Switzerland would be perfect. I place the money in a numbered account on deposit and provide you with a full responsibility letter from the bank confirming that it's there. Then when you give me the information I give you a document assigning the account to you.'

'Yes – I see. I——'

'Just think about it. I'll call you.'

Eddy walked back to his apartment through the hushed, opulent streets of Kensington. His assessment of Mark Price-Smith's attitude was seventy-thirty in favour of his taking the bait, and the same odds applied to the risk that he would go to Melldrum. It was a risk he had been forced into taking. He had spoken to three different computer experts and their answers had been the same. Without the code-word it would be virtually impossible to tap any of Melldrum's programs.

23

Dan had been three weeks in what he could only think of as solitary confinement. It wasn't so bad. During the day he was allowed to take some exercise by walking up the hill behind the house, though he was always accompanied by a little man in a sludgy-green uniform. From the top of the hill there was a glimpse of the sea in the distance – he assumed it was Deep Bay. A few hundred yards from the house was some kind of military compound – timber huts and concrete buildings behind high, wire fences. Trucks drove in and out of the compound at all times of the day and night.

He whiled away the hours by writing down every line of poetry he could remember from his days at San Jacinto High and was amazed at what his memory produced. He also spent a lot of time writing out a detailed account of the Greek gold transaction and Melldrum's part in it. But chiefly his thoughts would return again and again to Gina.

A woman brought him food – monotonous but tasty enough. After a lot of sign language he had managed to obtain a regular supply of some pretty vile hooch which took the edge off the boredom and uncertainty. One evening he had a visitor. At about six o'clock there was a knock on the door and the woman ushered in an old Chinese man. He had a wispy moustache and beard and somehow, despite his standard para-military rig, there was an aura of opulence about him.

'Good evening, Mr Daniels,' the old man said in excellent English. 'I have come to bring you some news – good news, I think.'

'From Cabererras?'

The old man didn't reply immediately and when he did, he didn't answer the question.

'These quarters are somewhat primitive,' he said. 'But you will not remain here for very much longer. That is the message I have for you.'

'How much longer?'

'That I cannot say precisely. Three or four days – no more.'

'Have you any other message – from Cabererras or my partner?'

The old man shook his head. 'That is all,' he said.

'Can you tell me where I am? That light in the sky? Is it Hong Kong?'

The old man looked out of the window, nodded, and smiled for the first time.

'The golden glow,' he said. 'It is some atmospheric phenomenon, of course – but the peasants of this region believe that the streets of Hong Kong are paved with gold, that all the buildings are covered with gold-leaf, and that the light in the sky is a reflection of a golden city in the clouds.'

'They really believe that?'

'Oh yes.'

'Well, I suppose, in a non-literal sense it's true.'

The old man laughed.

'Well, I have delivered the message, Mr Daniels, and now I must be on my way. When the time comes you will join the tourist train at Sham Chun and your documents will show that you have been participating in one of the regular, organized tours. There will be no difficulty. Good night to you.'

And that was that. Before Dan could ask him any more questions, he was gone.

An hour later, as he was eating his dinner, it came to Dan who the old man might be. He remembered Eddy's description of Tan Han Yu – the Gold King But what the hell was the biggest gold dealer in Asia doing in Red China, dressed like Mao Tse Tung?

George Roberts was a man of regular habits, who prided himself on his punctuality. He arrived at the large suburban branch of the Central and Shires Bank, where he worked, on the dot of nine o'clock every morning, Monday to Friday. People said that you could set your watch by Old George. He had got the three-mile drive from his semi-detached house in Hendon down to a fine art. His travelling time never varied by more than three or four minutes, whatever the traffic or weather conditions. With equal regularity he walked out of the bank on the stroke of noon and strolled up the hill to the Green Man pub where he ate a chicken-in-the-basket or sausages and mash, and drank two pints of bitter and three or four large whiskies.

George Roberts was a drinker. The fact was known to his employers and recorded in his confidential file. It had been noted by several supervisors that George Roberts's work in the morning was very different from his performance in the afternoon. It was an open secret that when George Roberts left the bank at five-thirty he went back to the Green Man and stayed there, drinking, until half-past seven or eight. It was a miracle, people said, that he'd never been breathalyzed. George Roberts's drinking habits were the reason why he had been passed over for promotion for the last five years. He was forty-five and his prospects for advancement were regarded as nil by his colleagues. He was not particularly good at his job; in the afternoon, especially, he often made serious errors. But Central and Shires treated its employees with an old-fashioned paternalism, and it was doubted that Roberts would ever be given the sack. The general view was that he'd mark time for another ten years and then take an early retirement.

Although George Roberts was a drinker, he was not a convivial man. More often than not he drank alone. The Green Man was the nearest pub to the bank and, at lunchtime, it was usually crowded with bank employees, but Roberts kept aloof from them. When he did join in the gossip about office politics and personalities, he revealed a sarcastic wit that was hardly endearing. He had one or two cronies in the bank, and sometimes he sat with them at lunchtime, but in the evenings he was invariably alone.

And then, people noticed without very much interest, George Roberts acquired a new friend. He was an American, with reddish hair and a beard, who was apparently some sort of university lecturer on a sabbatical. Several people from the bank had struck up a casual, pub acquaintance with him after he had begun to frequent the Green Man regularly at lunchtime. But for some reason he had very soon latched onto George Roberts and day after day they were to be seen talking quietly together in a corner. The American seemed to be able to make Roberts laugh and he certainly bought him a great many drinks.

And then, one day, a strange thing happened. George Roberts broke his routine. Instead of leaving for lunch at twelve o'clock as usual, he stayed behind in the computer room, saying that he was way behind and was going to skip lunch. He was alone in the room for twenty or thirty minutes.

He didn't skip lunch, as he had said, but he didn't go to the Green Man. He went somewhere else – nobody knew where. Even more curious, he did not go to the pub after work either.

The next day, however, he resumed his normal routine. Had anyone been really interested in George Roberts – and nobody really was – they might have noticed a change in him. He drank rather less, and was generally more sociable. His comments about the bank and its hierarchy grew less acid. The chip, once so visible on his shoulder, seemed to have disappeared. He no longer grumbled about his supervisor and the manager, but only mocked them lightly, as if he felt superior to them. His work improved and he actually received promotion, with a rise in salary and the use of a car.

It would have taken a really persistent investigator to realize that his new affluence could not be wholly attributed to his increased pay. There were one or two of his colleagues who wondered how he could afford certain things. But they assumed that George Roberts had come into a bit of a legacy and envied him his luck. The American was never seen again.

24

On a Saturday morning in early March, Eddy hired a car and drove west out of London. He took the M3 motorway and then the A303. It was one of those days of fleeting weather-changes that only England seems to produce, with light rain falling from an apparently cloudless sky, moments of wintry cold, and moments of spring-like sunshine. As he skirted Salisbury Plain the sky was full of racing clouds that created shadow-effects among the sarsen pillars of Stonehenge where he stopped for twenty minutes. He wandered among the great standing stones, revelling in the fresh country air, and drawing in great lungfuls of it as if it had the power to lift the weight of exhaustion that lay on him.

Mark Price-Smith had taken two days to make up his mind. After a great deal of nervous prevarication he had demanded £150,000 for the information, explaining that he intended to disappear abroad, and that £100,000 wasn't enough to make it worthwhile uprooting himself. Eddy had agreed on condition that Mark did nothing to alert Melldrum's suspicions until he received word. He had received word that morning and was presumably on his way to Zurich.

It had taken Eddy ten days to find George Roberts, and a further ten days to get to know him well enough to be certain that he'd accept the proposition. He had found Roberts through a simple process. He had selected five target branches of Central and Shires in the London suburbs. He had found out which local pubs were patronized by bank employees at lunchtime and had begun to frequent them. When he came across Roberts he had instantly decided that this was his man. He worked in the computer room, he suffered from a galloping inferiority complex, and he drank. What Eddy wanted him to do was almost ridiculously simple: feed a code-word into the bank's main computer and obtain a print-out of the program. The reward he offered was staggering to Roberts: £20,000 to be paid into a Swiss bank account.

While he was wooing Roberts he had had the additional problem of keeping Melldrum in play. Using the code-word of the Austrian bank account – it was a joint account in his own and Dan's name – he had arranged transfers of money to two European locations, and had then passed on the information to Melldrum. He assumed that Melldrum had staked out the banks where Dan was apparently going to collect his money and he had been surprised at the patience Melldrum showed when nothing happened.

What with arranging the payments to Price-Smith and Roberts, and monkeying with the Vienna account, he'd spent half his life in Post Office call-boxes. But now that was all over. He had a copy of the computer print-out in his briefcase, and duplicates deposited with three separate lawyers.

Anthony Melldrum was nailed.

He got back into his car and drove on west. A few miles beyond the little market town of Ilminster he turned off the main road into a network of narrow lanes with high banks on either side where the first primroses and the last snowdrops made a brave display of yellow and white. The lane dipped and rose and twisted through bare woodland and orchards; it was an intimate, welcoming countryside where villages of warm, golden stone and tea-cosy thatches lay snugly in hidden valleys. He came to Hamcary soon after noon and parked by the church. He walked under the lych-gate through the churchyard, where five or six sheep were cropping the grass, and into the building. In the chancel there was an ornate marble monument, in the style of Nollekens, to the memory of Joshua Rawlins Esquire and His Wife Charlotte of Hamcary House and opposite was a stained-glass window in memory of Edward Joshua Rawlins, first Earl of Ilminster, born 1813 died 1895. Both the monument and the window incorporated the Rawlins family crest with its tiger rampant. The same motif decorated the sign of the village inn, the Rawlins Arms, where Eddy ate a ploughman's lunch, watching the old men drink their cider and listening to their soft, slow speech. He left the pub when it closed at half-past two and got back into his car. A few hundred yards out of the village he came to the gates of Hamcary House where the ubiquitous tiger was in evidence in the wrought-iron of the gates, and in stucco over the door of the neo-Gothic lodge. The gates were open and a drive curled away into woods. Eddy consulted his Ordnance Survey map and drove on, up the hill. At the top of the hill he pulled into a woodland track and got out of the car. He followed a path through the trees, climbed a stile into a steep-sloping meadow, and then stopped. Below him lay Hamcary House, its honey-gold stone glowing in the afternoon light, its restrained classical proportions perfectly mirrored in the lake. It was a rectangular building with a pedimented Ionic portico and a balustrade and dentil cornice that masked its grey, slated roof. Eddy could hear, very faintly, the cawing of rooks in the great trees of the park, and detected a flavour of the wood-smoke that was rising from one chimney.

'It's rather beautiful, isn't it?'

Eddy turned, startled. A few yards away stood a bay hunter, and astride it was a woman dressed in jodhpurs and a hacking jacket. He had been so wrapped in contemplation of the house that he had not heard the approach of the horse and rider.

'It's superb,' he said.

The woman leaned forward in her saddle and stroked the horse's neck. She was handsome, rather than beautiful, with russet hair tied in a bun and a beak of a nose.

'Ah, the accent confirms it. Are you interested in architecture, Mr Polonski?' she said. 'Don't look so astonished. My husband has described you to me. Lean as a greyhound and with a beard like a Goya grandee, I seem to remember was his description. Are you flattered?'

Eddy smiled. 'How do you do, Lady Frances.' There was a silence.

'The house was designed by Henry Holland and the park was laid out by Capability Brown. We're rather proud of it. The interior quite lives up to the exterior. Perhaps you'd like to see it? I assume you've come to talk to my husband?'

'Yes. Is he at home?'

She glanced at a rather mannish watch on her wrist.

'I should imagine,' she said, 'that at this precise moment he is buggering the new stable-boy.' She smiled. 'But he always finishes in time for tea.' Eddy gaped at her. He couldn't help it. 'If you drive and I ride, we shall arrive at the same time. See you in a minute.' With that she touched the horse's flank with her heel and rode away, down the hill.

The interior of Hamcary House surprised Eddy. He had expected a museum-like atmosphere, but though the place was stately, it was also very much a home. Between Gainsboroughs and Morlands there were insipid flower paintings and woolwork pictures by Victorian great-aunts; a yellow labrador was sprawled on a threadbare Persian rug; a half-round Sheraton table was loaded with gloves and hats and riding-crops. In the drawing room there was a portrait of Disraeli.

'Dizzy has always had the place of honour,' Lady Frances said, as a maid brought in a tray of tea-things. 'Wicked old Jew though he was. Thank you, Daisy. Milk and sugar, Mr Polonski? I see we have crumpets, how delicious. It was Dizzy who gave my great-great-grandfather the Earldom. My great-great-grandfather bought the entire county of Somerset for the Tory party at some election. Those were the days.'

Melldrum came in a few minutes later. He stopped in his tracks when he saw Eddy, but recovered quickly and kissed his wife.

'Mr Polonski has come for tea, darling,' she said. 'If it's some turgid business matter, I'll leave you to it. But perhaps I could finish my tea first?'

Melldrum looked at Eddy. 'Is it a turgid business matter, Mr Polonski?'

'Yes.'

Melldrum avoided his eye and Lady Frances said: 'I've been telling Mr Polonski about Dizzy, darling.'

They chatted about political skullduggery in the nineteenth century, sipped tea, and ate crumpets and fruit cake. Eddy felt a sense of unreality creeping over him.

Eventually Lady Frances rose and said: 'Well, I'll leave you two to talk. Don't forget the Berringtons tonight, Ants. Goodbye, Mr Polonski, so interesting to have put a face to a name.'

'Well?' Melldrum said when his wife had gone. 'You'd better have a damned good reason for barging your way in here.'

'I think I have.'

Eddy opened his attaché case and brought out a sheaf of photocopies. He handed them to Melldrum.

One swift glance was all it took to tell Melldrum what he was holding. His reaction fascinated Eddy. He conformed exactly to the old cliché 'went white'. The blood drained from his face and he looked physically ill. Then the blood surged back, so that he seemed to blush.

He cleared his throat. 'I see,' he said. 'You have been busy. How did you get hold of them?'

'I'll have to leave you to work that out for yourself. It doesn't matter very much. The point is that our legal advisers in the States consider these print-outs to be prime documentary evidence in support of the class action.'

Slowly, Melldrum was recovering his composure. He let out a

short, harsh laugh. 'My God,' he said, 'do you mean that you and your partner are still in cahoots?' Eddy nodded and Melldrum laughed again. 'I've seriously underestimated you, Polonski.'

'We told you when we first met that we required a settlement, Mr Melldrum. Now I'm telling you again. We want substantial financial restitution and the full backing of your bank in putting through the Greek gold transaction.'

Melldrum stood up. 'I'll see you damned first,' he said. Eddy made no reply, but sat quietly. 'What do you take me for?' Melldrum said. 'Do you seriously suppose I'm going to hand you a fortune on the threat of a few scraps of paper that no jury in the world will be able to make head or tail of? Do you think I'm going to let you walk all over me without doing something about it? Well? Say something.'

Eddy said nothing for a moment. 'That was the reason I wanted to discuss this with you in your own home, Mr Melldrum. I didn't think it was likely that you'd do anything stupid in your own backyard. When you've had time to consider things calmly, I think you'll decide that you have no alternative but to agree to my terms.'

'I agree to nothing,' Melldrum said. 'I'll fight you every inch of the way. Now get out of my house.'

'Stay where you are, please, Mr Polonski.' Both Eddy and Melldrum turned. Lady Frances was standing in the doorway. She walked towards them with a dry rustle of her jodphurs. 'I'm afraid I've been evesdropping,' she said.

'Frances——'

'Let me handle this, please, Ants.' She turned to Eddy. 'My husband is a trifle emotional, Mr Polonski. You can hardly blame him, can you? If I give you *my* assurance that Anthony will meet your terms in full, without question, will that satisfy you?'

'Are you speaking for your husband or your father, Lady Frances?'

She smiled. 'For the family, Mr Polonski.'

'In that case I don't think I need take up any more of your time.' He turned to Melldrum. 'I'd like to see you first thing Monday morning.'

Melldrum started. 'What? Oh – yes. I suppose so.' All the fight had gone out of him. Beside his wife, with her cool elegance and imposing features, he looked like a gangling youth.

When Eddy had gone Melldrum sat down heavily on a sofa.

'I don't understand how he got hold of the print-outs. I simply don't understand.'

'What on earth does it matter? You'd better pour yourself a drink. You look ghastly.'

Melldrum mixed himself a whisky and soda at the drinks table.

'Frances——'

'There's no point in discussing it. They've got you hanged, drawn, and quartered, my darling.'

'What's your father going to say about this?'

'Nothing. Look what you've achieved for the bank, for the family. It would have been a miracle if you'd got away with it without something unfortunate happening.'

Melldrum was calming down. Frances was right. Nothing could detract from what he'd done.

'I suppose there's no chance that if we pay them off they'll go ahead with the legal action anyway?' he said after a moment.

'How could they possibly?'

'No. No. It wouldn't be in their interest. What I still can't understand is how the hell Polonski got hold of those print-outs.'

The solution did not occur to him until later that evening when he was changing for dinner and Frances was luxuriating in her bath.

Mark.

Something that Ilminster had said came back into his mind: 'In my day, of course, it was the gossiping lady's maid and the homosexual clerk.'

'Ants?'

Frances's voice broke into his reverie.

'Ants – are you there? I want you to come and do my back.'

He went into the bathroom.

'What's the matter with you? I called you twice.'

'Sorry, darling. I was in the middle of a revelation. I've worked out how Polonski did it.'

'Well?'

'Mark.'

Frances tried to suppress laughter but failed.

'Do shut up, darling,' Melldrum said. But his wife continued to splutter.

'I'm sorry, darling,' she said, 'but it really is rather priceless.'

25

When Dan stepped out of the train at Kowloon station the first person he saw was Eddy. They shook hands.

'No surveillance? No hit-men?'

Eddy grinned. 'Everything's just fine. I spoke to Collins yesterday. He was cold but co-operative. I'll fill you in on the way to the hotel. You have a lot of work ahead of you, my friend. We have a transaction to revive.'

'Know what I want to see more than anything else in the world?'

'No? What's that?'

'A flush toilet.'

Eddy went to Tan that same afternoon. Mrs Kwei led him through the office to the roof-garden, where Tan was throwing food to his fish.

'Ah – Mr Polonski,' the old man said. 'I am indeed glad to see you. You will drink a cup of tea with me. Mrs Kwei, if you would——'

When they were sitting, alone, over tea, Eddy said: 'I've really come to thank you for what you did, sir.'

'What I did, Mr Polonski?'

'For my partner. He told me about your visit to him.'

'Ah yes. My visit. That was indiscreet of me perhaps.'

'Not as far as I or my partner are concerned.'

'No. I am sure of that.' He paused and smiled. 'You say you have come to thank me. I think perhaps you have another reason for seeing me. I understand that you are in a position to proceed with the transaction we discussed in the summer.'

'I am, sir.'

'On the same terms?'

'Exactly the same terms.'

Tan smiled again. He seemed to be unusually friendly.

'It may not surprise you to learn that as a result of the

remarkable events of a few months ago my stock of bullion is very low.'

Eddy was puzzled by the old man's frankness.

'I'm not at all surprised to hear that,' he said.

'I have a confession to make to you.' Tan said. 'I knew a little in advance that the price of gold would rise. I also knew when it would fall.' This was getting to be more and more bizarre. Why was Tan telling him this? The old man read his mind. 'You ask yourself why I tell you these things? The reason is very simple. I knew that someone was manipulating the market. It was obvious not only from the way the price fluctuated within the general rise, but also, of course, from the fact that I had been pre-warned of the rise and was made to pay very heavily for the information. I believe you know who did it, Mr Polonski – and *how* they did it. I do not want any names from you. That does not interest me. But if you could satisfy the curiosity of an old man you would carn my undying gratitude.'

Eddy smiled. He told Tan the whole story from beginning to end, and when he had finished Tan thanked him politely.

It didn't occur to Eddy until much later that for Tan to have begged him for the information in such a way represented a massive loss of face. It taught him another fact about the character of the Chinese. Curiosity was a greater passion even than face.

When Eddy and Dan had set out to revive the gold transaction they had assumed that it would be an uphill struggle. But it turned out to be the opposite. Tan's response was typical. In a few weeks they were back in the position they had achieved in mid-December 1979. Even John, who had emerged from the undergrowth as if by magic a few hours after the partners returned to Luxembourg, was eager to buy.

By the last week in March everything was set and the gold price was steady at around $480, though there were signs that it would soon start to rise. On All Fools' Day Eddy and Dan were in Zurich for a final meeting at Limmatbank with Schurch's successor, a completely unremarkable careerist called Rimmel, who treated them with great deference. Towards the end of the meeting Rimmel's intercom buzzed. Rimmel reacted with surprise to his secretary's message.

'Show him in – show him in immediately.'

A moment later the door opened and Maniatos entered.

While Rimmel grovelled, Eddy and Dan observed the Greek. If anything, he seemed younger and less haunted. When he turned to look at them his eyes held the faintest suspicion of a twinkle.

'I want show you something,' the Greek said. 'You have time? This afternoon?' He turned to Rimmel. 'Is all arrange?' Rimmel nodded.

The Greek's car called for them at their hotel after lunch, and they drove out towards the airport. Eddy was silent, remembering the last time he had taken that route, with Tania.

They were received by a deputation of bank officers and security men in an office-block, in its own fenced-off compound, well away from the terminal buildings. Two senior directors of Limmatbank, with the bank's security chief and two uniformed guards armed with shot-guns, accompanied them in the elevator. They descended two hundred feet to the vaults below the airport runways.

After three separate security checks they arrived at last in a square, high, concrete room. The sole feature of the room was a massive, circular steel door. The two Limmatbank directors asked them to wait at the far end of the room while they walked forward to the door and punched out combinations on the computer-controlled lock. There was the moan of an electric motor and the two hemispherical sections of the door slid slowly apart.

Beyond was a void. One of the guards entered and after a moment a faint light appeared. The second guard followed his colleague in. One of the Limmatbank directors came over to Maniatos.

'If you would come with me, sir.'

The Greek moved forward, followed by Dan and then Eddy. In the half-light the interior of the vault was like a vast library at night: straight rows of what looked like high, metal bookshelves formed narrow corridors that seemed to stretch away into infinity. But to the left was a brightly lit aperture at which one of the guards was standing. Eddy followed the Greek and Dan through the aperture, turned right, through a door, and then stopped dead.

It was as if that last small step had carried him ninety-three million miles across space and he had walked straight into the sun. A searing blaze of golden light engulfed him. For a moment his eyes could take in nothing but the golden fire that swirled and danced and licked around him. The fire burned all thoughts from his brain, save one: *I am standing at the heart of a star*.

He deliberately shut his eyes and waited. When he opened them he could focus again, the world was back in perspective. He was standing in a vast, low-ceilinged room, the size of a tennis court. In front of him were ten separate walls of gold, forming nine corridors, each at least twenty feet in length. The walls were thick and squat. They were about three feet wide – as wide as a single bed – and six feet high. They were made of four-hundred-ounce bars. The bars had been laid across each other, at right angles, but with regular gaps, so that the walls were not solid but gave the impression of heavy latticework. Overhead, arc-lamps beamed fierce, white light into the golden labyrinth which acted as a giant filter, transmuting that light into a molten, golden light, a light that contained the very essence of high summer, of pure dawns and sunsets and eternal noons. He could see the Greek and Dan moving like sleep-walkers down the central aisle. Dan walked unsteadily and when he himself took a step forward he was astonished to find that his legs were as weak as if he'd spent a month in hospital. At the end of the central aisle were rows of grey, metal trestle-tables. On the tables, neatly stacked, were square cardboard boxes. The Greek had opened up one of the boxes and was showing its contents to Dan. Looking over Dan's shoulder Eddy saw that the box held hundreds of sheets of paper. Some were as thick as parchment, yellowing, and covered with copperplate writing; others were flimsy and type-written. These were the certificates of origin and ownership that had to accompany each Good London Delivery bar of gold. Without such a certificate a bar was unsaleable on the Market.

The Greek had moved away and was again standing in the central aisle. He was wearing a suit of pale grey silk and the fine-textured fabric seemed to capture and hold the golden light radiating from the stacked bullion, so that he appeared stained – dyed with gold.

Eddy picked up one of the certificates. It was thick and brittle and even smelled faintly of must. The first name he read was that of the original refiner and assayer, Johnson Matthey. The date was 1899. The name of the first owner of the bar to which the certificate referred was Cecil John Rhodes.

Eddy made a rapid mental calculation. There had to be something like one hundred and sixty thousand certificates. Many of them would accompany bars of recent manufacture and stamp but there must be thousands that dated back to the early years of the century. The piles of innocuous-looking cardboard boxes comprised a data-bank, a store-house of secret information, a clandestine archive of who paid whom, when. The truth behind political coups, revolutions, macro-business transactions, even wars was buried in the boxes. The thought awed him. In an undertone he said to Dan:

'If you could analyze the information here you could re-write the history of the century.'

'And get it right,' Dan said.

'That is curse. Too many secrets. Too many.'

It was the Greek's voice. He had moved and was standing a few feet from them. His eyes were awash with tears. The tears were spilling very slowly through the crevices of his face, like water retreating over rock.

Two days later, on 3 April, Eddy and Dan sat in Stoffel's office at Euro-resource Bank in Luxembourg. It was just before half-past three in the afternoon and all three men were staring at a video screen. At the far end of the room two telex operators were standing by. In separate offices adjoining Stoffel's room a representative of Limmatbank and a representative of the buyers' lead-bank were waiting. On Stoffel's desk lay the irrevocable, with-full-responsibility letters of the seller and the buyers. At a minute past three-thirty the information flashed onto the video screen.

'They're fixing,' Stoffel said.

He waited for a moment, then looked at Eddy and Dan. They nodded. Stoffel left the room. Eddy and Dan did not exchange a word while he was gone. When he returned, he carried the closing letters of instruction from Limmatbank and the lead-bank. He went over to the telex and instructed the operator to dial the Federal Reserve Bank in New York.

The first key-test telex instructed the Federal Reserve Bank to transfer funds held in the escrow account of the lead-bank into the escrow account of Euro-resource. On receipt of confirmation from the Federal Reserve, a telex went to Limmatbank in Zurich. A few moments later two further telexes simultaneously transferred the ownership of the Greek gold into pre-designated metal accounts and instructed the Federal Reserve to transfer funds from Euro-resource's escrow account to the Limmatbank escrow account.

The balance in the account of Euro-resource was confirmed at one hundred and eighty-nine million, six hundred thousand dollars, and that money, less commissions amounting to fifty-six million dollars, belonged to Eddy Polonski and Dan Daniels in equal shares.

When they left the bank later in the afternoon, Dan stopped suddenly in the street, drew in a lungful of air, and let it out in a great sigh.

'Try it, Eddy. Try breathing. It's wonderful. I'd forgotten how wonderful it is.'

They walked on. 'Now I know what it feels like to get out of gaol,' Dan said. 'No more surveillance, no more subterfuge. Just freedom. What's the matter Eddy? You look as if you just *lost* ninety-five million dollars.'

Eddy forced a smile. 'We've still got to be careful, Dan. People who do what we've just done have a habit of winding up vanished. We know a lot of secrets.'

'Eddy – you're getting as paranoid as John.'

26

Over the next few weeks various things happened in various parts of the world that were apparently unconnected but were in reality triggered by the sale of the two thousand tons of gold in Luxembourg on 3 April.

A distinguished firm of Dallas attorneys, who represented the Convent of the Little Sisters of Charity, received an offer for the Barraclough ranch in the Davis Mountains which exceeded all existing bids by a million dollars. They urged their clients to accept the offer immediately.

In Houston, another distinguished law firm, Landau & Landau, received representations from a New York attorney who was empowered by his client to settle all his outstanding debts, with generous interest, in return for a complete retraction of the embezzlement charge against him. The financial terms were so extraordinarily generous that, in spite of a certain chagrin, Landau accepted them. There was another reason why he was relieved to be shot of the Dan Daniels problem: one of his employees, Walter Shipley, having had a visit from certain FBI agents who were still doggedly pursuing their investigations into links between organized crime and legitimate business, decided to make a full confession in return for immunity from prosecution. This was extremely embarrassing for Beauregard Johnson Landau.

In Hong Kong Mrs Martha Pearson, a leading light of the local Canine Protection Society, received an anonymous donation of $50,000.

One event which was not directly connected with the sale of the Greek gold, but which interested Eddy and Dan very much when they read about it in a discreet column in the London *Financial Times* was an announcement that Anthony Melldrum, International Treasurer of Central and Shires Bank, had been promoted to a key advisory position at the headquarters of a major Swiss banking corporation.

While all these things had been happening Eddy and Dan had remained in Europe. On 21 April Eddy flew alone from London to Warsaw.

In London it had been spring, but Poland was still in the grip of winter. The streets were full of hunched, plodding people in fur hats and long coats, almost indistinguishable one from another. Everything about his birthplace chilled Eddy: the seven or eight different types of police and military who outnumbered the passengers at the airport; the soulless housing estates along Zwirki I Wigury; the bleak pile of the Palace of Culture and Science that dominated the flat city like a huge watchtower.

The fact that Eddy was an American citizen with a valid visa, that the Soviets thought he was dead, that his name in Poland was as common as Smith, and the even more powerful protection of his wealth could not quite allay a quiet fear compounded of the memories of his childhood.

He hired a *taksowaka* which took him down *al.* Swierczewskiego, past the bear-pit, over the bridge, and into Praga. It took the driver some time to locate the apartment block where Mrs Wojek lived but Eddy finally came to her door. An old woman dressed in black, her head and feet wrapped with woollen scarves, opened the door a few inches in response to his knock.

'Mrs Wojek?'

She nodded, peering at him suspiciously.

'I am a friend of your granddaughter, Tania Larionov.'

'Who?'

'Tania. Your granddaughter.'

'Tania? She is not here. She has gone away. A long time ago.'

'I know. I am a friend of hers.'

'You - you are a friend of Tania?'

'That's right.'

She smiled. 'Come in, come in, come in.'

The cramped one-room apartment smelt of kerosene and cabbage. A mass-produced picture of Pope John Paul II hung among faded, nineteenth-century prints on the walls. Mrs Wojek fussed around brewing tea, talking with the rambling garrulity of the old and lonely. Her conversation was salted with a dry Polish wit.

'You must forgive me. I am without staff today. All my servants have gone to the opera.' When Eddy asked her if she had any news of Tania she looked at him intently over the rim of her tea-glass. 'It is surely the stranger who knocks on the door who bears news, young man,' she said. 'It is a month now since I have had a letter from Tania.' She fumbled in a pocket and drew out a flimsy, blue air-mail form.

'She's in America then?' Eddy said.

Mrs Wojek nodded and, seeming to forget Eddy's presence, became absorbed in re-reading the letter. Eddy waited patiently. She looked up.

'I wonder, could you tell me where the letter was posted?'

'I don't know – my eyes. I am waiting for the operation. Here you wait. I shall have a white stick before I see the inside of a clinic.' She handed him the letter. The postmark was New York; there was no address.

'Tania sent me money for the operation,' Mrs Wojek said. 'But it is not a question of money, it is a question of the surgeon's time, you understand. Every month Tania sends me money. She is a good girl.'

'Does the money come from America? Or Switzerland perhaps?'

Mrs Wojek folded her arms and poked her head forward. 'Why are you trying to find Tania, young man?' she said.

'I love her.'

'Ah – I knew it,' she said with an air of triumph. 'The way you say her name. Tania. With a little throb, like that. Have you quarrelled?'

'No. We haven't quarrelled. I think Tania may be in some kind of trouble. I haven't heard from her for over a month. I can't find out where she is. I want to help her.'

'Trouble? What kind of trouble?'

'I don't know, Mrs Wojek. It's just a feeling.'

Mrs Wojek shook her head. 'And you come all the way to Warsaw – in winter too – because you have a feeling? You were born here, weren't you? I can tell by your accent.'

'Yes I was. My father was a professor at the University.'

'Ah yes, the University. Were you here in the war?'

'I was only a child – but I remember. When I was seventeen the Russians took me. I studied in Moscow. Now I live in America.'

'Where did you meet Tania?'

'In Zurich. In a restaurant.' He smiled.

'A restaurant? I do not know who is to be trusted any more, I do not understand how people behave. Before, one knew. If I help you, how can I be sure that it will not be bad for Tania? What is this trouble you speak of?'

'I think she's being forced to do things – things she doesn't want to do. She's disappeared. I can't find her. I'm a rich man, Mrs Wojek. I've made a lot of money in the West. I know I could find and help her if I just had somewhere to start.'

Mrs Wojek's eyes, in spite of her cataracts, were penetrating.

'These bad things Tania has done? Has she done them to you?'

'Yes. Yes, she has.'

'And you still want to help her?'

'Yes.'

'I think you are telling me the truth. I think you love my Tania. But I cannot believe you yet, I cannot help you.'

'Why not, Mrs Wojek?'

'Because you have said nothing about Gregori.'

'Gregori?'

'Tania's little boy – her son.'

Eddy said quietly: 'She never told me she had a son. She never mentioned him to me.'

'Are you trying to tell me that you never went to Tania's flat in Zurich?'

'Of course I did. But Tania was always alone. She had no son. She didn't even have a photograph of a little boy.'

'I don't understand.' Mrs Wojek was suddenly cast down. The shrewd inquisitor became a bewildered, old lady. 'Where is Gregori? Where is he?' She rocked to and fro. 'I don't understand.'

'I don't understand either, Mrs Wojek. But you see what this means? Tania needs my help more than ever. Something's happened. I don't know what. But I'm the only one who can find out.'

Mrs Wojek stared at him for a long time. Then she rose abruptly and shuffled over to the far side of the room. She bent down painfully, pulled a box from under the bed, and then returned to her chair carrying a bundle of flimsy papers. As she handed them to Eddy she said: 'That is all that I have.'

Eddy examined the papers. They were receipts from the State Bank confirming transfers of small amounts of foreign currency from a Swiss bank into Mrs Wojek's account. The name of the Swiss bank was Henkel Frères. And Henkel Frères had handled his expenses at the outset of the Greek gold transaction. It was a subsidiary of Paul Delgado's Canyon Bank.

The taxi drove him back to the airport through the sickly, Eastern-bloc street-lighting. He felt that the whole city, the whole country, was blighted: a place of half light and half life. He saw now how Tania had tried to alert him – twice. That day by the Rhine: 'I never saw the mountains,' she had said, 'only the cities of the plain.' Again, that first weekend in the Vosges, when she'd vanished. She had tried. But he hadn't been able to understand. If he had he would have realized what a farce Stephany's dossier on her had been. Of course her story had checked out: a professionally constructed cover was designed to stand up to the kind of investigation Stephany had done. But Collins! That she should have been working for Collins – it didn't make any kind of sense. Yet the proof was there. Inescapable.

He thought about it throughout the flight back to London, but his thoughts went round and round in hopeless spirals. He was grateful for Dan's detached practicality when they met at the airport. Dan was flying home to Houston and Eddy went with him.

'There's nothing you can do directly or immediately,' Dan said. 'You go steaming into the Eldorado in Vegas and you'll blow the whole damned thing. It's going to take some very cautious investigation. We can start with my old buddy Walter Shipley. He knows those people. He can give us a lead. When we have some hard information, then we can make a move.'

'Yeah – but what kind of move?'

'I don't know. It could be as simple as giving Collins a whole heap of money. I don't know.'

'It could be as simple as staking that bastard out in the desert and giving him a terminal sun-tan.'

'You've got to relax on this, Eddy,' Dan said. 'We can handle it – but we have to be very careful about messing with those people.'

At Houston airport the partners separated: Dan to visit his family, see his lawyers about the completion of the Barraclough purchase, and try to make an initial contact with Shipley through friends in the FBI; Eddy to re-open his apartment and make the arrangements for Harvey Ravenscroft's pay-off. They agreed to meet again in two days' time, fly up to Barraclough, and then on to Ravenscroft at Blackwind.

Eddy called the Hayes's number to alert Barbara and Tom to

his imminent home-coming, but there was no answer from their phone. He hired a car and drove out to the apartment. The sight of familiar streets and buildings gave him no sense of being back where he belonged. He felt like an alien. He had been away too long, had seen, done, and felt too much. Houston wasn't part of his life any more. It was just a big, hot, ugly city where there were only memories of a distant past: no present and no future.

There was a real-estate agent's board on a stake stuck into the front lawn of the Hayes's house. There were no curtains in the windows. The place was empty. He fitted his key into his own door and then hesitated. He took the key out and pressed the bell. After a moment, Barbara Hayes opened the door. When she saw Eddy she looked shocked, stricken.

'Eddy——'

'I called you from the airport,' he said. 'I couldn't get an answer. I'm sorry——'

'Come in—— I—— we didn't know—'

He walked past her, into the living room. His furniture had been pushed back to accommodate two beds. The beds were unmade and heaped with unwashed jeans and shirts, record sleeves, and other teenage paraphernalia.

'What's happened, Barbara?'

Barbara began to cry. Eddy put his arm round her and tried to make some sense out of what she was saying.

'I wanted to tell you – I told Tom – we didn't know where you were. You called once, I know, and I wanted Tom to—— but he couldn't. He couldn't do it.'

Eddy left her alone, went into the kitchen, and made some tea. By the time he got back to the living room Barbara was calmer.

'We'll quit the apartment right away, Eddy. I promise you.' She said.

'Just tell me what happened.'

She shrugged and produced a shaky smile. 'Can't you guess? Tom made one of his brilliant investments – only this time he put everything we had into it and about a hundred grand we didn't have. I don't know how much he lost – he won't tell me – I don't know how much we owe. But we lost the house, even the car. Tom got fired from Exxon because he was drinking. It all happened so fast. We had to move in here, we didn't have any other place to go.'

'What did Tom do?'

'I don't know. Gold futures or something. You'll have to ask him.'

231

'Where is Tom?'

'Where he always is, where he spends his life. In the bar down the street.'

'Okay, Barbara. I'll go and see him. And don't worry about the apartment. You stay until we get things straightened out.'

'But we can't Eddy——'

'Look – why don't you fix some lunch. I'll bring Tom home and we'll talk about it.'

He found Tom sitting alone over a glass of bourbon in the neighbourhood bar. Tom made an attempt to appear pleased to see Eddy but it was obvious that he was terrified. He was drunk and full of self-pity. His story came out in dribs and drabs, but Eddy didn't need a narrative. He knew exactly what must have happened to Tom. It was the same thing that had happened to millions of small investors who had caught the January gold fever, had believed the headlines and the predictions of the brokers, and had bought gold futures. Tom had invested $150,000 of borrowed money. He had bought gold at $950 an ounce, convinced that in a few weeks the price would skyrocket to over $1000. Instead, it had nose-dived, wiping him out.

He supported Tom back to the apartment, Tom vowing that he would be out of the place by sundown, that all he had left was his pride, that he wasn't taking charity from any man.

Eddy spent the night in a hotel and first thing next morning went to see Nat Culver at Culver-Kahn.

'You sure as hell did me a favour over that gold, Eddy,' Culver said. 'Sold out at eight hundred and put the money into a trust fund for my kids.'

'I'm delighted, Nat,' Eddy said. 'Would you like to do me a favour?'

'I owe you one.'

Briefly Eddy explained Tom Hayes's position. 'He's a great accountant when he doesn't drink – and the drinking will stop when he gets a job. I'm prepared to pay his salary for three years and I want you to keep him on for that time whatever happens – within reason. If he's a disaster put him somewhere he can't do any harm. If he causes you any loss I'll compensate you in full. But I think you'll like him, I think he'll make out. There's just one vital thing. He must never know. It would destroy him if he found out. His name's on the books of several agencies. You can approach him through the normal channels. What do you say, Nat?'

232

'I say it's the craziest, most quixotic thing I ever heard of. But, okay, it's your funeral. I'll do it.'

'I'm grateful.'

'Anyway, how come you're so rich and powerful all of a sudden? Last time I saw you, you were a desperate man.'

Eddy smiled. 'Well we didn't all lose out in the gold rush, did we?'

Nat scratched his head. 'Damnedest thing that rise. I still can't figure out what made it happen. Can you?'

27

Dan's Beachcraft Baron touched down neatly on the big field in front of Barraclough and taxied towards the house. It halted a few hundred yards away from the front portico and the engines died. Dan climbed out and tapped off the fuel, and Eddy climbed out after him. With him, he hauled a heavy, squat, metal case.

'Well, what do you think?' Dan said, looking at the house.

'Sensational.'

'Yeah – it is. D'you want to carry that thing with you?'

'I'm not leaving it in the plane.'

'Eddy – the place is empty. There isn't a human being for five miles around.'

'It's just my habit. Security.'

Dan shrugged. 'They're your muscles.'

They walked on up to the house. The local attorney in Fort Davis had handed Dan a big bunch of keys, and he tried three or four of them before he found the one that fitted the front door.

'This is a big moment for me,' he said, as the door opened. 'Like a dream come true. I don't know – I feel kinda empty, though.'

They entered a square outer hall and went through some half-open double doors into the staircase hall, which was dimly lit by a dusty glass dome.

'Smells bad,' Eddy said. 'Musty.'

His voice, in the silent, empty house, had a curious echo.

There was a sharp metallic click, like a bone cracking. It was the unmistakable sound of a man cocking a machine pistol. Eddy and Dan froze.

'Hi, *kamerads.*'

John stepped out from the shadows of the staircase. He was dressed in his black raincoat. He was unarmed. He was smiling.

'Well that explains the bad smell.'

It was Dan who had spoken. John exposed more teeth. 'Behind you,' he said.

Dan and Eddy turned. The man with the machine pistol was standing in a recess to the right of the double doors.

'Meet Irving,' John said. 'Irving has instructions to act with extreme prejudice, one of you makes a move.'

Irving stepped out of the recess and circled towards John, halting at nine o'clock in relation to him.

'What is this, John?' Dan said.

'Patience, *kamerad*.' He moved closer to them, maintaining a safe distance.

'I'm about to move, John,' Eddy said. 'I'm going to put this case down. It's heavy.'

John nodded and Eddy put the case down on the floor.

'Will you tell me what this is about?' Dan said. 'What the hell are you doing here, John? What is all this bullshit?'

'It's what shoulda happened in Hong Kong, *kamerad*. It's going to happen here, now. You shouldn't go buying big, lonely old places in the mountains. Irving and I've been waiting for you since dawn, *kamerad*. Your lawyer man in Fort Davis was co-operative.'

'Hong Kong. It was you.'

John looked at Eddy. 'That's right, *kamerad*.'

'Tania Larionov——'

'Me again.'

'Why did you go for Dan? Why not me? You knew where I was. You knew every move I made, every word I said.'

'You're a valuable individual, *kamerad*. You're going to work for the Government.'

'Are you telling us that's who you work for, John?' Dan said. 'I don't believe it.'

'That's right, *kamerad*. Government service. Irving too. But you know that, don't you? You know a hell of a lot. You're a smart guy. You go nosing around in libraries.'

'This is crazy,' Dan said. 'You showed us the letter from your bank. You didn't have to do that. What did you expect? The US Government wants to buy two thousand tons of gold and you expect us not to be curious?'

'Sure I expected you to be curious. I wanted you to be curious. If you didn't know too much, I didn't get authorization to terminate the file on you.'

'You think we're going to go public? You think anyone would believe us?'

'I don't know, *kamerad*. All I know is that you have

information prejudicial to the American government – and I have a duty to perform.'

'Okay, John,' Eddy broke in. 'How much?' John shook his head. 'Don't make any hasty decisions, John,' Eddy said. 'Don't you want to know why my case is so heavy?'

'I know why, *kamerad*. It won't buy you anything.'

'Don't you want to take a look, John?'

'Sure. I was going to tell you to open it. Real careful, now.'

Eddy felt completely confident about what he had to do, what John and Irving knew he was going to try to do. There was a serene calm spreading through his body and his mind. It was as if the spirit of Master Lim and of all the generations of Wing Tsun Masters had taken over his own spirit. He knew that for this moment their power was his. It wasn't a mystery any more, how they created a minute out of a second, an hour out of a minute. It was simple.

He rolled the tumblers of the combination lock and flipped the latches of the case. Then he let the two halves of the case fall open.

Thirty bars of gold cascaded onto the ground. Light was released into the room, the primal light of gold. For Eddy, time decelerated to the slow-motion of *tai-chi*. He saw how Irving and John were fixated by the light from the gold, how – for a second or two – it burned everything else from their minds. For him those two seconds were an age, and the space between himself and Irving, between Irving and John was nothing – two points between which he could float or fly.

What Dan saw was a blur of movement. He saw Eddy launch a flying double-kick at Irving. He saw Irving go down as if scythed. He saw Eddy roll, somersault into a crouch, then launch himself at John, his arm flicking straight like a whip, his fingers formed into a spear-point. He saw John catapult backwards into the balustrade of the staircase. He heard wood splinter and saw John bounce off, slump forward, and lie still.

John came round, small vibrations of his eyelids signalling the return of consciousness. They had found some curtain cord in one of the rooms and had trussed him up. There was caked blood on the back of his head, where it had hit the balustrade, and grazes on his face. On his stomach there was a purple-yellow bruise. Irving, also trussed up, was still out. Eddy had examined him and reckoned that he'd remain out for at least another hour.

John opened his eyes, and let out a gasp as he did so. He blinked and wriggled, then looked up to see Eddy and Dan standing over him. Dan knelt and held a cup of water to his lips. John drank greedily, then lay back.

'Are you ready to talk?' Eddy said. There was no response from John. 'I want Tania Larionov and her son, John. I want them delivered right here.' Again there was no response.

Eddy left him and went over to check on Irving. He examined him briefly and then returned to John.

'Still out?' Dan said.

Eddy nodded. 'Listen to me, John,' he said. 'You're only alive because Tania means more to me than killing you. I'm prepared to buy her. There are thirty kilo bars in the case – that's half a million dollars' worth of gold. It's yours in exchange for the girl and her son. You can take it and disappear. The alternative is that I kill you.'

Eddy could read John's thoughts like a print-out. Rage, followed by greed, followed by fear, followed by the clincher – hope. The hope that if he took the gold and handed over the girl, the matter would not end there. Once he was free he would be able to plan a counter-move, either as a private vendetta, financed by the gold, or simply as Agency business.

John's voice was a croak. 'What about Irving?' he said.

'Irving is your problem. I don't care what you tell him '

John heaved himself up into a sitting position. He looked across at Irving.

'How long before he wakes up?'

'I don't know. Maybe an hour – two.'

'When he wakes – put him out again. Is there a phone?'

'Yes there is,' Dan said.

'Okay. I'll have to make a call. Before I do, I wanna see that gold.'

Dan opened the case and took out one of the bars.

'What do you want – an assay?' he said.

'I want to see the stamps. I'm not getting screwed on any Mexican crap.'

'There's the stamp, John. *Asarco Gold Amarillo Texas*. Is that good enough for you?'

John nodded. Dan and Eddy helped him to his feet and frog-marched him into the next room.

'Okay – where have you got them, John?' Eddy said.

'California.'

'Will they release them on your word?' John nodded. 'Then this is what you tell your people.' He gave John exact instructions. John listened sullenly. Then, while Eddy covered him with Irving's gun, he dialled the California number and relayed Eddy's instructions. When he'd finished they tied him up again, and dumped him in the hall. Dan guarded him with the gun while Eddy called Ravenscroft at Blackwind. An hour later four of Ravenscroft's toughest ranch-hands arrived in a jeep and took over the surveillance of John and Irving. Irving was still unconscious.

Eddy found John's car in a garage at the back of the house and drove it round to the front. He and Dan loaded the gold in the trunk. Then it was a question of waiting.

The sun was going down when they heard the faint clatter of a helicopter. Ravenscroft's men untied John and escorted him to his car. Eddy showed him the gold in the trunk, locked the trunk, and gave John the key. Then Irving was carried out of the house and laid out in the back of the car. One of the ranch-hands removed the ropes from him but he did not stir. John got into the car, behind the wheel, a gun still held at his temples.

The helicopter was in sight now, swooping in from the northwest. It passed over the edge of the forest, slowing, and sank towards the big field in front of the house, touching down five hundred yards from the Beachcraft.

A woman and a small boy climbed out of the helicopter, crouching, and shielding their faces from the rotor winds. When they had moved clear, the helicopter rose twenty feet and hovered.

'Okay, John,' Eddy said.

John's car pulled away. The minute it moved the helicopter began to rise. As the car burned off down the driveway, the helicopter climbed faster, banked, and vanished over the hill.

The woman and the boy stood in the field, hand in hand. Eddy walked down towards them. When Tania saw who it was she bowed her head.

The warm air was vibrant with the chatter of crickets and the hums of nocturnal insects. From the nearby corral came the contented burr of one of Ravenscroft's horses. There was hardly a breath of wind and a great moon sailed in the sky.

Dan sat alone on the back porch of Blackwind. He sipped at his drink and the ice cubes tinkled. He was happy to be alone for a time, happy to think about nothing, nothing but the utter peace of the mountains, the peace that was his now, that he would preserve at Barraclough for the rest of his life. Eddy came out onto the porch and sat down.

'Is she okay?' Dan asked.

'She's sleeping. Harvey gave her something.'

'And the kid?'

Eddy smiled. 'He didn't need anything. Went out like a light.'

'Great little kid.'

'Yes.'

There was a silence.

'Did you talk?' said Dan. Eddy nodded. 'Where was John holding them?'

'A place about a hundred miles out of LA. A private mental hosital.'

'My God. Who's running security in this country? The KGB? Did she tell you anything else?'

'Everything.' He lay back in the chair and closed his eyes for a moment. 'When her husband was killed she was working in the Soviet Consulate in Washington. In the commercial section. She knows as much about gold as you and I do. Gregori was in Moscow; she asked them to send him to her in the States and they refused. They kept him in a State orphanage. Her work was sensitive from a security point of view and they wanted a hold on her – a hostage.' Eddy laughed harshly. 'From their point of view they were right. Her work *was* sensitive – that's why John was interested in her. He made contact with her through intermediaries. He offered her a deal. He'd get the kid out of Russia, bring him to the States, if she'd go to work for him.'

'Kidnap a child in Moscow and smuggle him out of the country?' Dan said. 'How the hell——?'

'That's exactly what Tania's reaction was. She didn't believe it was possible. Until it happened. John did it. God knows how, but he brought the kid to the States. At the same time he had Tania picked up. They took her to the clinic and let her see her boy. Then John introduced himself. You can guess what deal he wanted.'

'It's incredible, Eddy. What kind of power does John have? How could any government department sanction a thing like that?'

'I don't know why. I don't know why they trust him to go

around buying billions of dollars' worth of gold – we just know that they do. He does a good job for them, there may be no limit to his power.'

'Including taking the kid as a hostage.'

'Exactly.' Eddy stood up and walked to the edge of the porch. Gripping one of the rough, wooden pillars, he stared out at the night. 'John planted Tania on me, having found out about the Greek gold from Delgado. All he had to do was stake out Limmatbank to find me. He had you under surveillance too. He was out to buy the whole two thousand tons for the Government and it freaked him. He was convinced that one of us would suss out who he was and who he was buying for. He planned to have us killed from the start. Tania knew that. She knew that when she picked me up in the restaurant. She knew it when she fell in love. She couldn't warn me directly so she tried obliquely and I didn't get the message because I didn't want to understand. What could she do? It was either me or her son. She had to make a choice and she made the right one.'

'Hold on,' said Dan. 'What about the Collins connection – the payments to her grandmother through Henkel Frères?'

Eddy laughed. 'Coincidence. Just coincidence. Henkel Frères happened to be the nearest bank to her apartment.'

'I'd almost forgotten that banks do ordinary business as well. My God.' Dan took a pull of his drink. 'John's still alive. Have you thought of that?'

Eddy nodded sowly. 'That's why he took the gold,' he said. 'It was the only chance to save his life. He doesn't care about the money – only the power it gives.'

'That's right. And he *has* power. Frightening power.'

'I wonder.'

'What do you mean?'

Eddy stroked his beard thoughtfully for a moment. 'There's something I couldn't tell you before,' he said. 'About Irving.'

'Irving?'

'You remember just before I spoke to John I went over to check that Irving was still out?'

'Yeah?'

'In fact I was checking to see that he was still wide awake. He's a wise man, Irving. He knows the value of lying still and waiting to see what will happen. He heard the deal we put to John and he heard John accept it. He knew the gold was in the trunk of John's car. I couldn't tell you because it was critical that John believe that Irving was still out cold. Otherwise he would never have got into that car.'

'You think——?'

'I don't know, Dan. But put yourself in Irving's position. How many people knew where he and John were today? The way John works – nobody. The helicopter guys were just glorified cab-drivers. You remember John's mania for secrecy? My guess is that nobody knew what he was doing or that he and Irving were together. So Irving is alone with him in the car. They're driving through totally deserted country. There's half a million dollars' worth of gold in the trunk and nobody knows. What would you do if you were a forty-thousand-a-year CIA agent and there was a chance to get out, right away, with half a million in the most readily disposable currency in the world?' Dan began to laugh quietly. 'I could be wrong, but my guess is that right now *kamerad* John is dead and *kamerad* Irving is on a bus to Mexico.'

Eddy was right.

Two days later the body of a man was found by a Ranger in a lonely gulch in the hills thirty miles north of Barraclough. The man had been garotted with his own necktie.

There was nothing on the body to identify it: no documents, no tabs in the clothes, nothing. A description of the dead man was circulated to every law enforcement and security agency in the country, including all branches of the Central Intelligence Agency. But no man answering to John's description was on file anywhere. The description was then released to the media, in the hope that some friend or relative of the dead man would come forward to identify him. Nobody ever did.

John was buried by the County in an unmarked grave.

It was John's death – the neatness, the economy of it – that prompted Eddy to fly down to Las Vegas a few weeks later. He told neither Tania nor Dan about where he was going or what his intentions were.

For the first time in his life he travelled like a millionaire, with all the trappings of a private jet and three bodyguards. The bodyguards were there purely to impress Jim Collins and to remind him that, if he had any grievances left over from the past, his best policy was to bury them.

Eddy had no fear of Jan Pienaar. Through a carefully selected intermediary – a former mercenary and agent for BOSS, the South African intelligence agency – he had given Pienaar a message: that any hostile move made by Pienaar or his company, or any group or individual associated with it, would result in immediate retaliation in kind. He had paid the intermediary twenty thousand dollars to put this across to Pienaar in one brief conversation, but it had been worth the money. The intermediary was a man who inspired belief – and fear.

Eddy had no apprehension either about Anthony Melldrum. He did not think Melldrum would seek revenge for the sake of it. He had made no attempt, for instance, to find Mark Price-Smith. The defeat Eddy had inflicted on him was a minor defeat in comparison with the victory he had won. Melldrum could be sure of Eddy's and Dan's silence and he would be a fool to initiate any action likely to stir up the past.

And yet Anthony Melldrum was the reason for Eddy's visit to Las Vegas. Melldrum's activities had resulted in the death of an innocent girl. The normal processes of justice could not touch him; but there were other ways in which justice could be served.

Collins was waiting at the same table in the Sun God Restaurant where, almost a year before, Delgado had handed him the letter from Limmatbank and he had learned about the Greek gold.

'Jim.'

'Eddy.'

They shook hands and sat down. Collins darted a glance at a nearby table where Eddy's three men were also taking their seats. He smiled.

'The rich man's travelling companions,' he said. 'I ordered you tea.'

'You have a good memory, Jim.'

'I do. Is that why you asked for this meeting, Eddy?'

'One of the reasons.'

He tried to read Collins's attitude. He could deduce a little from his appearance. He looked more relaxed, more confident than when he'd last seen him in Zurich. He wore his bow tie with the old, jaunty air. It was a fair bet that his bosses had decided to overlook the fact of Collins's multi-million lapse. The gold had been sold; Collins's people had been paid; they'd carved up the thirty-two million margin. They were cool.

Collins's next words confirmed Eddy's intuition.

'I do have a good memory, my friend – but it's selective. You always said that market forces would prevail. Well, they did. You were right. I'm satisfied with that.'

'It's good to hear you say that, Jim.'

'It's what you wanted to hear. What else do you want?'

'Nothing. I want to tell you something. I want to tell you what happened – why it went wrong when it did, why the gold price went crazy.'

Collins fingered his chin. He made no reply until the waiter who brought his drink and Eddy's tea had gone away. Then he said: 'Why? I mean, I'm interested – but why do you want to tell me?'

'I thought you might like to know the name of the man. He hurt you and me pretty badly. I don't know about you, but I'm still smarting. He had us both set up from the start. He used me but he also used you and the Greek.'

Collins listened to the story, showing no particular reaction, stirring the ice in his drink with a plastic stick. When Eddy finished he looked up.

'What do you want me to do about it?' he asked.

Eddy shrugged. 'I don't know. There's nothing I can do. I don't have the facilities. But maybe you should discuss it with your people. Whichever way you look at it Melldrum was your man; he broke the banking rules and so jeopardized your interests. He helped himself and his family – to the detriment of you and your family. If Dan and I hadn't succeeded in circumventing him and forcing him to put the transaction through, the Greek gold would still be lying in the vault.'

Collins nodded slowly and then tipped back the remains of his drink.

'Okay,' he said. 'I'll give it some thought.'

'Do that.'

Eddy rose and offered his hand. Collins shook. His clasp was dry, neutral. He smiled pleasantly.

As Eddy left the restaurant he looked back to where Collins was sitting. Collins was ordering a fresh drink from the waiter. Of all the people in the place, he looked the most ordinary and unremarkable.

At his first meeting with Jim Collins Eddy had drawn an imaginary picture of a family-man's home environment: a house out by Lake Mead, a pool, a barbecue pit, a wife who was a dedicated follower of European fashions. Though Eddy never knew it, his analysis had been astonishingly accurate. Collins did have a house near Lake Mead, and it did have both a pool and a barbecue pit. His wife did take an interest in European fashions and was, in fact, in Paris on the night when she became a widow.

Collins was alone in the house that night, three weeks after his conversation with Eddy. He had spent the evening as usual at the Eldorado, and had driven home after dinner, arriving at about eleven o'clock. By nature and by lifelong habit he was a creature of the night and so he didn't go to bed immediately. He mixed himself a drink then switched on the TV and hunted through the channels for a movie or a show that interested him. There was nothing. He switched off the TV and took his drink outside. He sat down in one of the cane chairs by the pool and thought about having a swim later on, when he'd digested his dinner thoroughly. He thought about putting a disc on the stereo – there were extension speakers out by the pool. But he was a little tired, and it was very relaxing sitting by the floodlit water, doing nothing. When, a minute or two later, he heard the faint sound of a man's step on the concrete paving behind him, he remained perfectly still.

'Who is that?' His voice was steady, though he could feel bile burning his throat. 'I'm going to turn round,' he said. 'Don't shoot. Please.' He twisted round in his chair and choked – with relief and release of tension. 'Jesus Christ, Painter. What the hell are you doing creeping up on me like that?'

Painter said nothing. He was standing five feet away, a tall, darkly good-looking young man in a black suit and white shirt.

'What are you doing here anyway? You've had your instructions. Has something come up?'

Again Painter made no reply. But he did react. He slowly raised his right hand, and in his hand, Collins saw, was his gun.

The knowledge that he was about to die closed Collins's throat; but his brain – the precision instrument that had carried him so far and so high – did not give way to panic. In those last few seconds everything connected as logically as it had done throughout his life.

He had given Painter the contract on Anthony Melldrum. Only one other man in the world knew about the contract: the head of the family himself. Therefore the head was protecting Melldrum. Therefore——

Painter's gun spat twice. A dull *phutt-phutt*. Collins was punched backwards and the chair toppled, tipping him onto the ground.

Painter walked over to him. He took aim at his head and fired three more shots, then he knelt down and checked that Collins was dead.

EPILOGUE

Half the teenage population of Hong Kong seemed to have flocked to the beach at Repulse Bay. The sands were a mass of basking bodies, the sea teemed with bobbing heads, arched backs, flailing arms. The white diving-raft, moored a few hundred yards out, just inside the shark-net, was a metaphor for the place: a speck of an island jam-packed with people.

Somewhere among the bronzed bodies on the raft were Annie and Joe, Dan's children, with Gregori. Dan raised his sun-glasses and squinted across the water.

'I wouldn't worry,' Eddy said.

'I'm not worried. Except Annie has a tendency to flaunt herself for the benefit of Chinese youth.'

'A natural tendency.'

A waiter came out of the bar and brought them drinks. Dan shifted his chair to catch the shade of the canvas awning. The sun was getting fierce. Eddy glanced at his watch.

'I wouldn't worry,' Dan said with a smile. 'Once Elizabeth gets under a hair-dryer she loses all sense of time. I feel sorry for Tania; here she is in the romantic orient for the first time in her life and all she's seen so far are the insides of restaurants, salons, and shops. Thanks to Elizabeth.'

'They seem to get on.'

'They do. I can't figure out why Elizabeth wanted to come.'

'You and Elizabeth seem to get on.'

'Things are better – but then I'm rich now. Anyway, the kids are having a great time. Did you see the King?'

Eddy nodded.

'And?'

'I don't know. Tania and I could be going to Peking next week.'

'Are you going to tell me what's in your mind?'

'I haven't got any clear ideas yet.'

There was a paper lying on the table. It was an air-mail edition

246

of the *Wall Street Journal* and it contained a report of a speech Anthony Melldrum had recently delivered at a conference of Western finance ministers.

'I get mad every time I think of Melldrum,' Dan said.

'I was pretty certain Collins would do something about him. It seems I was wrong.'

'We should do something. That argument we staged for him in London – it wasn't all acting, Eddy. I meant what I said. I've got a sense of justice.'

Eddy nodded. 'But what should we do?'

'You've gotten some ideas – or I'm reading you all wrong.'

After a moment, Eddy said: 'When I went to Vegas to see Collins I spent some time in the casino – just watching. Watching the people, watching them getting ripped off. The same sort of people were at the airport, going home to work for another year so they could go back and get taken all over again. The system Melldrum and his kind work is the same. People make money and it's called a boom. The Melldrums take it away and it's called a recession.'

Dan smiled to himself: he doubted if the world really worked on such simple lines.

'I'd like the people to know the truth for once.'

Dan shook his head. 'Not a chance.'

'For the truth? You're right. But what about fiction?'

'Fiction?'

'A novel. We could hire some writer to turn the story into a novel. Okay, he'd have to hype up the action, disguise the identity of the bank, invent a lot of it – but the core, the market manipulation, he could expose in detail.'

Dan looked towards the sea. Annie and Joe were in the shallows, playing about like dolphins. 'But would anybody believe it?' he said.

'If they knew anything about the gold market,' Eddy replied, 'they would see that it was the only logical explanation.'